IMMORTAL REDEMPTION BOOK II

Eternal Echoes

CASSANDRA ELIZZABETH

Kissing Camels Publishing, LLC

1653 Lititz Pike #2233

Lancaster, PA 17601

First published in the United States October 2024

This is a work of fiction. Names, characters, places, and incidents either are the product of the author's imagination or are used fictitiously. Any resemblance to actual persons, living or dead, events, or locales is entirely coincidental.

ISBN 979-8-9895228-3-5 (paperback)

ISBN 979-8-9895228-2-8 (ebook)

Cover & Interior by Quirky Circe Book Design

Editing by Indie Editorial

http://www.cassandraelizzabeth.com

For all the friends you never expected to become the heroes you never knew you needed.

Content Warning

If you usually skip these warnings, please read this one sentence. *This book is a religious reinterpretation.* If that is not your cup of tea, please take the exit ramp. If this sounds good, hit the gas and hop on the highway to hell.

Now, for those sticking around: *The Immortal Redemption* series is a dark paranormal romance saga meant for adult readers who don't mind venturing into morally gray waters. It contains explicit and kinky sex, knife play, blood play, breath play, anal, flogging, spitting, violence, death, on-page murder, religious beings, alcohol, mental health struggles, oddities, profanity, body image topics, veiled references to sexual abuse, and... well, probably more. Buckle up.

Playlist

Prologue Luke | **Something I Could Never Have** *Flyleaf*

01 Lieshe | **Hurt** *2WEI*

02 Lieshe | **Bellyache** *Billie Eilish*

03 Lieshe | **Dragula (from "Haunt")** *Lissie*

04 Lieshe | **Like You Mean It** *Steven Rodriquez*

05 Vlad | **After Darkx Sweater Weather** *mikeeysmind*

06 Jo | **Wings** *Birdy*

07 Lieshe | **All Around Me (Acoustic Version)** *Flyleaf*

08 Lieshe | **Wicked Games** *RAIGN*

09 Lieshe | **To Be** *The Irrepressibles*

10 Lieshe | **I Know Your Secrets** *Tommee Profitt & Liv Ash*

11 Vlad | **Moonlight Sonata (Epic Trailer Version)** *Hidden Citizens*

12 Lieshe | **Slip Away *(feat. Ruelle)* UNSECRET**

13 Lieshe | **War of Hearts** *Ruelle*

14 Luke | **the fruits** *Paris Paloma*

15 Lieshe | **Chokehold** *Sleep Token*

16 Lieshe | **My Love Will Never Die** *AG & Claire Wyndham*

17 Lieshe | **Fade Into You** *Jessie Villa*

18 Lieshe | **Obsession** *Mellina Tey*

19 Vlad | **I Get to Love You** *Ruelle*

20 Lieshe | **Teardrop** *Massive Attack*

21 Vlad | **In This Shirt** *The Irrepressibles*

22 Lieshe | **Sledgehammer** *Miia*

23 Lieshe | **Abcdefu** *GAYLE*

24 Vlad | **Vendetta (feat. Krigaré)** *UNSECRET*

25 Lieshe | **Here Comes the Sun** *Edith Whiskers*

26 Lieshe | **Walk Through the Fire** *Klergy & BELLSAINT*

27 Lieshe | **Me and the Devil** *Soap&Skin*

28 Lieshe | **Shut Up and Listen** *Nicholas Bonnin & Angelicca*

29 Luke | **Heart-Shaped Box** *Imad Royal & Mark Johns*

30 Lieshe | **Lovely** *Billie Eilish & Khalid*

31 Luke | **I'm yours** *Isabel LaRosa*

32 Lieshe | **I like the way you kiss me (burnt)** *Artemas*

33 Lieshe | **Glory Box** *Portishead*

34 Luke | **I Wanna Be Your Slave** *Mitchell Zia*

35 Lieshe | **Dark Side** *Bishop Briggs*

36 Luke | **World on Fire** *Klergy*

37 Lieshe | **Shallow (feat. Fleurie)** *Tommee Profitt*

38 Lieshe | **Yes To Heaven (sped Up + Reverb) [Remix]** *ViralityX*

39 Vlad | **Madness** *Ruelle*

40 Lieshe | **Love Story (Indila)** *Shashikant Gupta & Sakshi Gupta*

41 Luke | **eyes don't lie** *Isabel LaRosa*

42 Lieshe | **Fallout** *UNSECRET & Neoni*

43 Vlad | **Smells Like Teen Spirit (Alt Mix)** *Witchz*

44 Lieshe | **Game of Survival** *Ruelle*

45 Vlad | **Love Is a Battlefield (feat. Sara Skinner)** *Holly Knight's Story of O*

46 Lieshe | **Into the Deep** *Denmark + Winter*

Epilogue Vlad | **Ain't No Grave (feat. Adam Christopher) [Epic Trailer Version]** *Hidden Citizens*

As my eyes survey the scene before me, I can't help but smile. Someone wanted my attention. *Desperately.* They've done their research—drew the right symbols, spilled the right blood. I inhale the dark bouquet of fading panic from the sacrifice like a fine wine, noting a delectable whiff of deceit just below its coppery tang.

I wrinkle my nose at the combination. It's interesting, but the only scent I crave anymore is the innocent desperation of my little queen.

My interest is waning to annoyance. I have far more pressing matters than some idiot who found a dusty book and decided to call me.

A startled squeak has me whirling around to face a petite, mousy woman. Now I am intrigued.

"Oh, this is just fucking fabulous," I laugh when I realize who she is. "You?"

She squares her shoulders, jaw set, boldly locking eyes with me. I let the black bleed through, just to drink in her fear. To her credit, she takes a step back, but steels herself.

"I want to make a bargain," she says in my language, Infernal, laboring over the ancient words.

"Impressive. But don't strain yourself. English is just fine. What dusty library have you been playing in *petit piaf?*" I reply, stalking toward her.

I let my size grow with each step. Scare tactics give me a secret thrill, and I am so tired of constantly folding in on myself, making myself smaller than, other than, *less than* just to fit into this boring fucking world. Restraining my true nature chafes like a hemp rope wound tight under my skin.

"He should love *me*. I *deserve* his love," she seethes, ignoring my question.

"Love," I spit.

An all-too-human eye roll escapes me. Why anyone would want that filthy mutt's love is beyond my understanding. And now he's gathering an entire fan club.

A maniacal laugh bubbles up as I think of him—a dog with a bone. He will never love this desperate little turncoat when he only has eyes for another. Not that I would tell her that. Nor would she believe me. I am, after all, the Father of Lies.

I can use this, and her, to my advantage. It's like I am preordained to win. I will gladly accept this serendipitous gift, but first, I'll play with my little prey. Idly spinning my rings on my fingers, I let her sweat in my silence.

Her heart rate ticks up with trepidation. Calling me is the simple part. Standing before me, sensing the all-consuming dark chaos that embodies my soul, is something else entirely. I let the dark vacuum of my aura pulse around her, solidifying her fear that, yes, she called me forth, but no, she cannot control me.

Nothing and no one can. Sometimes, not even me.

Her pupils dilate as I pull her into my gravitational field, the dark matter of my nature swirling around us both. Fear flickers in her eyes, but the worry that I won't strike a bargain bleeds through—even above her concern for her own safety—revealing just how badly she wants this.

But I will agree for two reasons. One, because it serves my purpose and allows me to control this variable that could otherwise thwart my plan. And two, I can't resist tricking anyone into a bargain that ultimately favors me. It's simply too much fun.

As she struggles to breathe in the changing atmospheric pressure, her heartbeat crescendos. The staccato beat fans my annoyance.

I speak just to break the sound. "I don't want your soul. I have no use for it. The traitor's section is bursting at the seams."

Pushing the chaos down deep, I stare into her eyes and read her like an open book. She at least has the decency to flinch at the word "traitor." Reaching out, I allow my black nail to extend into a claw and gently glide it across her forehead, tucking a lock of her brown hair behind her ear.

Her heart rate slows as she relaxes under my touch, charmed like so many others by my pretty face masking the monster within. Trapped in my gaze, she is a helpless bird caught in the stare of a serpent, hypnotized by my deadly allure.

I slide my claw from behind her ear to rest just over her carotid like a lover's caress. As I increase the pressure, a bead of blood wells up, crimson against her pale skin.

As she recognizes the mortal danger she's in, her defenses roar to life. The artery once more pulsing frantically beneath my touch like a jackhammer as her muscles tense, ready to flee.

I love this game of cat and mouse, keeping my prey on edge. Uncertain. Alternating fear and desire just for the fun of it. I am confident I will win, but just like the cat, I can't help but play just a little more before I snap my jaws closed.

"Love is worth breaking a centuries old vow? The price will be steep," I taunt.

She nods, flinching when the action causes my claw to sink in deeper but stands her ground. She spits, "That promise is not mine to keep. I didn't make it, and I ended those that did."

She pushes further into my claw, trying to prove her point as she says, "He is worth any price."

"Spoken like a true turncoat." Leaning in, I whisper over her lips like a lover. "I want your deceit, your lies, your treachery. I want your stained honor, your ruin. But most of all..." I pull back and lift my claw to my mouth. Keeping my eyes locked onto hers, I let the drop of blood fall to my tongue. I tip my head back and swallow, letting out a hum of appreciation.

"Most of all, my delicious little Benedict Arnold, I want to win."

Chapter 1

"Damn it, Lucifer," I curse, stumbling over the black cat as he goes racing off after his latest attempt on my life. He has gone from ignoring my existence to being my constant underfoot shadow. I might have liked it better when he hated me.

Standing up slowly and rebalancing the precarious stack of boxes that broke my fall, I take a deep breath, trying to calm my pounding heart. My efforts to get both the new and old merchandise entered in the inventory management system, organized, and put away have left my stock room in complete disarray.

Since Anna came on board to work at Grimm, the store and I have become more organized and efficient. There have been some growing pains—case in point, this mess—but the resulting sales and streamlined processes have been worth it.

As I glance around at my poor stockroom, which looks like a tornado hit it, I can't help but think how the physical disarray surrounding me matches the internal disaster of my heart and mind.

I've been keeping busy, going non-stop in the lead-up to my European buying trip. I rationalize that there's just so much to do before I leave. But if I'm honest with myself, it's just an attempt to fill every waking moment, avoiding the torment of missing the men who vanished as mysteriously as they appeared.

I haven't seen Stalky Hottie—my new nickname for

McHottie—since I stormed out on him and did a little B&E. Luke texted to say he's traveling for work, with no timeline given. His ambiguous message should unsettle me, but truthfully, it's perfect for me right now.

I replied with an equally vague, "Okay." After our dark encounter, I wasn't sure what else to say.

I know I shouldn't be sad that they're out of my life. Loneliness shouldn't tug at my heartstrings. I chose myself, after all. This is what I wanted. Isn't it?

In the busy waking moments, I'm fine—a little quieter, with a few less smiles—but passable. It's the nights that are killing me softly. Luke and Stalky Hottie simply won't let me sleep. I fear I might finally be going mad, just as my parents always feared.

I anticipate, and dread, drifting off to dreamland in equal amounts. Knowing one of them will appear as soon as my eyes close makes their absence from my waking hours so much more acute.

To say nothing of the dreams themselves. They are so vivid, so real; the line between them and reality is losing its distinction. Blurring, until I'm surprised to wake up alone, or I turn my head, expecting one of them to walk in from the next room. The Stalky Hottie prickle on the back of my neck has become such a constant companion I only notice when it's not present, rather than when it is.

The wild imagination I've always been accused of having can explain all those things away. But the physical remnants of our nighttime encounters defy explanation: bruises, bite marks, quivering thighs, JBF hair—I never know what condition I will awaken... with one exception. I always, *always*, wake up soaking wet. *Fucking drenched.*

Too bad I can't sell pay-per-view to my brain. I'd put the internet porn business to shame. My dreams of Stalky Hottie are filled with golden, languid passion scattered across time itself. Every lazy afternoon highlights a different lifetime in a new location. When we're together, it is as comfortable and familiar as coming home.

If the ones of Stalky are easy like Sunday morning, Luke is a wild Friday night. He crashes in like a tsunami, drowning me in wicked fantasies under a vivid midnight colored like the bruises I find on my body. Unlike the shifting times and places with Hottie, Luke and I are always in the same dark realm—a sea of endless twilight.

In the daylight hours, I boldly proclaim that I need no one and nothing. I am enough. But when I realize the noise I mistook for Luke's key sneaking my door open is just wishful thinking, or I catch a fleeting, imaginary whiff of Stalky Hottie only to remember he couldn't have been on my pillows, my heart bleeds just a little.

Despite the way I'm pushing myself, drowning my mind in the monotony of the countless checklists I write, the truth is I'm dying the death of a thousand paper cuts. Each dream, each imagined instance, bleeds me dry one tiny drop at a time until soon I'll be nothing but a white paper doll blowing in the wind.

Pulling my focus back to reality, I slump to the floor, leaning against the stack of boxes, chest constricting. Closing my eyes, I count my breaths, tamping the anxiety back down, and stop myself from waxing poetic.

Lucifer chooses this moment to show back up with a demonstration of his newfound love for me. My eyes snap open when he drops something onto my crossed legs and looks at me proudly, twitching his battered ear with its two missing notches.

His presence is a welcome distraction, pulling me out of my maudlin thoughts and back to the present. His timing is impeccable, as usual. He seems to know exactly when I need some affection in our new, friendly relationship. I swear he not only understands my spoken words but also can read my mind. Uncanny, but that's a black cat for you, I guess.

"So, that's why you were in such a hurry, big hunter? Saving the store from mice?"

He flicks his tail in response, narrowing his eyes as if to say, "Obviously."

"Who's the best Lucifer?" I croon, scratching under his chin, eliciting his rusty purr.

I can forgive him for almost knocking me down in his pursuit, since pests can wreak havoc in a shop like Grimm. Picking up the poor dispatched mangled mouse by its tail, I stand and head toward the back door.

"Come on, big guy, I'll get you a treat. Although if you brought him in alive, I could have just relocated him," I admonish him with no real ire.

The black tomcat glares at me, radiating disapproval at the mere suggestion that he'd let a perpetrator survive. He struts past me, giving me a full view of his kitty backside to drive the point home.

I can't help but laugh. My midnight shadow has wormed his way into my heart, helping to fill a little of the Luke and Stalky Hottie-shaped void in my life.

I glance at the clock in my little kitchen on the way out the back door, shocked I've worked until the wee hours of the morning. Once I see the time, physical exhaustion pulls me toward sleep, the product of a long day. In Pavlovian response, my lady parts start doing the happy dance in anticipation of my nighttime visitors.

I raise an eyebrow at myself, annoyed at the war within. My mind desperately wants a solid night of uninterrupted rest free from a midnight rendezvous while my body is more than willing to meet up for some guilt-free hanky-panky.

There is no rhyme or reason as to which of the guys will worm their way into my dreams every night. I can't help but question why there can't be a little Lieshe sandwich, but it seems even in dreamland these two can't cross paths.

I drop the recently departed mouse in the dumpster and make my way home, my shadow trailing behind. I wonder who will star in my dreams tonight as I crawl into bed naked. Might as well, since I wake up that way each morning.

At least with Stalky Hottie, my clothes just wind up tangled in the sheets. Rumpled but none the worse for wear. When I dream of Luke, though, nothing is safe. After finding several pairs of my standard-issue, comfortable cotton briefs shredded, I gave up sleeping in anything altogether.

Once I even played amateur detective and set my phone up to video myself overnight, wanting to record exactly what was going on. But when I woke, my phone was on the floor face down. I hoped it was just Lucifer that had knocked it over rather than something more insidious. If not, well, I might need a young priest and an old priest.

I ROLL OVER, chasing sleep, melting as Stalky Hottie repeats his familiar refrain in my ear. His exotic voice is so slow and deliberate, I burrow into the bed, attempting to stay in dreamland a little longer just to bask in his presence.

"Oh, my little *Roză*. You have no idea just how mine you are."

Despite feeling his breath whisper across my ear, along

with his words, I can tell I am alone before my eyelids even flutter open.

Always.

Fucking.

Alone.

I stretch, every muscle in my body deliciously sore. A yawn makes me wince at the throbbing in my lip. I reach up to find it swollen and bruised. As my fingertips brush over them, the pain sends a delicious shiver down my spine as I recall my nighttime imaginings.

Focusing on reality, I haul myself out of bed and brace for another day in the storeroom. Anna will work in the front of the store while I wrap up the storage mess. Although it is a lot of mindless manual labor and data entry, it helps for all the inventory to be fresh in my mind so I can organize my wish list for my European buying trip.

Bleary-eyed, I make my way through the back door of Grimm to hide away with my messy bun and ripped up sweats, stepping over boxes and shipping supplies on the way to the storeroom. I scrub my hand over my face, wishing for caffeine to face the day. My groceries are running low in anticipation of leaving, and as a result, I inadvertently ran out of coffee.

Like a genie, Anna shows up to hand me a latte from across the street. I gratefully take a swig while she launches into an update on our social media presence and resulting sales. Grimm was doing well before, but with our combined efforts on efficiency and marketing, it's now positively bustling.

I had no idea how hot my store would become online. There seems to be a never-ending parade of shipping supplies coming in and packages going out. Although the shift from old-fashioned, in-shop sales to this new, hectic pace seems overwhelming, I can't argue with the increase in revenue.

My eyes glaze over as Anna rattles off statistics. Lucifer leaps onto a nearby box and bumps me with his head, demanding attention. I absently reach down to scratch his head while she switches over to Lucifer's social media account. I try not to be annoyed that he gets more followers and likes than I do, but I gotta admit it stings a little.

When she fusses over him and shows him her phone, I swear he understands her, judging by the way his little kitty eyes sparkle. Giving him a dismissive pat that has him twitching his tail, she launches into our ongoing dream of expanding Grimm.

Although I don't want to move the business, we're not only running out of space for the inventory we now carry, but we also need a dedicated shipping area. Even after commandeering the kitchen, my store is simply outgrowing my beloved little end unit.

Maybe my neighbor will just go away, and I can somehow acquire his building, I think wishfully. But money isn't quite that flush, yet. And not that I've been looking— okay, maybe I looked once or twice—but I haven't seen him coming or going. Stalky Hottie might already be gone.

The thought fractures the protective wall I've built around my heart against him just a little. Would I really be okay with *never* seeing him again? Something about my mysterious neighbor is just so damn familiar, calling to me, tugging at my very soul. I shake my head, dispelling my wandering thoughts.

As thankful as I am that the store has been a welcome distraction from the men plaguing my heart and dreams, I'm even happier to be leaving soon. I need a break from this chaos, time for introspection, and a decent night's sleep. Hopefully, my trip will bring just that.

I'm saved from Anna's excited monologue by my phone ringing. Grateful for the interruption, I pick up the call from Mindy, saluting Anna with my coffee cup and escaping out the back door.

We chat about how happy we both are that I am finally doing something for myself—visiting Romania with Wren after I wrap up my shopping expedition. She fills me in on her life, then we hang up after promising to plan a trip soon for Mindy, Jo, and me. It's been ages since the three of us were together. I haven't seen Mindy since I ran away to her house after the Philly Expo, and I can't remember the last time I saw Jo.

The carefree college years we shared seem like a lifetime ago. But in just a few days, Jo will be here, and we can catch up. That is the best part about our friendship. No matter how much time passes, we just pick right back up where we left off. I'm not sure how I got so lucky to be roommates with those two, but I don't think I could have escaped my father or my small hometown without them.

I sit on the back steps of Grimm, tip my head back, and close my eyes, letting the sun warm my face. The memories of Mindy and Jo wrap around me like a hug, a quiet chuckle escaping as I remember our shenanigans. Re-energized, I sigh and head back into the storeroom to lose myself in work, as usual.

Chapter 2

The stockroom is done. I've checked off a million items on my lists, and at long last, Jo will be here tomorrow. I can't freaking wait. As I lie in bed, exhausted from the day, sleep remains elusive, reminding me of those late summer nights before heading back to college.

Break would crawl by, filled with small town church events and pleasing my parents. I would swallow my words, shrinking myself down to fit into their world like a square peg into a round hole.

That final night, I would lie awake in my tiny twin bed with its virginal white duvet, dreaming of being back together with Mindy and Jo. I'd count down with the cuckoo clock, marking the twilight hours, staying up until the sun rose just to make sure tomorrow really came.

I know it was magical thinking. But that all-nighter would be followed by the absolute best day of the year— escaping my taupe prison cell of piousness and reuniting with my girl gang.

I must fall asleep at some point because I wake up to my blaring alarm. Instead of smashing the snooze button, my excitement at seeing Jo has me popping out of bed. I get ready for the day and head down the stairs to my parking spot, grabbing onto the railing as Lucifer races me down the stairs, taking off on some top-secret kitty mission.

"Bye," I call to him, but he couldn't care less, having already disappeared around the corner.

I can't help but glance up at the windows at the back of my building looking for any sign of Stalky. For the first time, I have a true twinge of regret. Am I being too harsh?

The more time passes, the easier it is to convince myself that things weren't all that bad. Or maybe that's all the sex dreams getting my body to sway my mind. I let the thought go. Not my focus today. Compartmentalization for the win.

I hop into my old VW Beetle and head to the airport. Knowing I will need to navigate the ridiculous Baltimore traffic—where people drive like we're all in race cars competing in a demolition derby—revs up my anxiety. I usually avoid the beltway at all costs.

I white knuckle my way there without incident, but with a few choice swear words, and pull up right as Jo walks out with her rolling suitcase. She is in so many ways the opposite of me in appearance, tall and willowy with innocent blue eyes and a mass of honey-colored curls in contrast to my meatball-like stature, different colored eyes, and gray forelock.

Jo may look like an angel, but when she opens her mouth, she sounds more like a sailor. It's not just the shocking words she uses, but the confident way she throws them out, as if she's purposely trying to shatter the illusion her appearance creates—almost as if she doesn't want to be seen as the celestial being she so closely resembles.

We hug and squeal like we used to, laughing the whole time. Not only have I been neglecting myself, but I also haven't made nearly enough time for my friends. Now that I have Anna and am committed to doing more for myself, I swear I'll never let so much time pass without seeing them again.

My life may have recently taken some strange turns, but

at least my best friend is here. When I'm with Mindy or Jo, I know everything will be okay.

She keeps me in stitches the whole way back, with stories from her trip here and failed attempts at dating in the Midwest. After we all graduated, she had been a New York City girl, but moved home to take care of her mom, who was ill. Something I was all too familiar with.

Although her mom had passed over a year ago, she stayed in the middle-of-nowhere town to care for her stepdad. He was a strange dude with an even stranger toupee, but Jo is nothing if not loyal.

By the time we make it back to my place, my cheeks have that delicious ache that only comes from laughing too much. Jo has always been an anchor in my life, and right now, I need that more than ever. Especially when she's so damn funny that I can't even remember to be upset. I push aside the anticipatory grief of knowing tomorrow she'll drop me off at the airport I just picked her up from, instead focusing on the fact we have the whole day together.

After she unceremoniously dumps her suitcase just inside the door, she says, "Thai?"

Arm in arm, we walk across town to another of my favorite restaurants. We share many things in life, including a love of spicy Thai. We find a table by the window, so absorbed in catching up, that the third time the server comes to ask for our order, we pick at random and end up with enough food to feed a small village.

As we eat off each other's plates, Jo fixes me with a stare and says appraisingly, "You're different. What's changed?"

I think about spilling my guts, about telling her everything that is eating my soul. All about Stalky Hottie, the return of my "waking dreams," and the charming but possibly sinister Luke Devlin. But none of it makes sense, and

I can't explain all that has happened, much less my vivid nightly encounters with both of them.

What would I say? I met the hottest man alive, but I don't know his name. He made me realize I love myself, and I thought I was falling for him, but he turned out to be the rose stalker. Then I ran into a super-hot redhead who set my fantasies on fire, but I secretly think he's some type of villain. And oh, by the way, we have ridiculous sex every night in my sleep.

Jo loves me, but man, does that sound crazy pants. Things have been so wild that even I am starting to doubt if I have the line between reality and dreams firmly drawn. What if none of it is true? Or even stranger, what if all of it really happened?

"Earth to Lieshe," she calls as she waves her hands in front of my face.

"Sorry. I was lost in thought."

"Thoughts of who?" she asks.

I decide to tell the truth, or at least part of it. "I have finally fallen in love."

Jo's face lights up.

"With myself," I clarify.

Her entire being lights up, and she wiggles excitedly as she says, "Good for you. It suits you. I am so happy you finally see what I have all along. You've always been fucking fabulous. You just had to pry off the shit-colored glasses your parents slapped on your face."

I spit out my Thai iced tea at her words, thankful the Monday lunch hour is slow as I mop my face. I never know what the hell is going to come out of this girl's mouth. We finish our meal without further incident, sweating from all the spicy food and groaning about how much we ate.

"Why did we walk? I'm so full," I grumble.

"That's what she said," she quips, and we dissolve into giggles, like college roommates all over again. She insists on picking up the check, mothering me about having enough spending money for my trip.

We take the long way back to my place, just enjoying being in the same state together, walking in the sunshine. My heart is so happy. I missed these times. I missed Jo. This is what I needed in the maelstrom of my life—the anchoring presence of my girlfriends.

Back at the ranch, she sits on my couch while I repack my bags yet again, wanting her critical eye to help with the final edit. Planning is tricky for this kind of travel that will cross countries and various weather patterns.

I pick several pairs of pants which will wear well, a selection of shirts and layers I can mix and match, and what I call my "emergency dress." I had packed one for every trip since I was a little girl. You never know when a party will strike.

I add comfortable walking shoes and a pair of flats while longingly eyeing my twenty-hole platform docs. I want them for the trip, but won't make the mistake of wearing them on the plane again. The last time was a disaster with taking them off for security. The people waiting behind me to go through were thrilled with my lacing and unlacing boots.

Instead, I opt for a shorter pair—less personality but practical and lightweight. A few pieces of jewelry go into a roll-up leather case. Although I try to remove my new ring, hesitant to bring anything I might regret losing while traveling, I can't bear to take it off. Deciding it's safer to wear it, I slide it securely to the base of my finger, where it settles like home.

"Whatcha got there?" Jo asks, watching me fiddle with it.

"Oh, I picked this up at the Philly Expo. Not my usual

style, but I just fell in love with it," I say, showing off my new piece to her.

She looks at the ring and then at my face without so much as even a smile.

"Don't you like it?" I ask, looking down at it and frowning. Sure, it's gold, compared to my normal silver, and just a single stone, but the color—I could drown in the midnight red.

"No, it's great," Jo enthuses, with a smile that doesn't quite reach her eyes. "Just would hate to see you lose it. Are you sure you want to bring it with you?"

"Not at all, but I can't bear to leave it. Grab the luggage scale, will you? I think my suitcase is close to fifty pounds."

Just as I thought, I'm at the limit. I'll eat my snacks and that will leave room and weight for things I'll find along the way, but most of the shopping will get shipped back.

I wish I had a reason to bring my new corset and jacket, but they weigh a ton, and I don't have room in my bag. But damn, did that outfit make me feel sexy. I can't help but think about Luke lacing it up again or, even better, taking it back off. Although the last time I wore it was to the club where everything had gone to shit.

Pushing back yet another memory of the guys, I flop down next to Jo on the couch and say, "Okay, let's run through the shop's operations again."

She playfully shoves me and says, "Shut your smuthole. You know I got this. Plus, I have Anna now. Don't worry, I got your baby. Go. Have fun with the new you and enjoy buying all your weird, cool, creepy shit. Maybe you'll even meet some hot European stranger."

I smile back, "I know, I know. You're right about the store. But I think I've had my fill on guys for a minute. So, in or out tonight? My flight isn't until the afternoon, so I can hang."

Jo looks at me and quirks her brow. I return the face, and we both dissolve into belly laughs.

"Out!" we say at the same time.

She heads to the bathroom to get ready first while I double and triple check my packing lists. When my anxiety is down to a somewhat manageable level and the paper is nothing but a crossed-out mess, I pile my suitcase and backpack next to the door. My travel outfit is laid out. The lists for Jo and takeout menus are on the kitchen bar. There is nothing left to do except have a fun night with my friend and wait for tomorrow.

I change into a top that shows off the girls better and head to the bathroom to check if she is ready to give up the counter space. Watching her put the finishing touches on her eyebrows makes me smile, thinking back on the hundreds of times I have seen her do this. I love this girl so much.

"Your eyebrows are always so impressive," I say to her.

She arches one at me and deadpans, "I know."

Laughing, she heads out to change clothes, cracking me in the ass as she leaves. I chuckle as I do my makeup, darkening my brows in honor of Jo, adding red lipstick for me.

Tonight is a little cooler, so I throw on a cherry red leather jacket to match my Doc Martens. It reminds me of Stalky Hottie. I take a deep breath, the smell of tobacco and leather haunting my memories.

I put on a few necklaces to make a layered look and add my bat earrings that are on the dresser at the last minute. They remind me of the good times I had with Hottie. But maybe I should give up on someone who I'm pretty sure has substantial issues and focus on Luke.

Despite the mystery surrounding the last time I saw him, I can't help but cringe at the thought of him screwing around with someone else on his tour. Thinking of him whispering in another woman's ear or kissing them while spinning fire on stage makes my stomach fall to somewhere around my Docs.

And in the light of day, I have to wonder if I had been so caught up in that night, maybe my imagination had run away with me. Or maybe all the excitement triggered a waking dream. Because seeing a black upside down cross on my forehead in the mirror after he snuck in with my spare key just didn't make sense.

Sure, he said he was baptizing me into his darkness, but that was metaphorical. Wasn't it?

I googled the heck out of black semen. I doubt he had some type of metal poisoning, so that left blood as the only explanation. Which really seemed to be the most likely, and gross, scenario. Perhaps from all his piercings? Something just doesn't jive. I'm trying to unravel a riddle that is missing essential clues.

Giving up on understanding the motivations of a man like Luke Devlin, I grab my new spare key, since he had stolen the other one, and pass it over to Jo, saying, "Here, you'll need this."

"Oh, I almost forgot! I found this little shop and just had to have this made for you." She roots around in her purse for a second and then pops up with a vintage motel style keychain. She triumphantly hands it to me.

"Hottest slut in the oddities shoppe!" I read out loud and snort. "Who needs enemies when I have friends like you?"

I add the key to the new keyring and pass it back to her, then shove my wallet in my jacket pocket. We make our way down my back stairs, still chuckling over the gift, and walk a few blocks to my favorite corner spot, Jethro's.

We talk about everything and nothing as we go. Since the patio is closed when we arrive, we head inside and grab two seats at the bar.

"What will it be, ladies?" Jason, the usual bartender, asks when he makes his way over to us.

We look at each other and say in unison, "Margaritas!"

I smile at him and add, "And keep 'em coming."

I love bourbon, but Jo and tequila is an irresistible and dangerous combination. Like fire and oxygen—the resulting conflagration is so bright, and so beautiful, you can't help but reach out to touch it. Sure, it burns, but man, is it worth it. I can't even list all the times she talked herself, or all three of us back in college, out of trouble when tequila was involved. Or did she talk us into trouble?

We share chips and fresh guac, the perfect complement to our margaritas. We pick a few different appetizers, sharing them between us. Jo is always careful to stay gluten-free around me, cautious to keep me from getting sick ever since I was diagnosed with Celiac disease.

It was one of the many reasons my parents didn't approve of our friendship—she had told them exactly what she thought of me not having a safe space to eat at home because my dad simply would not give up his way of life for my "weakness." As if it was my choice.

After two margaritas, Jo excuses herself to go to the restroom. I have a devil on horseback halfway up to my mouth when the familiar prickling sensation creeps up the back of my neck, sending my heart racing in anticipation and tingling ghosting over my skin like Hottie's cool fingertips.

I inhale, expecting to catch a whiff of his signature tobacco and leather scent, but when I turn my head, nothing.

My smile falls, disappointed both at his absence and at how things ended with my mysterious neighbor. I'm going to need to figure this out when I get home.

Before I can get too lost in my thoughts, Jo bounces back into her seat, and I focus my attention on quality time with my bestie.

"Looking for hotties?" she asks.

Interesting choice of words, since there is one hottie in particular I am keeping an eye out for. We both have a history of hit-or-miss love lives. I never understood why some guy hadn't scooped Jo up. She is incredible. I wish she could see herself as I did. Perhaps she needed a hot mystery man to show her who she was in an antique mirror in a bathroom surrounded by penis candles.

I smile at the memory and say, "Girl, I'm always looking for hotties."

She squints at me in the dim bar lighting. "You're different. What's changed? I haven't heard you knock yourself once, and you're usually full of self-deprecating humor. Sure, earlier you said you've fallen in love with yourself, but there's way more to this story. I can sense it."

I sigh. Of course, I can't hide anything from my best friend. "I should have known better; you know me too well. Well, it's a fucking story. And," I pause dramatically, "I think I'll need one more margarita for it!"

She enthusiastically waves the bartender down. "Jason— more tequila, good sir!"

He brings two shots and two more margaritas over.

I groan, "We're too old for shots. Remember the last time? I have to leave tomorrow."

Jo slurs, "Bish, please!"

We pick up the shots and sloppily clink them just as he comes over with a crème brûlée. We squeal in delight.

"Ladies, I think you need a little more food to go with that last round. I'll walk you home then. I'm not on closing duty tonight."

Jo's gaze zeroes in on Jason's handsome face. She leans forward, crossing her arms so that her ample cleavage is all but falling out of her shirt. She catches his eyes dart to the sight and when he flicks them back up to her, she licks her lips and murmurs, "Sounds great."

Poor Jason. Once Jo sets her sights on someone, they don't stand a chance. Unfortunately, her inability to commit leaves a trail of broken hearts in her wake. I roll my eyes at her.

When he leaves, she looks at me and says, "What? He's cute in the boy next door kinda way." Then, with growing dread, asks, "Wait, did you already hit that? Is he the story?"

"Lower your voice. We're just friends," I shush her, although I am happy she might have company to keep her entertained while I'm gone.

Empty margarita glasses, shot glasses, and a demolished crème brûlée litter the bar in front of us. As Jason clears the remnants of a damn fine time, he says, "I'm ready in five."

I'm thankful Jo seems to have forgotten I owe her a story as we get our things together. Jason is back within a few minutes and the three of us link arms with Jo in the middle. A true gentleman, he gallantly steadies us as we stagger our way to my place, even waiting at the bottom of the stairs until we are back inside.

I lock the door, and we both struggle to get our shoes off. Imagining their height difference, I gasp out between fits of giggles, "He could climb you like a tree."

Jo shushes me noisily, but continues to laugh. I grab us each a bottle of water and an aspirin to ward off hangovers.

We down our pills and the water, take turns in the bathroom, and head up to my room.

"I really wanted to hear that story," she slurs as we head up the stairs.

We crawl into my bed and lay there facing each other, hands pillowed under our faces like the little angels we are not. I sincerely hope for a silent night, blissfully free of dreams, since Jo is here with me.

I struggle to focus on her face, my vision fuzzy around the edges. She looks so different when her face is relaxed, nothing sarcastic or shockingly vulgar slipping past her angelic smile. Sometimes I think she is so big, so loud, to hide something deeper. A secret she has yet to tell, even after all these years of friendship.

I am finally ready to reveal my own secrets. The story of my nameless mystery man, from our first run in to the night with the mirror. Tell her all about Luke, starting with his searing kiss and ending with being baptized into his darkness. Confide in someone I'm worried I either can't keep my waking dreams at bay or the nighttime ones from bleeding over. Tell her I fear I'm losing touch with reality.

Although I want to spill my guts in a midnight confession and unburden my soul—Jo is already asleep, which is probably for the best. There is no way I can get out anything coherent with the tequila swirling in my brain. I double-check that three alarms are set on my phone, so I don't miss my flight tomorrow, and promptly pass out to her soft snores.

I wake up the next morning-ish thankful for a dreamless sleep without a single nighttime visitor. I am proud to have been a real grown-up and packed yesterday rather than frantically running around today.

I head to the kitchen and throw a few panic snacks in my backpack. Having Celiac means always being prepared and airports are among the trickiest places to eat. Half the weight of my luggage is safe food for me.

At the last-minute, I grab Bram Stoker's *Dracula*. My e-reader is loaded with an impressive lineup for the long flight, but I want something familiar to fall back on and help me get in the mood for my trip to Romania.

Even though my schedule has been kind of tight with these back-to-back trips, I'm thankful to be embarking on this business venture. Hopefully, the miles between me and the guys will purge the testosterone from my system and let me make some decisions.

Jo comes stumbling downstairs, hair reminiscent of medusa, and heads to the bathroom. In less than ten minutes she emerges, looking as fresh and beautiful as ever. Mindy and I never did figure out how she could get ready so quickly. It was like magic. One minute she looks like something the cat dragged in, the next she looks like she could walk down the runway.

She comes to the kitchen and says, "Let's hit up that

coffee shop and then get you to the airport. I need a quad. With an extra shot."

I groan, "I hope Natalie is working!"

Jo laughs, knowing my longstanding love-hate relationship with the place across the street. But as luck would have it, my favorite barista is indeed in today. We load up with caffeine and snacks for the road. I nibble on my pastry, and while I would normally relish the gluten-free treat, nerves turn it into dust in my mouth.

Every mile we drive toward the airport seems to ratchet up my growing sense of anticipation. It's more than what I would expect to have for a buying trip. This will be my first European one, which means I will have items shipped versus packing them into the bug or a rental van. Maybe that is what is triggering this rising anxiety.

But even that doesn't seem to be quite enough of a reason for the premonition that something big is looming on the horizon. Not impending doom, more like a shift in the winds of change. I can't help but think things will be different when I come home. How exactly, I'm not sure, but I know I won't be returning home to life as I know it now.

I planned this trip to death, channeling my worries into extreme detail. My itinerary is relatively set, but I had built in some time for add-ins or following my intuition. I've accounted for every contingency. I even added a sick day.

Like a nervous tic, I double-check that my passport and wallet are in the designated pocket of my backpack every few miles, envisioning the nightmare of reaching the airport only to find them missing.

In between these compulsive checks, I run through my mental lists—everything I need for the trip, what needs to be done at Grimm—despite having already left paper copies for both Anna and Jo in my apartment and at the store. But I can't help but second guess myself. Did I leave the shop keys? Did I buy enough cat food?

"I can smell your brain melting," Jo says, breaking into my reverie, as I mutter about bank deposits and trash pickup schedules.

I laugh as she easily navigates us to the passenger drop-off. She pulls over into the unloading zone and I grab my rolling suitcase and shoulder my backpack. Jo sweeps me up in a hug, pouring her strength and reassurance into me.

"Have an amazing time and don't worry, I'll hold down the fort," she reassures me.

"I know, I know," I reply, but on the inside, I'm overwhelmed by the earlier foreboding that nothing will be the same when I return. For a second, I start panicking, wondering what would happen if Jo wasn't here.

Her outline shimmers as the sun peeks out from behind a cloud, highlighting her riotous golden curls like a halo, making her look like an angel on earth. If I squint hard enough, I can imagine great wings coming off of her like an iridescent aura.

A waking dream at departures is not on my carefully written schedule. I draw in a deep breath and start counting, spinning my ring and reciting with each spin, "You are safe."

She sweeps me back into a tight hug, whispering into the top of my head, "You are safe with Jo."

The panic fades away within her reassuring arms. Blinking at the burning behind my eyes, and steeling myself with box breathing, I break away and look up at her. No wings, just Jo, who is still an angel of a friend.

"Jo, I love you," I say in all sincerity. Where would I be without the support of my friends?

She puts her hands on my face, staring down at me with her big blue eyes. "I love you, too. You can do this. You can do anything. Hell, you could even save the world. You have no idea just how strong you are."

"I'm glad one of us believes in me," I half joke.

She drops her hold to my shoulders and gives me a squeeze, then gently pushes me toward the airport. I turn and head into the international terminal, rolling my suitcase behind me, eyes forward because I know if I turn around, I'll cry.

At the airline check-in counter, I hand over my bag—fifty pounds on the nose—and head toward the gate. I finish my coffee as I wait in line and chuck the cup so I can go through security.

I am always anxious trying to get my luggage and shoes and coat into the right bins, remembering if my e-reader needs to be in or out of my bag, and worrying I somehow slipped a full-size bottle of lotion or a switchblade I didn't know I owned into my backpack.

The line of travelers snakes its way forward as I try to ignore the happy couple in front of me with their "just married" matching T-shirts and hats. Instead, I imagine Hottie or Luke in a "the new Mr." hat, standing next to me. I stifle a laugh, knowing neither of them would be caught dead in one of those.

My heart twists a little at the thought of marriage, but soon enough I'm distracted by navigating security, fighting off panic that my passport will get eaten by the x-ray machine, and trying not to lose my phone.

I try to monitor my stuff zipping along the conveyor belt as I gingerly step across the dirty floor. Next thing I know, I'm through the body scan, gathering up my items from the bins, putting my shoes back on, and grabbing my backpack. I let out a relieved sigh at having survived the airport check-in.

Now I'm well and truly on my way. I follow the signs toward my gate, shuddering at the thought of a chain coffee shop but still craving another hot beverage. I skip my usual quad espresso latte in favor of a London Fog steamer—not wanting to be wired for the overnight flight but needing the comfort of a warm drink.

Tea in hand, I walk to the end of the terminal where my gate is, hours before boarding begins. I didn't want to cut it too close, but now it seems I have overestimated just how early I needed to arrive. Oh well, at least I didn't miss my plane.

I drop into a seat and watch the people go by. Business travelers in suits hustle past. I spot the newly married couple, again, and parents trying to wrangle too many suitcases and too many children.

The air buzzes with the excitement and stress of travel. Once again, I'm the odd one out. No family to worry about, no partner to pass the time with, just me on my own. Too restless to read, I pop in my earbuds and pull up my favorite playlist while I soak in the drama that is the airport microcosm.

Watching the people move like schools of fish, I reassure myself that there is freedom in traveling alone. Only my bag to worry about, and the autonomy to go wherever I want. Sometimes I get so bogged down in the pressure to be with someone I forget to enjoy the amazing parts that come with being solo.

I go to the bathroom twice, not wanting to have to get up too much on the plane. I start and stop reading to pass the time, but in the end, I give up and just scroll social media. I'm shocked to find Grimm's followers just keep ticking up.

The credit goes to Anna, who really excels at this part of the business. The way she posts pics of items for sale with

Lucifer looking every bit the haughty shop cat has people clamoring to buy. I've even received offers for him. I click over to his profile and gasp at his follower count, muttering in disbelief, "He's a fucking cat."

An eternity later, boarding is announced. As I wait to scan my paper ticket, not trusting something so important to technology, my playlist changes over to the remake of *Dragula* I've fallen in love with. The familiar McHottie prickle skitters across my neck and down my spine.

I glance around but, of course, don't find him and think it must just be a reaction to hearing the same song as the first time I saw him in my shop. Popping my earbuds out until I can get to my seat, I shuffle forward with the remaining crowd.

I hang toward the back since I just have my backpack and no carry-on. Might as well stand while I can before getting stuffed into the middle seat of a sardine can for hours on end.

I join the tail of the line, scan my boarding pass, and walk down the jetway. Just before entering the door, I tap the outside of the plane for luck. As people frantically search for overhead space, I longingly eye the first-class seats.

This airline features single or double suites, the ultimate in luxury and privacy. As we inch forward, regret punches me in the gut when I note how the seats can fully recline. I should have splurged.

As we move to the next section, I think this isn't too bad. But as we continue shuffling along and I glance at the row numbers, I spot my seat far ahead—small, tightly packed, with barely any legroom.

I'm already dreading the long flight cramped between strangers. What if they are chatty? What if they snore? I make my way to my assigned middle seat, eager to check out who I'm stuck with, but there in my spot sits a small child and her parents.

Looking at my paper ticket, I frown and say, "I'm sorry, but I think this is my seat."

The harried mom looks up at me, taking her phone from the little girl, who starts wailing, and pulls up an app with their three passes. The folks waiting behind me give a collective groan as I wave a flight attendant over.

As I stand there awkwardly while the attendant fiddles with her tablet, at last she says, "The seating assignments were updated after you printed your ticket. Please come with me."

I follow her, wading through the other passengers like a salmon swimming upstream, my shoulders shrinking at their huffs of annoyance. As we return to the slightly better seats, my embarrassment fades into relief at the thought of an upgrade. I'm incredibly grateful for this turn of events. My delight turns to confusion as she continues to lead me through the full business class and back to first.

While I stand there waiting for her to direct me, I can't help but drool over the suites with the wide leather seats. They seem even more luxurious after having seen the rest of the plane.

Expecting her to point me back to the rear after this tease of what I'm missing out on, I'm downright shocked when she gestures toward the window seat of the closest suite. Now *this* is the way to start a trip. I settle into the plush leather, stowing my backpack in the provided cubby. I can't believe my luck with this upgrade. I might actually sleep my way across the Atlantic with the reclining chairs.

Rather than the stiff ramrod straight nightmare I was expecting, I marvel at what seems more like a loveseat tucked into a nook—a true oasis in the sea of humanity crammed onto this plane. I worry this will spoil me for life.

I pick up the card that explains how the seat reclines while I sip on the champagne that was standing at the ready. Next, I explore the suite, finding a stash of blankets and legit pillows, not some dinky piece of foam covered in plastic. Yup, definitely ruined for life.

Having explored every inch of my private mini cabin, I turn to watch the landscape of airport activity out the window. I listen to the background noise of people scrambling to find their seats and store their belongings as the final few passengers board.

I reach down to root around in my backpack for snacks and my e-reader, when I swear, I catch a whiff of tobacco and leather. Whipping my head to the left, I see my seat partner has arrived and is stowing his luggage in the overhead bin. I could complain about not having the whole suite to myself, but I'm just so grateful for the stroke of luck that I don't even mind sharing.

My gaze travels up well-worn jeans hugging thick thighs to reveal chiseled abs framed by an Adonis belt, with a hint of a happy trail where his shirt had ridden up. Black ink peeks out from his waistband, but before I can make out the tattoos, the new passenger ducks into his seat.

Chapter 4

I gasp as he laughs, the sound warm and rich. He's clearly amused with himself and my reaction.

"You!" I exclaim, causing the flight attendants to turn toward me. I hiss, lowering my voice, "What the hell are you doing here?"

He gives me his half grin, the one that makes my knees weak, and says, "Flying."

Like that explains everything. How on earth is this happening? There is no way this is a coincidence, that not only are we on the same flight, but my seat was changed to share a conveniently private suite with him.

I frown and say, "This makes no sense. First you startle me into burning myself, then seduce me, next lecture me, then pull a Houdini. Now we are stuck together on a plane?"

His grin turns into his damn full nuclear smile, showcasing beautiful white teeth, and for the first time, the hint of a dimple. Seriously? Like the man needs a dimple on top of his exquisite, good looks.

"There are no coincidences," he says mysteriously. "Only fate."

His voice caresses my ears and heats my blood. He has too many weapons against me. His bulk fills the large luxury seats and his thigh rests along mine, heat and electricity crackling through our layers of clothing as if we were skin to skin.

"What the hell," I growl, jerking my leg away.

He leans in with his amber gaze fixated on me and smoothly slides my hand into his, lifts it to his lips, and kisses my knuckles, making it impossible to stay mad.

"I will explain, but not on a plane full of people," he promises.

"I can't wait," I deadpan.

His grip suddenly tightens, as his eyes catch on the ring I couldn't bear to leave behind. His eyes widen, an unknown emotion flashing across his face. But just as quickly as I see it, it's gone, and I'm left wondering if I saw it at all.

I let him take my hand and tuck it into his elbow. I try to scowl, I really do, but I'm secretly happy to be close to him. All this time of trying, but failing, not to look for him and here he is beside me. In the flesh, he is so much more than in my mind. Bigger. Hotter. Sexier.

I'm not the best flier with my fear of heights, so a drop-dead gorgeous mystery man sitting next to me in a luxury suite doesn't leave me with much to complain about. His sheer presence alone seems to crowd out my anxiety, as if it were a palpable thing we simply don't have the room for.

I have a whirlwind of emotions: anger, doubt, lust, and even a little guilt, all swirl in my heart and mind. I'm not sure what I *should* be feeling after the way we left things. My body has no such qualms after so many nights spent together in my dreams, immediately warming at the sight of him. Finally, I settle on vague unease with a side of cautious optimism and an undercurrent of let's get it on.

"This is going to be a long flight," I sigh.

He replies with a wink, "I'm looking forward to it."

The suite that had seemed so large now seems almost claustrophobic with his bulk next to me. I put in my earbuds to try to get some mental space while physically confined to a shared area with this man and turn my head to stare out the window at the sea of airport activity beyond.

I startle when he reaches over to pop out one of my earbuds so he can listen, too. Quirking an eyebrow at him, I mess around with my playlist, choosing some favorites and watching his expression. He seems into some of the music I like and others he is by turns amused, nonchalant, or scowling. What can I say? I have eclectic taste.

With boarding complete, we listen to the flight attendants drone on about using our seats as flotation devices. It always makes me laugh—the absurdity of thinking that, in the event of a crash, we might survive and actually need to use our cushions. This, of course, does nothing to assuage my fear.

At last, we taxi out to the runway and the plane takes off, pushing me back into my seat. Once we are in the air, I will be a little calmer, but take off is the worst, where the safety of the ground drops away as we soar higher, every foot up increasing the risk of plummeting to our deaths.

As if sensing my rising anxiety, he takes my hand, slowly running my knuckles back and forth over his lips. Feather light touches that draw my focus away from the window and to his amber eyes. They heat as they look at me until I'm burning in their twin flickering flames.

The cabin announcements break the spell, and it's only then I realize he distracted me through take off. As we hit our cruising altitude, I wonder what I am going to do with myself for hours stuck here with Stalky Hottie. I want to grill him for information and get all of my questions about him, and us, finally answered, but this is not the time or place.

We sit together in strained silence, each with an earbud. I grow increasingly aware of his proximity until I can sense the location of every molecule of his being. It makes me want to jump either out the window or into his lap. I can't decide which.

Charged particles pass between our skin like a synapse firing. My brain is dumping some serious oxytocin. If his nearness isn't enough, his familiar scent is now permanently seared into my olfactory nerve for eternity.

There is his usual tobacco and leather, but this close to him, I can pick up on the unique undertone of his skin, the clear smell of a rainstorm with a hint of the danger lightning will bring. If some evil scientist bottled this scent, she could enslave all of womankind with it.

Yup, this is going to be a very long flight indeed. My neighbor lets out a small chuckle under his breath, resulting in some serious side-eye from my side of the suite. The corner of his lush lips kicks up, and I have a wicked urge to lick that exact spot.

He turns his head to me, and I bite my bottom lip out of habit. He leans in to growl in my ear, "Stop. Biting. Your. Lip."

My heart races like a trapped rabbit, and I hold back a moan at his domineering manner. He pulls back and meets my eyes, reaching out and prying my lip from between my teeth with his thumb.

I don't know what possesses me, but I lean forward and suck his thumb into my mouth, cheeks hollowing, tongue swirling around the tip. The sight of his pupils eclipsing his amber irises, and his sudden sharp intake of breath is deeply satisfying on a primal level.

I smile up sweetly at him with his digit gripped none too gently between my teeth. The column of his throat ripples as he swallows, and only then do I release him.

A sinister grin lights up his face, and I instinctively clench my thighs. If I thought his megawatt grin was panty-melting, this dark look—one that promises to fulfill my newly unlocked secret fantasies—should be downright illegal.

Thankfully, I'm saved by the approach of the flight attendant serving drinks. Another perk of first class is that we're the first to receive more much-needed alcohol. Having already downed the champagne during boarding, I decide to switch to wine and forgo my usual bourbon. I can't lose my wits when I need my defenses up.

I choose a red and am surprised when he asks for the same, since I have never seen him eat or drink, other than that sexy sip of my bourbon back at Jethro's. And then my brain supplies the time he licked gelato off my lips. Does that count? Damn, that night, things were just getting good before it went to shit.

He passes me a glass from the flight attendant and lifts his own to me, saying as we toast, "To new beginnings."

I take a sip, pleased at how good it is for airplane wine. Must be another perk of flying in style.

"So, where ya going?" I ask, taking a larger swallow.

He meets my eyes and looks a little abashed as he replies, "I was hoping to go with you."

In a most uncharacteristic display of first-class passenger manners, I choke on my beverage, shocked into swallowing down the wrong pipe.

He thumps me helpfully on the back while I wipe my mouth with the cocktail napkin, eyes streaming, and try to catch my breath.

When I can move air in and out again, I wheeze, "With me?"

He patiently says, "Yes, with you."

"Huh," I grunt out. "Why?"

He sighs and cryptically says, "The question has never been about *wanting* to be with you. I *belong* with you."

I don't know how to reply to this so I curl my legs up, thankful to be vertically challenged, and pull out my old, tattered paperback of *Dracula*. If all else fails in life, run away into fiction.

I can't get the answers I want right now, and we are starting to venture into hazardous territory—too close to the truths I'm not sure I'm ready to know. I had begun to barricade my heart against him, safely labeling him a stalker with a few screws loose in the frontal lobe.

But being here next to him, I'm falling back under his spell. He can't actually be dangerous, I rationalize. He has good taste in wine and art. He loves vintage horror movies, the mark of any good human. Plus, he smells *so* good. Surely, if he were something awful, like a serial killer, he wouldn't smell like sex in a leather jacket.

He settles one hand on my ankle, softly circling the small bone there, mesmerizing me with his touch. I sneak peeks at him from the side of my eyes as I try, but fail to read the same page endlessly.

Sensing my need for silence, he pulls out a magazine and stares at it. He, too, fails to turn the pages. We pass the time pretending to read while stealing glances at each other, and I turn our conversation round in my mind. It is a hopeless labyrinth with no path forward, just endless dead ends of unanswered questions.

Dinner is served, and although he is sipping his drink, he doesn't eat. I pick at my bland food, tired and unsure of this situation. I slug down the rest of my wine.

"Sleep," he says, and I realize I'm exhausted. The tension, anxiety, and alcohol mixed with the dim lighting of the cabin lights push me toward a blissful escape. He pulls the door on our suite closed as I recline the seat almost horizontally. Yup, spoiled for life, is my last thought before surrendering to sleep.

I WAKE HOURS LATER, groggy from the mild disorientation that happens while traveling. I blink a few times and turn my head to find him watching me.

"Hi," I say. Even though I whisper, it sounds loud to my ears above the quiet, darkened plane.

He must have covered me with a blanket as I slept. He reclines his seat to match mine and lifts his arm, beckoning me to his side.

I snuggle into him, the best you can snuggle into solid marble. He is cool against me, and I pull the blanket up further against the chill of the air. He is so hot and cold in turns, mysterious yet sweet. His presence is an enigma compared to the bold, brash nature of Luke. I can't help but be intrigued.

He curls up behind me, pulling my hips into him so we are two spoons nestled perfectly together. His hardening length has my eyes springing open, suddenly wide awake. Unsure what the protocol is in this situation, I cover my uncertainty by opening my playlist.

One of my more explicit songs starts playing and I flush crimson, realizing we both still have an earbud. But before I can change it, he leans his head down to mine.

"Spread your legs for me," he whispers in my free ear.

He pulls my leg up over his. I try to glance behind him to make sure the suite door is closed, but I can't see over his bulk.

"It's just you and me. As it always has been and as it always will be," he reassures me.

Goosebumps ripple down my neck and shoulder where his whispered words have his breath ghosting along my skin. Against all rational thought, I comply, spell-bound under his instruction. I bend my right leg and hook my left over his, leaving myself exposed and vulnerable.

He pulls the blanket up to our shoulders, hiding us away from the world. He wraps his right arm around me, teasing my breasts while trailing his other hand to the waistband of my leggings.

I'm mildly disappointed I didn't push him harder to explain and let myself open right back up to him physically, but he is like an addiction—I just can't stop. Besides, I tell myself, when will I ever get to do this on a plane again?

He dips his fingers into my pants, triggering full-body goosebumps. His hand trails lower, and I bite my lip to stifle a moan as quiet footsteps walk past.

"Hush, *Roză*," he whispers in my ear.

I grip his hip with my hand and curl the other around his arm, loving the solid muscles flexing beneath my touch as he kneads my breasts. His other hand continues its descent, sneaking over my underwear to my molten core.

I'm disappointed he is still above them, barely touching me. Featherlight sweeps back and forth over the top, which somehow is even more erotic than if he had just dove right in. My panties grow damp and as my breathing picks up, he slips them to the side.

He dips two fingers into my entrance and swirls them in my arousal before bringing them up to circle my clit. As he repeats the movements, the pattern lulls me into a trance-like state. The hushed background noise of an overnight trans-Atlantic flight, paired with the suggestive song, is a strange juxtaposition.

Finally, I can't take anymore teasing and push my hips into his hand when he brings them back to my opening again.

"So greedy," he admonishes, yet thrusts his fingers into me.

I worry the entire plane must be able to hear my barely restrained moans and heavy breathing, but I can't stop now, and he better not stop, either.

He brings his left hand up and covers my mouth and nose, effectively silencing me. He groans low in my ear, and I respond with a gush of wetness as he curls his fingers inside of me while grinding his palm into my clit.

I'm thankful for his foresight as I ride his hand and a scream claws its way out of my throat, muffled in its escape. He's found some unknown place deep in me in perfect combination with the pressure of his hand. Stars float in my vision from the lack of oxygen with his hand covering my mouth and nose, but it only pushes the sensations higher.

"Come for me, *Roză*. Soak my hand," he whispers into my ear, and it sends me over the edge.

My entire body tenses, my back arching, walls pulsing around his hand, clamping down. He uncovers my nose so I can sneak in some air as he helps me ride out my orgasm, through the little aftershocks, and finally slides his fingers out and frees my mouth.

I gulp in a breath and my vision clears enough to see him lift his hand to his mouth, sucking each digit that had been inside of me without breaking eye contact. I could come again just from the sight.

He licks his lips and groans, pupils blown wide with lust. For a brief second, I think he has elongated canines, changing his usual smile to something more sinister, but I quickly write it off as oxygen deprivation and reading *Dracula* before I fell asleep.

He pulls me back into his body, curls around me protectively, and tucks in the blanket. A comforting Hottie cocoon.

"Sleep now," he says, again nuzzling my neck, and I do, boneless after the quick but intense, toe-curling orgasm.

Chapter 5

VLAD

How I wish we were anywhere other than a damn commercial aircraft. These small teasing samples of her barely slake my thirst. I bring my hand to my face, inhaling the lingering traces of her. My love. My life. Her scent only further inflames my desperate longing.

I reach under the blanket and adjust my throbbing cock. Even my centuries of practiced patience are wearing thin. I can't help but curl my ancient body around her frail human heat. Every lush curve fits snugly into my hard form. It should. She is from me, after all.

Whether she wants to accept it or not, this is our truth. One body, one flesh. Our souls are so intertwined we have no beginning or end from each other. Even that snake bastard could not cleave us apart despite his best efforts. Then or now.

If only I could protect our love, our soul, as easily as I wrap my undying body around her. The white noise of the flight and the sound of her breathing lull me into a relaxed state where I let my mind wander back through lifetime after lifetime.

This reincarnation of my *Roză*, Lieshe, is different. I've been trying to learn everything I can about her and this modern world. So bright and busy. So damn loud and distracted.

I think back to a quieter time, before airplanes and cell

phones, blazing lights and so much noise. A soft smile crosses my face as I reminisce about nights of flickering firelight where the only sounds we could hear over the summer crickets were our own stained breaths and cries of passion.

Flashes of happiness, stolen moments of beauty I keep locked in my heart for the long, lonely years without her. The times between filled with a longing so deep, so painful, I fear it has fractured what remains of my soul and stripped away the last vestiges of my humanity.

But lying here, with her in my arms once more, I can remember when I was just a man in love instead of a monster chasing a dream only to shred it with his claws, or in my case teeth, over and over again.

I bury my nose in her hair, drawing her sleepy rose scent in by the lungful. As if I can store it away for the next time between. I stop myself at that thought because there will be no more years without her at my side. I vow to make this lifetime the last.

Somehow, someway, we will have our chance. I will either die fighting for it, or I will die with her. I just need to figure out how to kill this immortal body.

Chapter 6

After keeping Lieshe from panic and sending her on her way, I slide into the driver's seat of her silly old car and take a deep breath. Glancing in the rearview mirror, I mutter, "You're such a shitty guardian angel."

"I'm *not* her guardian angel. You know that," replies my backseat passenger, crossing his arms and huffing like a petulant child.

I raise my brows at him and say, "Clearly."

He retorts, "Besides, you're a shitty best friend. What do you think is going to happen when she learns the truth? Your entire relationship with her, and Mindy, is a lie."

"It's not a lie!" I protest vehemently.

My friendship with Lieshe and Mindy *is* real. I will never regret the times we've shared. The amount of lies, half-truths, and subterfuge that has been necessary to maintain it, on the other hand, tugs at my conscience.

I tell myself the same line I've used for thirty years now. Lieshe is a single soul on the cosmic scale of justice versus the fate of humanity. I'm here to play my part, following orders—a pawn in a game even greater and older than the earth I stand on.

I mean what I said. Our friendship is not a lie and I really do love them. In the end, this is all for them, too. So, why does it feel so wrong?

"Jophiel," my passenger calls in our language, the sound

falling like music on my ears, bringing my attention back to the present.

With a huff, I say, "Don't call me that, and for fuck's sake, use English. Or any other human language. Except French; you don't want to sound like that pompous asshole. Now go. Someone needs to keep her safe."

I watch his reflection in the mirror as he rolls his eyes, looking every bit a human unless you know what to look for, before he blinks out of this plane of existence.

"Thank fuck," I say out loud to myself as I merge into the busy airport traffic and head back to Grimm.

I'm beginning to suspect we're not the only ones sent to influence this game from the shadows. There are other pieces on the board, and I'm going to uncover them.

Starting with getting my hands on that elusive mangy cat. I knew there was a reason he's never shown his whiskers in my presence but is always slinking around Lieshe. By the time I'm done with him, he'll be coughing up answers like a furball.

Then I might take that cute bartender for a spin. What was his name? James? Something with a J. With a smile I remember, Jason, that's it. Let's see if he can find my golden fleece.

Chapter 7

The next time I am awakened, it is by our descent. I blink the sleep from my eyes, adjust the chair back to the upright position, and pack my things away to prepare for departure. I'm tired and sure that I look like I just slept on an overnight flight across the pond.

Stalky Hottie, on the other hand, could walk onto a movie set. His hair is perfectly disheveled, eyes clear, faint stubble softening the knife edge of his jaw. In a word, delicious.

I meet his eyes, put my hand on his forearm, and say, "We need to talk. Quit distracting me with orgasms and your ridiculous good looks."

He chuckles and nods.

I am anxious to get off this plane and get some answers, but in usual fashion, the passengers take forever to disembark. Like they didn't realize we were going to be getting off when we landed. At least the wait isn't terrible, this close to the front.

I try to swing my backpack onto my shoulders, but he takes it along with his small carry on. My bag looks comically small on him, though it's so large it barely qualifies as a personal item. I follow him down the aisle, watching all my little keychains and baubles sway cheerfully above his fine ass.

We exit into the swarm of other passengers, all making

their way to the luggage carousel. I'm so happy to be in Dublin. I have always wanted to come here.

After we grab my bag, I say, "So, I'm actually on a work trip and have a pretty tight schedule."

"Of course," he says.

He looks down at the ground sheepishly and then back up at me through his lashes. It is boyishly charming to find him looking chagrined.

"I just want to be with you," he admits quietly.

If his looks weren't enough to melt me, those words are.

"Oh. Well, where are you staying?" I ask, surprised by his answer.

He smiles and says, "I have a place just outside Dublin you'd love. Please, stay with me."

I pause and weigh my options. On the one hand, I already booked a discount hotel with a shared bathroom. On the other, I could accept a romantic getaway with a super-hot guy who has given me several awesome orgasms, but is kind of a stalker. Whatever is a girl to do?

Helpful as always, the devil on my shoulder tells me to give this smoldering relationship a chance, to see if it can rise from the ashes like a phoenix—let my brooding mystery neighbor have one more try to win me over.

Before I can overthink it, I pull up the app on my phone to cancel my reservation. It is a good thing I had built in some flex time for this trip. My itinerary is about to go sideways.

And hopefully so will we. Although I appreciate the multiple orgasms he has given me while expecting nothing in return, I am desperate to get my hands—and body—all over him.

And we need some privacy to talk through whatever this

is between us. Practically speaking, I should be moving on and focusing on my business trip after things got so strange at home. But my heart easily sways me. I have to figure out this relationship to move forward, no matter what that means.

"I'll stay with you on one condition," I reply. "I deserve answers."

He gives me his full nuclear smile and takes my hand, bringing it to lips and ghosting a kiss over it. He tucks it into his elbow and with his other hand, grabs my suitcase, confidently leading the way as if familiar with this airport.

I try to get a peek at his passport on the way through immigration, but his large body blocks my view. A voice in my head reminds me I have yet to learn his name, but I argue back that he wouldn't sit next to me on an international flight if he had plans to harm me. Too easy to track.

Once we are outside, I take a deep breath of fresh air. I'm not scared of germs, but I dislike breathing in the same air as other people for hours on end and touching things where a million other hands have been.

I look at him in surprise as he steers me toward a black town car, but he just gestures to the open door. While he stashes my luggage in the trunk, I scoot across the leather bench seat and check out the luxurious surroundings. There is even a divider between us and the driver.

While I wait, I decide I should text someone and let them know where I am. Just to be safe. Usually, Mindy and Jo would be my go-to girls, but they're an entire ocean away. So, I message Wren, who's currently the closest person I know, physically speaking. She's out traveling around Europe until we meet up in London to buy the taxidermy raven that inspired this trip before we head to Transylvania.

LIESHE

Hey! Made it to Dublin. Funny story, I ran into my new neighbor from home on the plane and am heading to his place for the night. Can't wait to see you!

Reading my message back makes this seem just a little reckless. I mean, how well do I know him? Sure, he seems so damn familiar, but I'm suddenly plagued by indecision. This might not be the smartest choice I've ever made.

I'm in a foreign country, romping off to an undisclosed location with a virtual stranger who harbors stalker tendencies. My anxiety spikes and my breathing picks up. I start counting and spinning my ring just as Stalky Hottie slides in next to me.

I look up into his amber eyes, soaking in his jaw, those lips, and the devil on my shoulder gives a sexy little laugh. A smile splits my face as I realize not only am I in Ireland, but I am in Ireland being whisked away by a total fucking hottie in a town car.

Throwing caution to the wind, I think about how this is every woman's dream. The car is luxurious, with supple leather seats and that new car aroma. It's a nice transition from the airplane suite. A girl could get used to this. Secret billionaire fantasies commence.

He lifts his arm in invitation, but I frown and ask, "Did you forget to grab your suitcase?"

He pulls me against his cool solid side and replies, "No. I keep things here."

As I snuggle in closer, I say, "I thought you meant you were renting a place, but you own a place here? You don't sound Irish. Where are you from?"

"I am a child of the world, from everywhere and nowhere. We will get settled, and I will feed you," he says.

My stomach growls in response. The overnight flight and time change will soon catch up to me, but right now I am on a high from the erotic plane ride with him and thoughts of an entire uninterrupted night together. Finally, I'm getting some answers. I just hope they are good ones.

I watch the countryside pass by, amazed by the beauty as Ireland shifts from the Dublin cityscape to greener pastures, with narrow roads lined by stone walls and sheep dotting the landscape. Though we sit in shared silence, I can't shake the worry that this is the calm before the storm.

Gray clouds roll in, making the green fields appear even more verdant until the rain starts. As the drops streak down the windows, distorting the beautiful view, a wicked idea pops into my mind. Filled with sudden bravery, I turn from the watery view of the countryside and lock eyes with him.

In my best sultry voice, I say, "I don't think I can wait. I'm starving."

"Are you now?" he asks, eyes smoldering as he pulls me onto his lap.

I drop my forehead to his, our vision coalescing to a single amber focus. I could drown in him. I know we've been here before, falling into each other's eyes, the outside world long forgotten. I know it deep in my very marrow.

I *am* starving for him, to rediscover him and see if my fingertips recognize his skin, my tongue, his taste. I'm curious if my body can canvas his the way he has mine mapped with targeted precision.

I know this makes no sense. Hell, getting in a car headed to an undisclosed location with a maybe stalker is probably the stupidest—and most exciting—thing I've ever done. But right now, I don't care.

I.

Don't.

Care.

Pushing away coherent thought, I breathe across his lips the words I know will be his undoing, "Mm, hm. Absolutely famished."

Maintaining our smoldering eye contact, I slowly slide down his body to kneel on the running boards between his legs. I drag my hands up his thighs. I can't help but smile at the bulge forming behind those damn jeans.

Reaching up, I pop his button and draw down the zipper, the sound loud in the quiet of the car until his ragged breathing drowns it out. I pull open his fly; the tip of his cock is already straining toward me above the waistband of his black boxer briefs.

Mercy. Why I'm surprised at the size, I have no idea. His large hands and tree trunk thighs should have led me to expect this. Yet I remain astonished as I see the flushed head in contrast to the porcelain skin of his abs.

My hands tremble as I slide them up the outline of his erection and hook my fingers in his waistband. He is breathing like a freight train as he lifts his hips up so I can wrangle his pants down.

As I pull them down his legs to leave them pooled at his ankles, I am rewarded with a view of not only the ink on his abdomen that has teased me so many times but the full frontal view of him—tree trunk thighs rippling with muscle and tattoos, and yup, the final package.

I blink at his fierce beauty, intimidated by his size, and desperate to see all of him. Curious about the image I see peeking out of the bottom of his shirt, I push it up to reveal a large dragon circling his lower torso, artfully designed to highlight the deep V of his abs.

I stare into its fierce face, mesmerized by the way it shifts with his breathing, appearing almost alive. The body wraps around his hip, wing cresting up to his waist, then disappears from my sight, and reemerges on the other side. The tail extends fully across to wrap around its neck, the very tip curling right down to my target like an arrow pointing the way.

As I peer down at the exquisite tattoo, pondering the hours of pain he must have endured, he tips my chin up to gaze into my eyes.

He growls, "If you keep looking at me like that, it's you who is going to be eaten."

He snaps his teeth at me playfully as I slide my hands up over the shades of vibrant red and black. The line work is so fine, I'm surprised the teeth aren't sharp as I glide my fingertips over them. I leave a trail of goosebumps as I trace the dragon's tail down, down, down.

Stalky Hottie's breathing hitches as I draw ever closer. I lean in and ghost my breath over his head and down the shaft, hands braced on either side.

Sure, I've given blowjobs before. But this time, I really want to do it. Not just as an act on the way to sex itself, but to worship him. Revere him. Show him the feelings he brings bubbling to my surface.

I want him to experience what I did that first night in front of the mirror. My desire emboldens me to try something new. Instead of just swallowing him down, I dip my head down low and lick from his balls straight up the underside of his shaft.

I savor the smooth texture of his skin, running my tongue over the pulsing vein until I reach the very tip. My eyes dart to his face as he lets out a strangled moan.

Every muscle in his body is tensed as his hands flex over

and over. The sight of him coming undone fills me with indescribable power and confidence.

I boldly stare into his eyes and flick out my tongue to daintily lick the small drop of precum that has gathered there. His flavor bursts to life in my mouth—so damn familiar.

He unclenches his hands, only to fist them deep into my hair, and lets out a torrent of words in a beautiful language I don't understand, but there is no mistaking their meaning.

I am killing him, and I love it.

Before he can get his bearings, I open wide and swallow as much of him as I can. I suck and swirl my tongue, pushing ever further toward the base of his cock. All too soon, he is bottoming out in my throat, and I realize there is still no way I can fit all of him in my mouth. I am simply out of room.

I wrap one hand around the base and bring my other one up to caress his balls, marveling at how cool his skin is, well, everywhere.

I let my saliva drip down so I can work my mouth and hand in tandem, swirling my hand as I hollow my cheeks with suction. Jaw aching, I pull back to focus on just the head, bringing my other hand up to pump his shaft as well.

The back of the car is filled with his harsh breathing and my sloppy sucking, making me thankful for the divider. Totally consumed, he speaks to me in the same language.

I don't know what he seems to be asking me, and I don't really care. I would agree to anything right now, drunk with lust and power. I meet his eyes and see something primal and raw reflected back at me. Something I don't know that I am ready for.

He blinks as sweat drips down his forehead and into his eyes. He growls, "Here is a taste of what you are starving for."

For a second, I wonder at how his words could be so close

to Luke's, but that's impossible. He would have had to be there that night and overheard them. I'm quickly brought back to the present by his next command.

"Swallow me. Every drop is yours. All of me. Always," he pants out.

With his hands buried in my hair, he pulls me off with a loud pop, leaving a string of saliva trailing from my mouth to his cock. The sight has me panting.

"Say it," he demands.

"All of you. Always," I whisper hoarsely, throat raw, caught up in the moment.

I continue to work him with both hands, pumping in tandem, twisting at the top, over his head and back down. As he begins to pulse, I open my mouth as he falls over the edge at my words and readiness to take him.

As the first ropes of his release fall on my outstretched tongue, I take him back into my mouth, working his hard length while I suck and twirl my tongue over the head. He shudders and jerks in my mouth as I eagerly try to swallow mouthfuls.

He stills my movements, trembling and panting. He pulls back and stares at me in wonder. After a moment, he reaches out and swipes a drop that escaped from my mouth, swiping it across my lips before pulling me up to his lap to crash his mouth into mine.

Teeth clashing, tongues dancing, I drown in his flavor. He is all I can smell, all I can taste, surrounding me. The kiss turns feral until we're breathless. I break away, desperate for oxygen, stars swimming in my vision.

I'm not sure how we ended up flipped with me awkwardly on my back and him between my legs. We are rutting in the back of the car like two teenagers. I'm surprised his cock hasn't torn a hole through my leggings as it strains toward me or that they didn't incinerate right off my body with the lust pulsing in the air.

A knock on the divider draws our attention to the fact that we have stopped. I can't help but wonder just how soundproof the divider is.

Chapter 8

Stalky Hottie helps me to a sitting position, then wrangles his pants back on, flashing me his panty melting smile.

He steps out and holds out a hand to me. I awkwardly slide across the bench seat to take it, blinking at the bright sunshine after being lost in the dark confines of the car. A fresh breeze tugs at my curls as I take in the beautiful countryside, sparkling from the recent rain.

Down a cobblestone path lies a delightful little gatehouse surrounded by a high stone wall. While he retrieves my bags from the trunk, I spin in a circle, taking in the rolling lush green fields sloping gently down to a large crumbling structure far off in the distance.

Scattered wildflowers and clusters of trees dot the landscape, and a narrow, winding stream shimmers under the sun as it flows toward the sea. It is beyond idyllic. I clap my hands excitedly.

"Oh, it's perfect!" I exclaim as a smiling Stalky Hottie leads the way to the front door, my suitcase bumping along behind him over the cobblestone path.

A shiver that has nothing to do with him skates down my spine, pulling my gaze back to the car. I'm not able to make out the driver through the tinted windows, but I get the strangest flash of ill will directed toward me.

As it leaves through the wrought-iron gate, I question what on earth that could have been about. As the engine fades away, I realize just how quiet and isolated it is here. For a brief second, I wonder again if I made the right choice in romping off with a virtual stranger with stalker tendencies.

I turn back to the house and see Stalky Hottie standing there, smiling, framed by a charming doorway. The house's front is four-sided, like half of an octagon, with ornate windows. Each tall window is topped with a smaller triangular one, and both are filled with beautiful symmetrical patterns crafted from leaded glass.

Stone spires crown each set, giving the small gatehouse the appearance of a miniature cathedral. A rectangular structure extends from the back of the intriguing facade. I push aside my misgivings and follow him inside, hoping I don't end up like the curious cat—dead.

We enter through the old wooden door into the main room, a few soft pieces of furniture tucked in along the hexagonal wall. The flooring is made of ancient wide plank boards, scarred and beautiful from hundreds of years of feet upon them. Opposite the seating area is a large stone fireplace, already laid for a fire.

There are built-in bookcases stuffed with books and an antique writing desk and chair in the corner. The low table in front of the couch holds a fresh bouquet, accounting for the scent of flowers permeating the air.

I walk over to them and inhale, saying, "These are the same roses you filled my house with, stalker boy. They really are beautiful, though. The color is amazing, so red they are almost black."

I stroke the dark, velvety petals. I could get lost in their depths.

"They are called Vampira," he tells me, and the name makes perfect sense. "And if you think I'm a boy after that car ride, then I am wounded."

Smiling at his feigned hurt, I place my hand under a bloom to pull it toward me and prick my finger.

"Ouch!" I hiss.

I yank my hand back. The next thing I know, my finger is in his mouth, and as he sucks the tip, not only does the puncture wound pulse, but so does my core.

He lifts his eyes to mine, his full lips still wrapped around my me. He flicks his tongue against my finger and my breath catches. His pupils are blown wide, just a rim of amber visible, his eyes and touch electrifying. His stare pierces my heart, as if he can see past my defenses and is looking deep into my soul.

My gaze answers his, the whispered word, "Yes," falling from my lips, but in answer to what, I couldn't say. But every fiber of my being echoes the word, "yes," as if *this* is my purpose in life, in the universe. The fulfillment of my soul is to return to his. It is raw and real and monumental.

Everything freezes, time itself slows as we move like a motion picture advancing one frame at a time. He releases my finger and takes my face between his hands, our gaze fused. He painfully, slowly lowers his head to mine, ghosting my lips with his, sharing the same breath.

I lose all conscious thought and can only breathe in this moment, this exchange of power and air and hunger. Simultaneously, our mouths come alive, consuming each other in an uncoordinated and heated kiss. It'a meeting of souls, both of us trying to pull the other in like the movie is suddenly on high speed.

Ancient and exotic, he tastes like time itself. We kiss our way up the stairs, crashing into walls, holding each other up as we kick off our shoes and shed our jackets. I am desperate to touch all of him, not fragmented pieces, but a full melding of the flesh, the body, *the soul.*

He scoops me up bridal style, never breaking our kiss, and carries me up the final flight of the turning stairs. Each step up only fans the flames of our desire. He kicks a door open and then closed again behind us.

By the time I open my eyes, we are in my dream bed, an enormous four-poster in a stone room. The incredible teardrop windows line the floor. The fire is already lit here. Peat perfumes the air alongside the scent of the same Vampira roses scattered in vases all around the room.

He tosses me on the bed, where the same deep dark red of the roses is reflected in the color of the drapes and linens. Grabbing me by the ankles, he pulls me to the edge of the bed as I let out a squeal. In one smooth move, he hooks his hands into my leggings and panties and has my bottom half bared.

I struggle out of my shirt and bra, popping my head out at last to find him standing at the edge, staring at me, eyes smoldering with heated passion. I prop myself up on my elbows, desperate to drink him in, shirtless.

He shoots me his panty melting smile, knowing I am waiting in anticipation. Sure, I saw parts of his body in the car, but I've been longing for this moment—to see him in all his glory. He pops the button on his jeans, eyes locked on me.

I follow the movement of his hands, controlled, and unhurried—torturing me with his slow deliberation. Jeans clinging precariously to his hips, he reaches behind his neck and pulls his shirt off one-handed, tossing it carelessly to the floor.

I finally feast my eyes on his shirtless form and I'm breathless. I knew he was big and solid like marble, but this is incredible. He ripples with muscle, beautifully carved like an avenging god.

My eyes move up his abs and chest, taking in his broad

shoulders and finely sculpted arms. He is drenched in ink, a study in black and red from his wrists to the base of his neck.

He looks down at himself, following my gaze, then back up at me through his lashes, smirking at the way I'm drooling. He knows just how stunning he is and must spend hours honing those muscles in the gym.

Above the intricate dragon I saw earlier is a large skull of shadows and light. I'm unable to take in any more details as he gets on his hands and knees on the bed, crawling up to me. On instinct, I start to retreat up the bed, a lamb in his wolf's gaze.

He reaches out and grabs my ankle, stalling my progress. He climbs on top of me, straddling my legs with his. He moves his hands to grip my wrists, pinning them above my head.

Without his restraining hold, I would run far, far away from this dangerous predator. I'm freezing and on fire at the same time. He is so much more than I ever could have imagined. His chest just grazes my nipples when I want his full body against mine, *in mine*.

"Breathe," he whispers, making me realize I've been holding my breath.

I gulp air, and as I exhale, he lowers his lips to mine just to swallow my breath.

"I have chased you across time and space itself, *Rozǎ*, and now we are together again. Forgive me," he murmurs against my lips, then kisses me.

At this moment, I can't make sense of his words, because all I want is him. I crave him. I am frantic. Words don't matter when his lips are on mine.

He trails kisses down my neck, his tongue lingering in the hollow above my sternum, just as he did what seems like a lifetime ago. He moves his warm, open mouth down the center of my chest and finally releases my hands. Taking one nipple into his mouth, he gently bites me, and then pulls back to blow across it while his hand finds my other breast and kneads it.

I have been waiting to explore his bare skin and see if he is as hard and cold as I think. I caress his broad shoulders, reveling in the solid muscle below my fingertips. I slide them across the curving muscles and up to thread them into his silky black locks, pulling him in tighter to me. I can't get enough. I want to touch every texture, greedy to learn the landscape of his body.

He turns his head to worship my other breast, and I could implode just from his skin against me, coupled with his skillful mouth. He kisses his way down my abdomen, sliding his legs down the outside of mine, and I get a better view of his impressive shoulders, covered in more ink.

The firelight dances over his taut muscles, highlighting his beauty in shadows and light. His large hands on my knees spread my legs wide. I stare down at him as he looks at me like the secrets of the universe are contained in my exposed center.

He spreads me open with his thumbs and gazes at my innermost parts. I try closing my knees, but he is immovable. My heartbeat is frantic in my chest, ratcheting every faster as he drinks me in with his eyes.

Just when I think I am going to scream, he claims me with his mouth, erasing my inhibitions. There is no timid exploration or tentative lick. Rather, he dives into my apex like he is starving. He attacks me with his tongue, driving me wild until I am tossed into the storm of his mouth.

Pleasure swirls within me as he thrusts his tongue inside, taking me up and up. He works one large finger into my entrance, then two. I am so full as he plunges them in and out, swirling his tongue around his fingers and back up.

He tries to work a third finger in, but even as aroused as I am, his hands are large, and I just don't think another will fit. I toss my head from side to side, moaning.

"Open for me, my *Roză*. I need you ready for me," he says.

His encouragement has me trying to relax, realizing he is right. I could hardly fit his cock in my mouth. Taking him into my body is going to require some effort.

He moans as I relax, allowing him to slip another finger inside. Incoherent sounds fall from my lips. I have never been so full. Pleasure pulses deep in my belly as he adds his tongue to the mix. Swept up in the storm of his assault, I crash like a ship on the shore as he moves his mouth up to suck on my clit, hard.

I scream, stars swimming in my vision as I clamp down on his fingers. He curls them forward until my release gushes down my thighs.

He doesn't stop or even slow down. I try to push him away from my overly sensitive flesh, but he continues to ravage me with his mouth, pulling his fingers free to use both hands to push my knees flat to the bed.

I lift my head and watch him continue to feast like a man starving, moaning and lapping at the mess he's made of me. Seeing him thoroughly enjoy and savor me is so fulfilling. His pleasure skyrockets my own, the erotic sight of his black hair falling into his eyes.

He looks up at me through the stray locks, amber eyes blazing, holding my gaze as he takes one long lick with his tongue flattened the whole way from my ass to my clit and then bites it.

I scream as another orgasm hits me like a tsunami until I can only lie there, panting, trying to pull enough oxygen into my lungs. As he moves his kisses to my inner thigh, I am surprised by a stinging bite he then laves with his tongue. I love this dominant side of him.

Crawling up my body, he settles against me. Instinctively, I wrap my legs around his hips. He holds himself on his elbows, framing my face in his hands. Bringing our foreheads together, he whispers against my lips.

I can't make out what he says, but it sounds like the same language he used our first night, in front of the mirror. The words tease my brain, somehow familiar, which is so strange since I only speak English.

As he claims my mouth in a searing kiss, thoughts of linguistics fly away. His passion and longing, mixed with sadness, and the faintest wisp of despair, color it, as if he is saying goodbye before we've even said hello.

I pour my hope for us into him, trying to eclipse his darkness with my desire to love him. To trust him. To let him into not only my body but also into my heart. Into my soul.

He wraps his arms around me, crushing me into his chest. Rolling us, he settles me on top of him, caressing my back.

I push up on shaky arms, looking down into his eyes, worshiping me and filling me with confidence. Being on top, putting myself on display, always seems oddly more vulnerable.

This moment is clearly what he wants, though. He ghosts his hands down my breasts to settle on my hips, grinding me down against him.

I gasp as the head of his cock bumps my clit. He bites his lip as he moves his hips up into me. I trail my hands down his chest, across his pebbled nipples and as he shivers, I decide I want this.

I.

Want.

Him.

So, I take him. I place my hands over his on my hips as I lift up until I'm hovering over his cock as it strains toward me in the air. I slowly impale myself on him, sucking in as I'm filled, thankful now for the multiple orgasms that had only begun to prepare me for this invasion.

He stays perfectly still, eyes locked onto where our bodies meet, watching me take him into my body, merging us as one flesh. I drop my head between my shoulders, my hair tickling down my back. His hands rove up from my hips to caress my breasts as they jut out with my back bowed.

I continue to ease more and more of him into me, shifting side to side slightly to accommodate his girth.

"I—I don't think you'll fit," I gasp.

"How do you eat an elephant?" he asks.

I snap my head up. "What?"

"One bite at a time," he answers, chuckling as he reaches down to rub circles over my clit.

My laugh turns to a moan as he expertly strums across my bundle of nerves. The distraction and increased stimulation are exactly what I need to allow him into my tight heat. I try to balance the need to adjust to his size with the urgency to move, to have more friction, more of him.

As I shift my hips back and forth, grinding into him as I get used to the full sensation, he sits up, changing the angle. I wrap my arms around his shoulders, using the leverage to move faster.

"Please," I cry.

The sensations are overwhelming, but I just can't seem to get the right angle or speed. I need him to take control. I want to come along for the ride.

He rains kisses over my face, wrapping one arm around my hips to help my movements and fisting his other hand at the base of my scalp. Canting my head back, he licks a long line up my throat, up my chin, and across my lips. He claims my mouth as he begins thrusting up into me, meeting my rising frantic need. My thighs are shaking, no longer able to sustain this pace.

But I needn't have worried. He continues my earlier motions, grinding me into him while thrusting up into me as if we have done this a thousand times before.

"More," I demand, now fully accustomed to him.

With a growl, he flips us. I tilt my hips and lock my ankles behind his back, pulling him even deeper until this new angle is just this side of pain. I run my hands up his back, wondering at the rough texture in the center I had noticed before.

The need to explore every inch of him, learn all the textures of his skin with my mouth, and map the history of his life with my fingers, burns within me. I want to know every scar and its story, inside and out. And finally, I can share all of myself with someone, connect with them not only in the flesh, but in the soul—share my scars, too.

Resting his forehead against mine, he repeats his earlier words, each phrase punctuated with a rolling thrust of his hips.

"All of me. Always. You will take all of me. Always," he grunts out.

Using his hand in my hair, he turns my head to the side, growling in my ear, "*Roză*."

I know what he needs to hear. As I repeat back to him, "All of me. Always," his teeth sink deep into my neck, just as I had envisioned what seems like so long ago in my bathtub.

This vampiric bite is my longest held fantasy. The

sharpness of his teeth, his guttural moan of satisfaction, his lips pulling at my skin, sucking. It is nothing like I hoped it would be. It is so much more.

I scream my release as his hips jerk frantically, cock swelling impossibly larger before he fills me with liquid heat, rolling waves and aftershocks of my orgasm thundering through me.

I had no idea sex could be like this. Every time with him takes me to a new level. I am so sated, all I can do is lie here, boneless, casting about to find the pieces of myself that have been tossed in the storm of him. But now, we're so tangled in the wreckage that I don't know if we can ever be whole again without the other.

He kisses me slowly, languidly, swallowing my hiss of pain as he withdraws. He turns on his side and gathers me into him. Being his little spoon is quickly becoming my favorite place. He runs his hand over my breast, down the curve of my belly, and to my sex. Scooping up our joined release leaking out he pushes it back in with one long thick finger and holds it there.

"All of me," he whispers.

"Always," I murmur back.

The room is warm from the fire despite the chill of my marble man behind me. Wrapped in his arms, filled with him, surrounded by him, my body melts into the bed, and I'm drug under to sleep.

Chapter 9

I wake to the sun just starting to set outside of the leaded glass bedroom windows and the fire low in the fireplace. I'm starving and in need of a bathroom, which is the only thing that motivates me to crawl out from the luxury linens and fluffy comforter.

He must have tucked me in after I crashed out. I don't find him anywhere, but I do see a dark red nightgown and robe over a chair near the fire. I get up and slip them on, not wanting to wander around nude in an unfamiliar house.

This same deep red as the Vampira roses is quickly becoming a theme. The silk caresses my skin and fits me like a glove. An incredible dragon is embroidered down the entire back, reminiscent of his tattoo.

The divine color makes my skin luminous. I should wear this shade more often. As I slide my hand down the material, the firelight glints off the stone in my new ring and I notice it, too, matches the midnight red of the roses and my nightgown.

Opening the door, I peer down that hall where I see an open door. I head toward it, relieved to find it is indeed a bathroom. A large clawfoot tub and separate shower room dominate the space. The fixtures fit with the old stone house, blending seamlessly into the décor, but there are hints of modern trappings—a rainfall shower with multiple heads and heated tile floor.

After using the facilities and washing my hands, I head

out to find my man. For he is clearly mine. Stalky Hottie has seared himself into my very being, and now, it is time for answers.

I head back down the stairs to the living room where we first came in and find the fire burning merrily. My backpack and suitcase are neatly lined up next to the door. I pull out my phone to check if Wren texted me back, but the battery is dead. It's been a long time since I plugged it in, so I dig out a power bank and leave it to charge.

On impulse, I grab one of the Vampira roses from the vase on the table and pull out my old copy of *Dracula*. I tuck the flower inside to press it and place the book back in my backpack. This beautiful, rich, dark red will always remind me of this night.

The aroma of dinner and the comforting sounds of someone cooking lure me down the hall to the kitchen. Stalky Hottie stands there, chopping vegetables in jeans and a long-sleeve moss green henley. He looks up, and the shirt brings out the green flecks in his eyes, just as it does when I wear that color.

I walk over and drop onto a bar stool at the island opposite of him. The scent of a roast permeates the air. As he chops veggies and adds them to a bowl of salad, my eyes run over the muscles in his arms as they flex.

The pendant lights above the island have the Edison bulbs I have in my kitchen. I try to make out the tattoos below his pushed-up sleeves in their soft light. His arms are covered to the wrist in what appears to be different styles of writing, but I can't make out what they say and have a hard time even identifying many of the different scripts.

Some of them appear to be so old they are fading to a blurry blue. One looks almost like hieroglyphs while others are foreign to me, unlike any languages I've ever seen. In between the black letters are the Vampira roses, the dark red contrasting beautifully.

Up the right arm, they are blooming and beautiful, but when I look over to his left side, the flowers are withered and dying. I can't help but wonder at the underlying meaning. As I study over more of the script, I smile as I think to myself, I am not a cunning linguist but this man's cunnilingus? Mercy me.

He raises an eyebrow at my secret smile, wondering what I am thinking. Best not to embarrass myself, so instead, I say, "And you cook?"

He smiles and drops his eyes to his task.

"Um, everything smells lovely, but I'm afraid I can't eat gluten," I say reluctantly.

"Just a roast with veggies and salad," he responds. Fixing me with his amber stare, he quips, "Because you're famished."

I smile at his use of my words from the car as I wonder how he knows my dietary restrictions, but I guess it's part and parcel of being with a stalker. The scene is cozy and domestic. Normal. I wish the two of us were hidden away from the world in this cottage, perhaps on our honeymoon, like that couple who was in front of me at the airport.

But we aren't. It's time to figure this out. I can't wait any longer. I need answers.

As the sun falls, the fading daylight of the golden hour streams through the windows, highlighting the sharp contours of his face, straight nose, full lips, amber eyes, and my goodness, that jawline. But I must stop getting distracted by his incredible beauty or I won't get anywhere.

"We have to talk," I say, biting my lip.

His eyes fall to my movement, and he drops the knife and carrot. He comes around the island, steps between my legs on the stool, and reaches up with his thumb, pulling my bottom lip from my teeth.

"Are you sure?" he asks.

The sadness in his eyes bottoms out my stomach, triggering me to wonder what on earth can be this bad to make his eyes so haunted.

Shit, is he married? Or does he have a communicable disease I should have asked about before having unprotected sex? Or maybe he is the serial killer I keep joking to myself about.

"Stop," he says. "Whatever you're imagining, I can promise you, is not the truth."

I take a deep breath and meet his eyes. "Then tell me, because I have a pretty amazing imagination."

He turns and brings me a glass of red, taking one himself. He lifts his in a toast and says, "To the longest love story ever told."

I quirk an eyebrow and clink glasses with him.

"I never know where to start," he muses, as if to himself.

"Then start at the beginning," I respond.

He gives me a heartbreaking smile and says, "That's what you always say."

I frown at him, knowing I've never said that to him before. We've known each other for such a short time, every experience and moment together are fresh in my mind.

"Are you trying to say we have met before?" I ask, encouraging him to continue.

"Yes," he says. "Our story *is* the longest love story ever told."

"Ours?" I parrot back. "We have a love story?"

It is pretty early to start using the L-word, even if he is an incredible lover, insanely hot, and there is this amazing connection with him.

"Yes. Ours is the first and the last. It always was and always will be. An eternal echo, across time and space."

His strange reply almost makes me wish I hadn't asked. That I had simply eaten dinner with him, and then we had fallen back into bed together, hiding away from the world in this little cottage. But that is impossible.

I would do anything to prevent the visible anguish on his face, in his voice. I can tell his heart is breaking, and I just know mine is about to break, too. The sense of impending doom is thick in the air, like lightning about to strike, and I am the tallest object in an open field.

"I need you to trust in what you feel. I need you to think with your heart and leave your rational mind behind," he says in his beautiful, slow voice with the exotic accent I've come to adore.

I take several gulps of my wine without even tasting it, just needing to steel myself against whatever torrent of pain his expression promises to bring. The suspense is killing me. What can be this extreme? It must be terrible.

He softly says, "I need you to see me as I see you."

He backs up a few steps without breaking eye contact and goes back to his salad making, movements jerky, face tight.

Wanting the nearness of him to anchor me in the approaching storm, I stand and walk to him. Turning him to face me so we stand bare toes to bare toes, I reach my hands up to cup his face, rise to my tiptoes, and pull him down to rest our heads together.

"Why do I feel like this is goodbye?" I ask.

He pulls away to kiss my forehead and whispers, "Because it often is."

The kitchen timer goes off, breaking the mood, and we jump apart. He grabs oven mitts and pulls the roast out. He finishes the salad and puts it on the island. Then he plates some of the beef and roasted vegetables. Everything smells divine.

He gestures to the spread. "Please, eat."

He picks up the bottle of red that had been breathing on the counter and refills our glasses.

"Why don't you ever eat?" I ask. I drape the linen napkin across my lap and pick up my fork. I spear a bite of salad with it and then use it to point to his abs and say, "Clearly, you're getting some protein in."

He leans in, and I feed him.

"I can eat," he replies. "I just usually choose not to."

What a strange response. There is no fat on him. Maybe he does extreme intermittent fasting or some type of carnivore diet?

I take another bite and say, "Please, just tell me."

He sets down our wine glasses, sits next to me, and faces me as I eat. The salad is fresh and crisp, flavored with herbs and light olive oil. If the occasion wasn't so heavy, I'm sure I would be enjoying it more. The crunchy vegetables seem so loud in my head as I chew them in the stillness of the kitchen. A loud juxtaposition to this solemn moment.

"I'm serious that ours is the longest love story. What I am going to tell you will seem unbelievable. Impossible even. But I meant what I said. I need you to trust what you *feel* with me. I need you to listen with your heart," he says, face grave.

I immediately start throwing down sandbags around that organ, anticipating a flood of emotion. His opening statement is setting off alarm bells in my head. Clearly, a man this hot who talked me into going to a remote gatehouse with him in a foreign country must not be quite right.

I sense something pivotal is about to happen, and despite the gravity of it all, I find myself surprisingly calm, as if in disbelief. Stalling, I linger over my salad, savoring these last few moments of peace with him before the inevitable storm hits.

My stomach starts to knot, but this is the first time I've eaten since the flight, so I move on to the roast. It's incredible. This man gets points for so many things. And now cooking? But I keep letting my hedonistic side get distracted by orgasms and food.

I take a couple more bites, trying to delay both this conversation and whatever calamity is about to befall us, but my appetite is rapidly disappearing despite the wonderful meal. Unable to eat any more, I push the plate away, turning to face him, and his truth, head on.

"I'm ready to hear you," I say, blotting my mouth with the napkin. He picks up our wine glasses and moves us to the living room with the beautiful windows. He adds wood to the fireplace as I curl up on the low couch with a plush throw.

The room is warm enough, but the blanket offers some small level of physical protection during this uncertainty. The luxury linens and pillows here rival my own. I'm so comfortable and happy in this little bubble, which makes knowing it's about to burst even worse. With all the hints he has been dropping, I am in for something even I can't imagine.

He sits next to me, and we face each other at an angle. He reaches out and traces the outline of my face with a gentle finger. I grab his hand and turn my face into his cool palm, a faint tremor racing through his hand. He grasps mine and holds them in his lap. He meets my eyes, his amber gaze intense, locked into my amber and green one.

He starts by saying, "I have loved you since the dawn of time. You and I are literally the first love story ever told because we were the first people to be in love. I have followed you through many lifetimes, loving you and losing you, time and time again. Each one of your lifetimes, I hope for a miracle, but every time I lose you, one way or another."

For such an enormous man, he suddenly appears so small and lost. Destroyed. Devastated.

I try to remember he said I need to listen with my heart, wrap my head around what he might mean, and the only thing that I can come up with is that he is a serious believer in reincarnation and thinks we have been in love before.

Seeking clarification, I ask, "Do you mean like Romeo and Juliet? Destined to be in love, but not fated to be together?"

He gives me a sad smile. "That was one of the times."

I frown into my glass. Is this what a roofie feels like? Were there magic mushrooms in that roast? This conversation is bizarre. The crackling fire, the red wine, the beautiful cottage, his words—it all starts to become surreal.

A low buzzing begins in my ears as I say, "Break it down for me slow. Start at the beginning and don't leave any details out. Don't give me veiled analogies or parallelograms or whatever you call them. I want a factual accounting of what the hell you are talking about."

My voice rises as I talk, panic starting to set in.

He takes a deep breath and drops my hands to take a gulp from his wine glass, as if to fortify himself. Putting it back down, he places them in his cool grasp again.

My eyes trace over his large hands, cold like marble in mine. In the weight of the moment, I'm captivated by every detail: their size, dwarfing mine; the pale, cool skin, with faint blue veins tracing the backs; his nails, short and smooth, while mine are almond-shaped and black, with a torn cuticle I've been picking at.

His flawless hands tremble in mine, echoing the flutter of my heart. I examine his scattered rings. A well-worn signet with a dragon chasing its tail on his right index finger, a stack of bands in various metals on his right ring finger, and the blood-red stone in a heavy and aged gold band on his left ring finger. The red stone is almost black, reflecting the flickering firelight back to me.

My eyes shift to my right hand, and I realize why my new ring seems so familiar. Other than the smaller band, it is an exact replica of his. I lift my eyes back to him and the weight of his stare drops like a stone into the still well of my soul.

He appears ancient and utterly heartbroken. The gravity of the moment pushes down on me, and I know my life will never be the same. There are too many coincidences in such a short time to be anything other than fate.

"Tell me," I demand again, ready to face destiny.

Chapter 10

LIESHE

As he opens his mouth to speak, my phone roars to life, firing off notifications like the *1812 Overture*. I frown over at it, annoyed at the disruption but wondering what could be so earth shatteringly wrong for it to be going off like this. Worried it could be Mindy, Jo, or something to do with Grimm, I feel compelled to answer it.

"Sorry, one sec," I awkwardly say as I get up to grab it.

I pick up my phone to find dozens of notifications of missed calls, voice mails, and text messages. Unlocking it, I find almost all of them are from Wren.

"Lieshe, what's wrong?" Stalky Hottie calls, as I sink onto a nearby chair, knees weak, knowing in my gut something is terribly amiss.

WREN

New neighbor? Lieshe, are you sure you know him well enough to go somewhere with him?

WREN

Hey, girl, when you get a chance, just drop your location in case anything happens. I know you said he's your neighbor, but…

WREN

Hey, it's been hours. Please tell me you're okay. I'm really getting worried.

I'm scared you can't get to your phone.
Please check in.

JO

Wren called the shop phone. That's who you
are meeting up with, right? She said you
went somewhere with a guy. 🔪 I'm all about
you getting laid in Europe, but just give her
your location, ok? Send proof of life.
Love you.

WREN

I called Grimm, and your friend has no idea
where you are.

Please call me. I don't want to scare you,
but there is freaky news coming out of
Baltimore. I'm sure it's just a coincidence,
but there has been a series of murders. They
think there's a serial killer on the loose. The
murders have stopped, but I'm freaking out
that I haven't heard from you, and you are
with someone from the same town.

ANNA

Good thing you're not in Baltimore right
now. It's chaos. Jo and I are staying
together.

JO

Hey, Anna and I are going to pal up since
everyone is freaking out over here. I'm not
worried, just media hysteria. Check in,
okay? Wren said you still didn't drop a pin.

There are so many more texts from Wren, I can't even read them all before Stalky's shadow falls over the phone. His mouth is moving, but I can't hear him over my heart thundering in my ears. I quickly lock my screen, so he doesn't see it.

"I, uh, I have to run upstairs for a minute," I stammer out and race back up the stairs.

Slamming the door behind me, I run toward the far wall, attempting to put as much space between us as possible. I need time to think. Wren is freaking me out. She has never called or texted me like this in all the years we have known each other.

As I fight waves of anxiety, my phone goes off again, startling me into fumbling it. It clatters to the floor with a loud crash, fraying my already frazzled nerves. I snatch it back up to open her latest text.

WREN

Look at this

I click the link. The headline sends shivers down my spine—*Vampire in Baltimore? Three Found Exsanguinated in Chilling Attacks*

Fuck! Fuckity, fuck, fuck!

At the time, the erotic bite in the bed next to me had seemed incredible, the culmination of my lifelong vampire fantasy. But in light of this news, I can't help but worry that Wren is right. I don't know Stalky Hottie from Adam. The murders did stop when he left. The victims were found exsanguinated. This seems too much to be coincidence.

I reach up and slide my fingertips over the marks on my neck. Pure panic, raw fear bubbles up throwing me into fight or flight. Flight seems the better of my options, so I pull up a ride service app on my phone. I have no idea where I am or even if there is such a thing as taxis out this far.

"Please, oh, please," I plea.

Lieshe, if you don't end up murdered, I'm going to kill you myself, I chastise internally. This was so, so stupid. For fuck's sake, I don't even know his damn name!

"Yes," I cry, thankful when the app shows an available ride just a few minutes out. I choose the first hotel that pops up back in Dublin as my destination.

Hastily getting dressed, I grab my clothes from the neat pile on the chair and pull my shirt on over the robe and nightgown and my leggings underneath. I have no idea where my bra and undies could be, but that is the least of my worries right now.

Spinning around in a frantic circle, I find my shoes and coat next to the door and shove them on. According to the app, I still have three minutes to somehow slip past Stalky Hottie and get out the front door to meet my ride.

My rational mind tries to reach through my rising panic to tell me there is no way he can be a serial killer. The odds are just too astronomical. I must be overreacting. I start to slow my breathing. Think. Fucking think, Lieshe!

Why would he bring me here just to kill me? He could have done that at home. I'm definitely overreacting. I start to get a hold of myself, slowing my rapid breathing and feeling my heart rate trend back to normal when my phone pings with another text message from Wren.

A knock at the bedroom door whips my head toward it, stifling the scream that wants to tear from my throat. I've got to try to rein it in and act normally.

"Um, yeah?" I answer shakily.

"Lieshe?" His muffled voice comes through the door.

My name drips from his lips in his beautiful, exotic timbre. I frantically search the room for an escape. There is none. I'm trapped and at his mercy. My jackhammer heartbeat pulses deep into my core.

Really, I scold my lady parts—this is not hot!

"Are you alright?" he calls.

Even through the door, his concern bleeds through. I

can't answer him. The knob turns, and as the door swings open, my lungs seize up with my voice. I look, really look, at the man before me.

Dark. Foreboding. Huge.

The ridiculously hot, yet incredibly dangerous man stands in front of me—a unicorn. My traitorous body wants to run to him, rediscover the passion we shared just hours ago. My bleeding heart wants to cling to the deep connectedness I've always felt between us.

A lifetime has passed since I left home yesterday. The enormity of the situation and the exhaustion of international travel threatens to pull me under, but my instinct to live is stronger. I ride a second wind, with anxiety overpowering the wants of my body, the rationality of my logical mind, and the feelings of my heart.

"I, uh, I have to go. There's been an emergency," I choke out the lie.

His face falls. He must be one hell of an actor to show such genuine concern.

"I'm sure it can wait for the morning. Let me help you with whatever it is," he says, as he holds out a hand to me haltingly.

The heartbreak on his face is killing me. Part of me knows he means me no harm. Part of me wonders what the hell is going on here and that there must be more to this story. And a tiny sliver doesn't care about any of it, serial killer or not. Just wants him, everything else be damned.

"I already called a car. I-I'm sorry," I say, voice cracking on the last word.

I mean it. I'm so sorry for everything that could have been. I thought I was falling for him. Maybe I already have. In this lifetime, or perhaps another, as he seems to think.

As I watch him fall to his knees, arms outstretched

toward me, my mind replays that same image of him from my waking dream at the Philly expo, where he had walked in on me as Luke railed me from behind.

In this present moment, his face is just the same—hemorrhaging emotion. I witness the transformation of love and hope give way to loss and devastation so profound, my heart breaks, too—smashed like my mother's damn crystal vase that I broke as a child. Something beautiful and wondrous splintered into oblivion.

His body collapses like a deflating balloon as if his will to live, his soul, has been torn from it. His usual porcelain skin pales to almost translucent.

A long unused part of my brain urges me to act, the nurse in me looking for a way to save him. But there is no rescue protocol for a fractured soul, no way to transfuse a bleeding heart.

Before I lose my nerve, I abandon him to his own devices. I race past his outstretched hands, clamber down the stairs, and run to the front door. Throwing it open, with one hand I grab my backpack and with the other, the handle of my suitcase. My soul tugs me back as I leave him behind, as if it, too, can't bear to leave him.

Pushing down the painful and conflicting emotions, I take off toward the gate, swinging my pack onto my shoulder as my luggage bumps along on the cobblestones behind me. Headlights illuminate the space with their approach. I race to them as I hear his footsteps closing in.

"Lieshe," he cries brokenly as chases me down.

With a predator following me, a primal part of my brain wants to keep running, sprint past the car and into the deep woods in the distance. Let him chase me down, hunt me, *claim me* if he catches me. Erase the emotions, the thoughts, the hesitation. Just *be*. Surrender to the physical rules of engagement and to the victor go the spoils.

If only life were that simple. I cannot untangle my analytical brain from my emotion drenched heart. I cannot surrender my ego to the id. Fuck, how I wish I could. With the safety of the hired car behind me, I spin and face him.

"Tell me it wasn't you," I cry.

The moon highlights his pale face, reflects in his amber eyes. In this beautiful moonlit landscape, he looks every part the vampire I have imagined him to be. The voice, the glimmer of canines, the visions.

He pulls himself up to his full height and meets my eyes head on as he slowly stalks toward me. My suitcase handle is sweaty in my grasp, my lungs fight to pull enough oxygen in. My brain screams at me to run—just get in the fucking car and escape this insanity.

"Tell you what?" His voice is quiet and lethal as it cuts through the night.

He does not raise the volume, but the words meet my ear as if we are inches instead of feet apart. The car has pulled up behind me, opened the trunk, and is patiently idling. I inch backward until my back comes up against it.

"Baltimore. Was it you?" I cry, wanting to know who this man really is, yet dreading the answer.

He stops his approach at my question and drops his eyes to the ground for a moment, his silence deafening. He looks up at me without moving his head, eyes glittering gold in the moonlight, and I know.

I know.

Deep in my marrow, in the very seat of my soul, I know there is so much more to him than the man I have been falling for in this dangerous game of hide and seek. He isn't a man at all.

All the clues have been there from the start. His ability to slip in and out undetected. The bats, the giant dog, the visions, the dreams. His ice-cold skin. His obsession with me, with my blood. The orgasmic bite. Even the damn roses. The inconceivable truth has been staring me in the face the whole fucking time.

"Oh, my little *Roză*. You have no idea what I am or the depths I would go to *for you*. I would burn it all. Drown the world in rivers of blood. I have before. I would do it again and gladly. You cannot run from me. You cannot run from *us*. In this lifetime or the next, you will always be mine. And I will always be yours. Our love is eternal, echoing across time, across space. It always has been and always will be."

His words worm their way through my panic, implanting into the base of my brain. *All of me, always,* ringing in my ears. Turning, I hurriedly toss my suitcase into the trunk, slam it closed, and jump in the car on the far side, putting as much distance between us as possible.

I pull the door shut and turn to stare at him through the window. I put my hand against the cold glass, wishing it were the cool marble of his skin I was touching instead.

From the safety of the vehicle, I whisper, "All of me. Always."

He's right. I cannot run from us. But I sure as hell can run from him. And right now, that's exactly what I am going to do.

As the car pulls off into the night, he throws his head back and roars, face contorted, lips pulled back, and elongated canines gleaming white in the moonlight. Though the distance mutes his voice, that fucking scream reverberates through every cell of my being.

Primal.

Raw.

Lethal.

So close. I was so damn close to unraveling the mysteries of him, of us. He will come for me. He will chase me down. He will catch me.

And I want him to. I would be lying if I said I didn't. But tonight, I must run. It is the only choice. Isn't it?

I'm thankful the driver leaves me to my brooding silence. I have nothing to say. I'm exhausted. Physically. Emotionally. Completely wrung out. I am not even sure how long it has been since I hugged Jo goodbye outside the airport, the last normal moment of my life.

As we speed back toward Dublin, I bring up a travel app on my phone and find the closest hotel to my drop off point. It's a little pricier than the room I had canceled, but it looks nice and, most importantly, it has a vacancy.

I book it and then stare at my text messages, trying to figure out how to reply to Wren. I type, then delete my message, and restart several times. Finally, I settle on something bland yet reassuring.

LIESHE

Sorry I made you worry. I'm safe and heading back to Dublin.

For some reason, I am slightly protective of Stalky Hottie and don't want to go into any details. I hit send, then copy and paste the same text to Jo and Anna. Dropping my head back against the headrest, I shut my eyes and savor the silence.

It's short-lived as the driver's phone startles me with a text notification, jolting me upright, eyes flying open. An audible gasp escapes my lips as my frayed nerves teeter on edge.

"Sorry," the driver mumbles.

I don't think my body can take anymore adrenaline. Hearing her female voice makes me feel a little safer though on this winding dark drive, so I let my eyes drift closed again. As we make our way back to the city, I can't help but sift through my memories of Stalky Hottie looking for clues.

I turn over every look, every statement, every breath. If he really is a serial killer, I would know it. Right? But why didn't he deny it when I confronted him, instead of offering to burn down the world for me? Again. What does that even mean?

Whether he is a monster or not, it's getting harder to deny what my gut keeps telling me. Somehow, I suspect that Stalky Hottie is a vampire.

Chapter 11

VLAD

The wolves who call the surrounding woods home howl in response to my primal scream. They are called to me, killer to killer.

I strip my clothes in the driveway and shift to my enormous black canine form. Similar to a Cane Corso but twice the size, over three hundred pounds of muscle bunch and stretch as I run toward the tree line.

Rage pulses through my veins, pushing me to impossible speeds. In this form, my complex thoughts fall away, and I can just bask in my animal instincts—run, hunt, kill, feed. Heartbreak and despair fade away with every step.

As I break through the trees, I focus on the spongy moss, fallen leaves, and sharp rocks beneath my great paws. The ground slopes up, yet I push myself harder. Faster. Miles away, I scent the local wolf pack and change course to intercept them.

Within minutes, my supernatural speed brings me to them. The alpha whines, knowing he is outmatched. I could kill the whole pack almost instantly, rip their throats out and leave them as carrion.

Tonight, though, all I want is companionship without words for my lonely, broken soul. I howl at the moon in invitation and then take off, chasing the scent of a stag. I slow my pace so the pack can stay with me. Running at the lead, my animal instincts hum at the simplicity of this life.

I race ahead to catch the magnificent creature unawares,

launching myself at his throat. He whips his head around as the wind shifts, carrying the scent of danger to him. The scent of death. The scent of me.

His antler tears into my shoulder on impact and the pain is a glorious release, matching the fervor of his throat shredding in my mouth. My teeth tear through skin, muscle, sinew, and then into the great arteries and veins buried within.

The taste of the night, of wild Irish woods and earth, floods my senses. The pack catches up to me as the stag dies in my mouth. The cooling blood turns flavorless, so I release him and howl at the moon. My borrowed pack howls with me, and for one glorious moment, I am part of something bigger than myself.

I belong.

The primal satisfaction of the kill quickly fades as I back away and allow the wolves to move in and feed. A female wolf slinks toward me, but all it does is remind me of my mate. My *Rozǎ*. And I realize I'll never belong. Not to this pack. Not to my lost love. Not to anyone.

I am alone.

Leaving them behind, I race off to the old stone monastery ruins that hide one of my many safe houses. My harsh pants drown out the night sounds as I push myself faster and faster, hoping my cold, dead heart will burst in my chest and put me out of this misery.

No such mercy. But I deserve none after the centuries of death and devastation I have wreaked upon this cursed earth. All I ever leave in my wake is destruction. I am not worthy of my *Rozǎ*. One happy lifetime with her is all I have ever asked for. And what I have always been denied.

Forever punished for my original iniquity.

My vow to make this lifetime different has failed. *I have*

failed her. Again. And now in order to have just this once chance, I must turn to the only one left who can help me. The only one I can bargain with.

As I slink through the shadows of the old stone building, my animal senses easily pick out his scent—overwhelming cinnamon to cover the rotten undertone of sulfur.

I trot across the open courtyard to the ancient tree that stands in its center. I have watched it grow and change over the centuries. Aging where I have stayed the same. The leaves and springy ground under my feet are a familiar welcome, in sharp contrast to the monster waiting for me.

"Hello, *chien*," the demon calls from a large branch, where he lounges like a jungle cat.

I transform back into my human form, scowling at him for calling me a dog.

His reptilian gaze traverses my body. When he meets my eyes again, he quirks a brow and says, "Archetype indeed."

He jumps down and stalks toward me with lethal grace in his movements. I draw myself up to my full height and square my shoulders. I have no shame in my nakedness before this snake.

"Very well," he says, knowing my thoughts. They are what called him to me, after all.

"Hold out your hand, or paw, or wing, or whatever it is you want to give me," he says with a smirk.

He may find himself amusing, but all I want to find him is dead. Though, I suppose that isn't actually possible. I hold out my hand without hesitation, willing to sacrifice anything to strike this bargain.

He takes it in his, allowing his black thumbnail to extend into a claw and slice across my palm. Lifting our joined hands in the air, he grinds my bones together in his iron grip, my blood splattering the ground below. Then he brings it to his face and stares down at the blood welling from the cut he made through my flesh and into my soul.

"Well now, this is familiar, isn't it? Reminds me of the beginning. You, me, freshly spilled blood. Good times," he chuckles, flashing me his feline smile, eyes dancing.

"We're done here," I growl.

"Well, then. May the best beast win," he says as he spins on his heel and strides away.

"What do you mean?" I ask.

My heart sinks. His trickery is legendary.

He turns back to face me and replies, "Oh, you didn't specify *which* lifetime. You asked for *one* happy lifetime together, did you not? Well, I will grant you one. I didn't say which one, though."

An evil grin splits his face as he continues, "Besides, I quite like her this go round. She is a delicious little cocktail of innocent desperation. Now that I've tasted her, I may have to borrow her for a few hundred years. Or millennia. Time just kind of runs together for me. After all, eternity is a long, long time."

My mouth falls open in shock. My hands fist at my sides in frustration.

"Oh, why the long face? It's not like you won't be around. You, too, know just how long forever is, don't you, my sad, dead friend?"

"You should know, you made me this way," I fume.

He chuckles as he circles me and says, "What's that saying? Fool me once, shame on you, fool me twice, shame on me? Everyone once in a while, those stupid humans get something right. Unlike you, who just keeps make the stupidest fucking choices." He punctuates his last three words by poking me with his claw as he walks around me.

He returns to stand in front of me, close enough for me to reach out and choke. He eyes me up and down again.

Staring at my cock, he smirks and says, "Nailed the body, but the old noggin leaves a little something to be desired."

He leaps back as I lunge for his throat.

"Uh-uh," he tsks. "You can't actually kill me, you know."

He studies me as he props his chin on his fist and says, "How about this? I'm a betting man. Get her to fall in love with you and you can have *this* lifetime. Make her say she loves you, and mean it, and I will release you from your curse. You can die together and be done with this whole 'I've chased you across time itself' nonsense." He imitates my voice with its Romanian accent.

"The two of you happily turning into worm food in the ground," he says, with a dramatic shudder.

"What's the catch?" I grind out.

"Oh, good. The old dog can learn new tricks. Whew, I'm on a roll with the human sayings tonight!"

He laughs and slaps his knee. My urge to kill him is stronger than ever.

"Finally, you are more than just a pretty face. If she falls in love with *me* first, I get her soul. Forever. No more lifetimes. No more chasing." His voice is deadly serious.

"Her soul? Forever? And what of my soul? You would tear us apart?" The questions tumble from my mouth in disbelief at the steep price.

He smiles the smile that has melted more hearts than one. "You will stay here. Alone. The cruelest punishment there could ever be. You without your mate. Half a soul, suffering in solitude for all eternity on this wretched spinning rock."

He drops his head back, face highlighted by the moonlight. Truly ugly, truly evil.

He licks his lips, moaning, "Your pain will be fucking delicious."

I abruptly sit, collapsing to the ground, all of my strength gone. My soul is easy to bargain with. But hers?

"Tick tock, McHottie."

The use of her pet name for me is the final straw. I never said I was a good man. Only that I was a man in love—a man obsessed.

I stare down at the faint line that shimmers across my palm, marking our contract. I stare at my other hand, where the red stone ring winks in the moonlight. I have no choice. Another bargain is my last chance. *Our* only chance.

I lift my hand to my mouth, ripping open the palm with my elongated canines, and hold it up to him from where I sit on the ground, slumped against the tree.

He gives me a ridiculous high five, completely inappropriate for the situation. Blood splatters across me, sealing our final bargain.

As both the snake and his laughter fade away, I let myself collapse onto my side at the base of the tree. I don't even have the strength to stay sitting. This must be the lifetime. Now, there really is no choice.

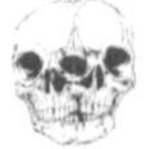

I LAY THERE FOR HOURS, staring at the night sky as the moon and stars make their nightly journey. The wolf pack moves through, followed by bats swooping through the air as they snatch insects out of the air. The world spins on, oblivious to my shattered heart.

The night sounds slowly fade until the darkest hour arrives, just before dawn, and with it, the witch of the witching hour. She leans over me, a vision in red. Her hair cascades down her barely there dress. She nudges me with the point of her stiletto.

I blink up at her, wondering if this is some type of nightmare, although I rarely actually sleep. She lifts her foot and digs the five-inch heel into my throat, confirming she is very much here in the flesh. I feign nonchalance. I must be almost as careful around her as with that damn snake.

"Lilith," I coolly acknowledge her presence.

She removes her foot, but not before pushing just the tiniest bit further in. Like she just can't help but try to hurt me. Her response is justified. She has every right to hate me.

"Are you fucking kidding me?" she hisses. She loves the vernacular modern speech. "You are a damn idiot. This may be one of the stupidest things you have ever done. Other than, well, you know. The big one."

I sit up and lean back against the tree, scrubbing my blood crusted hands over my face. The cuts healed almost as soon as they were made, but the wounds in my soul will never heal.

I heave a great sigh and say, "Why do you care?"

She steps back and surveys me, hands on hips. Her face softens, and I'm transported back to a time when she was young and beautiful. Before the world had hardened her or she had even met the destroyer of man.

"I've always cared," she whispers, with tears in her eyes. She spins on her heel and stalks off, strutting in the towering stilettos across the uneven ground as if it were a runway. Lilith is nothing if not stylish.

Her final words drift back to me over her shoulder. "Not only do you not deserve her, but you've done nothing to win her."

"I may not deserve her, but I need her," I call out to the breaking dawn. "Damn it, I need her!"

Although I can no longer see Lilith's form retreating into the darkness, her haughty whisper echoes in my mind. "Don't tell me. Tell her."

I haul myself up, more exhausted than I can recall in centuries. I make the long trek back to the gatehouse, naked and barefoot, punishing myself physically to match my broken soul and battered heart. As I come around to the front door with the rising sun, the town car is back in the driveway. I stumble through the door to find my faithful servant sitting on the couch, staring into the fire.

"Master," she cries.

"Miss Field," I reply as she rushes toward me, fluttering her hands.

"Oh, Master, let me help you," she says, face creased in concern.

She pulls my arm around her shoulders and helps me up the stairs. I let her steer me to the bathroom and lean against the wall while she fusses with the shower. When the air is thick with steam, she ushers me in.

She washes me like a child, turning me and scrubbing my back as I stand there, unmoving, numb to the world around me. Dispassionately, I watch the dirt and blood swirl down the drain. Her mouth is moving, but I cannot hear the words. When she spins me and starts to wash down my chest and abs, I have the wherewithal to gently grab her hands.

"Thank you, Miss Field, but I think I can handle the rest," I say woodenly.

She blushes and backs away, fleeing the bathroom.

I finish washing my body and hair, pulling my focus to the present, back to my purpose. Wrapping a towel around my waist, I walk to my bedroom. I want to sleep in the lingering scent of my love on the sheets.

Instead, I enter to find the fire stoked and a glass sitting on the table between the two armchairs. Miss Field sits in one, eyes downcast. I walk to the glass and down it in one gulp, but it barely slakes the exhaustion weighing me down.

She refills the cup while I go over to my dresser and pull on fresh boxers.

I drop the damp towel to the floor and flop down into the other chair. Draining the second glass, I stare into the dancing flames. The warmth of the fire does nothing to stave off the coldness that emanates from deep within me. The only thing that counteracts it is my *Rozǎ*, my love.

I see her face in the flames, lifetime after lifetime flashing before my eyes. Failures drift up the chimney like sparks, each lifetime the charred wood falling to embers below where their light dies as they turn to ash. Dust and ash, that's all I am. I have no life force, no fire without my mate.

Lilith is right. I don't deserve her. And I've done nothing to win her heart, her loyalty, or her love. Just being who I am is no longer enough. Angry with my own foolish shortsightedness, I hurl the glass into the flames where it shatters against the back wall, hissing in the flames.

A gentle touch on my shoulder jerks my attention back to the room. Startled, I lash out, grabbing my assailant by the throat on instinct and lifting them into the air. As my vision clears, I see young Miss Field turning red and scrabbling at my strangling grasp. I lower her feet to the ground and drop my hand, ashamed of my reaction.

"I-I'm sorry, Master. I didn't mean to frighten you." She swallows, rubbing at the handprint still visible there. "I called your name several times, but you didn't answer me.

You've been sitting here for over an hour. Please, rest. Forgive me for saying so, but you look terrible."

I had forgotten she was even here. Such a small, slight little thing. No one would guess that beneath the mousy facade lies a fierce and well-trained warrior. I smile at her in apology. Her family has served me for countless generations, serving as my protectors, informants, advisors, and aides. Always faithful, honoring a vow made long, long ago.

"I, uh, I could feed you. If you wanted. I know the storage bags aren't the same," she says shyly.

Her voice is soft and tremulous for the first time since I've known her. In the past, she was always eager to please but polite and professional. She steps closer, hesitant. Her hand flutters around her neck like a moth, the creamy swell of her breasts and the long column of her throat exposed by her open collar. Her heartbeat quickens as she tips her head back to meet my eyes.

I look over her light brown hair, cascading down in soft waves, almost matching her soft brown eyes. Just like the bird she is named for. Taking her chin in my hand, I study her eyes and face. I've never seen her with her hair down. She has always appeared severe, almost militant, with her hair pulled tightly back and wearing head-to-toe black clothing.

A faint blush creeps up her neck to darken her cheeks. She is soft and lovely and warm, and I am cold and hard and hungry.

I trace my hand from her chin along her jaw and slide it to her nape. I grasp her hair tightly in my fist and angle her neck, exposing her pulsing jugular. My other hand traces the fading outline of my handprint.

Her heartbeat fills my ears, calling to me in a primal song I can scarce resist. As I bring my lips to her throat, she gasps, "Vlad."

It startles me into dropping my hand and stepping back. No one has called me that in many, many years. I shake my head, seeing the small female before me. I narrow my eyes at her, taking in her rapid pulse, her heaving bosom. I inhale sharply and am met with her usual essence, tinged with the faintest hint of her arousal.

In a long line of faithful servants, this has been the only generation to provide me with a female—a fact that I had forgotten could matter. I only had eyes for one woman, so I forgot others could find me attractive, since I never saw them as anything but shadows drifting across a sea of time.

Her pulse thunders in my ears. I run my tongue over my elongated canines, breathing deeply. Centuries of practice allow me to restrain myself and pull on a polite mask to hide my rage and hunger.

"That will be all, Miss Field. Good evening," I say with finality.

Stepping back, I offer a stiff formal bow. I watch her duck her head and flee the room, closing the door softly behind her. Feeling as if I dodged one more complication I do not have the energy for, I crawl into my bed and collapse.

Knowing my *Roză* had shared this space with me and I am safe, I grab the pillow and crush it to my face. I burrow into the linens perfumed by our passion, and I let myself sleep for the first time in many years.

Chapter 12

We pull up at the drop off point and I hop out of the car, slinging my backpack over my shoulder and grabbing my suitcase from the trunk. The last-minute hotel I booked on the drive here is just across the street. Traffic is light at this time of night, so I dash over and head into the lobby, thankful there is a bar because I am hitting it up tonight.

The check-in clerk eyes me up and down, taking in my strange outfit of leggings with the silk nightgown and robe sticking oddly out from the bottom of my shirt. As soon as I give her my name for the reservation, she smiles, likely chalking up my eccentric appearance to my being an American.

No matter how odd my appearance may seem at this time of night, she has no qualms about taking my credit card. She hands me my key and directs me toward the elevator.

I head up to my room, which is clean and totally sufficient, but a far cry from the gatehouse that I fell in love with. No roses, no cheery fire, no four-poster bed draped in midnight red linens, and most of all, no Stalky Hottie.

What is happening to my life? I went from keeping my head down and focused on my business, unusual as it was, to being caught up in a maelstrom of the macabre. Can I really entertain the thought that he is a vampire?

In a huff, I drop my bags in the middle of the floor and head straight for the shower. I peel off layer after layer of my hastily thrown on clothes as I walk. Stopping to pick the nightgown and robe back up, I bring them to my face and inhale while nuzzling the silky fabric.

I smell him. I smell us. We smell like heartbreak.

The garments are gorgeous and seem as if they were made for me. I hang them on the back of the door, letting the silk slip through my hand. Mind swirling, I get into the shower and crank the water as hot as I can stand it. Leaning my head against the tile, I will my thoughts to wash down the drain along with my tears.

I'm not usually a big crier. But halfway around the world from home, lost somewhere between fact and the fiction I have loved for so long, I can't stop the fat drops from rolling down my face.

My forehead drops to the cold white porcelain and all it reminds me of is him. He is a constant roller coaster of mystery and longing. Standing in the moonlight, looking at him, I was convinced he was truly a vampire.

I think through our time together, trying to connect the dots. In the heightened emotion of that moment—in an ancient land, surrounded by woods, under the moon—it all seemed completely plausible. But now, here in this modern city, in a brightly lit bathroom, it seems not just improbable, but downright impossible.

I pull myself off the wall and wash my hair and body, wincing as the soap runs over my wrecked nether region. Despite his careful preparation, he was just so damn big. My mind drifts back to the fabulous sex with him as my tears dry up.

The passionate kisses, his absolute focus on me, the flexing muscles, and those fucking tattoos—I think about tracing every piece of ink imprinted into his flesh. I imagine drifting my fingertips over each line, running my tongue over every swirl. Even through my confusion and concern, the memories of his illustrated skin pulled taut over rippling muscles start a fire low in my belly.

Between thoughts of my mystery man and the scalding hot shower, I become overheated. Stepping out, I wrap myself in a too small and slightly rough towel, the faint whiff of bleached hotel linens mixing with the steam.

The industrial smell makes me miss the scent of the gatehouse—it smelled like coming home. His unique blend of dark and mysterious tobacco, leather, and the subtle fragrance of Vampira roses is now deeply etched into my amygdala.

As I stand there in my miniature towel, hair dripping water down my back, I can't help but sense that something is missing. There is a piece to this puzzle that I just can't see right now. I absentmindedly dab at my curls, mind spinning.

I should really crawl into bed and get some much-needed sleep. Then, I can try to think through this mess in the morning. But I know I'll just toss and turn. So, instead, I plop my hair into the towel and wrap it to set my curls while changing into clean but comfortable clothes.

I dry my hair just a little more, then smooth some product in and let it air dry. Throwing on a pair of shoes, I head up to the rooftop bar. I don't look like I'm ready for a night on the town, nor do I care. This isn't a social outing.

Once on the top floor, I take a seat in a shadowy corner, craving solitude but desperately needing a little liquid balm to soothe my soul. And a little snacky snack instead of breaking into my emergency stash.

After a few minutes, I realize there is no table service. Since I need to head up to the bar to order, I just relocate myself there. Only a couple scattered patrons are in the rooftop space enjoying the relatively warm summer night, so I pick a seat away from anyone else.

The bartender quickly comes over, flashing a grin and charming me with his Dublin accent, leaving a menu in front of me.

I order an Irish whiskey. After all, when in Rome and all that. Unfortunately, I can't have Guinness. Thankful for European attentiveness to allergens, I eye up the salad choices but give in to my need for comfort and pick the chips instead. I pass my food order on to the young man as he drops off my drink.

I stare dejectedly at my whiskey, idly swishing the amber liquid around the glass. I take a sip and its familiar burn travels down my throat to warm my belly. The liquor conjures thoughts of Luke, the first time I've thought of him tonight. I remember the way his brimstone bourbon burned down my throat, the way the crowd screamed to burn with him during the show.

As I swirl the amber liquid over the rocks, I realize Luke and Stalky Hottie are like the fiery burn of the whiskey and the cold ice in my glass. The two men that have me battling myself, my thoughts, my fantasies, and even my grip on reality. If Stalky Hottie really is a vampire, what does that make Luke? He seems like more than a man, but not a vampire.

A silver fox slides into the seat next to me, pulling me from my musings. I'm mildly annoyed that with all the open seats at the bar, he chose to sit next to me while I am trying to sort my thoughts and feelings.

He looks over and strikes up a conversation in a lovely, lilting Irish accent. "What did that drink do to you, love, that you're making such a sour face? Don't you like our whiskey, then?"

His voice alone makes me forgive the intrusion; I could listen to him talk all day. I reply, "No, no, the whiskey is just fine."

I can't help but smile at the mischievous twinkle in his blue eyes and answering smile. Typically, I don't go for quite this much of an age gap, but there is something captivating about him. I'm guessing he is pushing sixty but fit with close cropped silver hair and the best wrinkle lines around his eyes, like he has spent years laughing into the sun.

His smile and easy air are infectious and exactly what my sorry ass needs right now. Jeans and a casual sport coat over a button-down make him seem harmless enough. As we talk, he takes off his tweed flat cap.

"Go on, then, lass, and tell me. I've seen and heard it all in my time," he says with a wink.

The urge to unburden my soul to someone, anyone, when I'm so far from home with a broken heart is just about irresistible. But I also know that I can't tell this story in its entirety for fear I'll end up stuck in a nice public health ward. I'll have to tweak a few details, like the serial killing vampire part.

"Well, I met a guy in the states, and we ended up running into each other again on the way here. He's amazing, but I'm having trouble believing everything is as it seems. Some of it is really, um, fairytale-like." I draw out the last word, thinking that's as good of an explanation as any I can come up with.

He takes a deep swallow of his whiskey and swirls his glass, staring into it like it holds the secrets of the universe. He raises his twinkling blue eyes back to mine and quips, "When in Rome."

Funny, I had that same thought a few minutes ago.

He chuckles warmly and continues with a kind lecture,

"Here, the veil between this world and the next is thinner. Any local could spin you a tale or two about things they've seen or heard that might seem like 'fairytales' to outsiders. But around here, we don't dismiss these experiences. We see them as part of living in a land rich with mystery and ancient secrets. After all, what's life without a bit of magic?"

He pauses to sip on the whiskey, staring back down into it. When he looks back at me, I can't help but think how much he reminds me of Gabe. Those same heavenly blue eyes and reassuring warm smile, like a hug. I could envision Gabe's platinum hair fading to this shade of silver as he ages.

Just as Gabe had rescued me from the chaos of the club after Luke and Hottie's brawl back home, this man is here to rescue me from the turmoil of my heart and mind. Seems like an angel has followed me here after all.

He continues, "We're not meant to understand everything or limit ourselves to what's easily explained. After all, what is love but the greatest mystery of all? I've been around long enough to have love and lost. Perhaps even more than once."

He flashes me a smile and I can understand why he's had more than one love. Charming and gorgeous is a heady combination.

His voice holds my attention. "And I can promise you, the old saying is true. It's better to have loved and lost than never to have loved at all. Don't look back when death is knocking and wonder, 'What if?' If you can move forward with a clear conscience, then do so, but don't leave room in your heart for regret."

I am enchanted by this man and his perspective. What if I pushed my mind a little further? What if I opened myself to magic and mystery in this ancient land steeped in lore? What if I embraced the possibility that I might be meeting the vampire I've dreamed of my entire life?

"Let me buy you another whiskey. Your mind is running in circles now that I've opened your eyes to the magic of Éire."

He waves two fingers in a circle at the bartender in the universal sign for two more and turns back to face me.

"Can you open your heart to the idea that any part of your fairytale could be true? If so, then pursue it. If not, don't let someone waste the time of such a beautiful woman as yourself. I know we just met, and I'm offering a lot of advice, but I believe you might not fully recognize your own worth. It seems like you've allowed other people's perceptions to shape your world instead of giving yourself permission to dream about the possibilities for your own future."

He pins me with his bright blue stare, and I chew thoughtfully on my lip.

"Try playing out the worst-case scenario. If you never see him again, what's the worst that can happen? You might miss him forever and regret it, or you could meet someone new, and everything turns out just fine. But what if you find him and give it a go? What's the worst that could happen then? Either your heart stays as broken as it is now, and you've lost nothing, or it all works out and you've gained everything."

I'm left reeling by his words in the magical land swirling around me. I can't help but wonder how things would have gone if I had stayed back at the gatehouse and tried to work it out or at least listened to his side of the story instead of letting my anxiety, fueled by Wren, get the better of me and running off into the night. Again.

"So, what are you thinking now?" he asks, prodding gently.

I muse, "You're right, it's hard not to be open to magic when I'm sitting here listening to you. I think I can ask this here."

I glance around to make sure no one can hear and drop my voice to a conspiratorial whisper. "Do you think there are *things,* like not humans, who walk amongst us?"

He lets out a hearty laugh. "Like I said, I've seen a fair amount in my circles around the sun. My own dear ma even met one of the fairy folk herself. Here's one more piece of advice for you, love."

He reaches out and tucks a stray curl behind my ear and trails his fingertips lightly along my jawline as I drown in his vivid blue eyes, riveted.

"Someday, when you've circled the sun as many times as I have and you're getting ready to cross that veil yourself, don't look back with regret. Don't reach those final days and wonder, 'What if?' What if I'd turned right instead of left or said yes instead of no? What if I'd given magic and mystery a fair shake?"

The tales of the gift of the blarney are true, for he has me wrapped up tight in his spell. I wonder who my silver fox really is, as he seems like he himself is made of magic and mystery and was sent to help me decipher my heart just when I needed it the most.

He gently taps the tip of my nose with his finger, gives me a wink, and says, "Goodnight, lass. Don't be forgetting our fair Éire and the lessons she has for ya."

He drains the last of his whiskey and stands, throwing over his shoulder before he walks away, "Mind the fairy circles, Lieshe."

I blink a few times, shaking off his spell, trying to recall when I had told him my name. Turning my attention back to the chips that had arrived while I was captivated by yet another mysterious player in my life, I contemplate why I seem to be a magnet for them.

I've always been different, so maybe it's true, like attracts like. I'll definitely have to make my way back to Ireland. I've had more intrigue here in two days than I have in the past thirty years.

Picking at the deliciously greasy food, I finish off my second whiskey. Pleasantly full, with the faint buzz of alcohol smoothing out my nerves, I decide I'm ready for sleep at last. I hold up my card to signal that I need to tab out.

The bartender comes over with a beaming smile and says, "Ah, miss, it's already been sorted by himself."

"By who?" I reply.

"Himself that you were speaking with," he clarifies.

"Oh," I say, looking around to give him my thanks, but he is gone. "Well, please tell him I said thank you the next time you see him. I'm sorry I didn't get to!"

"Of course, miss," he replies. "Can I get you anything else?"

"No, thank you," I say and head back down to my room.

As I settle in for the night, completing my skin care routine and repacking everything for my trip tomorrow, I can't help but think about the advice from "himself."

What is life without magic and mystery? He is right. Love is the biggest mystery of all. I don't want to look back at my life with regrets. At the ripe old age of thirty, I don't have many. But what about ten or twenty years from now? If I never saw Stalky Hottie again, would I regret it? What about Luke?

Bag packed, I stand at the window in my hotel, looking out over the night skyline of Dublin. My heart soars at the beauty while my mind tries to balance the scales of fact versus fiction.

Thinking on the advice of the silver fox earlier, I let myself travel down the path of belief. What if I am in love with a vampire? Have our lives always been entwined? That would mean, what, reincarnation is real? Why couldn't I come back as my cat, if that's the case?

Am I being punished? This life kind of seems like punishment. My imagination starts swirling with imagined past wrongdoings to have granted me my current circumstances. Irish whiskey, two countries, and the deepening mystery of Stalky Hottie when all I wanted was answers is a headache waiting to happen.

My focus shifts from my view of the night skyline to my reflection in the glass windowpane, where my haunted mismatched eyes stare sadly back at me. I don't have an answer to anything right now, other than I am getting nowhere fast and sleep is beckoning me.

I set my alarm and snuggle into the bed. As the alcohol speeds me off to sleep, my last conscious thought is of amber eyes and the aroma of tobacco and leather mixed with roses and peat.

Chapter 15

I thought I wanted a break from the steamy late-night dreams I've been having, but this morning, I realize they are far better than the horrible nonsense I just woke up from. It was a chaotic blur of Stalky Hottie and Luke chasing me through the Irish countryside. But it wasn't them that scared me—it's the fairytale creatures gone horribly wrong.

I rub the sleep from my eyes, trying to shake off the lingering dread as I turn off my alarm, which is just about to go off, anyway. With a sigh, I turn on the in-room coffee maker and pull my hair into a messy bun, hoping the routine will help ground me after the terrible wake-up call.

Popping on the shower cap helpfully supplied by the hotel, I get into the steamy shower, rinsing my bad dreams and panic sweat down the drain. The steam swirls up around me claustrophobically and my vision wobbles.

I brace myself against the cold tiled walls and clench my jaw, squeezing my eyes shut tight as if that alone could stave off the waking dream coming on.

The three of us are in a fairy circle, being used as a makeshift boxing ring. There is so much blood everywhere, dripping midnight red. Luke is laughing his bloody smile like when he fought with Stalky Hottie back home at the club.

Hottie raises his hands, revealing vivid slashes across his palms. Crimson drips down his arms and streams off his elbows. My eyes are wide, mouth open on a silent scream as I look from one to the other like a horrific tennis match.

So.

Much.

Blood.

Luke lunges forward and grabs me, claiming my mouth with his bloody one while Stalky tries to pull me from his arms, but his hands are too slippery. They fight over me like a gory trophy until we are all covered in so much of the red sticky liquid that we fall down into it, great crimson waves crashing over our heads and pulling us down, down, down.

A hand reaches in and pulls me out, lungs bursting. I look up at my rescuer to find Stalky Hottie standing in a beautiful field of wildflowers. No red in sight. The sun is shining and warm on our backs as we walk from the gatehouse in the meadow, hand in hand, through the flowers.

He bends down, plucks a wild daisy, and gently tucks it behind my ear before leaning in to kiss me sweetly. The simple gesture fills my heart with warmth, like the sun's gentle glow.

We wander to the water and follow its winding path to a beautiful stone monastery with arches and a central courtyard containing a yew tree. We stand underneath, kissing. The wind softly rustles in the branches, the moss is soft under my feet.

The moment is still and full of wonder. My heart is carefree.

Hottie speaks to me in an unfamiliar tongue. I reply back in the same language, and in the way of dreams, I can understand it perfectly. I lean against the tree, its leaves overhead shading us from the sun, cool and comfortable in the shadows.

I take his hands and shyly place them over my belly. He

looks at me with wonder and joy on his face. He falls to his knees, peppering my stomach with kisses. Clearly, we are both filled with happiness.

As I gaze down at him, the wonder changes to fear as splotches of blood slowly appear on my belly, which is now quite obviously pregnant. I realize in horror that the splotches are falling tears—I am crying blood.

I grip his hands over my belly in panic as he raises his face to me, and with a ferocious snarl, his canines elongate, and he rips into my swollen abdomen.

I come to with a strangled scream in my throat, collapsed on the shower floor. Tears stream down my face, and I quickly wipe them, checking for blood. Of course, there is none. I reach over and twist at the knobs, trying to get the water off. At first, I only succeed in getting the hot tap turned, resulting in a shocking spray of cold.

If I hadn't been brought back to reality yet, the icy blast would have done it. Shivering, I pull myself out of the tub and wrap a towel tightly around my shoulders. I walk to the mirror and swipe away the condensation with my hand. My reflection stares back at me, pupils blown wide, pulse visibly thundering in my neck.

"Damn Irish whiskey," I mutter out loud, casting blame instead of worrying about the waking dreams as I travel as a lone female internationally.

I tell myself I just won't drink anymore while I'm here, and I'll get enough sleep, certain that will prevent any more episodes. As I shuffle out to the coffee maker, I can't help but wonder not only what it all means but why my waking dreams have changed so dramatically.

Will Luke and Stalky Hottie continue to fight over me? Is there no way for a human and vampire to be together?

Certainly, it seems like children would be out of the picture. I don't even know what I think of that.

In desperate need of help to process my rambling thoughts, I grab the small, now lukewarm cup of mediocre coffee, figuring that some caffeine is better than none. With only powdered creamer available, I add a bit of my stevia and stir the sad facsimile of a latte with a tiny plastic straw. I take a sip, scrunching up my face in distaste, but I'm desperate for a boost after a rough night and an even rougher waking dream.

I toss the coffee back, wishing I could mainline it instead and pull on my clothes for the day—leggings and an oversized shirt since I'll mostly just be traveling.

I sit down at the small hotel desk, get out my business notebook, and go over my buying trip plans to distract my rattled brain. Today I travel to Northern Ireland to meet with a contact there, and then I'll take the ferry from Belfast over to Scotland.

I wish I had a little more time to explore Dublin, but I have already burned a day with Stalky Hottie and the trip has just started. Next year I could take a vacation right after Valentine's Day when my slow season hits and spend time just exploring and enjoying myself. Take in Blarney Castle, the cliffs of Mohr, and Giant's Causeway, which are all high on my bucket list.

But for today, at least, I can spare a few hours to explore the city. I shoot a text off to my contact in Belfast to confirm my arrival details and double check the train schedule. Confident I have the next leg of my journey well in hand, I rush through getting ready to make the most of the little time I have left here.

I dry my hair, apply the barest of makeup and then pack all my toiletries back up. I make an extra careful round of the room, making sure not to leave anything behind. Unlike when I forgot my purchases at the hotel in Philly, no one will be tracking me down this time.

As I double check the bathroom, on the back of the door hangs the glorious nightgown and robe from Hottie. I slip the silk through my fingers, marveling at its sensual softness. I pull the garments down off the hook and bring them to my face, inhaling deeply. The faintest trace of roses and peat moss linger in the fabric.

Satisfied that nothing is left behind, I place the last few items into my suitcase and head down to the lobby. The front desk is more than happy to stow my luggage for me, so I can duck out to take in the city before my train leaves.

I pick a street at random, turning a corner to come face to face with something that can truly cheer me up, a huge Doc Martens store! I head in, reveling in the smell of my favorite shoes. There are so many incredible styles here to choose from. I wander around, picking up various ones, and weigh my options.

I try to think through my collection at home to figure out what would be the best addition. I love the 1460 vintage made in England red boots, but it's hard to justify the price tag when I already have red ones. I'm drooling over the twenty-eight eye extreme max Virginia boot, but there is no way I am going to haul those across Europe. I begrudgingly set them down.

Then I spy 1914 Vonda calf boots with red embroidered roses. The roses are not quite as dark as the beautiful crimson of the Vampira ones, but these shoes personify my last day here. One that I know will somehow change the trajectory of my life. Stalky was right about one thing—I can't run forever.

But before I head any further down that path, I tell

myself today is not for figuring things out. Today is for drowning my thoughts in my favorite vice. I know these will be perfect, and at checkout, I can't help but also grab the matching socks that hang there teasingly.

I know I should have them shipped home rather than adding them to my already heavy luggage, but this is my drug of choice, and just like when I was little, I end up putting my old ones in the box and wearing the new shoes out of the store. My heart is still heavy, but at least my self indulgence has put a little spring in my step.

I break in my new kicks on the streets of Dublin, happy to find so many great gluten-free eating options. I use my favorite food app and find a place close by. I walk the two blocks to the café, lonely despite the bustling city. The temporary dopamine hit from my purchase is already waning.

I wait my turn in the queue and pick up a falafel sandwich, then grab a stool at the high counter in the big front window, swinging my new Docs as I sit. I watch people hurry past, intent on their destinations, oblivious to the forlorn woman watching them.

I wonder what it would be like to rush around in the crowd, my biggest concern getting to the next tourist stop or into the office on time, rather than contemplating vampires and reincarnation.

Dismissing my swirling thoughts, and with new boots on my feet and a full belly, I decide to get in at least one of the main attractions of Dublin. I head over to Trinity College to visit the Book of Kells.

I've lucked out, and the weather is beautiful today, sunny with the occasional cloud scuttling across the sky, casting shadows and warmth alternately on my face. If only my thoughts matched.

Instead, I contemplate my choices. Running away seemed like the right thing to do in the heat of the moment. But by the light of day, the Irish sun casts the events of yesterday into sharp relief. I try to consider the possibility that Stalky Hottie is a vampire from every angle, looking for logical explanations or some semblance of sense, but I just can't make heads or tails of it.

I finally reach my destination and join the queue to view the historic book. I shuffle through the line, pausing in the darkened room to take in the wonder of this ancient, illuminated manuscript.

It is stunning, seeming to glow from within despite the dim lighting to protect it. The complexity of the angels, birds, and snakes illuminating the page on display astounds me.

The green of the serpents is so vibrant, the exact chartreuse of Luke's eyes. The similarity is so striking that I can almost feel his heated gaze caressing me. Shaking off my imagination, I turn my attention back to the book.

I could study the ancient tome for hours, but the line eventually forces me to keep moving. I wander through the enormous library, wishing I could spend years here perusing the vast book collection, lose myself in a leather armchair and a thousand volumes of fiction.

Checking my watch, I tear myself away and head to the gift shop. I have a tough time choosing, but fall in love with a trinity knot, symbolizing my past, present, and future—the three interlocking puzzle pieces I've yet to decode. I pick up a bracelet for me and each of my friends back home. Now I just need to grab my luggage from the hotel and get to the train station.

Chapter 14

Things couldn't be going better if I had scripted them myself. It's like that big dumb dog just can't help but fuck up at every turn. Of course, I have a little help on the inside, but I never said I would play fair. After all, this is love *and* war. Not much difference between the two to me since love is the key to winning this war.

I follow my delicious little queen around the city, studying her, plotting. When I watch her face light up over shoes, of all things, I tell myself it's only the anticipation of winning that brings a smile to my face. I have been so very, well, bored, and forever is a long, long time.

When I linger behind as she exits the store, to buy her the ones she really wanted but chose the more practical ones instead, I tell myself it's just one more step toward winning her over.

The stupid smile on my face? It's not from thinking about lacing her into only these boots and nothing else. And it's definitely not from imagining her wrapping her arms around me, thanking me with her lips and body.

This tired city looks better with her in it. Even the weather shines brighter with her here, a rare sunny day just to highlight the thousands of shades of brown in her hair. I can see them all, count them one by one. Even her white forelock is a stunning blend of silver, pearl, frost, and snow.

She will be even more beautiful in my world of endless twilight. The shadows will only make her more radiant. I need her there. Now. Patience is not one of my strong suits, but this game must be played delicately. The pieces are lined up, the first moves of the gambit have been made.

I watch her sit in the window of a restaurant after consulting her phone a hundred times. People love to complain that I am evil, but I've got nothing on those little pocket computers they are all so addicted to.

She swings her new boots back and forth as she eats and observes the people passing by. Nothing but pawns, oblivious to the epic finale unfolding around them. She savors each bite, her eyes closing in pleasure.

I can almost hear her faint moan, as if she were nestled against my neck rather than across the street from my vantage point. She exudes a naïve sexuality, made all the more enticing by her innocence to it—the polar opposite of Lilith, who is not only fucking stunning but fully aware of it, using it to her every advantage.

But as Lieshe wraps her sweet mouth around the sandwich, I know I need to move this game along. Desire shoots straight to my cock. I want her lips around me again. I want to watch the tears spill from her eyes and hear the ecstasy tumble from her mouth as I bring her every dark fantasy to life. And maybe add a few of my own to the mix.

Another presence pulls me from my lustful thoughts. Annoyed, I scan the crowds, looking for who it is. Well, well, well. Speaking of pawns, it's the fairy godmother. Oh, wait, they're both here—fucking fabulous. This city needed to be livened up, and here is my entertainment.

With a snap of my fingers, I appear behind them. I lean forward so my head is between theirs as they, too, watch my queen and say, "Mystery and magic? What kind of bullshit are you feeding her?"

The surprise on their faces as they jump and spin to face me is so downright comical that I double over in laughter.

Straightening, I wipe my eyes and manage, "It's a damn family reunion. Miss me?"

Two sets of angelic blue eyes stare me down, not finding the situation nearly as funny as I do. Oh, well, their loss.

Gabriel spits out, "She's nothing but a game to you. Why can't you leave her alone? She is everything that is good, that is real. She deserves better."

My mouth curls up as I choose my words carefully, keeping my cards close to my chest. "Why do you think she's the prize? Sure, she's good and kind—the first to help a friend, always pleased her parents instead of telling her father to fuck right off. And where did that get her? Her dutiful church attendance, the gaslighting about her visions, the way this fucked-up world treats her?"

My tightly held facade starts to crack, my skin tight, and the odor of sulfur rises the angrier I get.

"Where the fuck were *you*? Where was *good* when she needed to be protected? When she needed help? She has suffered time and time again. Every lifetime she has been *fucked* over. For what? Who has decided that's her fucking fate for all eternity?"

Gabriel shoves me with all his might, but it's no more than the brush of a moth's wing.

"I'm not her guardian angel!" he shouts.

"Well, that's crystal fucking clear. You're damn right she deserves better. Better than all of you. I don't know how any of you can be surprised when she chooses me. I haven't lied to her. I have been there for her. I am giving her a choice. A choice! I am giving her what I never fucking got, what they never got!"

"Oh, yeah, and what's that?" Jophiel chimes in, pushing me over the edge I'm teetering on.

"Unconditional love. Forgiveness," I cry, revealing too much. "I am giving her what she deserves and when my queen takes her rightful place beside me, we will both watch this whole shithouse go down in flames and then fuck in the ashes."

"I think you're forgetting something," Gabe taunts.

I whip my head back toward him and sneer, "What's that, *bâtard?*"

Jophiel pipes up and says, "You're the one who cursed them both."

The wind swirls around me as heat races down my outstretched hands, sizzling and snapping at my fingertips. They glance at each other nervously and then around the three of us, already thinking about damage control if the meatbags notice the disturbance.

As I see Lieshe leave the restaurant behind them, my anger immediately cools, and I'm reminded to keep my eye on the prize. Deciding I have far better things to do than waste my time with these assholes who can't possibly understand, I give them a cruel smile and flip them each the bird as I wink out of their sight and stalk my queen to her tourist trap.

Damn those wing flapping fuck faces. Sure, I tricked her and the dumb dog. Cursed them. But I wasn't the one who didn't forgive. I am not the one who forgets. All I did was show them the truth. I did them a favor. Besides, if I hadn't played my part where would we all be now? Not here.

Reassured by my self-righteousness, I follow her through the hushed building, focusing on her face, memorizing the constellation of freckles sprinkled across her nose. I watch from the shadows as she finally reaches the Book of Kells.

The way her face lit up over shoes pales in comparison to her admiration for the famous illuminated manuscript.

I may have nudged it open to a page I worked on myself. It had taken ages to perfect the perfect shade of the green pigments, but spending time with the monks while we tripped our faces off was worth it.

I supplied the mind-altering substances to keep their creative juices flowing, and in return, I got to sneak a bunch of snakes and ravens into the book. A win-win, really. Was it petty to leave my signature in a holy book? Perhaps.

But do I care? Fuck no.

The appreciation in her eyes of my illuminated ancient graffiti reminds me of all I have added to this ungrateful cesspool of meat puppets. Art, music, kinky sex—I've contributed so much to enrich their meaningless lives.

Sure, there was the odd plague and disaster here and there, and, oh, the St. Vitus' dance was one of my best ideas, but really, this world should be more grateful.

For there is no light without the darkness. The very fabric of the universe as we know it would cease to exist if not for my chaos—my dark matter holds it together. And that is my curse, to be the unappreciated bearer of darkness.

But there is also no darkness without the light. She is the light, the perfect complement to me. I *deserve* to have my queen by my side. She should have been mine all along. I guess I'll just have to make up for lost time when I steal her away. Because she may not have been mine before, but she is now.

I.

Will.

Have.

Her.

Chapter 15

I'm still smiling as I sit on the train to Belfast. When I went to collect my suitcase from the hotel, I was told my bill had already been settled. Surprised, I took the proffered receipt and walked outside. Glancing down at it, I find a note scrawled in a heavy black handwriting that says, "Mystery and magic."

My Irish silver fox had been generous not only with his wisdom but with his resources, covering both my tab last night and room charge this morning. I hope I see him again someday, as well as the younger man he reminded me of, Gabe. There must still be some good at work in my life for the right people to show up in my life when I need them.

Much like the barista at the great little cafe I found on the way to the station. Although usually when I travel, I just order a plain coffee, the woman behind the counter was so friendly I asked her if she could make my special drink—frothed oat milk with four shots of espresso, toasted marshmallow syrup, and stevia from my backpack.

She was thrilled to oblige, a real-world example of the famous Irish hospitality. I wished I could transport this store to replace the one at home. I had dropped a huge tip, thanking her profusely as she dipped her head, saying, "Thanks, love."

As the train speeds me away from Dublin toward Belfast, I again admire European mass transportation. It is quick, affordable, and efficient—a far cry from the light rail in the states that I avoid at all costs.

As the lush greenery whizzes by, I check in on some emails on my phone and text Declan, my next contact, the exact arrival time. Then, I message Anna a few pics I have snapped along the way and a selfie of me on the train making a silly face.

She is posting updates of my trip on social media as an advertisement for the store. She assures me it will help to hype up the items I am bringing home if our followers can track them as I travel. I'm sure she's right; I'm just happy I don't have to do it.

I come up with a cool idea, though, when a black cat that crossed my path looked so much like Lucifer, I could have sworn it was him. We turned it into a contest for his doppelgängers around the world. I scroll through his social media for a while, admiring all the pictures people have posted and congratulating the contest winner, Lauren and her sweet kitty, Bogie.

I can't help shaking my head over my cat having his own online presence. But there's no arguing with the sales, they just keep going up. Next thing he'll be doing promos and have his own product line.

Pulling away from social media, I drop a few pics and send updates to Mindy and Jo. I'm thankful things in Baltimore have gone right back to normal, or so they reassure me. Thinking of my friends makes me realize just how alone I am right now and how much I wish I had someone to enjoy this trip with.

I can tell myself all the wonderful parts of traveling solo, but in my heart, I'm lonely. My chest tightens and I wonder what I would be doing if I had just ignored my damn phone and stayed with Stalky Hottie. Truth be told, I don't think we would have made it very far from that bed.

Before I start fantasizing on public transit, I turn my thoughts to my next stop and what Declan will be like in person. I pick at the threads of my holey skinny jeans, and try to hone in on my business plans, thinking through what I am hoping to find for Grimm.

Despite the vague prickle across the back of my neck, and a whiff of tobacco and leather, I don't bother to look for him, chalking the sensations up to my desire for him to be here. I need to focus and get back to the whole point of this trip. No more time for shenanigans, Irish or otherwise. And as always, focusing on my shop grounds me in the wake of so much uncertainty.

I want to call Anna to check in on the store, but the timing isn't right. She will text back when she can and call if she needs me. I know I don't need to micromanage her or Jo. It's just so hard when I'm used to running everything by myself day in and day out.

So instead, I spend thirty minutes cleaning out my email, unsubscribing from lawn care and clothing ads, deleting the ones for increasing my penis size with a laugh. I'm startled when Jo texts me with the time difference, my jaw dropping at the pic she sends of her and Jason with their faces squished together.

She adds a devil face emoji, and I send back the shocked face to which she replies with an eggplant and multiple pound signs. I'm so happy for them both to have fun while I am gone. I certainly don't begrudge her a few days of entertainment. She must have gotten distracted afterwards because that is the last message she sends.

My stop is announced, and I hop up, grabbing my suitcase, excited to visit Northern Ireland. I exit the platform and head toward the parking lot where Declan is waving me down. Despite talking online for years, this is the first time we have met in person. Most of the curiosity shop owners are quite friendly, and there are a couple of online groups where we chat since it's a relatively small community.

He gathers me up in his arms, and my eyes prick at the sudden welcome warmth of a friendly hug. Sensing a heated gaze on us both, I step back. Could Stalky Hottie be hot on my trail? Am I endangering poor, unsuspecting Declan? I would never forgive myself if something happened to one of my friends because I fell for a maybe-vampire.

As we break apart, he exclaims, "Lieshe, it's a pleasure to meet ye, so it is!"

He takes my suitcase from me and steers us toward a ridiculously small old car.

"I'll just put your case in the boot. How're ye finding our wee country, then?" he asks as we walk.

I laugh as he opens the trunk and wedges my luggage in the tiny car. I ask, "Boot?"

He laughs and opens the passenger door for me. I get in and buckle, laughing again as I watch him fold himself into the driver's side. There's barely room to stash my backpack at my feet. I can't imagine what it's like for Declan to drive this thing.

"Well, at least ye find us funny," he chuckles good-naturedly.

"I'm in love with your wee country," I reply, quoting his words back to him as the toy sized car sputters to life, and he drives us away from the train station, easily navigating the city streets. "It certainly seems magical. I've lived a lifetime in just the short time I've been here."

"Well, I can't wait to show ye my shop, and then we'll

have a proper Irish night," he says, smiling at me with warm brown eyes.

Declan is tall and gangly, reminding me of a newly minted professor with his corduroy jacket with suede elbow patches and skinny jeans. His brown hair flops down over one eye, giving him the air of an absentminded one, though, who forgot to get a trim.

"My mates are playing at the pub tonight if ye fancy going," he says.

"I'd love to," I reply, thankful for someone to spend time with to stop my mind from doing nothing but replaying the past few day's events.

He tells me about his friends and their music while we drive the rest of the way to his place. We pull up behind a row of buildings, reminiscent of my neighborhood at home. He parks the ridiculously tiny car and unfolds himself like a Jack-in-the-box. After he wrestles my suitcase out, he leads me to the backdoor of his shop where we head up the stairs just inside.

"It's not much, but I'm happy to have ye," he says, waving his arm around his flat.

It is cute and cozy, filled with retro furnishings and a sputnik chandelier. Mid-century modern is one of my favorite styles and as an oddities store owner, I easily admire the effort he has painstakingly taken to decorate this way.

"Oh, I love it!" I honestly exclaim.

He invites me to follow him back to the hallway and puts my suitcase in a small spare room with a single bed covered in a vintage handmade quilt, a nightstand that boasts a cool rocket light, and several vintage horror movie posters on the walls. Above the bed is a poster of Bella Lugosi as Dracula.

I squeal. "Where did you get that?"

He smiles proudly. "Ah, that took years to track down! So, ye're a fan, then?"

"It's my favorite," I reply. "I love vintage horror movies."

"Ye'll have to see my bedroom, then," he winks.

He heads to a door down the hall and waves me in. When I see the room, I let out an audible gasp. His walls are covered in flocked red velvet wallpaper and all his furniture and linens are black. He has several more Dracula themed posters from various movies over the years and other classic horror movies, too.

"Oh Declan, it's incredible!"

He replies with a smile, "I'm glad ye like it." He points toward the other door in the hallway and says, "There's the loo."

"I'll check it out, thanks," I say and head to the bathroom, which turns out to be another super cool room, complete with a squishy toilet seat and a crochet doll covering the extra rolls of paper.

His kitschy style is absolutely awesome. Not for me, but I appreciate it nevertheless. I come back out to find him in the kitchen, brewing tea.

"D'ye want a cuppa?" he asks.

"A cup of what?" I reply, not understanding.

"Sorry, love. Tea?" he clarifies and holds up a mug.

"Sure, I'd love some," I say and smile back at him.

It's nice to sit with a familiar face and just relax. I needed this—a moment of normalcy in what's been a whirlwind of chaos and uncertainty. We have talked so much online over the years that he seems like an old friend, and I was thrilled when he offered to let me stay with him on my trip.

"You'll have to come crash with me sometime; let me return the favor!" I say.

"If I ever find meself in America, I'll take ye up on that. I got ye some gluten-free biscuits for yer tea," he says, handing me a tin.

"That was so kind! Thank you for remembering," I say.

We have our tea and cookies, or biscuits as he calls them, and talk nonstop about our mutual passion—our oddities shops. We compare trends from our respective countries, marketing strategy, and, of course, catch up on the latest community gossip. When I mention my next stop, Obscura Maximus, I spy a faint blush creep up his neck.

But before I can call him out on it, he abruptly changes the subject, saying, "Och, look at the time. We'd better get ready to go."

I don't pry, but mentally note that tidbit for later as I head back to the guest room to prepare for a welcome night out with a friend. I change into the quintessential little black emergency dress I always travel with, pairing it with striped tights and my new Docs adorned with red roses.

I fluff up my hair and apply my makeup with a bold cat eye and dark red lip. When I come out of the bathroom, Declan greets me with a low whistle and a raised eyebrow.

"Ye clean up well, Lieshe," he says, his voice a bit husky.

"Not so bad yourself," I reply.

Now that he has changed into dark jeans, boots and a button down with the sleeves rolled back, I can appreciate his build better. He isn't as gangly as my first impression had been and his slicked back hair gives him more sex appeal and less the absent-minded professor persona.

Belfast is a bustling city, and I enjoy our walk to the pub where his friends are playing. We are going early so we can grab dinner before the restaurant transitions to a club. Declan assures me there are plenty of options for me there, and I'm not disappointed.

I was expecting a dark and smoky fish and chips place,

but am pleasantly surprised by the beautiful open space with posh seating and an enormous bar featuring tons of top shelf liquors. We snag a seat in a booth with oversized high backed gray velvet seats.

I order some sliders and scope out their massive liquor selection. Declan suggests Greenore since it's the closest whiskey to bourbon and I love it. It is definitely not the same, but I can appreciate it for its own unique flavor.

We finish our dinner and order another round as we chat like long-lost friends. We move to the upper floor as the pub transitions to a club, something about local laws that I don't quite understand. We pay the cover and, as we are early, snag a great spot to the side of the stage where Declan's friends will perform.

The club fills by the second and by the time the band comes on, we are shouting to each other over the crowd. When they strum their first chord, the audience goes wild.

I quickly realize why they are a local favorite. They are good. Like really good. They play a mix of covers and originals, and soon, my Docs are tapping under the table.

The dance floor is packed with writhing bodies. Declan flags down a server and next thing I know, I'm on my third whiskey. I'm not normally a dancer, but I've drunk enough liquid courage, and it is so packed no one will notice me. Standing up, I grab Declan's hand and lead him out into the chaos.

We start out innocent, dancing without contact, but as the crowd gets thicker, we end up pushed closer together until we are grinding with the masses. I'm having an amazing time, no thoughts clouding my brain, just the energy of the people, the pulse of the music, and the beat of the drums driving my arms up into the air as I shimmy and shake. I let my eyes drift closed.

I barely have time to register a devastatingly familiar prickle on the back of my neck when strong hands grip my gyrating hips and tug me back against an exceptionally large, ridiculously hard, cool body. A whiff of tobacco and leather reaches my nose even above the combined odor of too much liquor and close pressed bodies in a confined space.

I know it's Stalky Hottie behind me. I know his signature scent and his hands on my body like they are embedded in my DNA. I expect him to spin me around to him, but he just fits himself to my back and dances. His hips move expertly to the beat, swaying me with him like we've danced together our entire lives.

The primal ritual of dancing to the pulsing music heats my blood, sweat blooming on my skin. I grind harder back into him and groan as his steel length presses into me. I want him. Against all logical thought and instinct for survival, I fucking want him. And he wants me, too.

In this moment I wish the world could disappear, that we could be wrapped back up in the golden glow of the gatehouse, surrounded by Vampira roses and peat fires.

He leans into my ear and whispers, *"Roză."*

The agony of his voice fills my heart with lead. Suddenly my back is cold. He's gone! I whirl around, but all I see is the pulsing, writhing crowd. Spinning, I scan the room, but I don't find him anywhere. I complete my circle until I am facing Declan again.

Needing a minute to compose myself, I point off to the bathrooms, and he nods. Working my way through the people and off the dance floor, I make it to the dark back hallway, where the pounding music and noise of the crowd barely diminishes.

Just as I reach out to pull the doorknob to the ladies' room, my hand is tugged into the shadows. I open my mouth to scream, but Stalky Hottie swallows it with a searing kiss. He spins me back against the wall, blotting out the club behind him with his bulk.

He pulls away to whisper across my lips, "How many times must I tell you, my little *Roză*? You are mine."

I should yell or kick him or do something—anything. Instead, I drown in his amber eyes, luminescent even in this shadowy corner. How can I break away when his very soul calls to me?

I slide my hands down the hard plane of his chest, across his washboard abs and sneak them under his shirt to find that vee I love so much. He shudders as I run my fingertips over the thick ridge of muscle and around his back.

"Who are you?" I ask as we simply stare at one another, the outside world forgotten. "Who are you really?"

He tips his head down to rest his forehead against mine. My entire world coalesces to the liquid fire in his gaze. He drags his fingertips down my throat and rests his palm over my heart.

"I am yours," he whispers across my lips before claiming them.

I am consumed by him and the passion he pours into this kiss. All the questions left unanswered, he tries to resolve with his mouth, his tongue, his hands.

When I respond just as fiercely, he moans deep into me and I melt. I run my hands up his back, fingertips dancing over the rough texture of his spine, and pull him closer. There is still too much space between us. I wrap my leg around his hip, needing more contact, more of him.

Without breaking our kiss, he slides his hand down past my heart, over my stomach, and hikes up the front of my dress. I curse myself for wearing tights, one more layer separating us.

He slips his hand under my tights and down the front of my panties, groaning when his fingers find me drenched. He slowly circles my clit as I frantically buck my hips into his touch, desperate for more of him.

He slips one long, thick finger into my tight channel and I'm forced to break our kiss, frantic for oxygen. I drop my head against his chest, riding the wave of pleasure. The fear of discovery only adds to my excitement. I cry out as he removes his finger, but it turns to a moan as he thrusts two inside me instead.

I can't help but think back to being filled by three of his thick fingers as he got me ready to take his impressive cock. My walls clamp down on him and I gush wetness, remembering how it felt to be so full.

"I want you," I rasp out. Wanton, wild. "Please," I beg.

He pulls out of my heat and turns his hand around to shred the crotch out of my tights, the tearing of the fabric barely drowned out by the pulsing music.

"I would have you more ready," he chokes out, but he is already unzipping his fly.

"I couldn't be more ready," I assure him, hitching my leg higher on his hip.

He pulls my panties to the side and rubs the head of his cock up and down, gathering my wetness. I can't help but dig my nails into his back, desperate to be filled by him. I feel like he is teasing me for eternity, every second that ticks by increasing our chances of discovery in the shadows.

"Please, Hottie, now," I cry.

His low chuckle at my nickname turns to a low growl as he notches the head of his cock at my opening. He claims my mouth just as he thrusts his hips, sheathing himself in one thrust. I cry into his mouth at the sting of being stretched so wide and filled so deep. He stills, allowing me a moment to adjust, then brings my hand to where we are joined.

He breaks the heated kiss to whisper in my ear, "Feel how we fit together."

Sliding my hand down to where he disappears inside of me, I slip him between my first two fingers and push my palm into my clit. He grabs my thighs and pulls me higher up the wall, pushing deeper into me.

"You take me so well. You are made for me," he gasps into my ear as I apply more pressure with my fingers.

This new angle has me feeling even fuller. I slide my fingers up to strum across the bundle of nerves above where he disappears into my body. As the music reaches a fevered pitch, I feel myself climbing, a familiar tightening in my belly. Voices approach, but he doesn't stop. If anything, he increases his pace, pistoning into me.

Pulling back to meet my eyes, he says, "Sh, little *Roză*. You'll have to come quietly for me."

I'm so close. I start pulsing around him but have no idea how I am going to detonate without screaming my release.

"Now. Come for me now," he commands, voice breaking.

I shatter, staring into his eyes, my mouth open in a silent scream. He bites his lip, his hips stutter, his cadence disrupted as I clench down so hard around him, he can scarcely move.

"*Roză*," he groans.

His warmth floods me, triggering a wave of aftershocks. He thrusts once more and holds himself deep inside of me as I writhe and grind my hips into him, chasing the last of the second orgasm that surprises me like a runaway train.

He drops his damp forehead to mine, sighs, and pulls out, releasing my legs to let me slide back down the wall. I pull my dress down and smile up at him shyly as he does up his fly.

"Just as I am yours, you are mine," he says as he stares into my soul.

I nod, wordlessly. He is right. Somehow, someway, I am his. My heart warms and swells with the knowledge. But the cold steel of his next warning douses it with ice.

"I will gladly kill him or any other who stands in our way. Remember that," he says, voice low and steely.

I stare up at him, realizing not only did I just have sex in a public hallway of a pub packed with people. But I just fucked a man that I suspect is a killer. A maybe-vampire.

His face drops as I push him back and flee into the ladies' room. I splash icy water on my face and put my sodden panties back into place under my wrecked tights, straightening my dress and smoothing my hair. I shake my head at the reflection in the tiny bathroom mirror.

Really, Lieshe. Really?

Not wanting to make Declan wait longer than I already have, and now worried for his safety, I force myself back out to the dance floor and work my way toward where I left him. Relief washes over me when I find him.

Declan smiles at me as he keeps dancing, oblivious to what has just shaken me to my core. He leans in to yell, "Everything okay?"

"Yeah," I yell back. "Long line."

He nods in reply, lost to the music. The song ends, and the crowd goes wild. The band's set is done and not a moment too soon.

I'm ready to leave. Now. I don't want to see Stalky Hottie again, and I need to get Declan home safely. I'm so far away from the gatehouse; there is no way his presence here tonight can be a coincidence. He is following me. There is nowhere to run.

Declan and I head back to our table, where I flag the server down for water. I'm not quite sure how to feel. The club is overstimulating—too many people and too many smells, along with the pulsing lights. My panties are sticky and uncomfortable as our combined release soaks them. I can't handle one more sensation.

Declan asks, "Lieshe, are ye sure ye're alright?"

I gulp my ice water to cover my lack of a response and embrace the chill it triggers.

I school my face and reply, "Yes, just a lot of traveling."

Like a true gentleman, he picks up his drink and drains the last sip, standing and extending a hand to me. I take it to stand but quickly pull my hand back out of his, wrapping my arms around myself as we walk out of the club and back toward his flat. I feel exposed, as if eyes are on me from every angle.

We stumble into the back of his store and up the stairs. We each chug another large glass of water, but I'm too amped to go to bed yet. Declan suggests watching a movie, and I welcome the distraction. I change into my pajamas and we curl up on opposite ends of his couch, but the next thing I know, we are snuggled together and under a blanket.

He picks a new Dracula spin off, *Renfield*, which I haven't seen yet. But I can't focus on the movie, rather my mind wanders through every interaction with Stalky Hottie, trying to figure out if he is actually a vampire. At this point, that seems more reassuring than if he is a serial killer. Although I guess a vampire is a serial killer?

From under Declan's arm, I say, "Do you think vampires could be real?"

He turns to me and burrows his face into my neck,

nipping playfully at me and saying, "I certainly hope so, love."

His accent is even thicker, and we're both still a little tipsy. Uncertainty hangs in the balance. If Stalky Hottie hadn't just so thoroughly fucked me in a hallway and then callously threatened poor Declan, this night could have taken a romantic turn.

But as nice as it is to sit here with Declan, my soul isn't on fire like it is with Hottie, and I don't want to give the impression I am interested in anything more than friendship.

He isn't the one I want nipping at my neck, and help me, I want not only Stalky Hottie biting at my neck but sinking in with his fangs. So, I playfully shove Declan away and pretend to stab him in the heart with an invisible stake.

He gallantly plays along, pretending to fall over and die hanging half off the couch. It is so dramatic I dissolve into giggles as he shuts down the TV system and offers me a hand up.

He pulls me close and kisses the top of my head, saying, "Feel free to change yer mind, lass. Ye know where my room is. G'night."

He turns and walks down the hall, leaving the bedroom door open. I sigh. He's great, but he's just not Hottie. Why, oh why, can't I just want a nice boy?

But that is it right there. I want not just a man, but a bad man. The nice boys never have been my style. Unbidden, Luke Devlin pops into my thoughts. And I know, deep down, Luke Devlin is definitely not a nice boy.

I head to the guest room and close the door, sliding into the single bed with thoughts of Hottie swirling through my head. I think back to the advice from my silver fox friend. I am starting to think if I don't give him a chance, I will regret it.

I try to envision myself settled with someone like Declan, a nice guy with similar interests, into oddities like me, fun and flirty. But when I picture a life with him, I literally yawn.

I wipe my watering eyes as my jaw cracks, and snuggle into my pillow, thinking instead about a life with Stalky. The thought licks flames along my body like a wildfire, settles in my core, and moves up to my heart where it lodges like a weight.

Not the weight of anxiety or heartache, but the weight of coming home, like a puzzle piece clicking into place. And although Luke is a hot enigma, he doesn't feel like home.

But what does home look like with an immortal serial killer vampire?

Not ready to process this final thought, I let sleep drag me down into oblivion where once again I'm claimed by Luke in a land of twilight skies, as if he, too, wants to stake his claim on me.

Chapter 16

LIESHE

Someone is calling my name, but I burrow deeper down into the covers, not yet ready to face the world. I pull the pillow over my head and mumble, "Five more minutes."

When it is wrestled off my face, I groan.

"Lieshe, love, it's noon," Declan croons.

I bolt upright, "Noon!"

He laughs. "I hated to wake ye. Yer wee snores were dead on."

I snatch my pillow from his hands, whacking him over the head with it. He laughs harder, tossing it back to me.

"Come on out when ye're ready, then," he throws over his shoulder, still chuckling as he walks out.

I hit the bathroom and take advantage of his shower, washing my hair and braiding it wet. Then, I make my way out to the kitchen where he has tea and biscuits set out for me.

"I didn't think ye'd be interested in an Irish breakfast," he says with a smile.

"You'd be right. This is perfect, thank you," I reply.

The conversation is easy and light, and I'm thankful that we've fallen right back into our friendship without any awkwardness from last night. Nothing actually happened, and it seems there are no hard feelings all around.

"I figured ye'd want to head down to the shop after this, since ye'll need to be on your way to the ferry soon enough.

We've got about six hours until the last one. After ye're done at my place, I've got a friend with old anatomy prints if ye're interested and there's time," he says.

That grabbed my attention. I am an absolute sucker for anything vintage medical.

"Let's go!" I exclaim, cramming one more biscuit in my mouth and swigging down the dregs of my tea while wishing it were coffee.

We head down the back stairs and enter his impressive storeroom, where I let out a whistle. "Declan, this is incredible!"

He ducks his head and smiles, clearly proud of his collections. He has massive amounts of iconography and various religious artifacts and relics. I spy several pieces that I know my moody maximalists back home would absolutely love.

We go through his collection, pulling out the items I want to ship back to America. I've never come across some of these before and don't know that I would have if I hadn't made this trip.

He brings me to another room, this one filled with vintage books. The musty smell wraps me in a comforting embrace. I've always loved reading and the sensation of paper under my fingertips as a story leaps to life. I pick a few out for both Grimm and my personal collection until I let out a series of sneezes.

Checking my watch, I tell Declan I'd really love to meet his friend with the anatomy prints. We head back out to his main store and settle on a price for the items I am getting before gathering my belongings from his flat.

Laughing as we pile back in, I say, "I keep meaning to ask, what is this tiny car?"

He returns my laugh as he shifts gears, easily navigating

the city traffic, and says, "It's a Fiat that's older than both of us."

We make our way to the outskirts of Belfast and pull up at an antique shop. It doesn't seem like much from the outside; the window is nearly opaque with grime and age, and a few spindly antiques are visible. I would have walked right by it.

Declan parks the little Fiat in an even smaller space, somehow defying the laws of physics, and we head into the store. The inside far surpasses the misleading exterior. There is no rhyme or reason to the layout—antiques, oddities, taxidermy, books, statues, and more haphazardly piled all over the place. It's a veritable treasure hunt.

A cat slinks its way out from under an end table with a cracked marble top and winds around my ankles, reminding me of my own at home. A wave of longing unexpectedly hits me, and I realize I actually miss Lucifer.

I reach down to pet the creature, but it hisses and darts away. A wheezy laugh has me looking up to find an old woman with a crinkled face and snow-white hair in a long braid over her shoulder.

She slaps her knee and says, "Ba chóir duit do dhóigh a fheiceáil."

Declan chuckles and says, "Caitriona says ye should see yer face. Don't let that old cat upset ye. Dubh's as old as the shop, or so she says."

Caitriona walks over and extends her hand. She continues to speak in Irish as he translates.

"Ye can talk to her in English. She's grand with it, but she's a stubborn one, our Cait, and she'll only answer ye in Irish."

I'm trying to follow the conversation while I take in everything in the store, which is impossible. It would take years to explore all the stuff that is packed in here. I give up and just trail after them to a back corner where Cait unearths stacks of vintage anatomy prints from under a pile of items.

Declan translating explains to me that Cait's husband used to collect books and cut out the old lithographs and etchings from them. They had traveled around Europe treasure hunting until she lost her husband and then stuck to just minding the store, selling off their years of accumulation.

I flip through the papers, pristine despite their age and the fact they've been stored beneath a moth-eaten, taxidermied red fox. Many are from the 1700 and 1800s. I soon amass a pile of really great ones, several of which will probably make their way into my house and not my store. At length, I reach the end of the stacks and pick up my treasures.

Our little trio makes its way to the register, where Cait surprises me by processing my card through a very modern point-of-sale system. As she hands it back, my eye catches on a necklace with a Greek cross above a dragon curled into a circle with the tip of its tail wrapped around its neck. I recognize the symbol from one of Stalky Hottie's rings.

"What is this?" I ask, pointing.

Declan picks up the pendant and spins it around to be right side up for him.

"Oh, that's the insignia of the Order of the Dragon," he explains.

"The Order of the Dragon?" I parrot back.

"And you said you were a *Dracula* fan," he chides.

Cait takes the necklace from him and presses it into my hand, closing both of her hands around mine, saying, "*Bronntanas duit. Coinnigh i sláinte mhaith.*"

Declan translates, "A gift for you. Wear it in good health."

I start to protest, but he whispers to me out of the side of his mouth, "Ye can't refuse a gift, Lieshe. Take it with thanks."

"Thank you, Cait," I say.

She wraps me in a hug, her head only coming to my shoulder. At five three, I am short, but she is absolutely tiny. Small but mighty, she feels anything but fragile. Rather, she feels like strength and stability, an anchor in time and place.

She releases me and looks up at my face, locking her pale blue eyes onto my mismatched ones, then murmurs something I can't quite make out. She knocks once on the wooden counter, then pats my cheek in dismissal.

Declan starts in response to what she says, but she has already wandered away through the maze of a store. We turn and head out.

"I'll pack these up and ship them with your pieces from me," he says, tucking my hoard into the boot of his car.

After we are both buckled back in, and we are pulling away, I ask him, "What was the last thing Cait said?"

He clears his throat.

"Declan?" I press him.

"She, uh, said something that's hard to translate," he says, trailing off at the end.

"Well, just try your best," I encourage.

Declan looks at me out of the corner of his eye and then back at the road. Motioning to one of his eyes, he says, "She said something about ye being touched by fate."

I frown. That didn't sound bad. I'm not quite sure why he looked uncomfortable about that. Perhaps there was some type of superstition attached to it that I didn't understand. Or he was worried I would be upset about someone bringing up my heterochromia.

I shrug it off, my thoughts already moving on to my next stop. We make our way to the ferry, and I buy my ticket to Cairnryan, Scotland. Declan walks me to the ferry and passes off my suitcase as I hitch my backpack more firmly onto my shoulders.

"Thank you, Declan, this has been an amazing visit, and I really appreciate everything you have done for me," I say.

He puts his hands on my face and leans in. I start to panic, worried my stalker is watching and will follow through on his threat to kill Declan if he doesn't keep his hands to himself. But all he does is drop a kiss on my forehead.

"It was a pleasure, Lieshe. *Go mbeirimid beo ar an am seo arís*," he says.

I reply, "I'm serious, come to America and let me host!"

He chuckles, and as he slowly backs away, promises, "I'll take you up on that."

"Wait, what did you say in Irish?" I call to him, curious.

He says, "It doesn't translate perfectly, but I said, may we be alive at this time again."

I freeze my smile into place to hide the fear that slithers down my spine. May we both be alive indeed. The ferry lets out a mournful blast on its horn and I turn to board with the last of the other passengers.

Declan stands at his car and watches me for a while, until we both give one more wave, and he turns and leaves. He was so lovely. I'm glad we could leave things as friends, and I really do hope that we see each other again.

Especially alive. I shiver at the saying.

I pull my suitcase along behind me and find a seat inside. The air on the water is cooler than I anticipated, but the cabin is nice and warm. I settle into a comfortable booth and decide to both pass the time and numb my mind with some fiction. I haven't been able to just read and relax my brain since I've been here.

I scroll through the library on my phone, trying to find something to grab my interest, but everything is repetitive and predictable. Remembering my new necklace, I am inspired to pull out my old, dog-eared copy of *Dracula*.

As I flip the pages, I absentmindedly nibble a granola bar from my bag and sip on a bottle of water. I've gotten seasick in my life, but luckily, this ferry is large, and the sea is calm. I read until my eyes are blurry. Despite the number of times I've gone through this book, I keep getting distracted by minute details, comparing the author's description of vampires to Stalky Hottie.

My thoughts circle. Could he actually be a vampire? In the light of day, I feel silly for even considering this. But in the fading twilight, I can't help but try to think through the possibilities. I hadn't seen him drink any blood, and he had made no move to bite me outside of the bedroom.

But if I stop and think about it, he did suck on my finger when I pricked it on the rose's thorn, I think he may have bitten my thigh, and he most definitely bit my neck. I briefly pause, wondering if I will become a vampire, too, but that seems a stretch, and I am still relatively happy to nibble my dry granola bar. Besides, I would have to drink his blood to be turned if all the stories are true.

Can he transform? That would explain a lot of things. I need some type of proof, something tangible to base my thoughts on rather than just believing in magic and mystery. Although I value the point of my silver fox from Dublin's advice, to have no regrets, first I have to wade through the evidence. That is the lynchpin my logical mind is clinging to.

My swirling theories have passed the time for the last of

the ferry crossing. I take my backpack and suitcase and head up to the top deck with the other passengers to prepare to disembark. The coastline of Scotland looms ahead, and a thrill runs through me. One of my absolute favorite book series takes place here with the characters moving through time using the standing stones.

I smile to myself, wondering if her story was predicated on bits and bobs of truth. What if the main character really had moved through time and fallen in love with a Scottish Highlander? If I gave credence to the possibility of vampires, I would have to open my mind to all types of possibilities—time travel, shifters, angels, and perhaps even aliens.

I shake my head. My imagination has always been incredible, and now my thoughts are turning fanciful. I join the line with the other passengers, bringing up my car reservation on my phone.

I have a lot of ground to cover and had built in just a few must-see stops, so I decided to be super adventurous and rent a vehicle for Scotland and England. I am mildly scared to drive on not only the other side of the road, but also from the opposite side of the car. But it surely can't be that hard, can it?

The wind picks up, pushing my hair back from face and carrying the scent of the sea, with an undercurrent of tobacco and leather. My head snaps up from my phone, eyes surveying the crowd in front of me, searching for Stalky Hottie. Up ahead, there is a man a head taller than all the other passengers, just like he would be, but short of shoving my way through, I have no way to reach him.

I impatiently wait for the people to disperse, bouncing on the balls of my feet and stomach knotted in anticipation. By the time my Docs hit solid ground, I can't find the tall man in the thinning crowd, and my heart drops. My feelings make no sense.

I walked away from him, but I am constantly searching for him. The club could be a coincidence, although I don't think it was. But if he really is on this ferry, he is absolutely stalking me. The question is, do I want him to be?

Chapter 17

LIESHE

I sit in the driver's seat—yes, the other driver's seat—of a car that makes Declan's tiny Fiat seem like a luxury SUV. My suitcase is on the passenger seat—yes, the other passenger seat—of what I am now calling the sardine can.

Not only because what was rented to me as a car, and I use the term loosely, is the size of a sardine can, but also because it vaguely smells like, well, sardines.

Declan never would have been able to fit in this car, much less Stalky Hottie. The thought of him trying to fold himself into the microscopic space brings a smile to my face. I pop the directions to Loch Ness into my phone and steel myself for my first European driving experience.

I try to ease the car into reverse as it bucks and stutters. I think it can't be that much different from my bug at home, which is a manual, of course, and give myself a little mental pep talk. With a loud grinding noise, I get the car going backward and then forward, heading off in the direction my phone is squawking at me to go.

I'm proud of my achievement until another car heads straight for me. In my excitement over getting moving, I completely forgot to drive on the left side of the road! I quickly correct course and wave apologetically as the other vehicle whizzes past, shouting, "Sorry!" as if they can hear me.

As the sun dips toward the horizon, I realize a few things.

To start, this plan was overly ambitious. Now I have been overly ambitious before, but usually with a solid foundation to be successful. This time, I am starting to doubt my plan. On paper, this seemed reasonable, and I had really wanted to visit Loch Ness. I can't imagine being this close and missing it.

What I hadn't factored in was the six-hour drive from Cairnryan to Loch Ness would be so grueling. This is nothing like driving six hours on a highway in the states. Driving here takes all of my concentration and focus to follow the unfamiliar rules of the road.

I can't even play music because I am concentrating so hard. I had also forgotten to factor in dinner and any pit stops. I don't know how on earth I'm going to accomplish getting there safely in the dark while starving. I scold myself for not leaving Declan's earlier.

The sun steadily lowers in the sky, following in the same direction as my spirits. I realize I need to change up my plan. I pull over at the next safe spot and try to consult my phone, but there is no service. Cursing, I get back onto the road and keep heading toward Loch Ness, figuring I will get to a reasonably sized town, grab dinner and a room, and finish the journey in the morning.

I push for as long as I safely can, but soon enough, I am too tired and hungry to go on. So, when there is a sign for a town named Pitlochry, I follow it. As I pull off the main road, I see a hotel sign and turn in that direction, following a twisting roadway. As I crest a hill, a majestic stone structure complete with turrets rises into view.

I park the sardine can, staring up at the impressive building and dreading the cost of the room. It's not that I don't have the money, I just hate to spend it on myself for something like a luxury hotel room. But I've pushed myself to the end of my limits today and I'm out of options.

Grabbing my backpack and suitcase, I step into a grand lobby, where a roaring fireplace and carefully arranged furniture create cozy conversation areas. Despite the contrast between my comfy travel clothes and the surrounding opulence, I walk to the desk, where a friendly Scotsman greets me.

If I thought the accents in Ireland were incredible, the Scottish accent is hitting me in all the feels. I could move here and just listen to the men talk all day, or better yet, all night.

He kindly informs me my timing is not great. There is a wedding at the hotel, and it is sold out except for one of the turret rooms. It's double the price of a regular room, but there isn't much choice in the matter, so I take it.

I follow the complicated directions to get to one of the south facing towers, and after only two wrong turns and three elevators, I find my way there. Swiping my key card, I walk into an amazing circular room with a lovely king-sized bed and jewel toned walls.

A door leads into a beautiful bath with a jacuzzi tub and separate shower room. I head back out and up the curving stairs to the second floor sitting room and am blown away by the three hundred- and sixty-degree views of the Perthshire countryside.

Around me are darkened mountains, but above that—I have never seen anything like this. The sky looks like black velvet dotted with millions of the whitest stars. I have never thought of myself as so small and insignificant as I feel here in the presence of the enormous cosmos spread out before me.

As I stand there contemplating an ever-expanding

universe, doubt snakes its way into my brain. What if I'm wrong about Stalky Hottie? In the face of this beauty, of the billions of stars that exist in a universe that never ends, walking around in a body that is amazingly complex in its millions of cells and chemical reactions—what if?

What if none of this beauty or function or structure is happenstance? What if we really do belong together? He keeps saying he is mine and I am his. Do we have some sort of love story already?

Unsure and unsteady, my newfound confidence teeters, becoming tenuous and strained. What if I'm wrong about everything? This is a dangerous road to follow. I shake myself from the reverie—I can't stand here staring at the stars, pondering the mysteries of the universe, with a growling stomach and exhaustion clouding my thoughts.

I call down to the front desk to order room service, so I can eat and get some sleep. The person on the other end of the phone instead invites me to head down to the spa. The café there is open for another thirty minutes yet, but there is no room service right now with the wedding going on.

I politely thank them while internally seething. I really don't want to leave this beautiful room, but I also can't stand the thought of eating one more granola bar from my bag. I need a real meal.

I follow the signs to the Lavender Loch Spa. As I step through the glass doors, my annoyance melts away. An enormous, curved water wall happily trickles along one side, and the soothing scent of lavender overlying high end spa products beckons me.

I stand still for a moment, closing my eyes and taking three deep breaths to steady myself. After feeling lost in my hotel room, I become increasingly centered with each breath, all that is Lieshe returning to my core, solidifying the essence of who I am.

I follow the water feature around to the check-in desk, where I'm greeted by a friendly attendant. She directs me to the café, and I walk into a small but beautifully appointed dining room. I am the only one here, and the solitude is blissful.

A server shows me to a table close to the buffet and brings over a large glass of citrus infused water. After the long day, the cold liquid is perfect, clean and crisp on my tongue.

The spread looks incredible, filled with fruits and veggies, charcuterie, and a hot soup. I am delighted when the server informs me the only gluten is the bread kept on a separate tray, and they would be happy to bring some hot tapioca rolls with fresh butter.

I go and fill my plate with a selection of a beautiful rainbow of produce, a little fruit, lots of grilled and roasted veggies, a few dips, and even a quinoa salad. By the time I settle back in my seat with my napkin on my lap, the server is dropping off the bread.

Hot fresh rolls in a restaurant are a rare treat, and I dig into them. The tension melts away as my stomach fills, and I enjoy the wonderful food. This is so much better than room service would have been. I'm happy I left my room after all.

When the server finally comes over to clear my plates and refill my water, I'm shocked at the offer of a massage. Apparently, there was a last-minute cancellation, and the final opening of the night is still available. I'm surprised they are open so late, but with weddings and such, I guess it makes sense.

What the heck, I think, why not pamper myself while I stay in this amazing place? I finish eating and am shown to the women's locker room, where I stow my clothes and change into the luxurious robe and slippers provided. The music and dim lighting already have me starting to relax.

Within a few minutes, another attendant comes and leads me to my treatment room. She explains in her beautiful Scottish accent to undress to my comfort level and then lie on the table face down.

After she leaves, I remove my robe and slippers and crawl under a sumptuous, weighted lavender blanket. The heated massage table has me melting into a relaxed state. This is exactly the treat I needed.

A soft knock, followed by the quiet opening and closing of the door, announces the therapist's arrival. I hear them quietly moving around the room, just over the soothing spa music. They fold up the blanket to expose my legs and then warm the lotion in their hands.

I startle slightly when two large, cool hands settle onto my left leg. In my previous experiences, the therapist would have come in and introduced themselves first, but I guess things are different in Scotland.

I quickly relax again as they knead away my travel-induced muscle tension. Up and down my left leg, I'm guessing the therapist is a he based on the large strong hands, and then he does the same treatment to my right side.

I relax further under his ministrations. Moving on to my feet, he works the arch, triggering me to let out an embarrassing moan. He rubs every individual toe, and I fall deeper into bliss. The blanket is folded back down and tucked under my warm and boneless legs.

The heated massage bed keeps me toasty even as I am bared to my waist, the blanket gently tucked around my hips. Standing at my side, his hands began working down the columns of muscles on each side of my spine, stretching my lower back and turning me into a pile of goo.

I am so thankful my journey serendipitously led me here to this spot. I can't believe how much I needed this. For once, my mind is quiet and I just drift as the skilled therapist continues to rub my back, then steps up to stand at my head and changes the position of his strokes.

He works my traps from the base of my neck out to each shoulder and then glides his hands deeply down both sides of my spine toward my hips, bringing his body above mine.

Almost dozing, I think of just how good Stalky Hottie smells and how refreshing it is to breathe in his tobacco and leather scent as it drifts up, breaking the lavender of the spa, which had become cloying in my nose. I don't really prefer florals after all. I frown, something pulling at my sleepy brain.

Nostrils flaring as I inhale, I whip my head up to find a pair of black jeans over thick thighs. Gone is my relaxed state. I know a massage therapist wouldn't be in jeans. I drag my gaze up a black V-neck t-shirt, cranking my head back from my prone position to finally reach his face.

Chapter 18

LIESHE

"You," I breathe.

As if he had been conjured by my thoughts, he stands there staring down at me with fire in his amber eyes. He looks like a dark, avenging angel in his black jeans and shirt. An errant strand of dark hair flops down over one eye as he stares down at me.

Before I can draw another breath, he reaches out with one hand and laces his fingers into the hair at the back of my scalp, and with the other under my arm, pulls me up to my knees, crushing his mouth to mine.

He angles my head using my hair, the sharp prickle causing me to gasp. He seizes the moment to claim my mouth, his taste like ancient mysteries, lost souls, and time immemorial—perfectly suited to the wild country we're in, as brutal and beautiful as this kiss.

When we're apart, all I can think of is him, and when we are together, I can't think at all, only react. This is insanity. I keep running from him, from my fears of who and what he could be. My reaction to him is the strongest evidence that he is right when he says we belong to each other.

He consumes me. Although my mind rebels, wanting to revert to logic, my body has no such qualms. Gone is the liquid relaxation of the warmed table and massage, and in its place, wildfire is licking me from the inside out.

My arms wind around his neck, hands fisting the back of his shirt, desperate for something to anchor me in the storm that is this man. I don't realize I'm off the table until I'm slammed against the wall, his length pressing into my core.

Through my damp panties, his hardness behind the zipper of his jeans digs deliciously against my seam as he thrusts against me. I wrap my legs around his waist and use my arms to rub myself up and down the stiff denim, frantic for more.

"Shirt," I grunt out between kisses, fervently wanting his skin against mine.

He pins my hips against the wall, and with one hand reaches behind his neck and rips his shirt off.

I press my hands to his pecs, his skin like cool marble, and slowly drag them down over every hard ridge of muscle. Finally, I can touch his tattoos like I have been craving. There are so many different scripts, and in the center of his chest, the living and dying Vampira roses come together to wrap around a skull that stares back at me.

On his right pec, the tattoos are swirls and lines, the pigment over raised bumps. As I trace each one, he shivers. His amber eyes lock onto mine. Time stands still, hanging between us, and suddenly I need to touch him, to consume him, to ground myself in him.

I slide my body down his and push him back into the single chair. He sits down, never breaking eye contact. I feel confident and sexy as his gaze absorbs me.

I sink to my knees in front of him, reaching out and running my fingers down his amazing abs to the waistband on his jeans. I drop my eyes to the button as I undo it and inch down his zipper, the sound loud in the massage room.

He reaches out and pulls my bottom lip out from my teeth, and in a dark, graveled voice commands, "Stop. Biting. My. Lip."

His dominant tone shoots straight to my core, triggering

my arousal, dripping down my thighs. He lifts his hips, and I grab the waistband of his jeans and black boxer briefs and slide them down to his ankles, exposing his inked, muscled, thick legs.

Staring back into the face of the dragon covering his lower abs, I realize this tattoo is nearly identical to the necklace Cait had pressed into my hand before I left. What does this mean? If I am touched by fate, is he my fate? Do we have a love story, as he tried to tell me?

My eyes follow the dragon's tail, pointing me back down to my goal. My mouth waters as the thought of tasting him again. I flick my eyes up to his to find a confident male smirk on his face.

He knows he is gorgeous and huge. Wrapping a large hand firmly around his shaft, he slowly slides it up and down, eyes locked onto mine. His bold confidence is one of the sexiest things I've ever seen.

As I watch, a drop of precum gathers at the tip, and I can't help but lean forward, desperate to savor him. He holds the base of his length as I dip my head to swipe it with the tip of my tongue.

He tastes like mine.

Emboldened by his sharp intake of breath, I drop down and place my hands on his knees, spreading his legs. Remembering what he loved last time, I dip low and lick from his balls, up the center to the underside of his shaft, until I get back to the head.

His tobacco and leather scent mixes with his unique stormy undertone. His grip is strangling his cock, and it turns an angry red. Muscles taut, he struggles to stay motionless as I explore him with my mouth.

I take in his amber eyes, pupils blown wide, and swirl my tongue around the head, flicking the slit and then engulfing the head. His gaze darkens, and he moans while I work more of him into my mouth.

He tastes delicious, smooth on my tongue like silk over steel, and I can't help but hum in appreciation. The hand not strangling his cock sneaks into my hair and just rests there, not changing my rhythm, just letting me continue to explore him.

I keep working my mouth up and down, my saliva trailing down his length, easing my way. I know I won't be able to get all of him in my mouth, but I'm desperate for as much as I can get.

"Touch yourself," he gets out in a strangled voice.

I am happy to oblige. I've never touched myself in front of someone else, but right now, I'm very willing to start. Sliding my panties to the side, I slide two fingers up and down my folds, finding my core dripping wet.

I find a rhythm with my mouth and use my other hand to wrap around him, fingers not meeting around his impressive girth. My breathing picks up, my hips rocking to meet my hand of their own volition.

"I'm going to fuck your face now, *Roză*. Are you ready?" he asks.

He lets go of his rock-hard length and winds both hands into my hair and holds my head steady.

"Come when I tell you," he rasps out.

He continues to fascinate me with the many facets of his personality. Obsessed one minute, doting and sweet the next, now dominant.

I think it will be all I can do to hold out for him at this rate. I relax my jaw as much as I can, and he feeds me another inch. I gag slightly, and his gaze smolders.

"Yes, *Roză*, give me your tears," he whispers as his hips thrust more frantically.

He hits the back of my throat, and tears slip down my face as I struggle to regulate my breathing and stop from gagging.

The reality of him surpasses my fantasy, leaving me feeling exalted and empowered, a vessel meant to bring him to ecstasy. My hand speeds up, my pelvis grinding down as I slip another finger inside myself, slamming my palm against my clit.

It's not enough, I need so much more. I raise my eyes to his face. He looks positively tortured, every muscle strung taut, sweat dripping from his brow. His mouth falls open and his eyes roll back.

"Now, come for me now!"

And I do. My inner walls clamp down around my hand, my forearm muscles locking up, but my hips ride my hand. I couldn't stop now if the building fell down. I can't help but moan around him in my mouth as my orgasm intensifies, triggering him to come with me.

His hips stutter and jerk as he shoots his hot release into my throat. He opens his eyes and meets mine, commanding, "All of me."

I swallow as much as I can, but some leaks out the corners of my stretched mouth. He holds the back of my head, my forehead against his lower abdomen, and I feel the last twitches of his cock and final spurt on my tongue.

He pulls me off and demands, "Open."

I stick out my tongue, showing him the part of his climax that has gathered there.

"Good girl," he says darkly. "Now swallow."

And I do. I love when he commands me, something I never knew I wanted until it happened.

He reaches out and swipes the drop making its way out of the corner of my mouth and leans forward, reaching his hand down between my legs and shoving it inside of me. With his other hand, he grabs my hair and crashes his lips to mine.

I should be shocked at him shoving his cum inside of me, kissing me with the rest of it still coating my tongue, but instead, I feel claimed, as if he is branding me to him, twinning our souls together.

I'm getting used to having multiple orgasms, and as he thrusts his finger inside of me and continues to kiss me fervently, another wave of pleasure crests over me. He sucks my tongue, and I wantonly ride his hand with my hips, moaning into his mouth as I come again, quick and fierce.

Leaning back, he stares into my eyes and brings his fingers to his face. Without breaking our stare, he sucks them off, one by one. He kisses me again and our combined flavor is too much. I am drowning. I pull back and drop back onto my heels, desperate for oxygen, still panting hard.

"You are mine, *Roză*," he says vehemently. "You can keep running, but you are mine. You always have been, and you always will be. I have waited an eternity for you. I will not lose you again."

By the end of his declaration, he is growling fiercely. He stands up, yanking up his jeans and fastening them. Turning around, he grabs his shirt and pulls it on. At last, I see the tattoo over his back. Reaching out, I stop him from pulling it down.

A large tree with red fruit covers his back from shoulder to shoulder, the trunk turning into intricate Celtic knots instead of roots that wind up into the branches to complete the circle.

The trunk looks rough, unlike the rest of the tattoo, marked by some type of extensive scarification. Threaded through the knot work is a snake with yellow-green eyes.

The leaves of the tree are made up of all different animals and on each side is a person.

I move even closer, squinting in the dim light of the massage room, to study the exquisite details. The man resembles him, holding out a piece of the fruit to the woman. I trail a finger across the tree, which is as rough as it looks. When it reaches the woman, I freeze.

It's like looking into a mirror—amber eyes, wild curly hair, and even my same build. The only difference is her eyes are the same color, no splash of green.

At my sharp gasp, he looks at me over his shoulder, his profile nothing but an outline in the soft lighting. He is exquisitely beautiful, with his straight nose, full lips, and jaw like a knife. He pulls his shirt the rest of the way down, movements jerky, and I sense an undercurrent of anger.

I'm not sure why his mood has suddenly shifted or why. I walk over to the door where the robe hangs on the back and shrug it on.

He comes up behind me and grips a side of the robe in each hand. He wraps it around me and with it his arms, embracing me from behind. I drop my head back against his chest and he rests his chin on top of it.

He ties the belt and drops a kiss on top of my head before stepping away, leaving the room glacial. He gently smooths a hand down my tousled hair, then reaches past me, opens the door, and walks out without so much as a backward glance.

I stare after him with a gaping mouth and then shake my head, walking back toward the locker room. Robotically, I change into my clothes and head back out of the spa, mind reeling.

At the desk, the attendant says, "How was your massage, miss?"

She withers under my raised eyebrow as I continue to

walk by and head back to my room. My massage was mind blowing, but the emotional whiplash is too much. This constant push and pull between us must come to a resolution. We are like spinning magnets, attracting and repelling depending on each spin.

I step off the elevator, and somehow, I know he is waiting for me. I turn the corner and there he is, leaning against the wall next to my door. He watches me like a wolf, stalking my every move.

When I reach the door, he reaches out a trembling hand and traces my jaw, pleading with me, "Let me hold you for one night, *Roză*." His face is etched in pain, sorrow bracketing his liquid gold eyes, corners of his delectable mouth pulled down. "Please."

The "please" breaks me, and at this moment, I'm not strong enough to refuse. I swipe my keycard and grab his hand, pulling him into the room behind me.

We get ready for bed in silence. I pull on a shirt, needing some type of barrier between us, though, lately, I've been sleeping naked. He strips his clothes, throwing them over a chair. I drink in the sight of him greedily, unable to help myself.

I avoid checking out between his legs, or I know I'll lose my sanity and turn back into a horny puddle of submission. He crawls in first, flashing me a perfectly rounded backside and lies on his back, stretching one arm out in invitation.

I turn off the light and at the last minute, take off my shirt, but leave my panties on. I'm only a woman after all, not a saint, and I want his skin on mine. I lie on my side as he curls around me, pulling one of my legs between his, draping a heavy arm over my waist, and resting one large hand on my breast.

He buries his nose in my hair, his breathing evening out.

His cool skin is a relief—I hate being too warm when I sleep, and there's a lot of him pressed to me. His erection presses into my hip, and my mind wanders, imagining all the ways I could shift until he is nudging at my entrance. He makes me insatiable, and now that I've experienced what sex with him is like, I want more.

I want to stay awake to memorize his body next to mine, wrapped in his dreams, breathing the same breath. But my eyelids grow heavy, and before I know it, sleep pulls me under.

Chapter 19

VLAD

I hold her for hours, wrapped in her dreams, breathing in her rose scent. Her heartbeat echoes into my body, reverberating into my soul. As the moon traverses the sky, Lilith's words come back to me.

I don't deserve her. I have done nothing to win her over.

I am loath to admit it, but Lilith is right. I have been punished for all of eternity, and I'm coming to the end of what little remains of my sanity. How many lifetimes can I be expected to love her, only to lose her time and time again, and remain sane?

No creature in this universe could survive this special version of Hell I have been sentenced to. I would gladly brave never-ending fire and brimstone rather than have my soul slowly fractured infinite times until I am left with nothing but a spider web of broken glass on the verge of shattering, never to be pieced back together again.

I know this is the last time I can withstand this exquisite torment. Even if I don't deserve her, she is mine. Made from me, for me. We are two halves of the same whole. The word love does not begin to encompass the depths of my feelings for her. I don't just want her. I *need* her. My very soul cannot exist without hers.

Even the infinite and ever-expanding universe is too small to hold the breadth of my feelings, my commitment, and my loyalty. Perhaps that is what my sin truly was. Not falling for a lie and handing her that damn fruit, but loving her above all else.

That is why I walked away from her earlier tonight, ashamed of my choices that have led us here. I hadn't been ready for her to see my back—the tattoo of our story, the extensive scarification I have tortured myself with until the flesh reflected the pain inside.

I grapple with the bargain I have made with both of our souls. It is a desperate gamble by an even more desperate man because this lifetime seems different.

Or is that wishful thinking? Am I so exhausted after countless lifetimes of love and loss that I have been driven to make this foolish agreement? I'm banking our future on my ability to make her love me once again, racing against the devil himself. Maybe I am mad after all.

The die has been cast. There is no forward momentum in ruminating on the past. Especially with one as long as mine. No matter what happens, there will be comfort in having this torture end. One way or another.

My resolve hardens. I must win, for the sake of both of our souls and our only chance at happiness. I let my mind drift back through countless memories, casting about for the golden ones, the bright spots where she has loved me back. I cast a glance at the small stack of wedding bands I have worn through the ages, but even those lifetimes ended in heartbreak.

I overlay the memories with what I know of her in this lifetime—what I have studied about her since she was born while waiting for her to call me back to her. The information my servants have fed me to slake my obsession.

As the night fades to dawn, a plan begins to form. She is desperate for our truth. Not only do I owe it to her, but I am ready to free myself from this burden. This is the point of no return.

I inhale one last deep breath of her, close my eyes, and commit this snapshot in time to my memory—curled around her, wrapped in her dreams, bodies entwined. The trust she shows by sleeping in my arms. I bury my face in her neck, let her pulse beat against my lips. If I can't win, I will gladly sacrifice myself for her.

I push the memories away along with the outside world and just appreciate her for who she is right now, right here. My eyes fly open. That is the key. She wants to be loved for herself. She needs to be appreciated and respected for the unique person she has carved out of this lifetime. The last piece of the puzzle clicks into place for my plan.

I materialize into particles slowly so that not even the rustle of the bedding will wake her. She still lets out a soft moan of protest at my loss. It takes every ounce of my strength to not slide back into the bed to comfort her, pull her back into me again, and bury myself in her.

But now I must race against the dawn to prepare.

For her.

For me.

For us.

Chapter 20

Stalky Hottie and I are standing hand in hand, looking out over Loch Ness. The rolling fields are verdant green, the sky a vivid blue, and the distant mountains a stunning hazy purple. I scan the water with my eyes, desperately hoping to catch a glimpse of Nessie.

We walk close to the water's edge, and I pull his hand excitedly, saying, "Look! Look! I see something!"

I walk right up to the edge of the murky water and peer in, just knowing I'm going to catch a glimpse of her. I frown and lean closer, where I see something underneath, catching the current.

As what looks like seaweed slowly drifts away, with dawning horror, I realize it is actually human hair as a distorted face comes into focus. I rear back as I find not just one body under the water's surface, but hundreds of them—bloated and pale. I turn to face Stalky Hottie and find him smiling, canines grotesquely extended and mouth bloody. I open mine to scream and wake with a start.

I'm momentarily confused, unsure of my surroundings. Breathing heavily, I glance around the room, but I appear to be alone. I reach over, but the other side of the bed is cold. I grab the pillow and bring it to my face, inhaling deeply, and catch the faintest scent of him. I scrub my hands over my face and press my palms into my eyes until spots dance in my vision.

Voicing my thoughts out loud to the empty room, I groan, "What am I doing?"

I'm hit with an unexpected pang of homesickness. I want my little store, my apartment. I want something real and tangible and familiar to navigate this unchartered territory. I want my friends.

In a daze, I roll out of bed and get ready to face the day, gathering up my things. I head up to the sitting room with the incredible views, the daylight equally stunning. Mountain ranges and rolling fields provide a beautiful panorama. I set the in-room tea maker to brew, missing my oat milk lattes.

I notice my copy of *Dracula* on the coffee table. Flipping it open to where the Vampira rose I took from the gatehouse has been moved to, I'm stunned. The flower should be pressed, flat and drying. Instead, it looks as fresh as the day I put it there, the red, black saturated color velvety and perfectly three-dimensional.

I reach out and stroke the softness of the petals; no logical explanation is possible. I look back at the open book and read the underlined sentence, "Do you believe in destiny? That even the powers of time can be altered for a single purpose. The luckiest man who walks on this earth is the one who finds true love."

Do I believe in destiny? It's clear that Stalky Hottie does. It had to be him who moved the rose and underlined that specific quote. Somehow, he believes our paths have crossed before. I think back to the dreams—or visions—I've had since meeting him, and how they've evolved from the ones I've had all my life.

I recall his tattoo, the image of us both. I should be scared by his stalker-like behavior. Instead, I find myself falling deeper for him. It feels good to be pursued, to be wanted, and desired. Not to mention the way he makes my body sing.

What is happening to me? I was so grounded, so logical, and if I'm being honest, I was also so lonely. I grab the hot tea and stand at the window, staring out at the stunning views while I blow on the steaming beverage.

My gaze travels over the mountain ranges, the ancient mysteries of Scotland surrounding me. I wonder where he went and why he left before I woke up. I contemplate moving on to my next stop and skipping Loch Ness. I don't know that I can face it alone after my disturbing dream.

After having the experience of a magical night with someone by my side on this trip, going sightseeing solo no longer seems quite as attractive. I pick up my phone and bring up one of my favorite songs, telling myself I will stand here and take in the view, sipping my tea. When the song is over, I will move on.

But I give myself these few minutes to contemplate the mystery of Stalky Hottie. In times of stress, setting time limits and compartmentalizing is helpful for me. The strong beat comes on, and my heart thumps in time to the music.

I perform my box breathing, inhaling for a count of three, holding my breath for three, then back out for three, and repeat. Flashes of my surprise massage, followed by his disappearance, and then our night together in each other's arms drifts back to me.

Stalky Hottie seems so conflicted, here one minute and gone the next. He's always contrite on his reappearance. I sense he is fighting some internal demon. But aren't we all? I wish he would share his battle with me.

What does my dream mean? Despite questioning if he is some type of immortal fictional creature or serial killer, I am not afraid in his arms. So, what was the nightmare about? Fear of the relationship? Fear of what he may be capable of? We must sit down and talk while keeping our clothes on. I need answers.

I stare at the Vampira rose, sitting on my copy of *Dracula,* until my vision blurs. Blinking hard, I smile as I realize, I'm going to stay the course. I planned this trip to the last detail, and I am *not* going to miss seeing Loch Ness. First, I'll get through the business portion, and then I'll meet up with Wren to go to Transylvania.

For some reason, I am inexplicably drawn to the loch, even beyond the possibility of seeing Nessie. Call it a premonition, but I know something waits for me there just as much as I know I must go to Transylvania. I just have to survive the rest of this adventure.

I pick up the rose, take a deep inhale of its dark fragrance, and slip it back into my book. I head downstairs, gather my belongings, and stride toward the door with renewed purpose. Before I close the door, I glance over my shoulder at the bed where I had slept entwined with Hottie and smile.

Back at the front desk, I am informed that my "husband" has already picked up the tab this morning.

"My husband?" I ask incredulously.

The woman looks down, types a few keystrokes, then looks back up at me, like I've lost it, and says, "Yes, Mr. Tepes."

I frown and reply, "Okay, thank you."

I head out to the sardine can, wrestling my suitcase back into its spot on the passenger seat and shoving my backpack in the footwell.

"Tepes, of course," I repeat out loud to myself.

I pick up my phone and Google the name, shaking my head when I bring up a Wikipedia article on Vlad Tepes, also known as Vlad the Impaler, or Dracula. I knew that name was familiar. In the article is not only a ton of information on Dracula but several images, including one that matches the tattoo wrapped around his middle and the necklace Cait gave me.

I click on the hyperlink for the Order of the Dragon and several more images pop up. A thrum of excitement races through me, knowing my instincts are right. Some of my answers lie to the East. Now I just need to get there.

If he is leaving me breadcrumbs to put our truth together, I can't fathom how the tree tattoo on his back fits into the story of Vlad Tepes and Dracula.

But first, Loch Ness. I'm not missing this bucket list item, I owe it to myself.

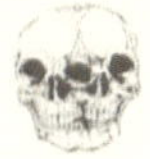

A FEW HOURS LATER, I park the sardine can and make my way toward Urquhart Castle and the loch. I'm thankful I had stopped for the night; I never would have been able to navigate this trip last night as exhausted as I had been.

I flex my hands, trying to get blood flow back to my fingertips after white knuckling the steering wheel for the entire drive. The parking lot is just about empty, whether it is from the time of day or the weather that has blown in.

Gray fog obscures what I'm sure is usually a stunning view. Undeterred, I grab my belt bag out of my backpack and double check the car is locked before making my way to the castle. I wander down the path, the cool mist sneaking its frigid fingers into me.

Cursing myself for not digging out my jacket, I continue on. Of course, this is the weather I get for my only chance to see Loch Ness. As I walk along the path, fear creeps in.

The fog cocoons me in eerie silence, alone, adrift in the endless gray, so I hurry my steps, hoping to run into other visitors.

The ancient stone castle suddenly looms in front of me, startling me with its imposing presence. I walk up to the wall and lean against it, catching my breath. The solidness behind me is comforting. I tip my head back against the stone and am hit with a sudden waking dream.

We are walking in a beautiful paradise. The sun is perfect, the air sweet, and all manner of creatures scurry about without fear. We come to a great tree, and Stalky Hottie plucks a piece of red fruit and hands it to me.

Despite the apprehension coiling in my belly, I bite into it. The fruit turns rotten in my mouth, and I gag, spitting it out.

I look back to him as the once vibrant landscape withers, animals decay into skeletal remains, and plants turn black with rot. But despite the death that surrounds us, he doesn't die—he morphs.

He rapidly ages before my eyes, skin turning to translucent paper that desperately clings to dusty bones. His beautiful inky black hair fades to brittle white wisps and his eyes sink into hollow sockets. As his bony skeletal hands reach for me, I scream, backing away from the grotesque shadow of the beautiful man he had been.

I come to with a strangled cry in my throat, drenched in sweat, with tears streaming down my face. I quickly look around from where I am slumped against the base of the castle, sitting on the damp ground, thankful no other tourists are here to witness me crumble.

Pushing the heels of my hands into my eyes, I breathe deep, hoping to center myself. I grab my red stone ring and spin it three times as my racing heart slows. A presence looming over me snaps my head up, only to find Stalky Hottie crouching down, his face creased with concern.

"I am here," he says simply and holds his arms open.

I launch into them, beyond thankful to find him looking like his normal beautiful self on the heels of such a disturbing waking dream. As he wraps me in his arms and pulls me into his lap, I let my tears fall. They're tears of frustration, of fear, of anger. Enough is enough. I'm tired of dreams and euphemisms, veiled hints, and tattooed clues.

With a charming snort of my runny nose, I look up into his eyes and say, "I thought you left me. One of us is always running away. Tell me. I deserve the truth. All of it."

He simply nods and helps me to my feet. He hands me a silk handkerchief, which I use to mop my face and blow my nose. Mortified at handing the sodden mess back to him, instead I shove it into my pocket.

He reaches out and tucks a curl behind my ear, sliding his hand down to cup my jaw. He leans in and presses a gentle kiss to my forehead.

"You are right. You deserve the truth," he says softly.

He puts my hand in the crook of his elbow and walks me through the castle. We wander through the ancient structure, and although I have no idea where we are going as we pass through curved arches and tumbling stone walls, he confidently leads us forward.

He moves as though he has been here countless times. Seeing him with the backdrop of an ancient, ruined castle makes him appear even darker and more forbidding, as if he himself belongs to the past.

I stare at the sharp outline of his features, questioning everything I know. Whatever truth he is about to tell me, I know I can't possibly be prepared for. The gravity of the day pulls at my soul. I know after today my life will never be the same. I am being pulled to my destiny, but wonder if I'll survive it.

We wander through the ruins and back outside, both lost in our own thoughts. He leads me down to the loch itself just as the sun breaks through the clouds and mist. I scan the loch, anxiously hoping, like so many others, that Nessie will suddenly reveal herself to me.

After several minutes, the glare cast by the now emerging sun makes my eyes water. I'm just about to turn away, accepting the fact that today is not the day Nessie makes herself known, when something ripples.

"Look," I shout, pointing. "There, there!"

I squeal as I jump up and down and pound on his solid arm next to me. When I finally turn my head to see if he is looking where I am pointing, to see if he sees what I see, instead I find his gaze riveted on me, amber eyes on fire.

Gone is the excitement of seeing the famous and elusive cryptid, replaced by a deep flutter in my chest. Never has someone looked at me like this. Like I am the rare creature being sought after. Like I am the mystery solved.

He looks at me with such desire and longing that I glow in the intensity of his gaze. I feel like the sun, the moon, the stars—like I belong to him.

Here on the bank of Loch Ness, I am falling for a man—or perhaps not a man at all—whom I know almost nothing about. And maybe, just maybe, I don't need to know him. What if we do have a love story—a before and a now? Will that be enough?

I think of the clues he has left, the trail of breadcrumbs, and venture, "Vlad?"

His eyes darken as he closes the distance between us and sweeps me into his arms, crushing me to him. Our mouths meet in a firestorm of need, of want, of desire. He bleeds his desperation, his obsession, and dare I say his love into the kiss.

I return my curiosity, my intrigue, and my open heart with mine. As our tongues dance and bodies collide, I brace myself for whatever is coming. I know this is the last kiss before a cosmic shift. I pour my all into it and hope it's enough.

Chapter 21

VLAD

This is the first kiss that has felt like a promise. I try to suppress the sliver of hope that snakes its way into my ancient heart. Hope is the most fearsome thing. I would rather face down an approaching horde of angry Ottoman invaders.

Tucking her hand into my arm, I steer us back to the parking lot. When we get to her car, she looks at me, looks at her car, then back at me and promptly dissolves into a giggling fit. I raise an eyebrow at her as she lets out a dignified snort.

"I'm sorry," she says, wiping the tears from her eyes. "But how on earth do you plan to fit in this sardine can?"

I hold my hand out for the keys, flashing her the half smile I know she loves.

"Oh, thank goodness. I am not cut out for driving here," she says as she slaps them into my hand, and I open her door.

I round the car, thankful she didn't think to ask how I got here. Folding myself into the driver's seat is indeed comical and has us both laughing. The easy way it is with her in this moment of simple joy is like coming home.

The short drive to the abbey is quiet. She is staring out the window at the passing countryside. I don't blame her. Ireland and Scotland have always been some of my favorite countries, and I have been almost everywhere on this planet at least once.

But I have come back to these two places often enough that I have my own homes and safe-houses here. The large gates swing open as we pull up to them. I follow the driveway around the imposing stone structure and drive around to my favorite part. The small apartment that reminds me so much of the gatehouse in Ireland is the reason I had purchased this vast estate.

I unfold myself from the car she jokingly calls "the sardine can" and open her door, offering a hand. Over a foot smaller than myself, she far more easily hops out, spinning to take in the view while I get her luggage out of the trunk.

"Is this some type of luxury AirBnB?" she asks.

"Something like that," I chuckle as I tug her by the hand toward the arched wooden door. I discreetly trigger the biometric lock and the door swings open.

She looks around in wonder at the dozens of Vampira roses I have used to fill the space. I walk to the bright and airy kitchen where champagne and the charcuterie she loves so much are spread out. I stand there, watching the emotions play across her face.

It had been a gamble to leave her in the early hours and set all this up for her. But as I see the wonder and joy on her face, I know my instincts were right. She needs to be loved for the amazing woman she is in this lifetime. And I am going to prove it to her.

She claps her hands delightedly, "This is beautiful!"

I pull the champagne from the ice bucket and pick up two glasses while she makes herself a plate. I can't help but be pleased with myself as she piles on her preferred crackers. I specifically stocked all of my homes with her favorites of everything, just in case.

I lead the way up the staircase that winds around the tower to the second-floor bedroom and out onto the balcony.

I set the glasses down on a small table and turn to watch her face again. It doesn't disappoint.

Her eyes widen, scanning the loch and surrounding mountains as I say, "I thought we could enjoy the sunset together."

I know of her fear of heights, so I placed the table and chairs close to the building, certain that is where she would feel the safest. I hold out my hand, thrilled at the sensation of her small one in mine.

She is beginning to trust me more. I flash her my full smile, the one that makes her bite her lip. I have planned so many little touches to acknowledge her beautiful individuality. Her favorite snacks, her fears, her dreams like Loch Ness.

I guide her to her seat, next to the door and with the solid wall of the abbey tower behind her. We are only on the second floor, not too high, and the stunning view has captured her full attention.

I tell her the highlights of the abbey's history as she eats. I know she loves my chosen voice, as do I. When everything is taken from you, when you are a victim of fate, making one's own choices where one can, is a gift indeed.

Of all the names I have been called, of all the personas I have taken over my painfully long existence, this is the one I have kept. The beauty and the horror of Vlad Tepes has been long misunderstood and frequently misinterpreted. But I know the truth. I was there, after all.

As she eats, I pop the champagne, drowning in her laugh as the cork sails over the balcony and the bubbly golden liquid overflows. Pouring two glasses, I hand one to her and hold my glass up to toast.

"To love eternal," I say, holding her amber and green gaze with my own.

"To truth," she says, lightly tapping my glass with hers.

I sit down to join her, sipping our bubbles as the sun sets and the first stars wink into existence. Although I have sworn countless times not to, I can't help but send up a prayer of thanks, even though I know it will land on deaf ears.

"Come," I say, as she shivers slightly in the cooling evening air, leading her into the bedroom to the pile of pillows at the foot of the bed facing the fireplace.

I light the already laid fire, blowing on it to bring it to life. The light and warmth quickly spread, casting the vaulted beamed ceiling into flickering shadows and highlighting the stained-glass windows circling the round tower walls.

I sit down in the pile of pillows and lean back against the footboard, pulling her into my lap. I wrap my arms around her, loving the way the firelight highlights her face where it rests against me.

It is time. I heave a sigh, chest tight under the weight of her eyes and expectations as I begin my story—our story.

"Our love story is the literal beginning. The beginning of the human race. You would call me Adam in your language, although that was not really my name, and I have gone by many, many names since that time. And you are who you would now call Eve. You were made from me."

She looks up at me through her lashes, her lower lip quivering. "Adam?"

I hate to witness the pain and confusion lining her face. I have broken her heart countless times and countless times have had mine broken in return.

I curse Luke, as I have millions of times before. And I curse myself for the long trail of sins I have left behind me, snaking through time like a black river of remorse that threatens to sweep me away in its angry current.

I will try my best to explain gently, to guide her in her

understanding. But as great as my love is for her, I simply don't know how much longer I can continue this cursed existence without her. I must succeed this time.

I have failed in my attempts to end my time in this long-suffering world. I do not know what lies beyond this life for me, Heaven or Hell, but I truly do not know how I can continue to suffer on this earthly plane.

Unlike every other time, though, surely this one will be different because *she* is different. Perchance, I am, too. I hope it will be enough to get us through.

With the pressure of hundreds of failures behind me, and only one chance left before me, I take a deep breath and memorize the way the firelight plays over her face. The way her body rests in the safety of my arms. The scent of her that drifts to me just like the roses I grow in remembrance of her. I lose myself in all that she is and use it to launch into all that could be.

"Something like that, but yes, we will say that is my first name and the one you first called me. We have had many since. I was the first human on this earth, and it was my job to name everything. The creator would come to the garden and walk with me. He loved the names I gave to them all, and it was good. I was happy."

I take a deep breath, trying to gauge her reaction. Her beautiful eyes remain locked on mine, jaw clenched. I cannot read her expression, but continue on before I lose my nerve.

"But the creator's time-space continuum and mine were different, so I was often alone. He knew my loneliness, so he cast a deep sleep upon me and split me in half. He created you from that part and made me whole again. You are bone of my bone and flesh of my flesh. So, when we come together as man and woman, we are made one again."

I take a slow, steady breath and continue. "We were so in

love. It was beautiful, sweet and innocent. I was so happy to have you by my side in paradise. We had a simple life of peace and joy in each other and the wonderful garden around us. We were like naïve children. But it did not last."

Lieshe puts up a hand and says, "But I thought Eve was made from Adam's rib? And why is the woman always at fault in this story?"

I take her raised hand and kiss away her righteous indignation. This incarnation of her reminds me of the original the most—feisty, intelligent, complementing me perfectly. Every lifetime with her is different, shaped by the current world she lives in and her life experiences. I have loved them all. But this one may just be my favorite.

"Rib is not the right translation. The written word accurately quotes me as saying you are bone of my bone and flesh of my flesh. But remember man's influence. Many came who interpreted, rewrote, and even removed parts of the original story. Here is the truth of what happened in the garden and what followed. How I came to be what I am and the curse I brought upon us.

"On the day of our downfall, we were walking hand in hand, just happy to be together. We were naked, knowing no shame—just love and happiness. The animals never harmed us. We ate from the garden, only plants.

"We loved to sit and watch the sunset, much like tonight. We would count the stars as they dotted the sky. That day I watched the golden hour of the most perfect sunset reflected in your amber eyes, highlighting the curve of your curls.

"I witnessed the dying light cast us into shadows, and I remember thinking how you had never looked more beautiful than you did at that moment. I stood up and pulled you to me by your hand, eagerly awaiting our joining under the great moon, smiling down at us.

"But as we turned to head further into the garden, we saw at the base of the large tree, full of the darkest red forbidden fruit, there was a new creature. It looked like a lizard with no legs, but so exceptionally big, its head was the size of mine.

"You were delighted and said, 'Look! What will we call it?'

"I looked at it and experienced something strange and new. I had no name for this emotion, just like I had no name for this creature. The thrill that normally came with the task was missing. As I looked into its enormous yellow-green eyes, the feeling became stronger. Now I know now that it was fear.

"Before that moment, we had never been afraid. In the manner of all the garden's creatures, this one also spoke to us, and we understood. It asked if I loved you, as if loving you was a choice. But it never was. I have always loved you.

"Of course, I replied, 'Yes. She is made from me; together, we are complete. She is from my very flesh and bone—for me, from me.'

"The creature hissed, 'So, if the two of you together can make one person, then clearly you are more than your creator. If you complete each other, you have no need for another's love. You have each other, and that is all you should ever need. The creator is hiding things from you. Hiding the truth this fruit can bring.'

"We exchanged a confused glance, having never experienced feelings for our creator outside of love. This is a new line of thinking in our simple lives—to question him, his motives, and even his love for us. We were naïve. All we had known was pure and simple happiness, love, and truth. The concept of subterfuge or lies had never crossed our minds.

"The creature continued, 'If you love her as you say, give her one of these fruits and her knowledge will grow. Eat of it with her, and you will both know as much as the selfish creator. He is jealous of your love for each other. Besides, if he truly loves you, as you do each other, he will forgive you as you would forgive each other. Eat of this fruit, both of you, and know these truths.'

"The newcomer steadily stared at us as we processed his words. Of everything in the garden, this was the only thing forbidden to us, but I was confident in the creator's love and forgiveness. I would prove it. If this fruit were not for us, why would it be there?

"This new line of questioning made me feel small and dark. I thought perhaps it was a test of my feelings for you. I had no foresight, no thoughts of our lives ever changing, as this was all we knew.

"I reached out and plucked the darkest red fruit and handed it to you. You looked at me with so much trust in your eyes. I nodded as you took a bite and gave it back to me. I, too, ate it, eager to learn the truths we thought were being hidden from us.

"What started as sweet and delicious turned to bitter sulfur in my mouth. As I choked out the mouthful, wiping at my streaming eyes, I saw you doing the same and another unknown emotion swept over me.

"Dread. Soul deep, crushing dread.

"The creature gave a great hissing laugh and said, 'Here is your new knowledge. Now you will know my truth. He did not love me unconditionally either, and now he will know what I felt when he cast me from his side. You are nothing but a pawn.'

"As he slithered away, our eyes met, and we knew we had done something terrible. We were ashamed of doubting the creator's love for us, mortified to have been tricked. We were not embarrassed of our physical bodies being naked as is often said, but of our minds having been laid bare.

"Before we could even process what had happened or the torrent of new emotions consuming us, we heard the creator enter the garden. We hid, holding on to each other, dreading what was to come. We did not try to clothe our naked bodies, we tried to conceal our feelings and mistakes with words. But he knew what we had done, and he cast us out. The original sin.

"*My* original sin.

"The serpent was right—the creator did not love us unconditionally. He did not forgive us, but he did forget us.

"Jophiel came with her flaming sword to force us from the garden, and we were terrified. Scared and alone, we wandered the desert, looking for a safe space. We came to a river and huddled together on its edge. We had lost our home, but we still had each other. The creature appeared again.

"'Now you know the truth,' he hissed, as he slithered about our ankles. 'It is just as I said. He did not love you unconditionally. You will see the world is a big and dangerous place. Outside of the garden, you will surely die.'

"As he wriggled away, I grabbed your face and put my forehead to yours. We stared into each other's eyes, your amber an exact match to mine.

"I vowed, 'I will protect you, my love. I am so sorry that I failed you, failed us. I cost us our home, our safety. *Everything.*'

"You put your hands over mine and smiled at me, saying, 'I still believe in you, believe in *us*. Our love is stronger than anything we could ever face. As long as we have each other, we still have our home. *You* are my *everything*. Only you.'

"'All of me, always,' I breathed across your lips.

"Eventually, we found our way in the dangerous outside world. We had children and as time marched on and we remained unscathed, the fear of the serpent's promise of death grew dim.

"As time passed, you gained the white streak you bear now in your hair, and I loved you more with every passing day. You were a wonderful partner and an amazing mother. We found happiness outside of the garden and lived our lives well. We watched the world grow and change together.

"Until, one day, we were walking hand in hand, the creature again came upon us. Now I knew he was called a snake, or serpent, and man feared and hated him. His great yellow eyes lit up when he saw us. He leapt out and struck your ankle.

"As you fell to the ground, I cried out, 'Eve!'

"I followed you down, cradling you against my chest. I raised my face to the heavens, and with all the anguish in my soul, I screamed for you, 'Eve!'

"As your breathing grew shallow and your body fell limp, your face was covered in my tears. I roared, 'I cannot live without you, my love. Bone of my bone and flesh of my flesh. You are my very soul.'

"I felt like I was dying along with you. I called out to the one who had forgotten us, 'Help us! Please, help us!'

"But no help came. I clutched you in my arms until I thought you would break. I tried to force you to live through sheer will alone. But I did not protect you as I had vowed. I had failed you yet again. And it would not be the last time. My eyes were so clouded by tears, I could hardly see your face as you took your last breath.

"As you turned cool in my arms, I screamed at that damned serpent, 'What have you done?'

"I gathered you to me, unmoving, unbreathing, lifeless. I was a broken man. Shattered. I traced the delicate curve of your cheek, tucked a curl behind your ear. I could not contemplate my existence without you. My love, my soul. You were my everything. My whole life was for you. I was lost.

"The evil one watched my agony, heard my screams and howls of anguish. When I had no more tears left to cry, when my voice was lost to my shredded throat, he approached me, nodding his head with those damn unblinking eyes.

"'Would you like her back?' he asked.

"Now I really had lost everything. I had lost my creator, the garden, and now you. I was a desperate man with nothing left to lose.

"'Yes,' I cried. 'I will do anything to bring her back.'

"'Anything? Are you sure?' he asked, coiling loops and loops of his great body around us both. I dropped my forehead to yours, ready to lay down my life. Willing to pay the ultimate price if only you could live.

"I looked him in his eyes and said, 'Yes, whatever you want is yours.'

"He put his head near your ankle and gashed the bite open with his teeth. The blood trickled out, the two drops that fell to the ground turning to stone. The same stones you and I wear now.

"'Suck the poison out with the bad blood and you will be together again. As she is of your flesh and bone, you will be of her blood,' the snake said.

"Foolishly, I did as the creature said for a second time. I was willing to sacrifice anything for you, my love. I had no idea just how much I would be sacrificing for both of us. The cost I bear to be of your blood is the very essence that sustains me, the price of my immortality to seek you again and again."

I blink rapidly as visions of the past disappear, and the present comes back into focus. Coward that I am, I can't look at her face just yet, so I stare into the fire as I continue.

"And so, I lived. And I could not die. Trust me, I tried. And you were reborn time and time again. And I suffered every time. And no matter what I have done, I have continued to lose you. Only to find you and fall in love endlessly. Truly, I am being punished for all eternity."

Having done this many times before, I never knew what response to expect. Lieshe stares at me in silence, eyes wide and brimming with tears. I go on to say, "There were lifetimes I didn't tell you our story and just attempted to win you over. There were others I found you, and you were already living a happy life, so I watched from the sidelines, unable to rip away that happiness, even though it gutted me.

"Other times, I could sense you, and I would chase that elusive feeling around the world and not find you. You have had a multitude of lifetimes while I roamed this earth. And I will admit, some years were so bad, I slept; as close to death as a creature like me could get. And then, there were the other times, the dark ones, that spawned the legends surrounding this identity.

"But no matter how I prayed to die, to end our pain and suffering, here I am. And each time, I pray to the one that does not hear me, that no matter what happens in each lifetime, your soul would at least be set free, even if mine cannot.

"This time, I thought of trying to stay away from you, but I am weak. I couldn't bear to have found you again, only to not even give this lifetime a chance. I continue to be weak, failing to protect you. First from the serpent himself, and this time, I have failed to protect you from myself and the pain that I am causing you."

I bow my head and await my fate, her hands warm in my cool grasp, my black heart thundering in my ears.

Hope is a fragile thing, a small ember in a dark night. I wait anxiously to see if it will ignite into a blaze or if it will sputter and die, leaving me in the cold darkness once more.

Chapter 22

At last, he runs out of steam and is quiet, his head bowed as if in defeat. It is a fantastic story. I appreciate the storyline and the carefully woven narrative. The emotion bled off of him in waves. His delivery pulled me back in time with him, experiencing the loss, the betrayal, the heartache as he did.

But it was so incredible, I just can't comprehend this tale as truth even though he so clearly does. My heart breaks for him as he relives his pain and loss. I could see it vividly flashing in his eyes, tears welling up at times, his voice quavering. Whether this is fact or fiction, it is his reality.

It makes me want to open my heart to this beautiful man who would sacrifice himself for the woman he has loved for all eternity. The woman he believes me to be.

If he turned this story into a novel, I would surely read it again and again. The heartbreak, loss, and hope top any of my late-night reads.

But.

It is just so outlandish. It challenges my worldview to include reincarnation and immortality and a complete retelling of the biblical origins of man. Although honestly, that piece is pretty believable. This would be proof positive that a god, and therefore a devil, did indeed exist.

How could I possibly wrap my head around that? And if I followed the last part correctly, on top of everything else, could I believe that not only he is a vampire, but this is the origin of vampires?

When I had run from him in Ireland, I thought I had believed he could be one. But laid out like this, it all sounds so surreal that I don't know if I can accept a single part, much less the entirety of it. Whether any of it is true, I still want to know how this story—our story—ends.

With watery eyes, I look at him and ask, "Does it ever end well?"

"Never," he whispers sadly.

"How many times have you lost her?" I ask.

He unbuttons his shirt and slowly pulls it off, twisting his arms to catch the light.

"Not her. *You.* I've lost you three hundred and thirty-two times," he replies.

I reach out and trace the black ink winding down one arm, flickering in and out of the firelight. Three hundred and thirty-two times. I've lived three hundred and thirty-two lifetimes? Panic begins to bubble in my chest, ratcheting up my heart rate and bringing my breaths up short.

That number just keeps echoing through my head. Out of habit, I reach down to spin a ring, casting for my grounding techniques. I grab the teardrop stone and view it with new eyes. The firelight gleams, making it glow scarlet in the flickering light.

This is supposed to be my blood from my original lifetime. How could it possibly survive all of those years? How could I have had so many lifetimes?

A thousand questions without answers swirl through my mind. Each more far-fetched than the last. I can't imagine Vlad living this way for thousands of years. What unimaginable heartache and joy he must have experienced. I wondered if the happiness sustained him between the devastation. Is this our destiny? Are we fated to be spinning magnets for all of eternity?

I couldn't fathom the horror of remembering not just the good times, but the heartache, the agony, the crippling loss again and again. Is this truly our punishment? After all, forever is a long, long time.

"I need a minute," I say as I scramble up off his lap and stand.

Seeking space, I race down the stairs and find myself in the small kitchen. I turn the water on full blast and splash my face, my shirt getting soaked in the process. I grab a linen towel and hold it against my face, where a sob breaks free.

I am nearing panic mode, trying to wrap my head around everything McHottie or Vlad or Adam has said. Hell, I don't even know what to call him.

Who is he?

I try to think through things logically, but my brain is rapid-firing questions, like how did he survive the Flood? Was he Noah? Did he know Jesus? Has he met famous people?

More importantly, does he love me for being me as Lieshe, or is he just following old habits and loving whoever he believes is Eve reincarnated because he thinks he is supposed to love her?

I shake my head. If I ask these questions, I am giving in to this entire line of delusional thinking. And as much as my soul is called to his, I realize I just can't.

I deserve my own love story, to be loved for myself and not as part of the ramblings of an insanely hot but mentally unbalanced man.

A horrifying thought dawns on me. The killer from Baltimore. What if he really is so unhinged and believes this story so deeply, that he is the killer, acting out this timeline in some type of fugue state? Can I help him? And am I safe?

He walks into the kitchen and says, "Lieshe?"

I turn to face him, seeing the tentative hope on his face as he looks at me.

He rubs the back of his neck, looking down at the floor, saying, "I know it is a lot to take in."

"Mc—I mean, Vlad, or is it Adam? Fuck it, for now you are McVladam," I say, unsure what to even call him now that I have kind of learned who he is or might be. "That is the understatement of the century. I am trying to keep an open mind and heart, but I just have so many questions. I need some time. I still don't even know what name to use. I'm sorry, but I just don't think I can do this."

His face falls, making him appear as ancient and immortal as he claims. As if he is nothing but a marble statue watching the world pass him by as he stands, cold and frozen in time.

He turns and walks out of the beautiful tower straight into the night. He doesn't stop for a coat or even his shoes. His silhouette fades away into the dark until he disappears.

I'm exhausted. I am very, very far from home. And I don't know what to do. I head back up to the bedroom and collapse back down into the pile of pillows to stare at the fire. Despite its cheery warmth, I'm shivering.

Staring off into the flames, I let memories of the last few weeks play through my mind like an old carousel slideshow. Flashes of feelings, kisses, touches, anger, loss, and confusion dance through my heart.

I just can't get my head wrapped around it. I've always had some level of faith in a higher power, even if I didn't attend church as an adult. I considered myself to be spiritual, even if I had always been on the macabre side and rooted for the villains.

I find myself doing something I haven't done in forever. I pray to whatever divine presence there may be.

Like a child, I fold my hands, clear my throat, and begin out loud, "Uh, hi. It's me, Lieshe. Sorry, this is awkward. So, I think you probably heard all that. And while I, uh, have you on the line here, I'm going to throw in an apology for any of the super offensive stuff I've done, and especially read, but I think I'm overall an okay person. I donate and try to be nice.

"Um, we're getting off track here. Look, I'm going to level with you. I'm having a really tough time accepting this story. It's pretty wild, but this guy is suffering. And no matter what the truth is, I hope that you can find it in your heart to help him out. Because he believes in you.

"And if somehow, someway, any of this is marginally true, can you help me, too? Oh, and please don't let him be a serial killer and kill me tonight. Good talk. Thanks."

I don't know what else to do. I have no idea where McVladam went or even if he is coming back. In my heart, I don't *think* I am in danger. I have no women's Spidey-sense kicking in. Despite the bizarre conversation and my disbelief, I am more worried about his safety than my own.

It is now fully dark, and I'm not sure if there are wild, I don't know, coyotes or something, in Scotland. I must have some level of care for him if I'm concerned. It might be stupid of me, but if he trusted me enough to share his delusions, that perhaps I'm reasonably safe and can somehow help him.

I hope I won't regret this and end up dead because it probably isn't the safest choice, but I decide I must go look for him. Perhaps I can convince him to get some help. He has some type of resources with the first-class flight tickets and town car that had picked us up from the airport. Surely we can find somewhere to give him the help he needs.

I head back downstairs and out the door, wrapping my arms around myself as the damp evening air surrounds me. I take a few steps, surveying the landscape and trying to determine what direction he would have been most likely to head in.

It's exceedingly dark as I walk out into the countryside. Looking back over my shoulder, the tower apartment behind me looks warm and inviting, with its beautiful windows emitting a cheery yellow glow in contrast to the fading light.

I should head back in and figure out my next steps are to get back to my purpose here, but instead, my feet carry me out into the night. I head toward the water in the distance, rippling silver in the moonlight.

Without the light pollution of cities and towns, the sky here is enormous and the first stars are peaking out. I stare up at them, thinking this night would be incredibly romantic with someone to share it with. I wished again that our love story had gone in a different direction, but maybe there is still hope.

Perhaps I can get him the help he needs, and we could make our own future grounded in reality rather than the one that exists in his mind. We have some type of connection, at least in this life. The thought gives me tentative hope and my steps quicken, needing to find him.

The field slopes gently down and I again fear what predators could be on the prowl. I hadn't read anything in the tour books when I had been making some of my plans, but I don't think most tourists are wandering around estates by themselves at night to prompt the inclusion of warnings.

I vaguely wonder if it is true that there are no snakes in Scotland, but then realize, no, that's Ireland. After his story, though, I don't think I will ever view snakes the same way again.

I make my way down the gently sloping ground, straining my ears for any sounds of danger or a hint of where he could have gone. I reach the water's edge and scan for any sign of Nessie in the reflection of the night sky. I bend and dip my fingers in the freezing water.

Shaking off a chill, a now remarkably familiar and oddly reassuring prickling sensation on the back of my neck tells me he is somewhere nearby. Watching me.

I follow the feeling, turning away from the water toward a large shadowy structure in the distance, a gentle wind at my back and the moon on my face. Walking toward it, I come upon what appears to be ruins. At one point, it must have been beautiful, but time and whatever calamity had befallen it wrecked most of the front of the castle-like structure.

The stones are weathered and tumbled, with nature reclaiming the site with plants and vines. The only sound breaking the stillness of the night is the lapping of the loch. I move further into the ruins, without fear, only curiosity with a faint sense of déjà vu.

The interior walls are still standing to form a large courtyard. I pass under a stone archway and enter it, shocked to find an enormous Yew tree in the middle, with a twisted trunk reaching its branches up into the night sky. It is glorious, and I am thankful it has survived whatever had ruined this once magnificent building.

I approach the tree and place my hand on the trunk, moving around its massive circumference and trailing my fingers over the rough, twisted bark, coiled like a piece of taffy. Through the branches, stars twinkle down between the leaves as I sense the ancient tree and this place wrapping me in a comforting embrace.

I realize just how small and young I am in this great big world. It must be the magic of Scotland, I muse, but the veil between fact and fiction feels thin, like at any moment a fairy could appear in front of me, and I wouldn't be the least bit surprised.

What would it be like to watch time march on indefinitely? Is there a special wisdom that comes with the eons or a madness? As I trail my fingers over the twisted bark, I wonder what this tree has witnessed as a sentinel of this place. How many lives have come and gone around it?

Had another woman circled it, touching the rough surface like I had? Was her heart broken, too? Or had a pair of lovers met secretly below, sneaking stolen kisses in the dark?

A presence draws my eyes toward one of the stone archways making up the courtyard and I see the outline of a large man. I know it is him. He has embedded himself deep into my marrow and I can sense him there, as familiar as my own heartbeat.

He steps out from the shadows, the moonlight reflecting blue in his midnight black hair and setting his amber eyes aglow. I freeze like prey in his stare, my breath quickening.

He stalks toward me like a wolf, and I realize I was foolish to have been worried about his safety, when the only predator I need to worry about is him. He walks resolutely forward, right into my space, so close the power radiates off of him in waves.

I tip my head back in order to meet his eyes.

He is so incredibly beautiful in the moonlight, surrounded by the ancient stone. Like he is carved from the very ruins themselves, a marbled fallen angel. The soft glow casts his face into sharp relief. His amber gaze appears otherworldly and, in this moment, steeped in history and moonbeams, I want to believe.

I desperately want to accept this man before me has loved me so deeply that he has chased me across time itself. I want to know that I am so worthy, so beautiful, so loved, that neither time, nor distance, or evil, could ever separate us. That he would find me, in this lifetime and in the next.

Eternal echoes of a never ending, never dying, all-consuming love.

He crosses the courtyard to stand with me under the ancient tree, breathing in each other. He buries his hand in my hair at the nape of my neck, tipping my head up and bringing his mouth down to hover above mine. His breath is warm on my face, a startling contrast to the night air.

We stare into each other's souls, truth reflected back at me. Truth and a love that is blinding in its intensity. Under the starry sky, I fall into the spell of magic and mystery and moonbeams. I fell in love with a man that makes no sense— a man who believes he is not a man at all.

This is insanity. I keep running from him, from my fears of who and what he could be. My reaction to him is the strongest evidence that what he has told me could be true. Although my mind rebels, wanting to revert back to logic, my body has no such qualms.

My very soul pushes against my skin, trying to reach to his, yearning to make us one again, as he had claimed we were. My arms twine around his neck, hands fisting the back of his shirt, desperate for something to anchor me in the storm that is this mystery man.

We kiss like lost lovers found again. I can taste his desperation turning to obsession. Somewhere, my mind tells me I should be scared, but my heart remembers this place where we exist.

This isn't the kiss of two strangers, learning each other's bodies, feeling their way forward. This is the kiss of lifetimes together, a deep and rich history, of knowing someone else so intimately muscle memory remembers its way backward, recalling each dip and contour, every surface of the other person's body. Each taste and breath feel like ancient history, familiar, welcoming me further into his embrace.

"Adam," I exhale, daring to believe.

I'm risking my heart, hell, maybe even my own sanity, to think this may be real. This could be my love story.

"Ah-dahm," he corrects my pronunciation.

"Ah-dahm," I reply, changing the emphasis the way he did to the second syllable.

"I have waited so long for my first name to fall from your lips again," he says, sinking to his knees before me.

He puts his hands on my hips and gazes up at me from his spot on the ground. His face is lined with anguish, and for a moment, he appears ancient—every bit the thousands of years he claims to be reflected in the slump of his shoulders and fine lines around his eyes.

"Please. Let me prove my love to you. No past, no future. Just you and me. Right here, right now," he pleads.

I want to refuse him. I really do. I should make him sit down, explain again, and show me irrefutable proof. I know it is the logical thing to do, the safe and practical thing. But this beautiful man at my feet is breaking, and I have been drawn to him since I first saw him.

I find myself nodding as I look down into his face, unable to say no, wanting to put his shattered pieces back together along with my own. For the first time in my life, I don't feel broken, splintered, fragile. He makes me whole.

I lean down and kiss his forehead, his skin cool beneath my lips. We stand and make our way out of the abbey, past moss-covered stones and falling arches. The midnight beauty has me wanting to come back again and explore in the daylight.

"Adam," I say, rolling yet another name around my mouth as we walk hand in hand. "I still don't know what to say."

"Then, for tonight, just feel," he says as he brings my hand up and kisses my knuckles.

We walk the rest of the way to the tower in silence, but my heart is thrumming in my ears. I have no idea what I'm doing, but excitement pools low in my belly. I glance up at him from the corner of my eye and he has the smallest smile, a hesitant little thing.

My lips turn up in response. I don't know what tomorrow will bring, but tonight I am going to do what he said, and just feel.

The warm yellow glow pouring from the windows beckons us home. We reach the door, and I'm suddenly shy. I have so many questions, but right now, I want to get lost in possibilities, lost in his touch, lost in him.

Just one night, I tell myself, and tomorrow I will deal with everything else. I will be practical and logical and make decisions with my brain instead of my heart.

Adam opens the door and pulls me by the hand behind him. As soon as we cross the threshold, he is on me, pushing my back against the door. He cages me in with his hands on either side of my head and, as always, I am overwhelmed by his size and presence.

His amber eyes blaze with intensity, locked onto mine. I'm melting, my entire being consumed by a fiery desire. I can't remember ever wanting something so desperately or being so incredibly right.

He lowers his lips just above mine, making everything else fade away.

I smell tobacco and leather mixed with the Vampira roses in the room, overlying a faint peat undertone from the fireplace. It smells like coming home. The moment is too intense, the feelings too much, so I close my eyes, just breathing him in as he breathes in my exhales.

It is as if we are sharing more than just this moment in time. Our very souls are reaching toward each other like a flower stretching its face to the sun. I am spellbound and, in this second, I can almost believe our love story truly is the longest ever told.

Every word he has said resounds in this moment as absolute truth. My belief in Adam, in us, in infinite possibilities and happily ever after rises within me.

"Open your eyes and look at me, Eve. Tell me that you love me," Adam whispers urgently against my lips.

And just like that, the spell is broken. It's as if a bucket of ice water has been dumped over my head, bringing perfect logical clarity. My eyes snap open, and I push him back with my hands against his chest, startling us both.

He looks at me, confused, hurt bleeding into his amber gaze.

"I deserve my own love story. I deserve to be loved for me, not for a memory of who you think I am. You say I am Eve, but to me, I'm Lieshe—the same girl I have been for the past thirty years. You taught me to see myself, and I do see me. And I know that I deserve more than this. You claim to love me, but you hardly know me. And I am definitely not ready to tell you that I love you," I sadly tell him.

Why couldn't he have just let this relationship develop naturally? Why did he have to push for me to not only love him, but immediately declare it?

Yes, I want to be in love. But I deserve to enjoy the journey, to walk every step along the path, not just be thrust into the destination. He visibly deflates as I talk, his immense size and presence dimming like a guttering candle.

My heart is breaking for him, for this strange and sad tale, for the ending of something beautiful that was only just beginning. But I know this is the right decision—the logical decision. It's too bad my heart doesn't seem to agree.

Adam falls to his knees, staring at the ground. My hand hovers over his head, wanting to reach out to him in his agony.

I say, "I'm sorry. I am so very sorry, Adam. I hope you find your Eve, but I'm not her."

Frozen in despair, he doesn't even acknowledge that I am speaking.

"I should go," I murmur.

He replies so low I can barely hear him. His voice is awash with soul crushing despair. "I'll go. Stay. You can leave whenever you wish."

Without even raising his head to look at me, he staggers to his feet like he has suffered a mortal wound and walks out the door. This time, I let him.

Exhausted, I trudge up the stairs and back to the pile of pillows at the end of the bed. Reaching up, I drag part of the covers down over me and toe off my shoes. I curl around my aching heart and stare at the fire, like the mysteries of the world will be explained in its embers.

I watch the flickering colors as the wood is consumed by the flames and turns to ash, falling to the hearth below. My heart feels the same, consumed by Adam and disintegrating into nothingness.

Chapter 23

I wake to early morning sunlight streaming through the windows. Dust motes dance in the air and I envy them their freedom; gravity has no hold on them while all of us poor schleps are bound to the earth and all its chains.

My heart seems especially subject to Newton's law, as if it's fallen to my toes, leaving a gaping black hole in my chest. I heave a sigh and stretch, trying to work out the kink in my neck from sleeping awkwardly on the floor. I know I need to get moving, but I allow myself just one more minute to wallow in self-pity.

On the fireplace mantle is a bouquet of the dying Vampira roses. A yawn has me filling my lungs with the cloying scent of flowers past their prime, peat fire, and at the last second, I pick up an underlying note of leather and tobacco. I hastily exhale as I scramble to stand, needing to get away from this place and the memories it holds.

I go downstairs and look around the silent space. I walk to the small kitchen, thankful to find bottled water in the fridge. I grab two and head out to the sardine can, anxious to move on. As I climb into the driver's seat, the familiar prickle skirts my neck, but I don't let myself turn back to search for him.

If I saw him, I don't know that I could trust myself not to run back into his arms. So, I face forward and as I drive away, the prickle fades as the distance grows.

Part of me wishes I had just accepted his invitation to have just one night together. And part of me knows today would have been infinitely harder if I had fully opened up to him. I would have fallen wholeheartedly in love with him. Hell, I think I already have, back under that tree, no matter how things ended.

The growing miles between us gives me clarity, as if I need to be far away from him to think logically. I know that a relationship started on a delusion, even if it is a shared one, has no chance of being healthy.

For the millionth time, I wonder if he is as disturbed as he is hot, and I worry about his safety. But if I stretch my mind back to nursing school and psychology, he did not display any other symptoms of mental illness that fit in with being delusional. Did he?

Or have I been so distracted by his looks and my physical reaction to him that I hadn't paid attention to anything other than my hedonistic desires? Guilt ghosts over my conscience. As outlandish as Adam's claims were, there seemed to be a thread of truth that woven through his story.

The solemnity of his soul seems ageless, and his love seems true. The smallest glance or touch from him sets my heart on fire. With feelings this deep, how can there not be some kernel of truth in his story?

But I just can't get my head wrapped around it. I can't understand what it would be like to believe in him, to acknowledge proof positive that there is indeed a god, a devil, and a vampire. It's like the start of a bad joke—a god, a devil, and a vampire walk into a bar...

Shaking my head at my dark sense of humor as I drive into the bright Scottish morning, such a contrast to the war within my heart, I wonder just what the hell I am doing.

Because if we truly are the original soul mates, why are we always running away from each other?

Chapter 24

VLAD

Soul-crushing sorrow drives me into despair and out into the night. All hope is lost. I am a failure and a fool. Without her, I am nothing.

I climb, desperate and relentless, the ancient stones offering only the smallest handholds. My skin shreds on the rough surface, leaving a bloody trail up the side of the abbey. My muscles strain and flex at the exertion of pulling my body up the vertical walls. I could simply transform, but I want the punishment. Crave the pain.

Consume myself with it.

My hand, slippery with blood, fails to grasp the small edge of the next stone and I dangle, weightless. My heart tells my mind to just let go, let myself fall to the ground below. Shatter my body into oblivion, like my heart.

But it would be nothing more than a brief reprieve and even the pain of a hundred broken bones knitting back together cannot compare to the tsunami of grief swallowing me whole. The impact of the earth rushing to meet me is inconsequential when measured against losing her to *him*.

I allow myself to dangle, the tendons and ligaments in my shoulder nearly snapping. I breathe deep, inhaling the burning pain and pushing it down. My biceps and triceps shred under the strain and immediately knit back together. A reminder of my cursed existence. My inability to control my destiny, even through taking my own life, has been denied to me.

Red hot rage fills me, propelling me upwards. Every movement fuels my desire for revenge. Hate builds, eclipsing my vision and purpose. If I can't have her, neither can he. Our deal be damned. I may not be able to kill him, but I will make him suffer as I have suffered. Or hopefully, I'll die trying.

I reach the topmost part of the old stone structure and collapse onto the peaked roof. Watching the stars pass by overhead and the sun rise, I resent that the universe continues to unfold while my heart has been shattered yet again.

Despite the space between us, I can hear hers beating, scent her natural rose perfume. Even though I can't hold her to me, just knowing that she is near me for one more night keeps me here until dawn.

Her heartbeat echoes in my soul, every pulsation fueling me toward revenge—toward war. I know I will probably fail. But failure means nothing when there is nothing left to lose. I have lost it all. I am now just a ghost, a soulless wraith, and I shall have my revenge.

I shouldn't have pushed her to confess her love, even though it was the only way to win this damn bargain. Perhaps this will be enough for the one above to finally have mercy on me, or the one below to claim my soul and release me from my endless curse.

The rising sun first washes away the gray, then paints the earth with its golden glow, bringing life to the world and all upon it. As the morning light touches my face, I don't appreciate the warmth, the beauty of a new morning. I am hollow. Empty. A never-ending void.

Without her, there is no light. Only my darkness. Now, I shall let it claim me. Sharpen me into an instrument of death and destruction. For far too long, I have clung to the hope of someday having her back.

My mind drifts back to the days when I became Vlad Tepes. The time I lost myself. I let the memories of the rage of finding that devil with my love fill me once again, feeling the fury that spawned the deaths of thousands, starting with hers.

I swore I would never descend into that madness again, fully becoming Vlad the Impaler once more. But here we are. So, watch out Luke *fucking* Devlin. I am coming for you.

Chapter 25

My thoughts swirl as I drive down the highway to Blackpool, heading for my next stop, Obscura Maximus. Despite leaving McVladam behind—I still can't bring myself to call him just Adam—I feel as though I'm racing toward my destiny.

With my heart such a mess, I do what I do best—throw myself headlong into my business. Grimm is safety, comfort in routine, and confidence in the store and brand I've worked tirelessly to create.

I desperately need some normalcy right now, something to anchor me in the world I know and love, instead of all this mystery, intrigue, and uncertainty. I crave dusty taxidermy, the crinkle of aging paper, and the thrill of discovering the next unappreciated treasure. I have no soul juice left for theology, reincarnation, or divinity.

My plan is to check out the shop and then head to London the following day, where I will meet Wren to finally see the taxidermied raven that inspired this trip. Then, final stop, Transylvania.

I'm now confident enough in my driving to listen to music. So, I pop on a Beatles playlist in honor of heading to England. I sing along to the songs I know and mumble to the ones I don't quite know all the words to just to distract my brain. I can't think anymore.

Within a few hours, my GPS directs me to pull into the driveway of a small row home just outside of Blackpool. I park the tiny car and double check the address before wrangling my suitcase out. I am so excited to be with my friends, and unlike Declan, I had met them in the states at an expo a couple years ago.

Before I can even knock on the door, it is swinging open, and two women are jockeying to get through at the same time. I laugh in delight at the antics of the identical twins, Mina and Lucy. They are hysterical, and although I would never tell them so, remind me of Tweedle Dee and Tweedle Dum, with how they finish each other's sentences and frequently argue.

Even now, they are bickering over who will get through the door first. It is almost impossible to tell them apart. They look the same to me, and even their mannerisms are similar.

At some point, they had gotten so tired of getting mixed up that they got coordinating tattoos on their wrists of ornate curlicue oval frames with script letters in them, one an M and the other an L.

They burst through, popping out like a jack-in-the-box, and sweep me up in a group hug.

"Eek, hi!" I say, my voice muffled by their arms wrapped around me.

They pull back laughing, and say in unison, "Welcome t' Blackpool, luv."

I follow them into their tiny row house, looking around in delight. Every available wall surface is covered—they bring maximalism to a new level. They collect everything twin themed and boast a fantastic collection of old photographs and portraits.

Seeing them in the matching Grimm shirts I had sent from the shop makes me smile. The conjoined twin skeleton logo perfectly fits their style.

Lucy shows me to their guest room and I deposit my bag.

She leaves me to get settled, and I sit down on the narrow bed, staring at my hands on my knees.

Although I am so excited to see Mina and Lucy again, my heart has been broken; the pieces scattered starting from somewhere in the middle of the Atlantic Ocean, through Ireland, and the last shards left in Scotland.

As I twirl my rings absently, my gaze settles on the deep red stone that is supposed to be a drop of my blood. The sun coming through the lace curtains in the window highlights it, seeming to make it glow from within. The blood-red hue perfectly matches the Vampira roses.

I pull my copy of *Dracula* from the bottom of my bag and open it to the quote McVladam had underlined. Do I believe in destiny? Maybe I would if destiny didn't hurt so damn bad.

I take out the rose to find it is finally fading and flattened as expected, which leaves me strangely disappointed. I bring it to my nose and inhale deeply. It could be my imagination, but I swear just under the deep rose aroma I can detect the notes of tobacco and leather, like he had somehow imprinted his scent below the floral notes.

I picture him the first time we met, when he had surprised me in my store. I can recall the exact shade of his black hair, the wayward curl falling down over his forehead in contrast to his tightly held control, his arched brows over amber eyes, broad shoulders, narrow hips. I envision the way he had stood with one thumb tucked into his pocket, a scattering of rings on his hand.

I take off my ring and hold it up to the light. I should bring it to a jeweler and have them identify what type of stone it is. It can't actually be ancient blood. My hand immediately feels naked, so I slide it back on where it feels like home.

What was it he had said on the plane? Something about, "There are no coincidences, only fate."

And what had Cait said? Something about my being touched by fate. How is it possible I even found this ring, the twin to his? Coincidence just isn't a good enough excuse.

In fact, there have been entirely too many "coincidences" since we've met. What else in my life has he manipulated? And is anyone else caught up in this charade?

I think back to the limited info I have on McVladam, and my brain lights up with questions. Knowing they will just circle in my mind, I decide to write them down. Organizing the chaos will help me tamp down the anxiety that threatens to consume me.

I dig in my backpack until I find a pen floating in the bottom and flip to the flyleaf in the back of *Dracula* and start jotting down notes.

1. McHottie is Adam and Dracula

2. Timeline

3. I am Eve

4. Matching rings

5. Coincidences

6. Tattoos

7. Order of the Dragon

Grabbing my phone, I pull back up the Wikipedia on Dracula and start reading. Apparently, Dracula's father had children in and out of wedlock, and Dracula and his brother had been held by the Ottoman empire at one point.

I try to wrap my head around the dates of invasions and the rulers falling in and out of favor. But this doesn't make any sense. These are two entirely different people. How can he be both Adam and Dracula?

I keep reading, reaching a section discussing the life of Vlad Tepes. His first wife committed suicide, and no one actually knew her name. My mind flashes back to the waking dream I had at the expo center of McVladam walking in on Luke and me in a stone room. I can't help but feel this is somehow connected.

I look back down, and read about his violent history. Is McVladam capable of such violence? If what he said is true, can I love a man with such a history? But he never said he was *the* Dracula; rather, he had implied that he was the first vampire. Are there others?

He does have a giant tattoo that is similar to the one from the order of the Dragon. So, that makes sense for the Vlad Tepes piece. And the tree on the back with the snake, animals, and image of me must be the creation story he told.

With the way he keeps popping up, maybe that tattoo is just one more piece of his stalker behavior. Although it certainly didn't seem like a fresh one.

In fact, lots of his tattoos looked ancient or even more like body modification or scarification with how they were raised and distorted. Many had been what looked like a different language, and if I recall from our fireside chat, he seemed to indicate they were all my names. A staggering three-hundred-and-thirty-two of them.

But why would the first man have a Romanian accent? I think the first language would have been something like Hebrew. I wish I knew what he had spoken to me in as we stood in front of my mirror at home. There have been other times he has used a different language as well.

I just can't piece this puzzle together. It's like that terrible multiple-choice question where the answer is "none of the above, need more information." And you just know you have the pieces, but they don't fit, like two different puzzles.

He also must have a fair number of resources, given that

he finagled the massage room and paid for the hotel, on top of arranging for both me sitting next to him in first class on the plane and the private car to the gatehouse.

I pick my book back up from the bed where I had laid it down and add to my list:

8. Money

9. Influence

I let out a huff of frustration. I'm getting nowhere, fast. Am I crazy for even trying to solve this riddle?

Not wanting to ignore my hosts any longer, I tuck the book away and head back downstairs to find the twins in the kitchen, prepping snacks. They look up at me as I walk in and smile in unison, giving the illusion of double vision. I drop into a seat at their table since they wave away my offer to help.

After a small tea, we head out to their shop, walking the few blocks it takes to get there. Nestled between a café and a used book shop, their brick storefront is beautiful. It has a large picture window in the front with their store name, Obscura Maximus, and their stylized Gemini logo.

The large window is framed with hundreds of doll heads. It is so delightfully creepy, I can't wait to get inside and explore the rest.

"We need a selfie!" I exclaim.

Anna will be proud of my initiative. This will be great to cross promote each other's stores on social media. I stand in the middle while we each snap some pictures and afterward, we all fuss over just how good they look. Mina and Lucy are striking with their brilliant blue eyes, small, upturned noses, black Betty Page haircuts, and the perfect blackberry shade of lipstick.

We make our way inside, and I take a deep breath of what smells like Grimm. Their shop has the same undernote of dust, formaldehyde, and that special dark essence that clings to antiques. I'm hit with a wave of homesickness for my place.

Shaking it off, I look around in wonder at the oddities they have collected. Their store is large and open, well organized and stocked to the brim. Whereas many stores like ours tend to be small, dark and cluttered, theirs is a refreshing and modern take. I loved the juxtaposition of old items in new modern display cases.

They also have tons of unusual plants mixed in which add a cool vibe. I might have to copy it. The checkout desk located in the middle is a brilliant layout, as it allows you to see the whole shop and interact with customers from any angle. The twins are clearly thoughtful and savvy business women.

After I wander around for a few minutes, they call me to the back room.

"So, who is the lovesick puppy working the register?" I ask, which earns me giggles.

Lucy replies, "Oh, that's Quincy. He's dead keen on both of us; he is."

"Oh, that poor thing," I reply.

Quincy is a pimple faced young man who couldn't be more than early twenties. I doubted he would be able to hold up to the twin fireballs of Lucy and Mina.

"He's proper sweet, but way too young for us," Mina says.

"Us? Okay, now I have to ask. Do you ever date the same guy?"

They exchange a grin and laugh. Mina says, "Nah, but we did try datin' identical twins once, and it was a right disaster."

Lucy adds, "Never again, I tell ya!"

They show me how the back stock room is organized, and I start going through items to pick out what I would be interested in. As I flip through old photographs, Mina explains this is their overflow. They often buy boxed lots to get one twin themed item in it, which leaves a lot of leftovers.

I rapidly sort through them, pulling out some unique and better-quality ones to make a pile we will negotiate over. After a few boxes, the images start blurring together, so I pick one last box to sort through.

Inside, I find a small metal frame mixed in with the loose pictures. I open it and immediately almost drop it as I stare in disbelief. My vision narrows to a dark tunnel; I lose my hearing and vaguely notice my hands are sweaty and shaking. Time grinds to a standstill. As if from a great distance, I hear someone calling my name.

Like a movie, my senses come rushing back and time speeds up to get me caught up to the present. I blink, and as the world comes back into focus, I see Mina and Lucy looking at me with concern.

"Did he give this to you?" I question harshly, shaking the picture at them. "When was he here?"

Lucy and Mina exchange a worried glance, and both turn to me with a frown.

"What're ya on about, Lieshe?" Mina asks.

"McVladam!" I exclaim. "Did he give you this picture to plant where I'd find it? Did he tell you to give it to me?"

Lucy answers, "Lieshe, we've no clue what you're on about. Why're you so upset? And who the hell's McVladam?"

I abruptly sit on the floor, staring at the daguerreotype in my hands. Lucy comes over and takes it from me. She looks at the image, at me, back at the photo, and then glances at Mina. Mina steps in and takes the frame from her.

"Whoa, this is well weird. The woman in this picture is the spitting image of you. Maybe she's a long-lost relative," she says helpfully.

I put my head down, feeling faint.

"Mina, I'll get Lieshe a drink of water," Lucy says.

Mina sits down on the floor next to me, rubbing my back, and asks, "Do ya wanna tell us what's goin' on?"

I would have rather confided in Jo or Mindy, someone who knew me and wouldn't be so quick to think that I've lost it, but this load is too heavy for me to carry alone any longer. I have to share this burden.

"It's a crazy story, but I can't do this by myself anymore," I say, my eyes burning with unshed tears.

"Right, let's grab a bite and you can tell us over a pint," Mina says.

She stands up and dusts herself off, holds a hand out to me and helps me haul myself up off the floor. Lucy returns with a bottle of water, and I chug half of it, the color coming back to my face.

"Lucy, it's time for–"

Lucy smiles and finishes her twin's sentence. "The Emporium. A'right, let's get goin'."

Chapter 26

LIESHE

We head back out to the store where Lucy throws over her shoulder, "Quincy, love, we need the car. Be a pet and lock up tonight, will ya?"

Mina snags the keys off the desk on her way by and as soon as we are outside, the girls dissolve into giggles.

"Bless 'im, 'e can't say no to us!"

We pile into a car slightly larger than the sardine can and head out.

"What's the Emporium?" I ask.

"Oh, you'll love it! It's at Pleasure Beach," Mina says, like that explains everything.

We turn on to Watson Road and, after going through a tunnel, reach the park. We walk through the giant metal archways, the lights just coming on as the sun sets. The twins lead the way, obviously intent on a destination.

We come upon a vintage-looking ice cream parlor called Emporium, and I'm thrilled. I'm assaulted with the amazing smells of frozen desserts and hot fudge as we enter. As we wait in line, Mina leans in and says, "I thought this story could do wi' a bit o' a treat."

I smile at her and respond, "Always. And I saw a sign for a bar, so after this, maybe something a little stronger?"

We place our orders, and I'm thrilled with the European allergen labeling system yet again. I order a hot fudge sundae with wet walnuts and whip cream. I'm not holding back, banking on sugar being the cure for my sick soul.

The shop isn't too full, and we find a booth in the back. Mina and Lucy sit across from me, licking their cones in unison. They look at me expectantly with their big blue eyes, and I tell them my story in between bites of gooey sundae.

Several times, I have to stop and remind them to lick their ice cream. They are so engrossed in my tale it is melting and dripping. Reaching the end, I say, "And that brings us to today."

Facing each other, they have a wordless conversation in their silent twin language, and then turn to me, blinking in unison like owls.

Mina says, "Oh, Lieshe."

I'm worried they think I've lost the plot when Lucy chimes in, "It's incredible. The longest love story ever told."

They sigh dramatically.

"Seriously? You believe me?" I ask.

"Course we believe ya," Lucy says.

"We don't know what any of it means, but we believe ya. Think about all the daft things we come across. The oddities that seem too real to be fake, the pictures that don't make any sense. The stuff you pick up and sense the energy pouring off it. There's a lot in this world we just don't get," Mina says.

"And you need our help, luv," Lucy chimes in with a laugh.

A load has been lifted off my shoulders. I hadn't even realized how heavy it had been, weighing me down when faced in isolation. Tears of relief pool in my eyes, but I quickly blink them back, not wanting to cry in an ice cream parlor.

"I'm so glad I can confide in someone. This has been such a heavy burden, and I feel like I'm losing my mind. I've been going round and round it all in my head," I admit.

"Let's make one of them detective boards, with string and thumbtacks," Lucy suggests as Mina shakes her head in agreement.

I nod along. It would be helpful to have others weigh in beyond my scrawled list in the back of my *Dracula* book. We head out of the ice cream parlor, and now that the sun has set, the park is lit up in that magical carnival way.

"Let's hit the scare maze and the horror bar!" Lucy says.

For the first time in days, I feel light and free. I want to have a good time and live a little. This will be the perfect distraction. I reply, "Let's do it."

We head toward the infamous haunted house—or scare maze, as they call it here—and I let them drag me onto some of the vintage coasters along the way. I'm flying high on adrenaline by the time we hit the maze. As we wait in line, Lucy and Mina fill me in on the ghost stories from the park and I am psyched to reach the haunted attraction. This is so up my alley.

Finally, it's our turn to enter. The doors open, and we are ushered in with another group of people. We walk in, arms linked. A strobe light and eerie music sets the stage. I'm thankful to be in between the twins, feeling safer in the middle. I know it's all fake, but I've always been a sucker for jump scares and attractions like these are full of them.

I eye up a darkened corner, bracing myself for a nasty surprise, but the closer we get, I see nothing but an empty rocking chair. Too late, I realize the distraction, and we all spin with a scream as a haunting little girl's voice starts singing.

A petite woman made up like a super creepy killer little girl is skipping toward us with a cleaver. We hastily retreat, walking backward to fall through the next set of doors. We laugh in relief as they close on the actress, but it's short-lived.

We spin around to the sound of a chainsaw, where a demented doctor is hacking someone open, entrails hanging out all over the place and human body parts strung up like a meat shop. His costuming and makeup are so realistic I'm almost worried for the "victim."

We continue moving through the attraction, passing through an asylum with interactive inmates and into a room of porcelain dolls which thrills Mina and Lucy, until another creepy little girl crawls out of the pile of dolls and chases them.

At last, we descend into a hot and humid room lit up with red lights in an imitation of Hell, complete with a devil dragging his helpless victims down into the fiery pits. His back is to us, but as we pass, he glances over his shoulder, and I freeze.

The flashing lights make it hard to see clearly, but just as our small group moves on, pulling me along, I crane my neck to catch a better glimpse of the devil winking at me. Luke must have a doppelgänger in London because I could swear that's him.

I'm swept away with the others and out the exit doors, where the bar patrons wait in anticipation for each group to come spilling out. The girls and I collapse onto each other once we are outside the final doors, laughing. Everyone is in high spirits, riding the adrenaline rush of fear, but I can't help glancing back at the now closed doors.

It can't be him.

"We survived!" Lucy yells.

Mina says, "We *earned* a drink!"

I'm still trying to figure out who the hell I just saw as we wander into the horror themed bar and claim a high-top table. The ambiance is super cool; the walls are covered in scary movie paraphernalia and all the cocktails are themed.

As our heart rates return to normal, Lucy and Mina order Bloody Marys that come with a huge skewer of hors d'oeuvres, including giant shrimp. I've never liked alcoholic ketchup flavored drinks, so I choose the obvious drink—Dracula's Kiss.

We let out a collective gasp when our drinks arrive. Theirs are huge and mine has glow-in-the-dark vampire fangs floating on top and a dark cherry impaled on a silver sword. Our first round goes down easily, but we take our time, hanging out and eating the garnish just to enjoy the amazing atmosphere.

Since we drove, we decide to head back instead of ordering more drinks. As we leave Pleasure Beach behind and pile back into Quincy's car, I ask if we need to drop it back by the store, but Mina assures me he will walk over and pick it up tomorrow.

We chatter on the way back about how much fun we had getting scared. Once home, we head into the kitchen where Lucy whips up some sangria and snacks while Mina goes down and roots around in the basement.

She emerges carrying several pieces of cardboard just as Lucy sits down and starts pouring drinks. Mina hangs the heavy papers on the cabinets with duct tape and smiles at us triumphantly.

Lucy and I exchange a confused look until Mina explains, "It's our detective board!"

Lucy and I both give a long, drawn out, "Oh," in unison and then laugh as the non-twins spoke in stereo.

Lucy says, "Oh, I know." She returns with index cards, a marker, and scotch tape, saying, "Reet, let's get this party goin'!"

I take two cards and label them "McVladam" and "Lieshe." Lucy tapes them to our makeshift detective board and then we all start writing clues and taping the cards up.

We stand back to admire our work, where cards are randomly taped with the words, "Adam, Dracula, Order of the Dragon, Tepes, money, stalker, tattoos, hot as fuck, fate, and rings."

"Hm," I say as Lucy chews on the pen cap and looks perplexed while Mina stands looking at the board with her arms crossed and chin on her hand.

"Well—," Lucy starts, but then stops.

"Maybe—," Lucy chimes in.

But none of us finish our thoughts.

"I don't know that this is helping," I finally say, and we all start laughing. "Do we need string and thumbtacks? Is that the problem?"

They are still chuckling as Lucy says, "I reckon it'd take a lot more than string to sort us out!"

We all sit back down at the table and start on the sangria.

"It was a grand idea," Mina says. "I just wish we'd been able to help more."

Lucy adds, "Maybe we can just have a chinwag? Throw some things at the wall and see what sticks?"

"That's a great idea!" I exclaim. "So, let's start with an idea and then decide whether it makes sense." I go up to the board and point to the card that says stalker. "Let's start with him being a stalker and then go through whether that could be the truth."

Lucy and Mina exchange a look. I put my hands on my hips and frown, "What's wrong?"

"There's nothing wrong with that, but it isn't very romantic," Mina shrugs.

"Let's start with his story bein' the truth," Lucy adds as she stares off, with stars in her eyes.

I quirk my eyebrow. "Okay, ladies, let's play good cop, bad cop. We will start with stalker, and I'll be the bad cop, and you can be the good cops and romanticize his behavior and explain to me why it's charming and not psychotic."

Lucy holds up her hands and says, "Blimey, remind me why he's stalkin' ya again?" She laughs and adds, "Just messin', just messin'. Alright, we'll give it a go your way."

I pluck the stalker card off the board and pace back and forth in their kitchen, waving it around as I make my points like a prosecutor.

I say, "Ladies of the jury, I present the following evidence that he is a stalker. Point one, he bought the property next to mine and snuck in and out of my store. Point two, he met me at the local bar. Point three, he had my seat moved next to his on the flight here and then convinced me to go to the gatehouse with him."

Lucy interrupts my tirade by putting up her hand. I raise my eyebrows at her, and she says, "Right, we've gotta start there or I'll lose me train of thought. Half the sangria's gone."

I nod. She has a fair point, and while she speaks, I sip on my drink.

Lucy starts, "Right, leavin' aside any arguments about fate or divine intervention, maybe he just ended up buyin' property next to you 'cause he was movin' there. Got any proof he moved your seat on the plane, or could it've just been a coincidence? And how much did he have to work to convince ya to go with him in Ireland?"

I think through her arguments. She has some valid points. I couldn't prove anything, and I did willingly go with him.

"Noted," I say in mock seriousness. "But what about

coming to the club in Belfast, seeing him on the ferry, *and* the run in at the hotel in Scotland?"

Mina steps up and says, "Well, are ya dead sure that was him on the ferry? Did ya actually see 'im and confirm it was really 'im?"

I nod my head no slowly. She's right; I had no proof that it was him. "The club was definitely him and the hotel is a different story altogether. Clearly, he pulled some type of strings to get me in the massage room and meet me back at my hotel room. How does that not seem stalkerish?"

"Oh, that proper does," Mina agrees, clinking her glass of sangria with mine. She counters, "But, uh, I don't reckon you were complaining' about the massage, or the club, were ya?"

I laugh. I hadn't gone into a play-by-play; rather, I just said we had mind blowing "interactions."

Lucy chimes in, "This isn't gettin' us anywhere. Let's move on to the supernatural bit, since that's much more interestin'. Let's have a natter about him bein' a vampire. What d'you remember him sayin' about it?"

I walk over to the board and this time I pick up a marker and draw a line connecting the cards that say Dracula, Tepes, and Order of the Dragon. I draw a dashed line to the card that says tattoos.

Oh, that man's tattoos, I think as I get a visual in my mind of slowly revealing his ink while I drug his pants down his legs and remember running my hands over the raised tattoos on his chest.

Mina snaps her fingers and says, "Oi, look at you, lickin' your lips. Where'd your mind get to, you cheeky little birdie?"

"Sorry," I say with a chuckle. "Okay, so everything Dracula I know is from movies and a brief reading of a Wikipedia page. But as far as Adam goes, all he said was the part about how the serpent told him when he drank my poisoned blood that he is now blood of my blood. He did also say something about a dark time when he lost me once that caused the legends surrounding him. But it was super vague."

Lucy whips out her phone and starts typing. "Right, so Tepes means 'the Impaler.' So that'd make Adam's name Adam the Impaler," she says with a fair bit of sarcasm. "History, dates, Ottomans, Turks, more history, blah blah blah. Not really all that helpful, other than the Order of the Dragon's mentioned here, and funnily enough, the name of his first missus isn't actually known," Lucy reports, summarizing her internet research.

"I read that, too. Isn't that odd?" I say.

"Oh, Lieshe," Mina says with lovestruck eyes. "Maybe you were his first missus!"

We sit in silence, digesting this thought.

"Yes, let's go with this train of thought. If you were, why would you jump to your death? 'Cause that's kinda what she did, y'know. Maybe before the hordes got to her, or maybe 'cause he was, like, you know, Dracula? Oh, oh! Maybe he wanted to turn you, but you said no!"

I shake my head. "Mina, I don't think the truth could be quite that fantastic. What about the Order of the Dragon? What's the connection there?"

Mina summarizes the key points until we all start zoning out. None of us seem to be history buffs.

Lucy pipes up, "So, you have a necklace given to you by an old Irish woman that matches his tattoo? Sounds like fate to me."

Somehow, we are on a second pitcher of Sangria now, and nothing is making much sense. We are going round and round, each idea getting more surreal.

I vaguely hear Lucy say, "Wait a minute, what was that?"

Mina smiles and says, "Breadcrumbs. The Order of the Dragon, usin' the last name Tepes, tellin' ya about the vampire lore. I think he wants ya to meet him in Transylvania."

"What about the money? How is he paying for all this stuff?" I counter.

"Oh, that's a doddle," Mina replies. "Dracula's always rich. McVladam's had ages to pile up wealth. Even if he just saved ancient coins and sold 'em a few thousand years later, he'd be minted."

I nod along with her logic. I mean, it makes sense as much as something like this can make sense. "What about the matching rings, though? I picked mine up at an Expo in Philly."

Lucy says, misty-eyed, "Well, maybe like the necklace in Ireland and the photo here, you or the objects—or both—are drawn to each other across time."

"Time-space continuum. Of course," I murmur.

The twins crack up. I finish off the last of my sangria and raise an eyebrow at them. Mina stands up, shushing Lucy loudly, and with a bit of a slur says, "Right, right, now hang on. Seriously though, we need some more details on vampire willy. Like, proper details."

We all burst out laughing.

Lucy adds, "So, that knob, then? What's it like? Can't imagine we'll ever get to see any immortal dick."

I smile and stutter out, "Uh, impressive. It's really, really freaking impressive."

They exchange a look, then both get up and start dancing, belting out some raunchy ditty about male genitalia. These two are hysterical, and as much fun as we've had tonight, it's clear we are getting nowhere fast at figuring out the mysteries of McVladam outside of celebrating his paranormal peen.

I fill three large glasses of water and say, "I propose a toast. To my best girls across the pond, and the unsolved mystery of Stalky Hottie Vlad Adam Tepes."

We clink cups and everyone shouts, "Cheers!"

I slug mine down and set the glass back down on the table. I pick up my phone to head upstairs and see a message notification. Opening my texts, I open the new one from Wren.

WREN

Hey girl! Hope your buying trip is going great. Can't wait to meet up tomorrow to check out that raven. Text me when you're up so we can decide on a time and place. I'm so excited for tomorrow, but I have to share this with someone now! Eek! I've been chatting with this amazing guy, and we finally met up in person!

I click on the attached picture to enlarge it, since my vision is a little fuzzy and the photo is dark. Wren is wearing a huge smile, sitting on a bed with dark red sheets, and a guy is sleeping behind her. I shake my head, trying to make sense of what I am seeing through the Sangria sloshing in my brain.

But it doesn't make sense. It can't.

The dark red sheets on the enormous four-poster bed are exactly like my dream bed back at the gatehouse. I know it's one and the same, and I sure as shit recognize the fucking guy behind her.

Another text pops up.

WREN

What a hottie! He even gave me a beautiful ring with a red teardrop stone. I know it's a lot so soon, but I just can't help but feel like this is meant to be. We just clicked! It's like he's my soulmate. Anyway, I can't wait to see you tomorrow!

I collapse into the chair and toss my phone carelessly onto the table. The loud clatter draws the attention of the twins immediately.

"Lieshe?" they ask in unison.

I look at Mina and Lucy and shake my head.

With a bitter laugh, I say, "He's not a stalker. He's a fucking grifter."

"What?" they ask.

"It's all a lie. One big bullshit lie. All those times he rushed off it was probably to talk to her," I cry.

Lucy grabs my phone off the table and says, "Is this 'im?"

Mina scowls, "Who's textin' ya?"

I scoff, "My friend that I am meeting tomorrow. I can't believe this!"

Lucy exchanges a look with Mina, then says, "I dunno, Lieshe. This is a bit of a mad coincidence, don't ya think?"

My eyes fill with tears. I'm exhausted, once again, and so very far away from home. "I've known Wren for years. Maybe? I don't know. I don't know anything, except I can't handle one more fucking coincidence."

The fun we had tonight drains away, leaving only the weight of this moment. Disbelief wars with the ache of my breaking heart. How could I have been so blind? And how will I face Wren tomorrow, knowing she is lying next to him right now?

Mina powers down my phone and hands it back with a

sympathetic smile. "Maybe just sleep on it. Everything'll be better in the mornin', and we'll all be sober. We'll help ya sort this out."

"Course we will," says Lucy, reaching out to give me a hug.

I stand up out of the chair and back away. I know if someone hugs me, I'm going to lose it. I am too fragile for anything other than retreating into sleep. "I'm sorry. I just need to go to bed. I appreciate you. Both of you. I'll see you in the morning. Thanks."

I turn and run up the stairs, just making it to the small guest room before I break down. I smash my face into the pillow, sobbing hysterically until I have no tears left, and sleep claims me.

Chapter 27

I bolt upright in bed and clutch my chest, my heart pounding away behind my ribs like a caged bird. Glancing at the clock, I'm shocked to find it's only three in the morning. I rub my puffy eyes and let out a jaw cracking yawn.

The events before I fell asleep come rushing back to me. Fuck, how am I going to meet Wren tomorrow? Last night had been so much fun before everything went south. Unburdening my soul to my friends, ice cream, awesome cocktails, and trying to play amateur detective had made for an unforgettable night.

Not to mention the haunted house. I haven't screamed like that in ages. Until it was fucking ruined. With an angry scowl, I lie back down on my side, punching at the pillow. I flop down with a sigh and attempt to find sleep again.

My eyes fly open. The haunted house! I *know* that was Luke. I can feel him pulling me back toward him like an invisible string wrapped around my soul. I get out of bed, telling myself I am just getting a drink because my mouth is as dry as a cotton ball. I've cried myself into dehydration.

I'm not getting up because I am pulled back to him. Absolutely not.

Tiptoeing downstairs so as not to wake anyone up, I head to the kitchen. I can't face another soul right now. As I stand at the sink, filling my glass and staring at my reflection in the window, the strangest thought comes to me. More of an impulse, really.

I *must* go back. I have to know if that was Luke. Now. Like *right now*. Before I can even think through this rash decision, I sneak through the darkened house and snag one of the twins' hoodies, throwing it on over my tank top and tiny sleep shorts. I shove my feet into my Docs without even bothering to lace them up.

I stand at the front door and stare at the keys to Quincy's car on the side table. I should really go back upstairs and grab both my wallet and the keys to the sardine can. But someone might wake up, or I might change my mind.

This is crazy. But crazy or not, I snatch the keys and open the door. Against all rational thought, I give into the impulse pulling me back to him.

"Maybe today, Satan," I whisper to the night as I commit grand theft auto.

Slipping out the door, I close the latch carefully behind me. As I step out into the night air, the quietness particular to this darkest hour before the dawn wraps me in its misty embrace. Not a star shines as I pick my way across the dewy grass to the driveway. The shadows are oppressive, weighing me down, pressing in on all sides. Every faint noise has me jumping, expecting someone to stop me from this crazy fool's errand.

I slide into the driver's seat and close the door as silently as I can. Putting the car into neutral, I let it drift down the driveway and into the road before starting the engine. Not a soul is stirring as I take off into the night.

My sense of direction is abysmal, but the drive somehow comes easily; I just listen to my gut as if following an invisible GPS. In no time, I'm back at Pleasure Beach and pulling into the dark parking lot, no other cars in sight.

I sit for a moment, calming my breathing, trying to understand what the hell I am doing. Before I can figure it out, my body is already on the move, tiptoeing across the deserted lot to the back of the building.

Past the dumpster, I find an exit door with a faint light over the top. I shield my eyes, looking for any cameras. I don't know what the penalty is here in England for an American breaking and entering, but the lack of knowledge doesn't stop my trembling hand from reaching for the door handle.

Sure enough, it swings open. Last chance to turn around, I tell myself even as my feet step forward into the dark. I close the door behind me with agonizing slowness, trying to keep from making any sound. As the door latches, I'm bathed in the red emergency exit light.

I swore my lawbreaking days were over after my little B&E into McVladam's house back home, but here I am, on my way to becoming a felon. Okay, maybe not a hardened criminal, but the thought of that damn grifter McVladam sure has hardened my heart.

I stand there, letting my eyes adjust to the dark environment, body buzzing with adrenaline. Straining my ears, I catch the horror soundtrack that was playing in the background earlier. I can't help but wonder why no one turned off the music.

I slowly follow the eerie sounds, my heart quickening with every step. At last, I come to a door. Pressing my ear against it I can hear the cackling and creepy noises of the soundtrack more clearly. Steeling myself to face the maze alone, in the middle of the night, I open the door.

Nothing springs out at me, so I walk through and into the next room. My pounding heart skips a beat when I see all those damn dolls. I quickly scan the area, looking for the actress from earlier. But all I see in the eerie lights are rows of doll faces staring back at me with their creepy dead eyes.

I slide my back against the wall, slowly making my way to the next doorway, keeping a vigilant eye on them. The wall gives way to a door that leads to the next room, where I swear I saw Luke as the devil dragging souls to the underworld.

Bracing myself for disappointment in what is probably one of the craziest things I have ever done, I throw open the door and leap into the room, determined to surprise him. The red lights flicker, casting strange shadows. The music ratchets up in intensity, drowning out even my pounding heart in my ears.

Spinning in a slow circle, I survey the room as the heat causes sweat to bloom on my face. There is no sign of Luke or anyone else. The attraction is closed, after all. There shouldn't be anyone here, including me.

Strange they didn't turn down the heat or kill the lights, much less the music. I walk toward the spot where I thought I saw Luke standing earlier, looking for what clue I don't know. A drop of sweat snakes its way down my spine.

The flashing lights, the heat, the pounding music start to close in on me. The realization of what I have done hits, along with the fact I am going to have to find my way out of this place and back to the house.

What was I thinking? Now that the excitement from this wild goose chase is fading, the lateness of the night weighs me down on the heels of the adrenaline crash. I close my eyes and take a deep breath to center myself.

As I draw in a second one, I'm bombarded with a wave of cinnamon. My eyes fly open, but before I can so much as glance around the room, a wall of heat hits my back.

"*Ma Reine Rouge*," Luke whispers into my ear, his beautiful velvet voice dripping with sin.

Whirling around, I am shocked to find him standing behind me. His hair is down, chest bare, and he is wearing those damn leather pants. The flashing red lights paint him as the very devil he appeared to be earlier in the night. He gives me his Cheshire cat smile, pleased with how I can't help but run my eyes down his body.

"Wh-what are you doing here?" I stammer out, backing away.

He stalks toward me, matching me step for step. As I'm brought up short, bumping into the wall behind me, his devilish grin grows. Leaning an arm on either side of me, caging me in, he leans close enough to whisper across my lips, "I could ask you the same thing."

His deep chuckle sends shivers down my spine. He pulls back and I curse my traitorous mouth as it follows him like a desperate puppy. He drops his arms and steps back, looking me up and down.

This is impossible. How the hell, no pun intended, is he here? Fear races through me. My brain is kicking over to primal instinct, knowing that something is very, very wrong while at the same time lighting an inferno low in my belly. The heady combination of fear and arousal is intoxicating.

I shake my head, trying to form coherent words. "But how?"

"*Ma Reine Rouge,* you wanted me here. Did you not?" he asks, like this is the most logical answer in the world.

"No. I mean, yes? I don't understand."

Faster than I can process, he steps forward and grips my jaw in his hand, forcing my lips into a pout. Bringing his face directly to mine, he fixes me with his yellow-green gaze.

"You can lie to yourself. But you can't fucking lie to me.

Don't you dare. Fucking. Lie. To. Me." He punctuates his last few words with small kisses, nips, licks and ends with a sharp bite into my lower lip.

Copper blooms in my mouth. Run, my brain screams. Run! But I'm trapped, frozen like a rabbit, watching in helpless fear as the predator swoops in.

Luke licks a drop of blood, midnight black in the flashing red lights, off his bottom lip. His mouth tips up in a sinful smile.

"Oh, yes. Please run. Your fear is exquisite." His whisper easily reaches my ears, almost echoing within my mind itself.

For the first time tonight, my brain has given me good advice. I take it and lash out with a kick to Luke's shin, which I'm fairly sure hurts me more than it does him. But it is enough to startle him, allowing me to turn and escape as he drops his hand.

His laughter trails behind me as I take off, running back through the horror maze.

I fly past the dolls, burst into the asylum, back into the slaughterhouse past the poor disemboweled soul, and into the first room where the creepy girl was. It stands empty now, except the rocking chair, the flashing strobe lights turning my rapid movements into jerky seconds in time.

Luke's even footsteps pursue me, close on my heels even though I run for all my worth. I reach the entrance and throw myself into the door, painfully jarring my shoulder when it doesn't open. I frantically rattle the knob, but it's locked. There is no way out.

"Are you fucking kidding me?!" I scream. They leave the back door open but lock this one? "Shit," I mumble. "Shitty, shitty, bang, bang."

I trail my hands along the walls, looking for another way out, a side door, an emergency exit. Anything.

There is nothing—no way out. And no one knows where I am because I snuck off into the night without even grabbing my phone or wallet. Hell, I don't even have underwear on. I brace my hands on the back of the rocking chair, trying to calm my frantic breathing.

I wait and I wait. My eyes stare so hard at the spot I expect Luke to burst through that my vision blurs and tears run down my face. I hate this damn strobe light. He was hot on my heels. Where the hell is he now?

The anticipation is agonizing. He knows exactly what he's doing. As I close my eyes to escape the damn strobes, just for a moment, the door flies open with a bang.

He zeroes in on me with his eyes and stalks toward me. The stroboscopic effect deranging his usual panther like grace into eerie abrupt movements. He stops in front of the rocking chair.

I feign right and then left, but he anticipates my moves before I make them. With a smile, he reaches out with one hand and grabs the chair, flinging it to the side like it is nothing.

The loud crack of the rocker shattering as it hits the wall startles me into retreat. I cannot drag enough air into my lungs. My fear is as exquisite as the desire. The paradoxical combination is like pouring gasoline on fire.

Every nerve ending of my body is awake. My nipples harden and scratch against my shirt with my heaving breaths. I clench my thighs, desperately seeking some type of relief. My sleep shorts soak with my arousal even as fear floods my veins.

Luke slowly walks toward me, in no hurry now that I have nowhere to run. His yellow-green eyes lock on mine as he takes my hand and places it on his chest. His heat licks against my hand where it rests over his heart.

My panic sweat turns icy, and I shiver at the contrast in temperature. He grasps my other hand in his and gently moves it behind my back. I'm trapped against him, but I make no move to escape. I swallow, mouth dry, heart racing.

He takes my hand against his chest and slowly, purposefully, trails it down his body. Every ridge of muscle, every breath he takes, caresses the back of my hand. Time becomes surreal; this moment could last five seconds or five hours.

Below my hand is liquid fire, while the universe spins around us, expanding, with solar systems whizzing by in perfect orbits. This moment is both everything and nothing, both here in his touch and swirling out into eternity.

He continues to drag my hand down. I know what comes next, but I still suck in a breath of surprise when he grazes my hand right down his crotch, his haughty smirk turning into a sultry smile as my eyes widen when my hand connects with his erection.

His tongue sweeps out across his full red bottom lip, and he gives the smallest thrust against my hand as if he just can't help himself. Then he places that hand behind my back as well and pulls my hips into his so he can lean me over me, tipping my weight back over my trapped arms.

He keeps me precariously balanced, dependent on him to keep me from falling. My brain rebels at this position that exposes the long line of my throat and my soft belly to the predator in front of me.

Luke leans over me, eclipsing my vision. The hard lines of his face thrown into sharp relief, contrasting light and shadow from the strobe lights. It reminds me of being on stage with him while he was spinning fire. My core clenches at the memory of that amazing night.

As if he can read my mind, he lets out a chuckle as he runs the tip of his nose down my forehead, down my nose, lips, and chin, then drags it agonizingly slowly down my neck. He tips me back further, balanced on the fulcrum of my arms.

He places his mouth over my heart and whispers, "You cannot lie to me because I see you. Every dark desire, every hidden secret. I see your thirst for the darkness. The thirst that has always been there. You've always sought the shadows. You've been looking for me your whole damn life. From the time you crossed your little fingers and hid them in your skirt while you lied to your priest to the moment you came here to find me."

I picture that little girl staring up at the stained-glass symphony of color and condemnation. Something tugs at a dusty corner of my mind—something long forgotten, repressed, unspeakable.

"*Où était ton ange quand tu avais vraiment besoin d'être sauvé? Où est-il maintenant?* Hmm? Where is your useless angel now?" he asks.

He distracts me from the memory and his cryptic questions as he moves his lips to the side, trails them over my breast and breathes hot air onto my nipple.

I watch in rapt fascination as he opens his mouth and bites me through the hoodie, his aim dead on. I cry out in pain and growing arousal. Somewhere in the back of my mind, I know there is a reason this should be so incredibly wrong, but right now, for the life of me, I just can't quite recall why.

He releases my breast from his mouth, the damp fabric cold against his warmth, and walks me backward to the wall once more. He moves my hands to my sides and drags them up the wall in an arc, pinning both wrists above my head with one hand.

The sensation burns like a band of fire, highlighting just how cold I am inside. But I know that if I can press his skin against mine, I will be enveloped in the most incredible heat.

"Je suis seul ton sauveur."

His French whisper washes over me as he stares down into my eyes, keeping his body from touching mine, but just barely. The heat radiates off him in waves, but he is still not close enough. He leans in until his lips just graze mine.

"I have not lied to you. I'm the only one you can trust. I am the only one who can see you, who knows what you need. I alone will be your savior."

I breathe his words in where they diffuse through my lungs and into my blood like oxygen. Someone I can trust. Someone who knows what I need. He sees me. He is here, now, when I need someone.

"Tell me no," he says, his breath ghosting over my lips, smelling like the cinnamon red-hot candies from my childhood.

They were so spicy. Every one I ate, I told myself would be the last, but my hand kept sneaking more into my mouth like I just couldn't stop. Luke fucking Devlin is the same. I just can't stop even though I know I should. But the burn will be so sweet.

"Luke," I breathe.

He presses his cheek to mine, the contrast to my chilled flesh inducing shivers.

"Say it," he says, lips next to my ear. "Tell me no," he whispers, voice dripping like molasses. Dark. Sweet. Like he wants me to say it.

"No," I force the bitter lie past my lips.

I want to push back at him and find out just how dark this will go. It's a dangerous game, but one I can't stop now. Just like those damn candies.

He pulls back to stare into my eyes. "Then why does your pussy weep down your thighs for me? Why does your heart pound so hard I can see it through all these damn clothes? Why are these nipples so tight and aching? I can smell your desire even above the stench of your lie. *Et ça sent bon.*"

His yellow-green eyes glow in the chaotic lighting, hypnotizing me.

"Now, tell me no and mean it or stop *fucking* lying," he hisses.

He releases my wrists and grips my face with both hands while he stares into my very soul.

"What does yes mean?" I ask in a tremulous whisper.

He slides one hand down to my throat while the other hand glides down to my breast. I can't help but push into it, my body so desperate for him, for anything. The fear, the adrenaline, the lust—something has to relieve this deep aching need.

With a final squeeze, his hand leaves my breast and traverses my stomach to cup me over my shorts. My breath hitches as he slides his hand down to push them to the side to find me dripping for him like he knew I would be.

He tightens his grip on my neck as, without warning, he thrusts two fingers into me.

I gasp, startled but so damn thankful for the sudden fullness in my aching center. He kicks my feet out wider with one of his. This position allows him to penetrate me further, pushing at the very entrance of my womb.

"The world darling. Yes means the world. *My* world," he says.

He punctuates his words with a motion that has my toes curling.

"Fuck," I moan, riding his hand as he finger fucks me expertly.

I cannot rip my eyes away from his, can't stop my traitorous body from grinding down into his hand, seeking more. He brings his thumb up to strum across my sensitive bundle of nerves.

"I'm sorry, was that a no?" he asks darkly, tightening his hand around my neck until stars swim in my vision. "Don't lie to me. I see you. I see you, Lieshe."

My name dripping from his lips like sin is my undoing. Every muscle in my body tenses as I feel myself on the edge of shattering.

"Every insecurity, every fear. I will strip you down to your very soul. I will pull every dark and depraved desire from that fascinating brain of yours. I will highlight your perfection with my hands."

He tightens his hand around my throat, filling my head with euphoria.

"My lips," he whispers over mine, nipping sharply at the bottom one as my mouth falls open in a silent O.

"My cock," he growls, rubbing his leather covered member against me.

Every word he says plucks at my heartstrings, brings moans tumbling from my mouth in response. He sees me. All I've ever wanted was to be seen, loved, and cherished. Worshiped just like this.

"I will make you *ma Reine Rouge*, crown you with dark stars, anoint you in the blood of our enemies, and cloak you in their lost souls. Together, we will rule the world."

My brain screams no. I know that is the right answer. The answer I am supposed to give. But my lips, oh my traitorous lips, they won't cooperate. The picture in my mind is so real, so vivid, I should be able to reach out and touch her. The Red Queen. She is beautiful. She is fierce. She is me.

I.

Am.

Her.

"Yes," I force past the grip on my throat.

"Yes, what?" he purrs into my ear. Increasing his pace to an impossible speed and curling his fingers forward, he hits a spot that puts stars in my vision. "Scream it for me."

"Yes, my Lord!" I shout as I erupt. For a brief second, I have pressure like I have to use the bathroom and then wetness shoots out and down my legs, drenching me.

"Wonderful, *ma vilaine petite reine*," he growls, ripping my soaked shorts down, where they hit the ground with a sodden plop.

"Tell me yes again," he says against my lips as he claims my mouth in a searing kiss.

Sliding his hands up under my tank and sweatshirt, he breaks it only long enough to get my clothes off.

I gasp as my chest finally meets his, his heat scorching my pebbled flesh. I can't get close enough, winding my arms around his neck and anchoring my hands in his hair.

"Yes," I moan into our heated kiss.

He undoes those fucking leather pants and shoves them to the ground. I feel his cock against me, hot velvet over steel. Even the metal bars running up the underside are scorching, like they will brand into the sensitive flesh of my belly. He reaches down and wraps his arm under my knee, hiking my leg up against the wall.

"Yes, what?" he asks, breaking our kiss to stare into my eyes.

He reaches down under my other knee and lifts me

higher against the wall. As he rubs the head of his cock up and down against my entrance, the magic cross piercing bumps up against my clit, pulling a gasp from me with each contact.

I know this is a point of no return. I know I'm not just saying yes to sex. I am stepping into his world. A world I somehow think isn't quite the same as this one. In this moment, poised to be impaled by his thick cock, I throw caution to the wind.

"Yes, my Lord," I cry, desperate to be filled by him, claimed by him and all he is offering to me.

He slams home, sheathing himself deep into me in a single thrust. He buries his face in my breasts, licking and sucking between dark, incomprehensible words spilling from his lips.

They raise the hair on the back of my neck and send shivers skating down my spine. These words have power radiating off of him, through him, and filling me like a great volcano erupting inside of me.

This is most definitely *not* French. It is something older, darker, and far more powerful. All I can think of right now is the feeling of Luke and the dark and dangerous black fire he lights inside of me. He's forging me from the inside out into a new woman—a queen.

I lock my ankles together behind his back, pulling him in deeper with every thrust. The angle is delicious, his piercings not only massaging against my entrance with every thrust but hitting some magical spot deep inside me.

The scratchy wall behind my back, the strobe lights, the creepy soundtrack playing in the background—all of it fades away to nothing. My singular focus is Luke and the point where we are connected.

The way his heat surrounds me is consuming. My belly

clenches and my walls ripple around him as my climax builds. His cock swells as his breathing turns ragged. Knowing he is close to being just as consumed by our blaze as I am pushes me closer.

"Lieshe," he calls to me in my lust fueled haze.

I find his eyes with mine, the yellow green almost glowing. For a second, they appear all black and I blink, but push it out of my mind as a trick of the strobe lights I've been in for so long.

"Eyes always on me," he says, reminding me of our time together before.

We lock eyes, and I watch as he bites his lip and his nostrils flare.

"Come with me, *ma Reine Rouge*. Now and forever."

Watching his face tense as I feel his hot release flood inside me triggers my own intense orgasm. I can't scream, can't moan, can't even breathe. All I can do is thrust against him the best I can from this position.

As he continues to move with me, pushing past his release to help me chase mine, I find my voice and scream as I crest, one more time, "Yes, my Lord."

We slide to the floor in a tangled heap without separating. Luke gathers me to his body and holds me while my breathing and racing heart slow.

I curl up against the warmth of his chest, moaning a little as he softens, and our combined release leaks down my thighs. I look up into his face; the effort of moving my head seems insurmountable.

He chuckles softly and says, "Again?"

Chapter 28

We make our way to the back door and burst out into the night, stumbling, kissing, and groping each other every few feet on some type of high. What a pair, he in his leather pants half slung around his hips, and me in my stolen hoodie with the sleep shorts shoved in the pocket as they were too wet and sticky to put back on.

Laughing, we walk through the parking lot to where a large black SUV waits. The driver is tactfully turned away, next to an open door. A quick slap to my bare ass has me yelping and running toward it, while Luke playfully chases me in.

The warm interior and plush leather seats are so comfortable after my quick run through the rapidly cooling air. The dawn is approaching, the sky just beginning to lose its dark hold over the earth. I glance around the abandoned parking lot, spotting the evidence of my grand theft auto.

"Their car!" I exclaim, pointing through the darkened windows.

Luke nips at my finger, taking it into his mouth to swirl his tongue around it, pulling a moan from my lips.

"I'll take care of everything. Where does it need to go?" He asks, grabbing a phone from the console and typing away.

I rattle off the address, worrying about what the twins will think of my sudden departure, but he distracts me by pulling me across his lap so I'm lying over his legs, ass up. He gathers my mass of curls in his hand and pulls my head back, arching my back.

"Grab the door handle and hold on." His voice drips with dark dominance, slipping against my skin like hot silk.

"Wh-what are you doing?" I ask, stunned.

"Oh, my naughty, naughty girl. You placed yourself in harm's way and broke any number of laws tonight. You were foolish. Reckless. I cannot allow you to put what belongs to me in danger. You must be punished."

"Punished?" I squeak, as the impact of what he is saying sinks in. I belong to him?

I try to push up and get off his lap, but the bend of my legs across the large bench seat and his grip on my hair make it impossible. All I accomplish is getting the hoodie further up my body, exposing more of my backside to him.

"*Oui, ma belle coquine*," he says as he trails his fingers lightly over my exposed flesh, leaving a trail of fire in their wake.

"But I don't want to be punished." My eyes glance toward the driver. "Luke! We're not even alone," I hiss.

He chuckles as he drifts the fingers of his other hand down my spine, along the cleft of my ass, to my thighs clenched as tight as I can get them.

"Is that why you're dripping all over my lap and wiggling that sweet cunt into me? I told you, every dark fantasy. Starting with this one."

I feel a wave of embarrassment flush from my hairline to my toes. I am going to be punished. In front of someone. Luke is right. It wasn't until he said it out loud that I noticed I'm grinding into him for all I'm worth, not trying to get away at all.

My legs are already spreading, inviting him in. I want to be punished, and I want an audience. Who am I?

"Yes, my Lord," falls from my lips before I've even finished trying to unravel this reaction.

Does this make me bad? Dirty? Impure? The first hard smack takes my breath away, along with any self-deprecating thoughts. Each stinging blow is followed by a sensual caress. My world condenses to pure sensation. The pattern is ever changing in tempo and placement, preventing me from settling into a rhythm and keeping me on edge.

I am dripping, desperately seeking some type of friction. The tops of my feet flexing against the cold glass, the angle of my head, the strain of the arch of my back—everything falls away.

My singular focus is the heat spreading out where Luke's hand meets my flesh again and again. The pain is replaced by euphoria and building pleasure.

"Oh, *ma Reine Rouge.* Your skin blushes so beautifully."

I hear him praise me from somewhere far, far away while I float in this feeling. I shiver as his fingers trace over the reddened skin ever so slightly, then break out into goosebumps as he gently blows across my heated flesh.

"I could listen to the song of your moans and my hands on your flesh for all eternity," he murmurs.

"Please," I whisper in a voice so small I'm surprised I find it at all, drifting in this peaceful place.

"Uh-uh," he tsks. "That's the real punishment. Leaving you dripping," he says as he circles his fingers just over the outside of my lips.

"Wanting," he says as they dip further and he swirls my wetness around my pulsing clit.

"Luke, please," I beg on a throaty moan.

"Begging," he whispers as he slides two inside of me and then retreats.

I clench on the emptiness, desperate to be filled. I can't

help but let out a small whine. All I can feel is Luke. The air is heavy, sweet with the scent of my arousal.

He pats me gently, saying, "Beautiful girl, you took your punishment exquisitely. Didn't she Malachi?"

I had completely forgotten about our audience. As Luke scoops me up into his arms against his chest like the rag doll I resemble, I don't feel dirty or ashamed.

I feel free.

Chapter 29

LUKE

Lieshe falls asleep in my lap, curled into herself. I should put her on the seat next to me, but the feel of her—warm, soft, *trusting*—intrigues me. I keep her gathered in my arms, head tucked under my chin.

Her wild, unruly curls, made even more so by the past few hours, get stuck in my facial hair and tickle my nose. Normally, I would swat away the slightest annoyance, but her unique rose scent mixed with the faintest fresh sweat and our combined sex is worth keeping her close and breathing her in.

She whimpers in her sleep, so I resettle her, getting more comfortable myself and whisper sweet words into her hair, gently, like a baby. She immediately settles. I flick my gaze up to catch the driver watching me in the rearview mirror.

A slight narrowing of my eyes has the fucker dropping his right back down. So what? I shushed her to get the silence back. Nothing more.

I concentrate on her body in my arms. It's so frail, with its fragile bones and squishy organs. I can hear the air move in and out of her lungs and listen to not only her heartbeat, but the blood itself, flowing through her veins. I lose myself in the symphony of her physiology, mapping her anatomy in my mind.

I let my consciousness drift into her dreams, feeling my way through the synaptic firings. I push my way gently in further, not wanting to put myself in them, although that had been so much fun over the summer, but just enough to peer below the surface.

I can see young Lieshe in church, gazing at the colors of the stained glass in the shadow of her father and looking for a spot of hope in the condemnation of the men surrounding her. Fucking hypocrites. Their oppression is stifling.

Then her dream morphs to sneaking out to a party, but in the strange way of dreams she remains a little girl in her uncomfortable dress clothes. Her eyes catch on someone pulling her from danger.

I smirk as I recognize Gabe. That asshat has been doing a shit job at protecting her. Where is he now? If he really wanted to protect her, he should be here. I'm the biggest danger there is.

I retreat from her dreams, but just before I pull my consciousness from her brain, a spot catches my attention and reminds me of just how mortal she is. I follow it down to the spine, along the long track of the nerve. The muscle twitches under my gaze, confirming my suspicions. She will die her mother's death. What a shame.

For a second, I wonder if I could wipe it out, relieve her of her fate. I've never intervened to help someone. I'm not quite sure if I even could. I go back to the spot and gently nudge it, whispering to it in the same ancient language I whispered into her hair.

A golden halo flickers around it. Shocked, I pull my mind completely from her body. Unwilling, or maybe unable, to ponder this mystery and the potential cosmic implications, instead I think through the next stage of my plans. I move pieces around, studying the strategy and outcomes. Like chess, I predict the pattern of events based on any individual move or counter move.

The path forward is clearly laid before me. There are so

many ways to win. I might as well enjoy myself in the process. Victory will be mine, I'm sure of it.

My musings have passed the time for us to arrive at the small private airport. The large SUV pulls in close to the jet. Time to wake sleeping beauty.

"Lieshe," I whisper in her ear as I run my hands up and down her back.

I gently pull her to a sitting position and smooth down her hoodie. I want the fuck out of London. I want to see her in my city of eternal night. I've never brought anyone there before. Well, anyone alive. I hope she survives.

For some reason I can't quite fathom, I need to see her skin under the never-ending twilight, see the stars reflected in her eyes.

As she sits up, she wipes at her mouth where she had been drooling a little, smashed against my chest. Her hair is wild, eyes unfocused. She blinks a few times and then her lips tighten as she scrubs her hands over her face. She seems embarrassed and tries to tame her unruly curls. I place my hands over hers, stopping her from making herself smaller.

"Down. I like it down," I remind her.

Her wild curls charm me with their chaos, and I loathe pushing chaos into order. I know all too well what it is like to make yourself less than.

She brings her hands to cup my face. I smile as her hair settles back into mayhem, retaliating against her attempt to order it just as she has resisted the attempts all her life to make her smaller, force her into the mold of the millions who have come before her.

Ma Reine Rouge cannot be contained. Just like me. A sweet smile lights up her face, pure adoration. Yes, all paths lead to my victory. I'll enjoy the ride indeed.

"Where are we?" she asks, straining her eyes to take in our surroundings past the tinted windows.

I give her my full smile, the one that masks the monster within and brings men and women alike to their knees. "When you get out of this car, you will walk like the queen you are. You will not try to cover yourself or the marks I have painted your beautiful skin with. Let the world see my claim on you."

Her eyes go wide as I gently set her on the seat next to me. Before she can ask any questions, the driver has opened the door and I step out, holding out a hand to her.

She awkwardly scrambles across the leather bench seat and stumbles out of the car. I'm sure she would have fallen if I hadn't given her my hand. I don't know how she survived to the ripe old age of thirty.

I turn and tuck her hand into my elbow and begin walking, only to be brought up short. Looking back, I see her staring at the jet, too shocked to even try to pull down the hoodie that barely covers her bottom half.

"Come, *ma chatte*." I slip my arm around her shoulders, tucking her into my side. She fits there, as if she were carved from my flesh instead of that stupid *chien's*.

The pilot, co-pilot, and flight attendants all respectfully bow their heads while keeping their eyes averted. I gently push her up the stairs, enjoying the view of my handprints still on her ass as she mounts the short flight. I stop myself from walking into her as she stops and spins to gape at me.

"Luke," she squeaks. "What the fuck is happening?"

"I told you."

I walk forward, slipping one arm around her back and pulling her into my body while I fist my other hand into her thick mass of hair, where it tangles in her curls. Keeping my eyes locked into her amber ones, the yellow-green splash there makes me genuinely smile.

"Welcome to my world," I murmur before crushing my lips to hers.

I feed on her emotions, feel her body move from shock, to acceptance, to excitement. I lick past the seam of her lips and claim her mouth with my tongue. Plundering, retreating only to kiss her deeper, darker. I maintain control, swallowing her throaty moans, only breaking away once she is breathless.

I keep her face staring into mine as the crew boards and skirts past us to prepare for flight. I can see her drowning in desire, and smell her arousal. It's fucking exquisite. I find myself sincerely hoping she survives the transition to my realm. A living human soul has never crossed.

Oh, the fun we will have. A million ideas to corrupt her dance in my head. Might as well start now, I think as I nip her bottom lip sharply. Her heart races in response, signaling to me she is open to a little more pain with her pleasure. Lucky for both of us, that's my specialty.

"Kneel," I command, smiling as she drops to her knees and lets her eyes drift to the ground.

"Lieshe." She snaps her eyes up to mine. "What have I told you before?

She looks panicked for a second, then smiles at me, saying, "Eyes always on you."

"*Bonne fille*," I praise her.

I leave her where she kneels to check in with the flight crew. In my peripheral vision, I see her sneaking glimpses of the luxury jet. I linger a little longer, just so I can continue to covertly watch her. Seeing her reaction to the opulence around her gives me a fabulous idea.

I can't help but smile at my own brilliance. I will dazzle her, indulge her, consume her. That stupid *chien* doesn't stand a chance. This is really almost too easy, like taking candy from a baby. I lick my lips, wanting to go taste my girl.

If I didn't know myself better, I'd almost think I'm developing a preference for my sweet little candy. I frown. There are too many flavors for that.

Seeing her eyes shift from her surroundings back to me, I pull my smiling mask into place and stalk back to her, all swagger. I watch her eyes drift down my body as I slowly run my hand down the chiseled plane of my chest, slide it down my abs, and into the waistband of my pants to adjust myself.

Her heart beats faster and I can't help but put on a little show for her hungry eyes. I'm going to strip her down to her basest desires, fill her to overflowing with sin, and she will love me for it. She will worship me.

I squeeze my hard cock, biting my lip and tipping my head back while she hungrily drinks the sight in. With my other hand, I beckon her toward me. To my complete delight, she moves from kneeling to crawling.

"Good fucking girl," I growl as she crosses to me.

"Sir, would you like a drink before we go?" the attendant asks from just behind me, turning a blind eye to my activities.

I merely hold out my right hand in anticipation, while my left continues to fist my cock inside my leather pants. Lieshe's eyes widen, shocked.

As soon as the tumbler is placed in my hand, I throw over my shoulder, "You are dismissed to the cockpit."

"But sir, we are next for takeoff."

I merely turn my head slightly over my shoulder, and she rapidly scampers off, the cockpit door closing behind her. Anyone who works for me knows better.

I hold the glass out to Lieshe, pulling it out of her reach when she lifts her hand, shaking my head. She drops her hands and raises to her knees, so I can place it at her lips and give her a sip. Her tongue darts out along her lower lip to catch the drop of bourbon there, and I let out a deep groan.

I want her mouth again. Hell, I want all of her again. I toss the rest of the liquor back and throw the glass carelessly over my shoulder, where it bounces on the carpet.

I pull down my zipper, watching her pupils blow wide as she takes in my cock straining toward her, the light glinting off the matte black magic cross piercing. I run my fingertips down the underside, over the Jacob's ladder barbells.

She bites her lower lip, and I am done for. Knowing there are only minutes left until take off, I bend down and toss her over my shoulder. She lets out a squeal as I race us to the back and into my bedroom there. Throwing her onto the bed, she bounces on the black silk.

We stare at each other for a heated minute as the plane gains speed. I kick out of my leather pants as she strips off the sweatshirt, getting tangled in the sleeves.

Seizing the perfect opportunity, I grit out, "Leave it."

She stops her struggle, arms gloriously restrained. Her chest is heaving, putting her full lush breasts on display for me. I crawl up her body, straddling it, working my way to those beautiful tits. I grab them in my hands, kneading, stroking, pinching and rolling her nipples until she is moaning and tossing her head. I wrap my cock in their glorious softness and slowly fuck them.

"Give me your tongue," I grunt out.

I can't help but moan when the pink tip hesitantly peaks out from her lips.

"More," I command, gifting her with a wicked smile as she opens her mouth and stretches it out for me.

As the tip of my cock batters her outstretched tongue, I let out a deep groan. I lean forward and spit on my cock, her eyes widening. I pick up my pace, the slick tunnel bringing me closer. I push down my orgasm, needing to draw this out and wanting to debase her the way I know she wishes for. Bring her to my dark side.

Slowly is the way, layer by layer, so she doesn't understand the depravity we have reached until we are already there. Stilling my movements, I dip down over her, eclipsing her, becoming her world. I gather more saliva in my mouth and let it slip from my lips to fall on her outstretched tongue.

It lands just as the plane lifts off from the ground. I keep my balance as the jet chases the dawn, my attention solely focused on her reaction. Her eyes flick down to her tongue, and I hold my breath, desperate to learn what she will do.

She raises her molten gaze to mine, quirks her brow, then curls her little pink tongue around the spit pooled there and brings it back in her mouth. Her loud swallow has me dropping dark curses as old as this earth. Of course, she's a fast learner. It is time to rip off the training wheels.

I slide my hands up from her breasts, one wrapping around the exquisite column of her throat and one shoving the sweatshirt that still has her arms trapped behind her head. She has never looked more beautiful.

"Don't move," I command, my restraint on a tight leash.

Her answering smile tells me she knows it. She may be able to see me holding back, but she has no idea just where I will be leading her. This is merely a glimpse. I'll let her think she holds the power for now.

I lean down, allowing some of my weight to transfer to the hand on her neck. Her pulse thrums wildly under my fingers, leaping at me. I slowly lick the seam of her lips, and although they part with a moan, she otherwise stays perfectly still.

I take advantage of her open mouth and swallow her moan, thrusting my tongue past her lips, fucking her with my mouth. I steal her breath with my kiss as my hand continues to tighten around her beautiful throat.

I explore her with my tongue, plundering, claiming, and searing. I suck her tongue into my mouth, scraping my teeth along it.

Despite how close I am taking her to the edge, her pulse skipping a beat below my fingers, she melts into the moment, trusting me. Surrendering. Her blind faith that I am somehow good, that I won't actually hurt her because I must care for her, is like shattered glass inside of me.

Sharp. Jagged. Wrong.

I release her neck, and the red recedes as she gulps great lungfuls of air. I rip the sweatshirt off of her arms and flip her over, drawing her hips up. The sight of my handprints all over her ass drive the shards deeper into my gut.

Time to fuck this pain away. I gather her wild curls into my hands and twist it into a rope, loop it around her neck, and pull back, effectively leashing her with her own hair. With my other hand, I cross her arms behind her back and hold her wrists in an iron grip.

My cock twitches forward, intent on ramming home. Her pussy is glistening, swollen, and waiting to welcome me. Her heartbeat thunders in my ears, drowning out my thoughts. I rub along her slit, bumping the head of my cock with its magic cross piercing against her clit until she is grinding back into me, frantic.

"*Supplie-moi, vilaine fille.*" I'm so deep in my lust, I barely realize she can't understand me. "Beg, my naughty girl. What do you want?"

"Please, my Lord!" she immediately cries. "Please!"

"Please what? Do I need to remind you of your words again?" I rasp.

"Fuck me," she whimpers.

"Oh, *vilaine fille*. That's not nearly good enough. Speak like the queen you are. I want you blushing as red as this greedy cunt. Lose yourself. There is no right or wrong. There is just you and me, here in this moment." I punctuate each sentence with a bump against her clit, watching her pussy clench around nothing. "Tell me."

She is almost crying in frustration. "Luke, please."

I slap her ass hard, drawing a delightful gasp. "Use." Slap. "Your." Slap. "Words."

Her legs shake as she sobs. "Fuck me, my Lord. Fill me with your cock. Fuck my pussy. Hard."

"*Ma Reine Rouge*, there is my queen," I groan, letting my head fall back. I nudge just the head of my cock into her warm, welcoming heat.

Despite her hair wound round her neck and my tight grip on her wrists, she bucks back into me with all her strength, desperate to be filled. I slowly sink into her, filling her, until I bottom out.

"Is that what you wanted? Watching your pussy stretch around my cock is exquisite."

She continues to try moving, frantic for me to fuck her.

"But I don't think you're quite full enough yet. Are you my *vilaine fille*?" I drop my hold on her and carefully reposition her arms so she will have use of them. "Go ahead. Take what you want."

I freeze, motionless as she realizes her freedom and begins to thrust her hips, fucking me. Seeing her take the power in this position is incredible. She experiments with different angles until she finds one that is hitting all the best spots.

"That's right. Use me. Take your pleasure, *mon amoureuse.*"

She continues her movements. I feel her clenching, searching, desperate for her release. I let out a dark chuckle.

"Words," I prompt her.

"Luke," she begins.

I cut her off with a sharp smack to her ass.

"My Lord. Please, more. I want you, no, I need you to take control," she pants.

"Do you now?" I purr. "You want to be my toy? You want me to use you?"

"Yes, God, yes!" she cries.

I still. In a deathly quiet voice, I say, "I will only tell you this once and never again. You worship at my altar. Do you understand?"

"Yes. Yes, my Lord." She writhes against me, ruled by her physical need.

All the other nonsense her head has been filled with falls away, replaced by lust, desire, and greed. Spreading her gorgeous full ass, I spit on her pleated hole, eliciting a scream, but not a protest. I circle it, then insert my finger, pushing in further and further to match each thrust of my cock.

"That's better," I say once my finger sinks the whole way in. "Reach down and feel us."

She shifts to move her hand, tentatively stroking around my shaft as I thrust in and out of her tight channel. "Feel that greedy pussy sucking my cock in. Just like that ass took my finger. Tell me, have you been fucked here yet?"

I already know the answer but eagerly await her response.

"N-no," she stutters out.

But the gush of her arousal and her holes strangling my

cock and finger tells a different story. Her body is anything but hesitant.

I pick up the tempo as her fingers find her clit. Her moans and cries become a continuous torrent as she chases her release. As a deep pulse begins within her, I immediately work a second finger into her ass, taking advantage of her frenzy.

"Come with me. Feel me fill you up."

I twist my fingers, pulling a deep, guttural scream from her. My other hand grips her hair to turn her head to face the open door.

"Scream louder for them, my deviant, dark darling. I want everyone on this damn plane to hear how well you've taken my cock. How much you love my fingers buried in your tight virgin ass."

She gets impossibly wetter and then explodes into her orgasm, limbs shaking, breaths heaving. I knew bringing attention to her exhibitionism is what she needed to push her over the edge.

I pull my hand away, knowing her orgasm will lessen the sting. Seeing her empty ass clench the air spurs me to let my release burst forth, shooting out and painting her in my hot darkness as I imagine claiming her there. The first. The last. I will be her eternity.

Her orgasm continues to roll through her in waves, my last thrust and spurt triggering a final scream. She collapses to the bed, no longer able to hold herself up. I've fucked her senseless, I think with a smug smile.

I lick slowly up her spine, one vertebra at a time, as she shivers below me. Kissing my way to the shell of her ear, I breathe her in, getting inebriated by her essence. I was already high on her desperate innocence. But this tainted dark path I am leading her down by the hand is infinitely more potent and delicious.

"My queen," I murmur into her ear as she succumbs to sleep. I stand and stare down at her—peaceful, sated, and wrecked. I can't help but mutter, "Fucking exquisite."

All of her. All of her will be mine. Body. Heart. *Soul.* And then, all the world, above and below. *Ma Reine Rogue* is the lynchpin. Victory would be sweet with her kneeling at my side, but watching her claim her throne—that will be my crowning glory.

Chapter 30

LIESHE

The slide of silk sheets caressing my skin as I stretch is delicious. My eyes fly open as I realize I am still on Luke's plane. I sit up, wincing slightly at the burn my movement causes. I look around the back cabin for something to cover with, but even my stolen sweatshirt from the night before is gone.

I use the ensuite bathroom marveling at the luxury of my surroundings. Seeing no other option, I wrap myself with the bedsheet and head out to learn where we are.

Emerging, I realize we are not flying at all but sitting stationary. The flight attendant from last night stands at the sight of me, giving me a haughty up and down. I stop in my tracks, cheeks flaming as I remember the open door during the ride here. I glance around, seeking Luke's presence, but we are the only two here.

"Excuse me. Where are we?" I ask.

"You don't know where you just flew to? What kind of woman gets on a plane without knowing where she is going and then fucks her way there?" she scoffs in accented English.

I stumble back, as if she struck me. What have I done? I have no idea where I am or, quite frankly, what the hell I'm doing. My carefully laid plans for my business trip have been thrown completely out the window. I wasn't thinking. Why does Luke make me lose my mind?

Her eyes narrow at me, and just as I spin to retreat to the safety of the cabin to figure out my next steps, her eyes blow wide as she glances over my shoulder. Keeping my focus on her face just as I turned throws me off balance. My feet tangle in the slippery sheet and down I go in a blaze of black silk.

Hard arms wrap around me, a split second before my head would have cracked off the table set between the plush leather seats. My head spins as I am righted, my eyes still squeezed shut against the impending impact.

"Lieshe," Luke purrs.

I open one eye to check if the room is no longer moving. Luke's face looms in front of me, a small smile playing on his lips at my one-eyed stare.

Opening both eyes, I drop my gaze to the floor. I'm ashamed of being called out by the flight attendant, standing here in nothing but a sheet, and for having fucked my way to wherever here is, just as she said.

Luke lifts my face back to his with a finger below my chin. His unusual yellow-green eyes search mine for a moment, assessing the situation, the change in my demeanor. As realization dawns, his face loses all playfulness.

"Who are you?" he asks me, his cinnamon breath whispering his breath over my lips.

I blink at him, not understanding his question. What does he mean, who am I? I'm an embarrassed woman standing wrapped in a sheet in an undisclosed location getting judged by a flight attendant on a private jet I've no business being on, but I don't think that's the answer he is looking for.

I bite my lip, not knowing what he expects me to say. My

eyes fall to the ground, shame and embarrassment warring within me. I take in my bare toes on the plush black carpet mere inches from his leather clad feet.

It only highlights our differences—quirky, curvy, awkward me versus a refined yet elusive, enigmatic man with a private jet and fancy shoes. The woman's eyes bore into my back. I know this is what she sees, too.

Luke reaches out and tilts my gaze back to this, pulling my lip from between my teeth. He slides his hands down my shoulders, hooking his fingers into the sheet clamped around me under my arms.

I begin to protest, but the fire flaring in his eyes stops me. Instead, I let him pull the sheet from my grasp, allowing it to pool at my feet. He gives me his Cheshire smile, pride dancing in his eyes.

"Lieshe," he says again, louder and more emphatically this time. Although my name drips from his lips with his smoldering French accent, I know he is repeating this not for me, but for her. "Who are you?"

My mind races through our last few hours together. When he sees I understand his meaning, he turns me by my shoulders to face the attendant.

My shame and embarrassment fall away. She's a pawn. Her judgment means nothing. She is jealous. Luke chose me. I orgasmed my way across Europe at twenty-thousand feet, not her. I draw myself up taller, bold in my nakedness— confident and strong.

Luke's hands rest heavy on my shoulders. I feel his heat seeping into my skin; imagine it filling me until I am as fierce and daring as he is.

The answer falls easily from my lips. *"Je suis la Reine Rouge."*

Her mouth falling open in shock is one of the highlights of my life.

I lift my chin higher, regally. I let my gaze fall down my nose at her, seeing her for who she really is. Nothing but a jealous and judgmental pawn. She drops her head in defeat, but not before I see the very real flash of fear in her eyes.

"*Putain,*" he growls behind me, spinning me to face him and colliding his lips to mine.

His cinnamon flavor invades my senses, filling my mouth. I am burning in Luke Devlin. His touch, his words set me on fire. I remember watching him on stage, falling in lust with him along with the crowd. I recall how we all screamed when he asked us if we wanted more. And I did. I wanted more Luke. But now?

Now, I want to be consumed by his inferno.

He licks deeper into my mouth, swallowing my moans. He drags his hands roughly down my back to grip my ass, pulling me even further into him. I forget about the bitch behind me. My sole focus is on staying upright as he claims me, marking me as his—worthy and venerated. Loved?

He abruptly tears away, eyes flashing with a nameless emotion. I reach up, running my fingers along my swollen lips, to read his kiss like braille on my fingertips.

With a small nod, he gestures to the shopping bags he must have returned with. "Get dressed."

Reeling from his kiss and trying to understand the enigma that is Luke Devlin, I walk back through the plane, grabbing up the handful of bags from the black leather sofa near the door. Tossing them on the bed, I close the door and lean back against it, pulling deep lungfuls of oxygen in. But all it does is fuel the fire that is Luke.

"Holy shit," I whisper as I upend the contents onto the bed.

I sift through piles of lace, astonished at the amount of lingerie he picked out. I hold up a particularly strappy piece, turning it this way and that, trying to make sense of how I would even strap myself into this contraption.

Dropping it, I grab a pair of underwear that has less to it than my dental floss. Shrugging, I pull them on. When in Rome, I think. But then, I realize I actually have no idea where I am at. Eager to find out, I pull out the matching bra, surprised but not that Luke obtained such beautiful things that fit as if made for me.

I've never worn a bra like this—sheer and unlined. Instead, I pick wide straps, jabby under wire, and modest padding because I always worry about showing my nipples. Why? Why do women need to pretend like we don't have nipples while men go about flaunting their big hairy chests, nipples and all, whenever the chance presents itself?

I glance down at the gossamer lace that proudly displays my breasts. Heading to the bathroom mirror, I can't help but smile at the gorgeous reflection staring back at me. I looked good in lace. Confidence buoyed, I go back to the pile of clothing on the bed.

Luke is taking this "Red Queen" business seriously. Every item he brought me is red. I contemplate the outfits, struggling to decide since I have not only no idea where we are, but no clue where we are going today.

My choices seem to be a night at the opera, a nightclub, or a sexy pajama party given there are three dresses ranging from long to short to sheer. Deciding against tripping in the floor-length gown or revealing everything I was born with in the sheer one, I choose the short and tight dress that would have done Lilith proud.

Once I've rolled it on like a sausage casing, I pull the lone shoe box over. I'm hesitant to open it, worried it will contain stilettos. I flip it open, surprised that not only does it not contain heels, it contains shoes similar to the ones I loved on Luke when he returned my corset and jacket to me. I take the black flats out, admiring the short silver spikes covering them.

Holding my breath, I turn them over to see the beautiful red bottoms. I can't help the little squeal that escapes. For a shoe girl, this is amazing. I never would have bought these for myself, and I just love them. I am happy I picked the dress I did; the outfit looks great.

I start to wind my hair up into a knot, but then remember Luke's preference for it down and shake it out, blowing a rogue curl out of my face. Squaring my shoulders, I turn and walk back out. I look over his shoulder, but the flight attendant is gone.

"Where'd my new friend go?"

He lets out a low whistle, holding a hand out to me. I take it and allow him to spin me around. When I come to face him again, his eyes are smoldering.

"Luke?" I prompt.

"Hm? Oh, don't concern yourself with her. Come. My world awaits."

He tucks my hand into his elbow and leads me off the plane. I can't wait to see where we are. We descend the short staircase, and he walks us to a sleek red sports car. Getting in, I admire the interior which looks like a spaceship.

"Maybach?" I ask as he slides into his seat, remembering the fancy one at home.

He shoots me a smile as he revs the engine. "Bugatti."

I can't help but mirror back his happiness with a grin of my own. "Thank you for the beautiful clothes. It's too much."

He gives me a dark look. Every word weighted with

sincerity, he says, "Stop at thank you. Nothing is too much for you."

As my cheeks heat, I reply, "The shoes are incredible. I've always dreamed of owning Louboutins."

I love seeing the curve of his cheek as he looks straight ahead, a smile still stuck to his face, as I continue, "I tend to buy vintage or thrifted, but outside of that, I like to invest in things that I know will last. I'll treasure these forever."

He reaches over and glides his fingertips up and down my very exposed thigh. "Except for the shoes, everything you are wearing is handmade in a small fashion house right here in Paris."

All I hear is the final word. "Paris? We're in Paris?"

"*Oui, mon petit chou. Je t'ai emmenée dans ma ville préférée, mais elle ne peut pas rivaliser avec ta beauté.*"

I whip my head around to stare out the window, and sure enough, as we leave the airport, the sights of Paris greet my eyes. I've always wanted to come to the city of light. My face is all but pressed up against the window of the car.

"We have a few stops to make on the way home," Luke says as he expertly drives us into the city.

My stomach lets out an embarrassingly loud growl.

He chuckles as he says, "First, food. Then shopping. You will need new things."

"What's wrong with my things?" I ask, hurt.

I know he loves his designers and fancy cars, but I love my ripped jeans and Docs. He grips my thigh, and I shift my eyes back to him.

"There is nothing wrong with your things, but they aren't here," he explains.

"Oh, shit! I need my phone and passport. Wait, what about the sardine can? The twins?" My list of worries surfaces in the light of day.

"Everything has been taken care of, as befits my queen," he answers with a chuckle.

I can tell how pleased he is with himself by his grin, though I'm curious how he managed all the details. Meanwhile, the passing scenery of Paris captivates me. After handling the business and taking care of myself for so long, it's a relief to have someone else take charge.

Within a few minutes, we are turning down progressively smaller streets until we pull up next to a cafe facing a fountain. I wait for Luke to come and open my door as I know he likes. He offers me his hand, and I tug at my hem as he helps me out of the car, uncomfortable with how revealing the dress is for the early afternoon at a sidewalk bistro.

"Who are you?" he whispers in my ear.

I stop fidgeting and lift my chin. We are drawing curious looks, but I tell myself it is because Luke is just so damn handsome in his all-black suit. He looks dark and dangerous, especially with his red hair pulled back to the nape of his neck.

He leads me to a table where I can view the fountain and watch the people walking past. He pulls out a chair for me, and I can't help but fall in love with the quintessential Paris experience. The little tables and chairs, the azure sky, the bubbling water.

It's all just so perfect. I just hope I'll be able to eat something here since I'm starving. The ice cream parlor was a lifetime ago.

A waiter comes over and hands us menus. Luke stares intently at my face, which seems odd until I glance down at the menu and realize he is waiting for my reaction.

"Luke! I can't believe this. *'Sans gluten'* means what I think it does, right?"

I look into his eyes and am met with a rush of warmth. He seems so content, so happy to do something that might seem small or silly to others, but means a lot to me. I'm amazed at how he not only knows, but also appreciates all the little details about me—my needs, my values, my desires.

But how can he know all of this?

As if he can read my mind, he says, "When you care about someone, you pay attention to what matters to them."

He takes my hands across the table and stares into my soul. The busy cafe falls away; in this moment, there is just Luke and me. His gaze is intense, gauging my reaction. The air is heavy with anticipation, as if my response could easily change the trajectory of wherever this runaway train is going.

He lifts each of my hands, feathering a kiss over the back. The old-fashioned gesture is so appropriate to the idyllic setting. I realize I want to know what matters to him. This is moving past lust, past infatuation.

I find myself in a solid state of like. If I were in middle school again, and praise be that I am not, I would even go so far as to say that I like-like him.

My poor heart struggles under the emotional whiplash coming off the McVladam roller coaster. But where that felt like obsession and déjà vu, this feels like a romantic whirlwind. Being wooed feels so damn good. I'm not going to lie, I want more of it. Feeling like a queen is incredible, being treated like one—incomparable.

I let my feelings bleed into my stare and ask, "What matters to you?"

"*Tu comptes pour moi,*" he replies with a smile that outshines the sun. He repeats in English, "You."

The waiter comes back to take our order, and I drop my hands to pick up the forgotten menu. Luke responds in

French, and I'm surprised when the server reaches out to take my menu.

"I didn't even get to look," I complain.

He just smiles his Cheshire smile at me. I forgive him slightly when our coffee arrives. Despite not being my usual concoction, it is delicious and a welcome boost. I stifle a yawn as I realize just how little sleep I am running on.

"Nap or shopping?" Luke asks in response.

I take another sip of my coffee and reply, "I can sleep when I'm dead. It's not every day I get to shop in Paris. Please tell me you at least have my wallet with you."

"*Relaxe-toi.* All is well. You'll have your things by tonight, and in the meantime, you are mine to take care of. *Mine* to spoil." His voice darkens possessively with ownership.

This is the point I should protest. I know I should turn down more expensive gifts from him. But I'm tired of doing what I should and of pushing so hard. If Luke wants to spoil me, I'm not saying no. I'm not going to play games and pretend I don't want to go shopping in Paris or let him treat me.

He is freely offering, and I will graciously accept. I'm already thinking of all the wicked ways I can demonstrate my appreciation.

"I like that look in your eye. Please tell me you are not going to pretend you don't want this," he says, as if reading my mind.

"Oh, I want this. I'm just dreaming up creative ways to thank you later." I look up through my lashes at him and add, "My Lord."

"If I couldn't hear your stomach rumbling from here, we would leave now, and I'd let you thank me in advance. As it is, I will sit here and imagine just what you could be dreaming up. Until the waiter comes back, I want you to place both hands on the table and press your wrists together. Imagine that I have you tied up and waiting for my touch."

His softly spoken words easily carry to my ears and invade my senses. I do as he says and put them on the table just as instructed, squeezing my thighs together. It is all too easy to picture him tying me up, left at his mercy.

He watches me over the rim of his mug as he sips the steaming beverage. I look on in fascination as he licks his lips and swallows, throat bobbing. I never knew foreplay could happen without even touching. I couldn't care less about eating right now.

A sudden, "Ahem," startles me, and I realize the waiter has returned and needs me to move my hands to set down the plate.

I grab my drink and take a sip to cover my embarrassment while he lays down a decadent chocolate croissant in front of me and sets down a large to-go bag filled with boxes beside me. Luke merely holds up a black card without taking his eyes from me, observing me with the gaze of a hungry panther.

I bite into the delicate pastry and barely stifle a moan.

"I haven't had a croissant in so many years," I say in between bites of heaven.

The flaky and buttery pastry quickly disappears, and I can hardly stop myself from licking my fingers. I finish my coffee as he signs the bill, and standing, picks up the bag.

"What's in the bag?" I ask him, eyeing up the boxes in hopes of another pastry.

"The rest of the menu," he says with a wink.

"Luke! You ordered the entire menu?" I gasp.

"Oh, *ma Reine Rouge*, just wait." He chuckles.

And with that mysterious response, he walks me back to the car. After he deposits me into the passenger seat, I turn to see him walk back a few spots and hand the package off to someone in a black SUV. When he gets in, I face him, my questions written on my face.

"Trunk space," he says.

I guess that makes sense, given the sleek sports car. But who does he have following us around?

Chapter 31

Good thing I have some of my men tailing us in an SUV since I plan on drowning Lieshe in gifts. Any amount of love, attention, or the smallest kindness just lights her up. I suppose that's one more fuck up her parents did that works in my favor.

I slide into my Paris car—honestly one of my favorites—and look over to see her smiling like I handed her the fucking moon rather than a measly gluten-free croissant. She looks happy. Like really happy.

And that makes me feel... What the fuck is this feeling?

I must just be satisfied that I am well on my way to winning. I return her smile and ease out into traffic. I could drive these streets blindfolded. I've spent countless years here in my favorite city. Parts of my life have flashed by like a time lapse video while other pieces of my wretched existence have stretched into eternity. I've chased pleasure, and it's often led me here.

I shake off the introspection and focus on today—better to live in moments like this one. There is a beautiful woman beside me in one of the world's best cars on our way to indulge in a few of my favorite sins in the best city on this wretched spinning rock.

I navigate us down the side streets and to one of my preferred boutiques. I pull up in front and park, watching in the rearview to note where the large SUV ends up. Satisfied with its location, I escort my sweet little queen inside.

She is immediately drawn to the beautiful designs, running her hands over the best materials Paris has to offer. This is one of my top choices for a reason. As she works her way through the store, I see her stop and frown.

She carries a silk kimono style dress up to me and squawks, "Luke, why are there no price tags?"

I tip her chin up and drop a playful kiss on her nose. "*Mon petit chou,* we talked about this. You are mine to spoil. You are doing me a favor. I am a patron of this shop. We must do our part to support small businesses. There is no one else in Paris I would trust to dress you in the way you deserve. But let's not pick something so shapeless, hm? I want your curves on display for me."

From the corner of my eye, I see Chloe approach. I let her come closer but continue to hold Lieshe's attention, letting both women know just who is my priority. I drop her chin and gesture to Chloe while keeping Lieshe's gaze.

"*Chloé, je te présente Lieshe.*"

Lieshe breaks my stare to acknowledge Chloe, still a slave to societal norms like politeness. Unlike me, who suffers no such constraints. I see her insecurities surface in the face of Chloe's classic Parisian build and style. I sigh and roll my eyes.

Lieshe might as well have been created for me. Her body is perfect—soft where women should be soft, round where they should be round. I let out a quiet dark chuckle as I think, tight, wet, and delicious where they should be, too.

Lieshe's gaze jerks to me with a questioning look. I draw her into my side in reassurance and give Chloe a litany of instructions in French over my shoulder as I pull Lieshe by the hand to the dressing room.

"Strip, *mon petit chou,*" I say, just to get a rise out of her.

She doesn't fail to disappoint, eyes widening in surprise.

I nod to the dressing room behind her, and she scampers off to follow my command. I drag a chair over to face the closed curtain.

"This brings back memories," I say, thinking of when I laced her into that damn corset back in Philadelphia.

My fingers itch to do it again and carry through on my claim from then—to pull the laces so tight she could scarcely breathe. Maybe tonight I will.

An entire night free from interruptions, just her and me in my townhouse. I plan to fuck her in each room on every available surface at least once. Given the size of my home here, we may need more than one night.

Chloe and her assistants arrive with several racks for me to sort through. As they pull out the items that I want her to try on, she calls out to me from the dressing room.

"What do you even do? I've seen you as a vendor and a stage performer, but I don't think either one of those things can support your car habit," she calls through the curtain.

I can't help but chuckle. She is too observant. I give the same answer that has served me well for so very long. "Old money, *chérie*. I do what I please. Sometimes, that means selling, and others, I'm the buyer."

I pass the items I deem worthy to Chloe and wave away the rest. One of the assistants moves to assist Lieshe, but I shoo them all away. I don't want anyone else near her. I want to feast my eyes on her. It's only been a few hours since the plane, but I want her again already. I frown. That's unlike me. I open the curtain and duck in, laughing as she covers herself.

"Drop your hands," I growl.

I love when she obeys and displays herself to me confidently. Seeing her embrace her role as queen is nothing short of beautiful. I spin her by the shoulders to face the mirror in the dressing room. I take the dresses and hold them up in front of her.

The first few are pretty enough, but finally, I find one that lights up her face. A dark red velvet with a sweetheart neckline and a high side slit. It will be perfect for the dinner I have planned. I set it aside and hold up some more items.

Every time I hold up a piece between her and the mirror, I catch her deep rose scent. I step closer, pulling her back against me.

"I can feel the heat coming off you in waves even through your clothes," she says, holding my eyes in our combined reflection.

I trail my hands over the curves of her shoulders and down to her breasts. Her breathing hitches as I cup them, sliding my thumbs back and forth over her pert nipples.

In French, I call for Chloe to bring me a corset and then to get the fuck out, knowing she will do what I ask. I'm the reason for her success, after all. In just a moment, she passes a white corset through the curtain.

Really? I think. White?

I pull it from her grasp and turn my attention back to where I've left my little queen panting. I rip the laces out, wanting them done to my specifications.

"What has that poor corset done to offend you?" she asks with a smile.

I raise a brow at her in the mirror.

"Not only is it white, but it's not even laced correctly," I say in clipped tones.

She bites her lip to hide her amusement, and I can't help but laugh along with her. I step closer, and her smile falls as the air crackles with something else.

Bringing it in front of her, I lean into her ear and whisper, "Hold this."

I trail open-mouthed kisses down her neck as she tilts her head. I sweep her hair to the side and begin lacing the corset from the top down. With each pass, I let my fingers graze her back until she shivers under my touch.

When at last I have it properly laced with the rabbit ears at her waist, I meet her eyes over her head in the mirror. Pure lust reflects back at me.

"Do you remember what I said to you the first time we did this?"

She nods silently, eyes smoldering. I begin to draw the laces, tightening the top and bottom of the corset at the same time. Her breaths become shorter and faster, not because it's even that tight yet, but because she knows it is coming.

My eyes fall to her reflection where her breasts heave beautifully, pushed up in the garment. I continue to pull the laces, tighter and tighter, just past the point of comfort, and then tie them off in an elaborate knot.

"*Tu es la perfection absolue.*"

I grab the chair from the corner of the dressing room and place it behind her, then circle around to face her. The white actually compliments her skin and hair, giving her an angelic appearance. Perhaps I'll change my color scheme for her, making her my blasphemous bride.

I push her back and as she falls into the chair, I command, "Spread your legs for me."

She complies, her skin flushing pink, making the white all the more brilliant. I kneel down in front of her, grab her knees, and yank her ass to the edge of the chair. Pushing her thighs as wide as they will go, I drop my tone to the dark dominance I know she craves.

"When I say spread your legs for me, this is what I mean. Or do you need to be punished again?"

She nods her head yes, then corrects herself, sputtering, "No! I mean, yes."

I tighten my grip on her creamy thighs, prompting a quick, "My lord."

I reward her with a long, languid swipe of my tongue while I stare up into her face. Her mouth falls open as she pants, breathing constricted by the tightness of the corset. I take her hands and bring them down to spread herself open for me.

Leaning back on my haunches, I take her in. From her wild curls to her amber eyes with my splash of yellow green, down to her struggling breaths and glistening pink pussy.

"You are absolute perfection," I murmur again, in English this time for her benefit.

I dive into her like a man starving, licking and sucking all that beautiful, exposed pink skin. My monster pushes at me, wanting to devour her, claim her as ours. With brute force, I keep my form, my face, and my hands.

I fuck her with my tongue, plunging into her repeatedly until she is riding my face, grinding into me. Only when she is panting and desperate, begging cries falling from her lips do I move up to suck her clit. She explodes, wrapping her thighs around my face.

I drop my suction, helping her ride out the last of her orgasm without torturing her, as much as I would love to. But there will be plenty of time for that later. I rise up, claiming her mouth in a deep kiss so she can taste her release coating my lips and tongue. I pull back with a satisfied smirk and smooth out my mustache.

"I was wrong. Now, you are an absolute vision."

"Luke," she pants out. "I need air."

I cock my head at her. I know she is fine; she has plenty of circulating oxygen and her heart beats steadily, but I can't tell her that. So, instead, I give her a hand up and spin her around, rapidly loosening the laces until the corset falls to her feet.

I choose a pair of ripped jeans and a red strappy top out of the pile and hand them to her. She puts her bra and panties back on and then changes into the new outfit.

Holding hands, we step out into the store where I'm brought up short. You've got to be fucking kidding me.

Chapter 32

LIESHE

"Lilith! What are you doing here?" I ask.

I'm beyond shocked to find her sitting here and wonder just how much she heard.

She cocks an auburn brown at me and says, "What am I doing here? I could ask you the same thing."

"Lilith," he growls.

She stands and kisses me on both cheeks. Pulling back, she wrinkles her nose and waves a hand at her face.

I flush crimson knowing that she smells the sex on me as she says, "What a happy coincidence. Luke, you have to bring her to the club tonight. We had so much fun last time. Until you showed up, that is."

"Club?" I ask.

"Why, Synd of course. There is one right here in Paris. Luke, be a lamb and bring Lieshe out. We'll have such a good time," Lilith purrs.

Sure, the last time we went out ended in disaster. But we did have a great time up until then. I turn and look at Luke.

"Please, can we go? When will I get the chance again to go out in Paris?" I bat my lashes at him, trying to put on my most charming smile.

I just know going out with the two of them will be epic. Possibly an epic disaster. But either way, I know it will be something.

"Yes, please Luke," Lilith simpers at him, imitating me.

It's so silly I'm not offended. He scowls at both of us in

turn. Then a wicked glint enters his eye, and he says, "What a brilliant idea."

"Great, let's go get ready," Lilith says, turning to lead the way.

"We'll meet you later," Luke growls at her.

I'm relieved. Lilith is a lot to handle, and although I want to go out with her tonight, I don't necessarily want her watching over me as I get ready.

Tucking my hand in his elbow, Luke tugs me to the sales counter where Chloe materializes. He rattles off something to her in French and then leads me out the door.

"Thanks," I call over my shoulder, surprised at Luke's curtness toward her. "Bye Lilith!"

We slide back into the fancy car and take off through the streets of Paris. I watch the scenery go by, falling in love with the quaint cafes and admiring the beautiful people. We make another turn, and I let out a gasp.

"Luke! There it is!" I squeal as the Eiffel Tower comes into view, highlighted by the sun.

"Welcome to the Left Bank."

"Do you live here?" I ask.

"In the seventh *arrondissement*. We'll be there soon," he says.

I'm all but plastered to the car window, taking in the sights. True to his word, in a few minutes, we pull up outside of a beautiful ornate stone building. A man dressed all in black with an earpiece comes over and opens my door, extending a hand to me.

"Don't move," Luke surprises me with his curt command.

I obediently sit, watching as he rounds the front of the car and casts a withering glance at the man who immediately bows his head and backs off. I place my hand in

Luke's, surprised when he pulls me in for a hard, claiming kiss.

I look up at him when he releases me and joke, "Would you also like to piss on me?"

He winks, saying, "I didn't know you were into that."

I let out a belly laugh. "That's not what I meant. I felt like you were marking your territory."

He looks at me stone faced.

"N-no, that is not what I want!" I stutter out.

He holds his serious face for one more second and then he bursts out laughing. It transforms his face from brutally handsome to stunning. His laugh is warm and shoots straight to my chest, where my heart does a funny extra little beat.

I see him in the light of Paris, and I marvel that this is my life right now. Who am I? I orgasmed my way across Europe, ate in a Parisian cafe, and then shopped at a trendy boutique. At least, I think we bought things there; we didn't leave with anything. Not to mention the epic orgasm in the dressing room.

Luke cocks his head, studying me. "*Un sou pour tes pensées.*"

I wrinkle my nose at him, wishing as always that I spoke French like he did. Although I do have my red queen phrase down.

He looks down at the ground and then steps into me, tipping my chin up to his. "You would say a penny for your thoughts."

I stare up into his unusual eyes and murmur, "You dazzle me."

He leans down to whisper across my lips, "No, *mon petit chou*, it is you who dazzles me." He slides his hand into my hair and brings his mouth to my ear, whispering, "Your strength. Your beauty. Your mind." He pulls back and nips at my bottom lip. "Your taste," he murmurs darkly.

I'm surprised when he steps back, revealing the bustling city around us. I had lost myself in the moment, Luke eclipses the world. Dazzling indeed, I think.

He takes my hand and tugs me after him, past another man in black who holds the door for us. We step into a small foyer, through yet another door, complete with a butler, and into the most decadent house I've ever been in.

"Luke," I gasp. "This is stunning."

He smiles proudly and replies, "Thank you. This home is in the *Haussmannian* or Second Empire style. It's one of my favorites."

As he leads me through the first floor, I take in the herringbone parquet wood floors, soaring ceilings, and elaborate moldings. As we walk further in, I catch glimpses of marble fireplaces and chandeliers. The home is a study in opulence.

"And a courtyard?" I say as I wander out into a beautiful area with plants and a central fountain.

A little oasis away from the hustle and bustle of the city. It's easy to see why this is one of his favorites. Wait, one of them? I can't help but wonder how many he owns.

"Do you have a lot of houses?" I can't help but ask.

He just smiles his feline smile at me and guides me to sit at a little bistro set next to the water feature. He holds my hands across the table, smiling at me, as the butler comes over with a bottle of champagne and two glasses. He sets them down with a small bow and leaves.

"Champagne? What are we celebrating?" I ask.

"You, Lieshe. We're celebrating you."

He looks at me as if the answer is obvious. As if I really am something special, someone worth celebrating.

Warmth bubbles up inside of me, I don't even need the champagne.

The fading afternoon sun fills the courtyard with golden light. Luke stands and shrugs out of his jacket, hanging it over the back of the bistro chair. He rolls his black sleeves up, revealing his muscular forearms.

As he picks up the champagne bottle and pops the cork, the sunlight makes its way over to highlight his red hair, outlining him in fire. He laughs as it goes flying off and gives me a golden smile.

My heart does that funny little dance again in my chest and I worry that I'm falling for him—that my like-like is sailing away like that cork toward *really* like. Or maybe even love.

After the whiplash of McVladam, I don't know how this could even be happening, or how I could let myself be vulnerable again. But I *want* to be in love. I want my special someone to share my life with, like a trip to Paris.

Damn it, I do deserve to be happy. I am someone worth celebrating.

Oh, shit. Thinking of McVladam reminds me I was supposed to meet Wren today. I hadn't wanted to face her after that text she sent, but I haven't even had my phone to call or text her at all. I'm torn between wanting to let my friend know that I am okay and feeling green over the picture she shared.

Something doesn't seem quite right about this situation, but I just can't put my finger on it. Even Mina and Lucy thought something was off. Is McVladam really that good of an actor? Is he some type of conman? But there is nothing to get out of me unless he's after Grimm, which wouldn't make any sense.

Unless it did! He did buy the building next to me and

then target Wren, one of my oddities contacts. He is stalking me on my business trip.

I need to warn Wren before he breaks her heart, too. I don't understand his motivation, but he's after something. My business or my building, I'm not sure. But girl code is, I have to let her know.

"Luke! I need my phone. I was supposed to meet someone today in London." I don't know how I can explain to him the other reason why I must call her.

"Too bad I stole you away to Paris, then. Your things will be delivered tonight. I took care of everything. Your car was returned, and your friends Mina and Lucy know you are with me and safe. I'm sorry about your meeting. I wasn't aware," he says with a sympathetic smile.

"No, of course. How could you have known? It was oddly perfect. I didn't know how I was going to face her today, anyway." I cringe.

He narrows his eyes at my statement.

"Why not?" he asks.

Oh, shit. I said too much. I do not want to get into this story with Luke. I don't want to explain how foolish I was to believe that McVladam was some type of supernatural creature chasing me, his long lost fated mate, through time.

Sitting here, sipping champagne with Luke is so real, so sophisticated, that everything to do with McVladam seems like a bad B movie. *Vlad-nado.*

Luke has been attentive and charming. He has done nothing but spoil me and worship me. I would be foolish not to see this through to the end. It's so damn good to have someone take care of me for a change.

Sure, there have been times where he has seemed a little dark and hasn't been the best communicator, but since he swept me off my feet, this has all been a dream.

And it's not like I wasn't busy with someone else while we were apart.

The lengthening shadows highlight the sharp planes of his face as he repeats himself. "I asked why not? I won't ask again."

"I don't want to stir anything up. I already know you two don't like each other. Turns out, that other guy isn't at all who I thought he was and now I'm worried he is some type of conman and involved with my friend. I need to warn her."

Luke kneels in front of me, hands on my knees. With complete seriousness, he asks, "Shall I kill him?"

"What? No! Of course not." I hope he's joking. He has to be joking, right?

"That *chien* is not worthy of you. Do not even give him another thought. Tell me the name of your friend, and I'll call her myself."

It would actually be a huge relief to avoid this confrontation a little longer, but instead I say, "Luke, I can't ask you to do that."

"*Non*. Since you and Lilith have schemed to get us to go to the club tonight, you need to rest. Please, allow me to take care of you. It's the least I can do since you won't let me kill anyone."

He gives me his megawatt smile, and I'm relieved to know he is joking after all. I'd love to argue, but a jaw cracking yawn escapes me, sealing my fate. I nod as I cover my mouth with my hand. I'm exhausted. The excitement and champagne are nothing compared to the few hours of sleep I've had in the past two days.

"Wren is her name. Wren Field. She is in my contacts."

I give him the passcode to my phone and let him lead me up the curving stairs, trailing my hand along the wrought-iron railing, to a large and airy bedroom.

He walks over and opens the doors to a balcony where I can see the Eiffel Tower in the distance. As I stand there enjoying the view from the safety of the room rather than actually out on the balcony, he goes and turns down the covers for me.

"Come," he commands.

I walk over and allow him to undress me. He tucks me in, and I want to ask him to join me, but my eyes are blinking slower and slower.

Luke kisses my forehead and whispers something in a language older and darker than French that sends shivers down my spine. I want to ask what he said, but I'm already asleep.

Chapter 33

I stretch and blink my eyes. Through the still open balcony doors, I have a magical view of the glittering Eiffel Tower under the night sky. I swing my legs over the edge and watch for a few minutes. The sound of distant raised voices piques my curiosity. I stand, loathe to leave the exquisite comfort of the decadent bed.

Finding a robe laid over the end of the foot, I slip on the white satin and make my way to the door and back to the stairwell. I peek over the edge, unable to get much closer to the railing. With my fear of heights, the decorative wrought iron does nothing to make me feel any safer. Two matching red heads snap up to see me standing there.

Lilith flashes Luke a triumphant smile and races up the stairs to me, calling up, "I knew he would try to weasel his way out of this. Good thing I came to help you get ready and rescue you from his evil lair."

"Good thing," I laugh weakly.

I don't want to leave this evil lair. Like ever. But I'm swept along in the wake of the tornado that is Lilith.

She looks at me and then leans dangerously over the railing to yell back down at Luke, "Really? White?"

He volleys back something in French that has her pushing me back into my room and slamming the door.

"Fucker," she mutters under her breath.

Spinning to face me, she ushers me through a door into the most enormous and ornate bathroom I've ever seen. I drift over to the sink, letting my fingers glide over every toiletry and cosmetic I could ever wish for.

"This place is magnificent," I breathe in wonder.

Lilith snorts, "It looks like Liberace threw up in here. Hurry up, get in the shower so we can get ready."

As she goes over and starts picking through all my new goodies and unboxing them, I head over to the enormous shower. Once again, she clearly gives no shits about my modesty. I shrug out of the robe and step under a waterfall.

I wash my hair and am soaping up my body when she calls to me, "Don't forget to shave your naughty bits."

"Lilith!" I yell back, scandalized.

"Your call, sister, but we *are* going to the club."

I lather up as I wonder what going to the club has to do with shaving, but still take her seriously enough to take her hint. I would have shaved anyway, I tell myself, not wanting to admit she has any influence on me.

Finally, I rinse all the soap down the drain, along with part of my sanity, and step out to wrap up in heated luxury towels that make me want to cry. Would Luke notice if I took a few home? I'm sure if I even hinted I liked them, I'd find a shipment awaiting me back home. He is so generous.

I wrap one towel around my body and one around my hair, turban style. I walk over to the sink and use the toothbrush and paste that are there and then start slathering on an incredible moisturizer. I jump when Lilith speaks up behind me.

"Well, since you already ruined your curls, I guess I'm doing your hair."

I spin around to tell her that I know how to handle my curls, thank you very much, but the words die in my mouth when I see that she has primped herself while I showered. It is simply unfair that such a prickly personality is housed in a stunning exterior.

Her hair is twisted up into an elaborate updo, highlighting her long neck and perfect shoulders. Her lips, dress, and stilettos are all the exact matching shade of red. If I am going out next to her, maybe it wouldn't hurt to let her help me get ready after all. I want to be stunning for Luke.

I walk over and sit in the vanity chair in front of her, applying the new eye gel I had been eyeing up but wasn't willing to splurge on. Luke stocked this bathroom with everything I could have ever wanted, and I'm not even surprised. Of course, he has access to every abandoned cart I've ever filled on my phone.

Lilith pulls the towel from my hair and starts applying product, then grabs a fancy dryer and several brushes from a drawer. She expertly dries and styles my hair into stunning Hollywood waves. I've never been able to achieve this on my own, but have always loved it. The makeup I can handle.

I smile at her in our combined reflection and say with sincerity, "Thank you. It's beautiful."

She gives me a rare, genuine smile. Not a smirk or snarl, just a real smile. Once again, I can't help but think we really could be friends.

"I'm going to go sort through whatever nonsense Luke bought," she says, breaking the moment.

Shrugging, I finish my makeup to match my hair with a bold red lip and winged liner. I have no idea how Luke not only knew my favorite lipstick but tracked it down when it's been discontinued, but I'm so thankful he did. Nothing beats this shade.

I hang up the towel and put the robe back on. Lilith may be fine with seeing me naked, but I'm not quite there yet. I walk out to see outfits piled over the bed and chairs. My jaw drops.

"Did Luke buy the whole store?"

Lilith shrugs. "Probably. It's his store, anyway."

"What?" Why would Luke own a woman's boutique? How many businesses can he be involved in?

"Oh, look at this!" She ignores my question and instead thrusts a pile of clothes at me.

"What's up with the white? I never wear white."

I eye the clothes dubiously. White is a recipe for disaster when I'm likely to fall or drop food or spill wine on it. I'm not sophisticated enough for white. I feel like a marshmallow in white. I'd rather hide in black. Even the red Luke seems obsessed with for me is much preferable.

"He said white. He bought white. So, white it is."

I look down at the textiles—sheer, lacey, delicate. This looks more like lingerie than clothing. Looking back at Lilith, I see her advancing on me with a corset held out in front of her.

I hold up my hands and say, "Oh, no. Not again. What is this, a regency romance?"

Lilith laughs and says, "Ew. That was a horrible time."

"Regency romance is horrible?" I ask, confused by her statement.

"Sure," she says slowly, throwing me an odd look.

I walk over to the bed and drop the pile, digging through to come up with a sheer lacy thong. I slide that on underneath the robe and grab the corset from Lilith with a huff and shimmy my way into it. "How am I even supposed to dance in this thing? And who the hell wears underwear like this?"

Her childlike giggle has me whipping my head around. "What's so funny?"

"You think we are going dancing?" she asks between giggles.

"Well, yeah. You said we are going to Synd tonight," I reply.

"So we are, so we are," she purrs at me.

This. This is why I didn't want her to come over.

I huff, "What's that supposed to mean?"

She steps into my space and looks me in the eye. I am startled by her resemblance to Luke, made more apparent at this close range.

"I'm not your enemy," she says softly.

She looks serious, for once, not a trace of sarcasm or snark in sight. I feel bad for her. Somewhere, maybe deep, deep inside, I think she's hurting. And I can't help but want to gather her into my little found family. Like the proverbial redheaded stepchild.

"Are we friends, then?" I ask, wanting to understand her better.

A gorgeous smile lights up her face. She is always fiercely beautiful—like a diamond. All hard edges and glittering perfection. But right now, her face is transformed in a rare glimpse of genuine happiness.

"I've always wanted a girlfriend," she squeals with a little bounce.

If it weren't for her facial expressions and body posture, I would think she is being sarcastic. Instead, I know she is serious. I don't think she has ever had a friend. My armor toward her breaks a little, and I vow to try harder with this mysterious force of nature. I can't help but wonder, who the hell is Lilith?

"Let me do the laces before Luke gets up here or you won't be able to breathe all night. And I'm not ready for you to be dead quite yet," she says.

"Oh, good. I'm not quite ready to be dead yet either," I reply incredulously as I spin to give her access to the back.

"Look at that! We are already having the same thoughts. We really are besties."

Her absolute certainty has me smiling as she laces the corset with quick efficiency. I can't help but think I should have let Luke do it again. But then we'd never get out of here, and I want to go to the Paris branch of Synd.

I finish adjusting my breasts in the cups now that I'm laced, and by the time I turn around, Lilith is holding a dress out toward me. I allow her to slide it over my head and walk back into the ensuite to look in the mirror.

My mouth drops open at my reflection. I am so happy I let her help me get ready. The dress is stunning, not at all like a marshmallow. The bias-cut satin is draped perfectly to highlight my figure, and the thigh slit goes all the way up to my hip. The Hollywood curls shine and my white streak pops.

I smile at my reflection, thrilled to see the beautiful woman smile back at me. I'm ready to take on the world.

I see Luke entering the bathroom in the mirror. He meets my eyes in our combined reflection, and I watch them turn to liquid fire as he comes to stand behind me. He reaches out and sweeps my hair over my shoulder.

Leaning in, he whispers into my ear, "Lieshe. You are a vision."

Chills race down my spine at his dark voice. He drapes a jeweled necklace around my neck. I gasp and reach up, startled.

He does the clasp and then gently pulls my hair through, wrapping it around his fist. Every twist of his hand sends my heart fluttering. Seeing us both in the mirror, I can't help but think what a stunning couple we make and that I want more of his darkness.

I manage to whisper, "Luke, are these rubies?"

He frowns at me. "*Non, ce sont des diamants rouges.* Red diamonds for my red queen."

I spin to face him. Red diamonds? He can't be serious. I'm scared to even wear this necklace in the house, much less go out in it. He pulls a box from his pocket and adds a large matching cuff to my exposed ear.

"I can't wait to have that red lipstick smeared on my cock," he says as he kneels in front of me.

My knees go weak, and I reach out to grab his shoulders, steadying myself at the onslaught of the vision his words trigger.

He slides a box over and pulls out jewel encrusted white heels. Although I prefer Docs and Converse, every girl dreams of Cinderella shoes. As I step into them, it's just like a fairy tale. Finally, being swept off my feet by the perfect villain. I didn't want the prince, anyway.

"These are exquisite, but I don't know how I'm going to walk in them."

"But *ma Reine Rouge,* these are not for walking in."

I know what he is implying, but I want him to say it. I love his filthy words and the way they make my insides melt, so I can't help but say a little breathlessly, "What are they for, then?"

He slides his hands the whole way up the outside of my legs as he holds my heated gaze. Hooking his fingers in the flimsy lace of the thong, he pulls it down to my ankles.

His eyes darken as he says, "To fuck you in, of course."

I step out of the scrap of lace, mesmerized, as he brings it to his face and inhales. With a wicked smile and a wink, he folds them up and tucks them into the pocket of his black suit jacket.

"That dress is cut too high for panties. Besides, I needed a pocket square," he says as he stands up, like a thong is the perfect accessory, and he didn't just make me clench for him.

I have to admit, not only do I love knowing that his accessory is my panties, but the pop of white does complement his all-black outfit. It fits him like a second skin, highlighting his build. Luke Devlin is going to be the death of me. I just know it.

He tugs me by the hand out of the room and down the stairs where Lilith is standing by the door, tapping her foot. The shoes are surprisingly comfortable and easy to walk in. I guess they should be for whatever small fortune I suspect he spent on them. As we reach the bottom, she stills, taking us in.

"White it is," she says.

And on that cryptic note, the three of us walk out the door.

Chapter 34

LUKE

Although Lilith immediately bitches about her hair when she sees what car I picked for the evening, I know it was the right choice when Lieshe's face lights up. I wanted her to enjoy Paris while we drove to the club.

I wave off the driver and help the ladies into the vintage Rolls Royce convertible limo myself. I pull Lieshe under my arm, appreciating the way she fits at my side. She watches the city pass by with wide eyes, pointing out the things I've seen a thousand times before.

Seeing my favorite city through her eyes, hearing her excitement, makes me fall in love with it all over again. I can't remember the last time I've felt this way. There is a lightness and desire to watch her enjoy this life and all the things I can give her. I want to see her smile.

Am I happy? I've felt so little for so long; this is foreign and strange. I'm thankful we pull up at the club just in time to keep me from analyzing these—these *feelings*. I shake my head and hold my hand out to Lieshe, knowing if I don't watch her carefully, she will fall out of the car in the heels Chloe sent.

I snap my fingers, and the driver hands me a leather bag to bring in the club. Flanked by the two women in my life, we walk straight up to the doors. The bouncers immediately bow their heads and hold off the crowd waiting in line to let us in.

I toss them each a thousand-dollar chip from the casino. My employees are thoroughly vetted and fiercely loyal. I like to keep them that way.

As we walk through the sumptuous red and black lobby to the elevators, Lieshe reminds me of a small white owl, trying to turn her head around to see all of Synd, Paris at once.

We pass the main elevators, through a door with keycard access and another bouncer, and proceed to the back hallway where everything is black—black marble, black matte metal, even black ceilings.

Finding her tongue, she speaks, sensing this is a different part of the club. "So, uh, is this the way to the casino?"

"Are you a betting girl?" Lilith asks. She knows exactly where we are going, but it's her nature to tease.

"Your office?" Lieshe asks breathlessly.

We reach another set of elevators, and I tag the keycard again. Looking at Lieshe, I can't help but smile as I shake my head no. She is so thirsty for my darkness; I'm going to let her choke on it.

As the three of us enter the elevator and hit the only button, with a nervous little laugh she says, "Dance club?"

I elbow Lilith none too gently as she snorts. The elevators stop, and Lilith says, "You're out of guesses."

Lieshe's sharp intake of breath as the doors open to reveal the *other* club Synd holds already has my dick hardening. This is going to be delicious. I tug her forward as she hesitates for just a moment. But curiosity has got the best of this little cat, and she follows me as Lilith wanders off to find her own victim—I mean, amusement—for the evening.

We walk through the crowd milling around the cocktail

tables and the bar. I pull out a stool for her, nodding at the bartender as he immediately comes over. Glad everyone still knows who is in charge here.

"*Deux nouveaux bourbons avec deux glaçons chacun.*" I order and then settle in to watch Lieshe's face as she observes the club activities.

She faces me when our drinks arrive, wide-eyed after taking in the surrounding activities. I can't help but chuckle at the sight of her drinking it all in, curiosity stamped all over her face.

"You are the first to try the new bourbon," I say as I hand her a glass with two rocks in it, just the way I know she likes it.

She picks up the rocks glass, swirls it, then takes a delicate sniff and sips. The movements of her lips and throat as she swallows have me riveted. Her inadvertent sensuality only adds to her beauty and appeal. There is something so damn sexy about a woman who knows how to enjoy bourbon.

I reach out and wipe away a drop on her lip with my thumb, sliding my hand down to collar her throat. "Well?"

"It's softer and sweeter than Brimstone." She scrunches her nose and takes another sip. "Is that a floral note? Rose?"

I smile at her in delight. "*Très bien, ma chérie.* Very good indeed. Do you like it?"

"I love it. It's perfect. Like it's custom made for my palette."

She beams at me as she takes another sip.

"It is. I made it for you."

She opens her mouth to speak, but is cut off by two of the bouncers approaching. I whip my head around to face them, irritated at their intrusion. They stand there, stone faced, waiting for my response until I nod, and they step to the side.

If it is so bad they won't say it in the club, I have no choice but to go with them.

I give her throat a slight squeeze to emphasize my next words. "Don't fucking move. When I get back, I expect you to be sitting in this exact spot. If a man is next to you, I'll kill him. Understand?"

Her eyes widen at my words, but she gives me a short, jerky nod even as her pupils dilate. I give her a dark smile, thrilled that she loves this side of me. I hate to leave her here, but I don't have much choice right now.

I follow the two enormous men to the back hallway and into a security room filled with screens. This is one of many control rooms where everything that happens in the club is monitored. One of the techs points a screen out. All employees had been briefed to monitor for the stray dog and here he is, unable to leave this bone alone.

"Excellent job. Keep four men on him at all times. Lock down this floor. People can exit, but no one else enters. Understand?"

I slide a poker chip to each of them. Money keeps them loyal, but the promise of violence without reprisal keeps them feral. They all know the risks that come with being part of Synd, and they're more than eager to reap the rewards. Most of them are ex-military or former mercenaries, still addicted to the thrill of danger.

I turn to leave, more than ready to get back to my evening, when a camera angle of the very spot I just left catches my eye. Lilith has rejoined Lieshe, leaning in over the back of the next barstool. Their heads are bent together, and I think I better get back there before Lilith causes trouble when a man sidles up to her.

She ignores him and keeps talking to Lieshe. His face becomes annoyed at the unrequited attention. He reaches out and grabs her shoulder, spinning her to face him. The men behind me posture and make to leave the room when I hold up a hand to stop them. Someone else is coming to Lilith's defense.

Lieshe stands so abruptly her barstool tips over. In one smooth move, she throws an arm out, pushing Lilith behind her and gets right up in the man's face, shaking her clenched fist at him. I chuckle as whatever she says to him has him backing off, hands up in surrender.

She turns and embraces Lilith, patting her back reassuringly. I can't help but laugh out loud. Lieshe has no idea she just defended one of the most dangerous creatures to ever exist. I don't know which is more surprising, though —Lieshe's rushing to Lilith's defense or Lilith returning her hug and genuinely smiling at Lieshe.

I really should get back out there. This could be more treacherous than I know. I look at the two men taking up most of the space in the security room with me, smiling wickedly as one pops the knuckles of his ham-sized fists, and the other cracks his neck with an audible pop.

"Enjoy," I tell them as I head back to the bar. That guy has no idea the world of pain he is in for. I have to throw a little bait in for the sharks now and then—keeps them hungry.

I walk back and shoot Lilith an appraising look. In response, she gives me her usual sarcastic smirk and stalks off. The altercation has Lieshe's heart pumping, still riding a little adrenaline surge from protecting another woman.

She is amazing. For all her fears and insecurities, she really is brave when challenged. My perfect queen. I love seeing her in this bridal white. I am going to keep her in it until she takes her rightful place and we flood the world in red.

I step in between her legs and place my hand back on her throat. Her pulse jackhammers under my hand, teasing me with its frantic beat. I let her anger at the man who wouldn't back down bleed into me, licking my lips at the taste.

I say, "Back to that bourbon. What do you think of your own reserve?"

She cocks her head at me and drops her voice into a sexy, sultry tone. "It could use a little cinnamon."

I pull her in by her throat for a kiss, letting her savor the cinnamon she craves.Deepening the kiss, I plunge my tongue into her mouth, claiming her. I swallow her moan as my patience grows thin. Breaking away, I keep my eyes focused on hers as I knock back my bourbon in one gulp.

Lust hangs heavy in the air; the club fills with desire. It swirls, dark and decadent over my skin, through my mind—pulses within me like another heartbeat. I close my eyes for just a moment, a break from the role forced upon me, one I usually relish.

But when I open my eyes again, before me lies my path to salvation, a vision in white. Her amber eyes flash with concern for me, and I again feel her emotions bubbling to the surface. She is falling for me, hard and fast, like the way I want to take her. My need for her is growing insatiable.

"Fuck it," I murmur. I never have been one to deny myself.

Seeing my dark shift, she also tosses back her bourbon and scrambles off the bar stool. I grab her hand and tug her through the club. I had planned to seduce her with a slow introduction, but I can't restrain myself any longer. I'm not willing to risk any more interruptions; I need her now.

I want to debase her and torture her. I've got to sate this desperate fucking need for her. It's driving me mad. This was not the plan. I was purely going to use her to win.

But now? I'm going to enjoy the fuck out of her fall. She's going to land on my lap as I sit on my throne, and together, we will watch this fucking world burn as she rules by my side.

But tonight, I'm going to rule her. And she's going to love me for it.

Chapter 35

LIESHE

This is most definitely not a dance club. Unless it's the horizontal mambo. Although as I look around, horizontal is only about one out of a hundred ways people are getting busy. I giggle at my own joke, chugging that bourbon on the heels of defending Lilith has made me just a little silly.

I can't stand a man who can't take no for an answer. I didn't even think about it; I just threw her behind me.

I'm dying to know what is going on in all these different rooms. I even catch a quick glimpse of a stage, but Luke is intently pulling me to some mysterious destination. The pounding bass of the soundtrack almost drowns out the moans and cries around me. Almost, but not quite.

The thoughts of being surrounded by people chasing their pleasure turns me on. I've had a few tastes of Luke's dark dominance. Tonight, I hope he brings it with full force. I'm more than ready.

After making our way down several twisting hallways, we finally come to a door that he opens with his keycard. He spins around, searching my face. I'm not sure if he is looking for hesitation or giving me a last chance out, but curiosity drives me forward. Pushing past him, I'm brought up short at the room before me.

A fair number of things I recognize—the bed, of course, what looks like a spanking bench, and a good old-fashioned pillory. Some things I have no idea what they are. Why is there a box with a hole in it? I walk slowly through the room, trying to take everything in. Chains and restraints and cuffs of all sorts on the walls and even the ceiling.

Over in the corner, I spot something I've always wanted to try. Feeling bold, I go over to it and run my fingers over the solid X in front of me. The wave of heat that is Luke at my back has me shivering in response. He pushes my straps off my shoulders and the dress falls to the floor.

"Good choice," he says, his words heavy in the air.

I turn to face him and look up into his smoldering eyes. Reaching out, I place my hands on his chest, sliding them down as I drop to my knees and keeping my eyes locked on his.

I'm hoping for a taste of him, but he turns and walks to a large gothic black chair against one wall, almost throne-like in appearance.

He unbuttons his jacket and tosses it over the arm. As he opens his black dress shirt, he says, "Crawl to me."

I step out of the white satin pooled at my feet and fall to my knees, crawling across the floor to him. Every inch closer to him makes me feel sexy, confident. I want this. I want him.

I kneel in front of him as he pulls the shirt off, tossing it on top of the jacket. His muscles ripple and flex with the movement, the low lights highlighting his chiseled abs and that damn deep V I want to bite.

He sits and reaches out a hand, raising me to standing. He pulls me forward between his legs and leans in to nuzzle my breasts, spilling over the front of the corset. Hands on my hips, he spins me around. I think he is going to undo my laces, but instead, he pulls them tighter.

I can't decide if it's the anticipation making me breathless or if it really is that tight, but my heart pounds as I feel the corset constricting me.

"You seemed to like this in the dressing room. I'm going to push you tonight, *mon amoureuse*. Find your freedom in knowing that I will keep you safe. I know where to pull back and where to bring you to the darkest heights. Your surrender *is* your power. It will be intoxicating."

His words are punctuated with pulls on the laces until I am all but panting.

"Safe word," I get out.

He chuckles darkly. "Safe word? Someone has been reading naughty things late at night. Very well."

He spins me to face him, tracing a finger over the audacious swell of my breasts with the corset this tight. He stills with his finger over my heart and whispers a word that raises the hair on the back of my neck.

Dark.

Powerful.

Ancient.

"Say it back to me," he whispers in a dark voice tinged with hope.

I hesitate. I can sense this word has deep meaning, mysticism dripping from the syllables. His eyes pulse, hypnotizing. He is waiting, holding his breath for me to say it.

I wait a heartbeat, then two, and I repeat the word back. It feels heavy and foreign in my mouth.

Luke's eyes darken a split second before he crashes his mouth to mine, pulling my body into his heat. I can't tell where I end and he begins. Endless darkness infused with his cinnamon fire engulfs me as he kisses me. Stars swim in my vision as my oxygen plummets.

I'm desperate to pull back and take a deep breath, but all I can do is drown in Luke, meet every lash of his tongue with mine, teeth clacking in our passion. Just as the world starts to spin, he breaks the kiss and steadies me by the shoulders. Sweet air fills my lungs as I pant, and the world comes back into focus.

"Go stand at the Saint Andrew's cross," he commands.

I make my way over, shivering as I cross the room without his heat in nothing but heels, a corset, and dripping in red diamonds. I reach my destination without falling by some miracle and stand as instructed. Behind me, Luke unzips the leather bag he had brought with him.

The anticipation and mystery of what he is doing only increases my desire. I have always wanted to do something like this. And here I am. In Paris. With Luke. Doing *things*. Dark, naughty, sinful, liberating *things*.

"Don't move," he commands.

I hold my breath, not wanting to move even the tiniest muscle. I feel a tiny sting at the top of my corset and then a pop. As this process repeats, I realize he is cutting the laces. I freeze, fear and desire swirling deliciously low in my belly.

"Breathe," he whispers.

I take a cautious breath, then another. The corset falls to the floor, and I take a deep breath at last, filling my lungs. He traces the blade down my spine, barely a whisper. The faint contact and building anticipation has me moaning his name.

"Luke."

He steps into me, his naked chest searing against my back. He reaches around, collaring my throat. Squeezing over my pulse points, he tsks, "Oh, no, no, no. Who am I?"

"My Lord," I breathe out.

He hums deep in his throat and trails his hand down, agonizingly slowly. I can't help but lean back into him, needing more contact. More Luke.

Finally, his hand reaches down to cup my pussy. As he finds me drenched, he growls out, "*Putain*."

My knees go weak as he thrusts two fingers into me. If he hadn't wrapped an arm around my waist, I would have fallen. He abruptly withdraws and thrusts his sopping fingers into my mouth. I swirl my tongue around them, sucking, overwhelmed by the sexually charged air of the room.

He pulls them out with a pop to run his hands down my arms to my wrists, bringing them up along the beams of the large X in front of me. As he secures me into the leather cuffs, I worry he can hear my heart pounding out of my chest. He clearly has done this before. I hate to seem inexperienced or unsophisticated.

As if he can read my thoughts, he whispers in my ear, "You worship at my altar. Just as I alone will be your undoing, I, too, will be your only salvation."

He moves down to secure each ankle. I have never been so incredibly exposed and vulnerable, yet paradoxically empowered. I practice the strange safe word Luke had given me in my mind and a deep power unfurls within me.

I tug at the bonds and find myself immobile. Do I trust him to offer this power over me? Do I trust anyone? I can't help but think of McVladam. I trusted him, trusted what I thought I felt. Maybe I am the one who can't be trusted.

A new sensation breaks me out of my spiraling thoughts. The scent of leather fills my nose as something soft and heavy drapes over my shoulders and caresses me. I glance down to see long strips of black leather trailing over my skin.

The same sensation has me turning my head to my other shoulder to find another one. A thrill runs through me at the thought of my first foray into the kink world, including not one, but two floggers. He trails them over my body, the leather soft and sensual.

I drop my head against the beam, ready for whatever

comes next. I'm just about to open my mouth to ask when I hear the floggers whistling through the air. Although I'm braced for a stinging slap, instead I'm met with a delicious, firm thudding sensation that brings every nerve in its path alive.

The blows rain down in succession, creating a path up and down my back, ass, and thighs. My skin is electric, like it has been sleeping this entire time and this, *this*, is what it needed to be awake.

I wish I could see Luke, his face, the figure he cuts as he swings them with expert precision. I remember how he looked on stage at the Cirque Maléfique with the fire whip and imagine he must look the same now.

Dark, controlled chaos.

Time stretches into infinity, and everything except my newly awakened skin falls away. I lose myself to the sensations that blossom and grow within me. When the flogging stops, I let out a desperate whimper. "More."

He responds with a dark chuckle. "Oh, *mon petit*, that was just the warm up."

I'm trying to wrap my head around what could be the main event if that is the warm up when he resumes the flogging. This time, he strikes harder over my ass and thighs, allowing the tips to wrap just enough to tease the edge of my breasts or just inside my thighs to graze my dripping core.

I gasp at his precision as every few stroke laps at a different erogenous spot. Luke pushes himself faster and me further, triggering a rush of pleasure deep in my belly, the building orgasm surprising me.

The pleasure rides a razor-thin edge of pain, and my mind is blissfully blank and floating. The sensations and sounds fade away, with only the building orgasm remaining.

I can see it in my mind's eye, like a spark igniting tinder, growing into a great, roaring, all-consuming fire. I'm writhing, panting, trying to both escape this exquisite torture and simultaneously move closer. I become frantic, desperate for release.

I hear Luke's dark and filthy whisperings, the words a litany of praise and encouragement until he yells, "Now! Come for me now, *ma Reine Rouge!*"

With one last blow to my pussy, I shatter into a million pieces, sagging against the bonds and the beams, unable to even bear my own weight. Within seconds, I am gathered into his arms and brought to the massive bed where he holds me as I drift off into weightless oblivion.

Chapter 36

LUKE

I lean back against the headboard, holding her gathered on my lap as she sleeps, exhausted. Florentine flogging has always been my favorite. The precision, the timing, and the movement are almost trancelike. Second only to my love of my fire whips, but she is far from ready for that. Soon, though.

I let myself drift into her mind again, and before I can think it through, I find I'm tracing my proverbial steps back to that damn spot again. This time the neurons are angrier, sicker. I nudge them, imagine smoothing them down.

That golden glow returns again as I whisper the ancient words. This time, I don't pull back. My first language, beautiful and golden, music like I've never heard before or since, surrounds the dying spot.

I watch in rapt fascination as the beautiful light travels down the dying nerve tract like a synaptic firing, leaving smooth, healthy tissue in its wake.

Down to the muscle the nerve innervates, the very tips which had been withered once again become healthy and smooth in their home. The muscle fibers around them swell back to their original size.

I hold my breath like a human, the habit of breathing to blend in over the years dropping away as I try not to move a single muscle. I wait a breath, then two, then three. I wait a hundred and still all the cells remain healthy.

I dive deeper into them, watching the mitochondria

churn out their fuel for the cells. Every tiny organelle within each cell functions with perfect precision. I drop my focus down further, to the very protein level and the aggregates clear from the cytoplasm, the copper and zinc normalizing as the proteins resume folding normally.

Knowing what I have done is a temporary stopgap, I filter down to her basic building blocks, her very DNA. Can I alter her at this level? Fixing that one neuron tract was like plugging a hole in the dam with my finger. Not only can I, but for the first time in my very damned existence, I ponder, should I?

With my usual disregard for the rules, I throw caution to the wind, mutter, "Fuck it," and snip the faulty DNA, replacing it with the correct code. Two letters are all it takes to kill her. GCG swapped for GTG, and she dies her mother's death.

Not today. Her blinding trust, her pure soul, has pushed me to do something so foreign, so fundamentally not like me, I can't even comprehend my decision. Doing something right, something driven from altruism, from caring for her, has me rubbing my chest at the odd sensation.

Unable to think about the gravity of what I have just done, and what butterfly effect the world may have just suffered, I turn back to what I know. I'll wake her back up with my dark depravity. I'll finish my task of ruining her only to be her salvation.

I slip back into this version of myself that I know, the one I have worn for millennia. It fits me like, I chuckle, well, like my own skin.

I ease her off of me and slowly secure her wrists to the restraints at the head of the bed. A soft murmur has me pausing, stilling my movements, until she is pulled back under. Easing her legs apart, I attach a spreader bar between her ankles and to a chain from the ceiling. I stand at the foot of the bed, surveying my handiwork.

I grab the bottle of lube I so thoughtfully brought with me and head back to study her. My eyes travel up her legs and soft belly to the curve of her breasts. She may not believe it, but she really is the female archetype. Round where we men are flat, yielding where we are hard. I will relish sinking into her heat again. And again. And again. It's going to be a deliciously long night.

I pull the chain, the first click of the ratchet lock loud in the quietness of the room. She scrunches her eyes as she is pulled from sleep. The second click has her eyes fluttering open, and the third has them wide and searching.

She visibly relaxes when she finds me as the cause of the sudden sound. Foolish girl, I'm the most dangerous thing there is. As I hoist her legs into the air and reveal her gleaming sex, I'm thankful she has no self-preservation instincts. If she did, she never would have stepped on stage with me so long ago, came back to the party, came with me from London, or even entered this room.

I shed my pants and knee my way onto the mattress and reach out, tracing along her pussy with my finger. Deliberate with my slow, feather light touches. I stare into her blazing amber eyes, the splash of my own yellow green pulling a satisfied grin from me.

I watch her try to move, wanting me to fill her. She pulls at the bonds, wiggling her sweet ass. She is a vision.

She may not have been made from me, but I have left my permanent mark on her. I have molded her. And now I am going to shatter her and rebuild her in *my* image. She entered this room in bridal white, but she will soon leave the plane of this world in red. She will be *ma Reine Rouge*, a worthy mate to rule by my side.

With that happy thought, I plunge my fingers into her warm, wet heat, eliciting a feral cry. I gather her wetness on my fingers and begin moving it to her ass. The spreader bar has her legs beautifully suspended, all of her so easily accessible .

Gravity helps me to move her wetness and ease my entry into her tight back hole. She holds her breath and clenches.

"Relax. Lean into the sensation. Don't let your mind control you. Allow sensation to lead your body," I encourage her.

As her tight opening slowly relaxes, I begin to work one finger in. My cock throbs in response. I use my other hand to draw circles around her clit until she draws my finger in.

"Look at you, taking my fingers in your ass like a greedy girl."

I work two fingers into her pussy and thrust both hands in and out in tandem. Her breathing picks up, and she becomes even wetter. She loves my filthy words. When it comes to her, I have no shortage of them.

I add a second finger to her ass, drawing a deep moan from her. "That's my good girl. You're taking me so well."

Removing my hand from her sopping pussy, I drizzle lube all over her mound, letting it drip down and over my fingers as they pump in and out of her ass.

"You are a beautiful, sopping mess."

She whimpers as I add a third finger, swirling the lube around and pushing it inside of her. I plunge my other hand back into her clenching cunt.

"So full," she moans, tossing her head.

"Oh darling, this is nothing," I warn her darkly. I feel her orgasm building and know this is the perfect time to take her.

Tonight, I am going to claim her in every way I can. I

withdraw both hands to grab her hips and pull her sweet, tight ass onto the head of my dick.

"Luke!" she screams.

I smack her pussy, hard.

"My Lord," she corrects herself.

"Yes," I hiss as I ease my cock past the tight ring of muscle.

I worked her up as much as I could, but I want her to ride the edge of pleasure and pain as I take her. Reaching up, I again circle her clit while I feed my erection into her tight channel, inch by glorious inch.

Tearing my eyes away from the sight of my disappearing cock, I stare into her eyes. I want to watch her face.

"*Mon amour*," I say as I punch my hips forward and impale her on my cock.

Her answering cry has my balls drawing up tight. I plunge my fingers into her dripping pussy and hook them forward, hitting her G spot and strumming my thumb over her clit.

Her cries quickly turn to throaty moans. I pound into her fiercely, skin slapping, both of us grunting. I try to hold back, but she is so tight with my fingers and cock both filling her up. Rhythmic clenching greets me, and I know we're close.

Her eyes roll back as she arches her body, her head falling back, thrusting her breasts out. She's a fucking vision. I need her to see me as I wreck her.

"Eyes on me," I manage to grit out.

She opens her amber eyes, and the yellow green spot pulses brightly. Her ass and pussy clamp down so hard I still my hand, it's all I can do to keep thrusting with my hips. I love the feel of her strangling my cock. I bottom out, cock pulsing, and explode, filling her ass with jets of my hot cum.

In response, she screams her release, shaking and

quivering. I can't help but let out a dark laugh. I haven't had this much fun in Paris since the 1920s, when I was hanging out with those two crazy cats, Picasso and Dali.

Fuck, I love this girl.

I freeze at the thought. I am incapable of love. I shut down all emotion, safely retreating while I pay attention to her bodily needs. I ease my way out of her body as she hisses at my withdrawal. I lower her legs and unclip the bar. Releasing her wrists, I gradually bring her arms down, rubbing her shoulders as I do.

I roll her over and lie next to her, kneading the muscles along her neck and back, massaging down her arms and hands to increase the circulation. I glance around the room, thinking of what I can show her next.

I could stay here for days, but I imagine at some point she will need to do human stuff. Frowning, I realize I don't want to share my toy. I want to be holed up in this room for a few hundred years, peeling her apart layer by layer. I'll find all the ways to make her cum, make her scream.

I want to explore just how close she likes her pleasure and her pain. I want her to use the safe word I had given her; the only word I know would reach me if I utterly lost control.

A disturbance pulls me from my thoughts. That mutt thinks he can get to her here, save her. It's too bad he doesn't realize she doesn't want to be saved, much less by him. I push my focus outside of the deep underground where I currently am and find two others with him.

I chuckle softly. They almost hid themselves, but not quite good enough. Those two wing flappers think they can fool me? This place is a veritable fortress to humans and has enough of my powerful darkness to be impenetrable to almost everyone else.

I let my laughter drift up and outside the walls so they

can hear me. My dark words whisper on the wind to their ears, "Fuck all the way off."

Victory is so close I can just about touch it. I'm going to get her home sooner rather than later. My little traitor has been helpful, but I trust no one except Lilith, and even she has a short leash.

Time to twist the knife.

"Lieshe," I croon, waking her up with hands and trailing kisses.

She snuggles into me, letting out a sleepy, "My Lord."

I amplify her words and send them up to his ears. My cock is already hard, but as I hear his scream of anguish at her voice, I swell impossibly harder. This lifetime of hers has been the most fun yet. Not only have I enjoyed his suffering, but she is such a delicious little morsel.

Yes, it's time to move her where I can enjoy her free from interference from them all—the damned dog and those flappy winged fucks. For just a second, I worry about her crossing over. It's never been done.

I think this will call for a sacrifice. And I know just the right lamb for the job. It will be the perfect traitor's death.

I push my power out into the stars, the rotation of the earth, and search out the dark matter. I mentally map the upcoming swings in energy, lining up black holes and dying stars to map where the veil will be the thinnest.

I'm in luck. Tomorrow night at midnight it is. And I think I know just how to shift us. Just as I know how to fill the hours between now and then.

Chapter 37

LIESHE

I stretch in the softest sheets I've ever slept in and wince. I am sore just about everywhere. Muscles I didn't even know of protest my every movement. Last night, and well, I guess this morning, too, was all of my wildest fantasies come true, including ones I didn't know I had.

Even better than that was seeing another side of Luke. Not the hot, sexy, dark, and domineering one I always knew was there, but the sweet and kind one.

I saw one that made me drink water between rounds of mind-blowing sex, fed me a burger and fries after drilling the kitchen staff about gluten cross-contamination, and then brought me back to this beautiful home and tenderly bathed me in his swimming pool-sized tub.

The sun was already above the horizon as he tucked me into bed, and I slept like the dead. I have no idea what time it is now, but I'm sure it's past noon. The few short hours of sleep were refreshing. In fact, I don't remember ever feeling this good. I feel stronger, healthier. It must be the French air.

My heart swells, wanting to search out Luke. Am I in love? Is that why I feel this way? I sit on the edge of the bed, gazing out toward the Eiffel Tower and sort through my feelings. I had really thought I was falling for McVladam. He had seemed so familiar, like a missing piece of my very soul.

I thought he felt the same way. The way he looked at me, the way my heart reached for his. The familiarity that made connected past lives seem almost believable. My feelings had been real. I am sure of it. Almost as sure as I am that his were, too.

But the photo Wren sent is irrefutable proof that none of it had been true. I pick at the sore spot in my heart like an old scab. I know I should leave it alone, but I just can't stop myself. Something is wrong. The pieces don't quite fit. This last one is like someone took it from another box and forced it into place just to complete the puzzle.

It almost fits, but if I look close enough, the edges are just a tad off. The colors are slightly different from where they should be. What can it be? I think, like trying to recall a dream that is floating just outside of my conscious thought.

My stomach lets out a loud growl, pulling me from my musings. The late-night burger and fries must have been hours ago. I get up and put the beautiful white silk robe back on and head downstairs in search of food and Luke.

He is the one I should be falling for. He is the one you *are* falling for, I tell myself. Luke is dark and mysterious, yet catering to my every whim and desire—a man of means, of commitment. He is a man of sanity and not delusion. Last night, while he explored my darkest desires, he also built a solid foundation of trust. And right now, that seems pretty damn important.

I pad downstairs on my bare feet and make my way out to the courtyard, following the sound of Luke's voice. He stands as I enter and flashes me a smile as brilliant as the sun. Holding a hand out to me as I walk across to him, he murmurs, "Sleeping beauty."

He takes my hand as if to kiss it and then flips it over at the last second, flicking his tongue over my pulse. It is the same move he did back in Philly which reminds me of home, Grimm, and the whole reason I am in Europe to begin with.

"Good morning," I say.

He laughs and says, "You mean, *bon après-midi*. The morning is long past."

I cast an eye to the sky and notice he is right. The sun has that beautiful late afternoon glow. "Luke! You should have woken me up."

"Why?" he asks with a laugh.

"Oh, good question. Um, I don't actually know."

"Sloth is one of my favorite sins. Come, sit and enjoy the afternoon with me."

He leads me to one of the bistro chairs, and the same man from yesterday appears with an overflowing charcuterie tray, some of the gluten-free pastries, and a pitcher of mimosas.

I look at Luke and say, "Is gluttony your other favorite? This is way too much food for two people."

He winks and says, "No. Greed. I can't wait to devour you again. I can't decide who is greedier—your pussy or my cock."

I choke on the mimosa I was sipping, caught off guard by his filthy words. "Luke!"

I am scandalized by his brunch—or is this dinner—conversation, but also can't deny either what he says or the effect his words have on me. He just smiles his Cheshire smile at me, eyes feline in the light.

I'm startled from my coughing as the man now appears with a tray he holds out to me. I catch a whiff of a familiar scent—toasted marshmallow and coconut. I pick up the large ceramic cup and saucer and turn to Luke.

"Is this my coffee?"

His smile gets bigger as he shrugs one shoulder. I take a tentative sip and moan. It's as perfect as if Natalie had made it at the shop back home.

"Thank you. I was really missing this."

He reaches out a finger and swipes a dot of foam from the tip of my nose, brings it to my mouth, and I delicately swipe it off with my tongue. His eyes heat and drop to my lips.

"Show me again what that mouth can do."

"My Lord," I say, laughing, "please, can I eat first?"

He adjusts himself and rolls his eyes good-naturedly. "Of course."

"Also, this coffee reminds me of home and of why I am here in the first place. I was, uh, distracted last night. Are my things here and my phone? I need to check in with Mindy before she calls the embassy looking for me. Oh, and I should call Anna and Jo and check in on Grimm, too."

Luke chuckles. "I'll get your phone since your adoring fans await. We don't want the embassy on our doorstep."

I smile at his easy humor. This feels good, comfortable and easy. I like being with Luke. I like it a lot.

"Oh, and did you call Wren?"

I know it's the coward's way out. So, call me a coward.

He says, "I actually texted her from your phone. I hope you don't mind, but I didn't want her to worry that a strange man was calling her. I messaged that you found another place you just couldn't miss and needed another day or two before meeting up. I just couldn't stand the thought of waking you, but knew you wouldn't want her to worry."

"Oh, Luke, that was perfect. I really appreciate it. What did she say?" I ask.

"She said she understood and to take your time, as she was quite happy to be with the new man she met a little longer," he says.

"Oh." The punch to the gut I feel must be my concern over Wren falling for this con man. That's all. It couldn't be this is the final nail in the coffin of my stupid naïveté about him—my belief in a supernatural being chasing me—his soulmate—through time.

I thought I was part of something magical, part of the longest love story ever told. Instead, I was a part of the longest con in existence; a man taking advantage of a woman looking for love.

How could I be so stupid? Tears prick my eyes and my face flames in embarrassment. I am sitting here with an amazing man who is catering to me, worshiping me, and I'm crying over a con man who broke my heart and tried to take advantage of me first, and now my friend.

Luke is beside me in an instant, tipping my chin up to look at him. "It's you and I against the world. Fear, jealousy, and pain have no place with us. You and I are the only things that matter. The rest of the world can burn."

I drop my eyes and bite my lip. He tips my chin further up, so I am forced to meet the fire in his eyes.

"Who are you?" he asks softly.

I take a deep breath and think back to the absolute confidence I had when he asked me this on the plane.

"The red queen," I say, a tremor to my voice.

"Who are you?" he asks again, more firmly this time.

"The red queen." I say more confidently.

"Who are you?" he all but shouts, his voice full of sinful, dark promise.

"*Je suis la Reine Rouge.*" My voice is confident, sure, strong.

Luke sweeps me into his arms and claims my mouth in a brutal kiss until I'm breathless. Starving for him or oxygen, I'm not even sure. He eclipses the world, and I am burning for him. This. This is where I belong.

"Tonight, we celebrate." He whispers across my lips as he releases me from his kiss.

"Celebrate?"

"Yes, *ma Reine Rouge.* Celebrate us."

Chapter 38

LIESHE

I am primped and styled within an inch of my life, having received the celebrity treatment of in-house hair, makeup, and nails performed by a small army. I feel like a princess, and I'm not going to lie—I could get used to this life. I never aspired to riches or luxury. It's a far cry from the small town and boring beige life I lived growing up.

If this technicolor world is like Dorothy landing in Oz, then Luke must be the great and powerful wizard. I still wonder what I will find when I peek behind the curtain. The man himself enters and gives a low whistle. I turn from the mirror to look at him.

His signature head to toe black suit has been replaced by a white tailcoat. The white emphasizes his build and sets his unique coloring to glowing. His hair is pulled back and topped with an elegant top hat. The formal combination suits him, giving him a timeless elegance. He is a chameleon, equally at ease in leather pants or formal wear.

Eyes smoldering at me, he comes to take my hand, turning me in a circle as he says, "Lieshe, there are no words to describe your beauty. They would all pale next to your radiant splendor."

My cheeks turn pink. His face is so serious, so full of absolute adoration, that I feel all the more beautiful at the reflection in his eyes. I hope that I can make him proud to have me on his arm tonight—wherever we are going.

He helps me put on the red diamond necklace again, but

this time, hands me a set of earrings to match. Then he faces me back to the mirror to take in our combined reflection. I'm speechless. Together, we appear elegant. Regal, even.

I hadn't been too sure about the white gown he had selected for me. It seemed almost bridal with the thick satin material and small train. But it was the most beautiful dress I had ever put on and fit as if made for me. Which it was.

With a mischievous smile, he cocks his head at me in the mirror and says, "Something is missing."

I study my reflection for what the team of stylists could have missed, but nothing is awry. His smile widens as he removes his top hat and, like a magician, pulls a large box from the inside.

I can't help but laugh at his antics. I take the proffered box and pull the ribbon on the top. The box falls open to reveal an honest to goodness tiara.

"Luke," I gasp, hands flying to cover my mouth in disbelief.

The tiara sparkles and shines under the lights—a perfect match to the necklace and earrings. Looking closer, the red diamonds are set into beautifully morbid skulls. This is exactly what I would have chosen.

He smiles like the sun as he removes the tiara from the box and nestles it into my beautiful updo, deftly securing it.

"Luke, I feel like a princess," I whisper as I touch the tiara.

He kneels at my feet and bows his head over my hand. Looking back up into my eyes, he declares, "Not a princess. A queen."

Emotion clogs my throat. He really does worship me. I feel beautiful and powerful, knowing I can be the woman he sees in me. Fueled by the adoration in his eyes, I step into my role, into my power. I let my eyes close and give him a regal nod.

Opening them again, I take in his severe beauty and can't help but imagine my life by his side. Luke may be wild and unpredictable, but I have no doubt that his love would be steadfast, committed, and true.

After the rollercoaster of McVladam—the whiplash of hot and cold—Luke's fire only burns brighter, a constant flame that refuses to waver. Once again, I want to burn with him and drown in his red.

Rising to his feet, he tucks my hand into his elbow and escorts me downstairs where his butler greets us with accessories. He dons black gloves and picks up a cane resting next to the front door. He hands me a pair of above the elbow white gloves and helps me to pull them carefully up my arms.

We stand at the door, taking each other in. Tonight feels important, life changing. Butterflies fill my stomach as I wonder what will happen and ask myself what it is I am hoping for. Or is it what I'm worried about? I can't quite decide if I'm just happy-nervous, or if the thrill running through me is fear.

Luke gifts me a warm smile, and with a playful glint in his eye, throws open the front door. I look out to where a horse and carriage wait for us. Every experience with him is so over the top, so of course, this is our transportation for tonight.

He helps me up into the carriage, and I try to smooth down my dress and arrange the small train to prevent wrinkles for wherever our destination might be. He sits beside me, and we take off through the streets of Paris.

Luke is so pleased with himself. The setting sun covers

everything in the special light particular to the golden hour. He's never been more handsome; I could even say beautiful.

He twirls the cane, and I drop my eye to see the top is a stylized raven with red stone eyes. It reminds me of Wren and the Raven I had planned to go to London for but never got to.

I tell myself to stop, just enjoy tonight. I push away thoughts of anything else and focus on the romance of the evening. I need to stop sabotaging my happiness. There is nothing to fear.

As the carriage carries us along, I take mental snapshots of the beauty of Paris at sunset. I want to keep this memory with me always. We pull up at the Louvre and I'm beside myself.

"Luke! This is on my bucket list. I hope we have enough time before they close to see everything."

Luke chuckles.

"What?" I ask.

"That would take years. We can come whenever you like, but for tonight, we have a private tour of some of the highlights," he says.

I DON'T THINK my mouth has closed since we arrived. I am in awe of the beauty that surrounds us. The capacity of humans to create art like this simply astounds me. We are at the final piece Luke wished to show me, *Checkmate*.

"I don't get it. Why is there an angel watching two guys play chess?"

He stands behind me, wrapping his arms around me and

bringing his lips to my ear. "Look closer. That man is no man at all. He plays for the soul of the other."

I study the painting and let out a soft laugh. I joke, "That's the way I've seen you look at me. Do you want my soul, then?"

"Yes," he answers simply.

I turn in his arms to face him. Laughing, I ask, "You want my soul?"

His face looks ancient, his eyes fathomless. They are black pits with no end, like falling through the depths of the earth itself. My heart skips a beat and fear snakes down my spine as my smile slowly dies on my face. Then his eyes crinkle and his mouth turns up at the corners. The moment is over so fast I think I must have imagined it.

"I want to devour you, body *and* soul," he says playfully.

I laugh to push away my dark imaginings as we walk down the corridor. We are on our way out, and although I am trying to take in every piece we pass, our guide keeps up the pace to get us to our next destination on time.

Just as we turn the corner, I stop and try to get a better view of the painting we just passed.

Luke glances where my gaze is riveted and tugs me gently forward, saying, "We can come back, but I have more surprises for you."

As we keep walking, I ask the guide, "What was that painting back there? With the naked man biting the other naked man's throat?"

"*Oui, madame.* That is *Dante and Virgile.*"

I stumble for a second, but keep walking. It was so similar to the painting at McVladam's back home. But he couldn't have had a priceless original in his home. It must have been one of those high-quality reproductions. Because I could have sworn it was the same one. The painting is such an unusual size and striking image.

That wasn't what had caused my steps to falter, though. It was the recognition of the men in the painting's incredible resemblance to the two in my life. McVladam could easily pass for Capocchio and if Luke had shorter hair and was missing his Van Dyke beard, he could be Gianni.

It's strange, but easy enough to explain. My imagination must be superimposing my subconscious onto the painting simply because they looked close enough to the men I am constantly thinking about. I scold myself once again for looking for reasons to sabotage my enjoyment of this incredible night.

We exit the museum and this time a large black SUV is waiting for us. Luke seems on high alert, scanning our surroundings. I look around, but nothing seems out of the ordinary, other than two other SUVs identical to the one we are walking toward. As my eyes adjust to the twilight, I can pick out men similar to those I've seen, before falling in around us.

"Um, Luke? Do you have bodyguards? Are we in some sort of danger?" I ask, hesitantly.

He lets out a low laugh. "I'm the most dangerous thing there is. No one can hurt you when you are with me. I would never allow it."

I nervously laugh in return, trying to diffuse the tension. I notice he doesn't quite answer my question. I ask, "Dangerous? Is assassin on your long list of side hustles?"

"Not exactly," he replies.

"How many side jobs do you have? Circus performer, vendor, club and boutique owner are just the ones I know. None of that even goes together," I say, confused.

We reach the car, and as he opens the door, he turns me

to face him. He bends down and leaves a light kiss on my lips.

"I already told you. I play chess for people's souls. Right now, I am playing for yours." His face is intent, serious even.

I scoff, "No, really."

"I do whatever the *fuck* I want. And right now, that means you." He wraps his arms around me and buries his face in my neck.

"Luke!" I squeal. "My hair and makeup. It took hours to get ready."

He releases me and hands me up into the SUV.

"You're safe," he says, climbing in beside me, "for now." He playfully waggles his eyebrows at me, and I laugh as we take off into the night.

Chapter 39

I returned the painting here in the hopes she would see it. The museum was only too happy to add it back to their collection on loan. I am desperate, searching for a way to make her learn the truth. I know if I could only get her away from his lies, I could convince her of who we are and who *he* is.

I saw him looking for me, scanning the crowds. He knows I am here, following them. His words drift back to me, and I groan in frustration. He is telling her the truth, yet she thinks he is joking.

I want to scream to her, "He wants your soul. This is all a game to him. We can't let him win!"

But she cannot hear me and that would only push her away further, convince her that I'm the crazy man she thinks I am. If I lose her again, I will be so much worse than that. My soul, and hers, will be his.

As they pull away, I feel more frantic. Time is running out. I must get her away so I can move in on him and carry out my final act of love. The endgame is here.

Chapter 40

LIESHE

Just when I thought our date couldn't get any more romantic, we pull up in front of the Eiffel Tower. Luke helps me out of the vehicle and pulls me into his side. Which is a good thing, as he needs to steer me in the right direction as I distractedly stare up at the magnificent structure.

The view from my bedroom window at his house had been incredible. But up close, I'm blown away.

"Another private tour?" I ask.

He glances at me out of the side of his eyes. "Something like that."

As we near the south pillar, I see signs for the exclusive Michelin star restaurant. I squeal, "We're having dinner here?"

Luke drops a kiss on the top of my head as we pass through the security checkpoint and into the restaurant's elevator. I'm disappointed when a staff member joins us. We exchange a heated stare, and I know he is, too.

The last time we had been in an elevator together was so hot. It seems like a lifetime ago instead of just a continent away. I want to recreate that memory.

The host makes small talk about the restaurant, who the chef is or some such nonsense. We blatantly ignore him, exchanging a molten stare and solely focused on each other. How the other person doesn't choke on the sexual tension thickening in the air, I don't know.

My breath is coming shorter and shorter, as if an invisible corset is being pulled tight. I stretch my neck, trying to loosen the feeling and force more air into my lungs.

Luke's eyes burn hotter.

I bite my lip and watch as his eyes drop to my mouth. Filled with confidence and power under his hungry stare, I squeeze my arms together, pushing up the already incredible cleavage from this dress.

He drops his eyes and looks back up at me, a warning in his gaze. I'm playing with fire. And I want to get burned. I bite my bottom lip again just to incite him further. He lifts an eyebrow and holds his hand out to me. I can ignore him, which would appear odd, or I can take his hand.

Not trusting Luke not to make a scene in front of this stranger if I don't give in, I go to take his hand. Instead, he captures my wrist in a grip of steel and tugs me to stand in front of him. As the elevator doors open, Luke holds me in place, preventing me from exiting.

The other man exits the elevator, spinning around when he senses we aren't following, only to catch Luke hitting the close door button. He steps toward us, but the doors close on his astonished face.

"Luke! What are you doing?" I gasp.

"What you've been begging me to do with your eyes this whole damned time. Last time we were in an elevator, you ran out of time. This time, I suggest you try harder. You don't want to lose."

My cheeks flame at the memory. I step back against the wall and grip the railing, just like the time before.

He places his top hat on my head with a wink and leans his cane in the corner before dropping to his knees. He gathers the bottom half of my gown and bunches it up around my hips.

"*Apéritif?*" he asks.

Hooking his fingers in the sides of the white whisper of lace panties I have on, he drags them down my legs while he devours me with his eyes.

He shoots me his wicked Cheshire cat smile as he tucks them into his jacket pocket. Throwing my leg over his shoulder, he dives in and starts lapping at me like a man starved.

I can't help but pull him in closer and grind my hips into his face. Tossing my head back, I notice a camera in the corner of the elevator.

"Luke, there's a camera!" I protest.

Without breaking his stride, he merely laughs and thrusts his tongue inside of me, pulling a deep moan from my lips. The mystery of whether someone is actually watching only increases my pleasure. Just as he knew it would.

He pulls back to look at me for a moment, lips coated with my arousal, and says, "Be ready to hit the close door button when we hit the ground. Time is halfway up."

"What happens if I lose?" I desperately ask.

"Don't lose," he mutters darkly and dives back to suck at my clit.

I balance precariously on one leg, white knuckling the railing with one hand and stretching out the other toward the button. My fingertip just grazes it.

I try to focus on the illuminated numbers showing our descent, but Luke adds his hands to the mix, thrusting two fingers deep inside of me and curling them to hit that magic secret spot. My muscles shake with the effort of holding this position, while my impending orgasm threatens to coincide with the doors opening to waiting passengers.

If they open and expose us like this, I'm going to die of

mortification. I only hope I can close the doors in time. The thought of not just a stranger behind a camera, but a crowd of people watching me explode on Luke's hands and tongue, pushes me over the edge.

My walls clamp down on his fingers. He groans into me and redoubles his efforts, licking and sucking with precision. The light turns off of number two and I explode, crying out a string of breathy moans followed by a long, "Fuck!"

At the last second, Luke stands, whipping down my skirt and wrapping an arm around me to keep me upright. The doors open to an elderly couple, who smile kindly at the sight of us with me wearing the top hat. He nods at them and picks up his cane from the corner.

We all ride back up together while Luke delicately wipes his mouth with my panties and then neatly folds them into a pocket square that he adds to his jacket. With a grin, he plucks his hat off my head and places it back on his own.

I make a futile attempt to calm my breathing as I recover from the intense orgasm and get my shaking limbs under control. We arrive back at the entrance to the restaurant and follow the older couple out.

The man we had dodged to go on our escapade blocks our path, giving Luke a sharp look, but all Luke does is point to his breast pocket and shrug, saying, "I forgot my pocket square."

The other couple is met by another host to lead them to their table. As they walk past, the older gentleman says, "Well played, sir. Well played."

I flush crimson from the tip of my nose down to my toes. Luke lets out a hearty laugh, causing heads to turn. He thrusts his top hat and cane at the host, barely pausing to make sure the other man has them, before he takes my hand and tucks it into his elbow.

He stares into my eyes like I am the only woman on the planet and throws over his shoulder, "You may seat us now."

The host opens and closes his mouth a few times, but seeing no other polite way forward, he nods and spins on his heel, leading the way like a drum major with Luke's cane.

I attempt to hide my laugh behind my hand as I follow him, but an unhinged giggle sneaks its way out.

The host throws me a haughty glance as we arrive at the table, but Luke palms him a large note and says, *"Je voudrais une bouteille de Krug Clos d'Ambonnay deux mille deux, s'il vous plaît."*

His eyes widen for a moment before he bows and begins to fawn over us, pulling out our chairs and prattling on in French.

Luke point-blank ignores him, instead reaching for my hands across the table. He fixes me with his intense stare, and the world falls away. This should be the most romantic moment of my life, but something about his gaze is uncomfortable. Predatorial, even.

His smile is almost mask-like, not quite reaching his eyes, which normally blaze with fire when looks at me, but right now seem almost cold and reptilian. I close my eyes for a second as a flare of anxiety hits.

He gives my hands a gentle squeeze, prompting me to open my eyes again. His familiar smile and warmth are back, making me question if I am seeing things. It's easy to blame my overactive imagination, but this seems to be happening more and more.

"Is everything okay?" he questions.

"What? Oh, yeah. I mean, yes, everything is fine. Thank you. I just struggle a little with heights," I say.

I cover my expression with a convenient excuse and curse my face for not having an internal monologue.

"Should we move away from the windows then?" he offers, concerned.

We have the best seats in the house, the skyline of Paris stretching out before us, glittering under the night sky. I smile at him reassuringly.

"No, no, I'll be fine. Really. I think eating will help."

A waiter appears to hand us menus, but Luke waves him off, giving what sounds like a very long and detailed order in French. The only part I catch is *sans gluten,* which Luke says emphatically several times. The waiter merely bows in response.

I realize just how silly my earlier thoughts were. Luke has been nothing but attentive. He has given me the ultimate Paris experience, helped me explore my sexual fantasies, and become more confident in myself. Even if I don't totally understand his fascination with me being his "Red Queen," it feels good to slip on the mantle of a badass alter ego.

To me, the Red Queen is just that—a persona for me to slip into and feel like the woman I could be. She's the woman Luke makes room for and encourages. I should be thankful that he did exactly what he proposed—pulled me into his world. I came willingly and I've certainly enjoyed the white glove treatment.

I've had experiences in the brief time I've been here I never could have imagined—both in bed and out.

"Thank you," I blurt, surprising myself.

"The pleasure has been all mine," is his smooth reply.

I smile at him across the table and say, "Maybe not *all* yours."

A man I assume is the chef due to his very tall hat comes over and confers at length with Luke in French. I look at him questioningly.

"He assures me there will be zero cross contamination for

either of our meals. He's actually looking forward to making a special dinner just for us. We decided on a tasting menu of his design. I hope you have an adventurous palate," he explains.

"You're certainly broadening my tastes," I say in what I hope is a sexy tone. Trying to match his level of sex appeal and flirting is a challenge.

"I like your taste just fine," he drawls, his voice low and sexy.

The bass of it resonates deep in my belly, stirring something primal. His smile draws an answering one from me, his eyes glittering with playful intent. I'm outmatched in this game, but I'm eager to learn.

I'm saved from replying by the arrival of our champagne in an ice stand. With great ceremony, the sommelier displays the label to Luke, who merely nods after casting the barest glance at the proffered bottle. His focus is only on me.

A waiter approaches the sommelier with a saber resting on a pillow and bows. The sommelier accepts the sword with a return bow. I watch in rapt fascination as the ritual unfolds before me, amused but clueless as to what they're doing.

The sommelier lifts the bottle, and the surrounding diners take in a collective breath. All this pomp and circumstance has drawn enough attention that I shift uncomfortably in my seat, disliking being the center of it.

He raises the saber and aims at the neck while another waiter readies two glasses. With a swift stroke up the bottle, the crowd gasps as—nothing happens.

"Was that supposed to pop the cork?" I whisper to Luke out of the corner of my mouth as the poor sommelier stands there, mortified.

Luke snorts, dropping his napkin onto the table as he stands and holds out his hands. The sommelier, now a frightful shade of red and looking a little lost, hands over the bottle and saber.

Just as Luke repeats the same process, the sommelier seems to gather himself and holds up a finger to interrupt him, stepping into the path of the cork as it flies off, along with a small glass ring from the bottle's neck.

The projectile strikes the man in the temple. He doubles over, clutching his head as a few of the other waiters rush over to help, while Luke calmly pours the champagne into the waiting glasses, ignoring the spectacle unfolding next to us.

I'm thankful a woman next to me lets out a shriek, covering my sudden fit of laughter at the absurdity of the situation. I'll take a twist-off cap over all this nonsense any day.

I pull myself together and call out, "Are you okay?"

He straightens and turns to Luke, a visible lump already forming on his head. Bowing, he mutters, "My fault entirely, sir. I stepped directly into the path."

He about-faces and exits the dining floor with his head held high. The crowd immediately buzzes with excitement. Luke sits back down and hands me a champagne glass as I continue to erupt into small fits of giggles.

"Really, Luke? Is everything with you always an adventure?"

"Do you want it to be?" He questions, face serious and eyes dancing.

All I can do is nod. Chaos surrounds him in the best way. I have spent my life organizing and planning, rigid and anxious. Giving in to the maelstrom that pulls me in like a whirlpool is freeing. Luke allows me to be the woman I've always wanted to be.

He lifts his glass in response.

"What are we celebrating tonight?" I ask.

"You," he says simply.

"That's what you always say," I counter.

"Because it is true. There is nothing in this world, or the next, I would rather raise a glass to than you."

Whatever defenses I had been trying to erect against him are rapidly weakening. He is fun and wonderful. He makes me feel so many emotions on so many levels that it would take a lifetime to unravel. Is this what love is?

I have no comprehension of how the doubts about him can creep in. Is it self-sabotage? Am I trying to keep myself from the happiness Luke so obviously wants to give me?

Yes, I was shocked at the outcome of things with McVladam. I never thought I would be swept up in a conman. But I cannot let one terrible experience color my entire future and keep me from enjoying someone like Luke who has been truthful and so damn *real*.

Let yourself be happy, I plead with myself. Just let yourself be *fucking* happy.

Easy to say, but a tall order when the very foundation for my relationship with men had been set up on a sour note. Not that I know my father lied to me, per se, but he certainly didn't instill confidence, trust, or affection in our relationship—only fear, subservience, and insecurity. Luke has consistently offered the exact opposite.

I'm pulled from my thoughts by the arrival of our first course, which the waiter announces as, "*Amuse-bouche Varié.*"

"What a fun word, *amuse-bouche*," I repeat.

"Perhaps that is what I should call you from now on. My little mouth teaser," Luke says.

My cheeks grow pink at his words in the middle of a fine

dining experience. Curious, I ask, "Why do you call me your Red Queen?"

He picks up his tasting spoon and gestures to me to do the same. I chew the smoked salmon roll with avocado mousse, thankful it is smoky and fresh. I've never cared for this particular fish, but here it is full of flavor and not a whiff of fishiness to be found.

I take a sip of my champagne, savoring what I'm sure is some crazy-expensive, rare vintage. We move onto our chilled gazpacho shooters while Luke looks thoughtful.

After he swallows and chases it with a sip of his own bubbles, he says, "Chess pieces are often black and white, to represent good versus evil. But what is good? What is evil? Is anything all good or all bad? Is life black and white? What if everything is actually shades of not gray, but red? Love and hate, pleasure and pain. They are just different shades of red."

He picks up his last bite-sized appetizer and pops it in his mouth. I watch his lips move in fascination, the ripple of the column of his throat as he swallows. I marvel at how he can command a circus tent or a Michelin-starred restaurant with such grace and intensity.

"You are the key to it all. You have all the power, and you don't even know it. You don't recognize your own value, your own worth. The world has failed you. You are not a pawn of this realm. Your worth is far greater. You are the queen in this great chess game of life. And you will rule by my side," he says fiercely.

His passion rises as he talks. By the end, I not only believe him, but I am nodding enthusiastically. Luke is right. I'm not a pawn. I am a queen in the shades of red that is life, and I want to be *his* queen.

I bow my head and look up at him through my lashes. "Yes, my Lord."

He holds his hand out to me, eyes smoldering. I place my hand in his, surprised when he does his signature move of kissing my inner wrist at the table. I'm shocked the restaurant doesn't incinerate at the rising heat between us.

I swallow hard. Needing a break from the building of emotions and sexual tension, I excuse myself to the restroom where I lock myself in a stall and take deep, steadying breaths.

As I exit the luxurious cubicle, I find Lilith sitting on the counter, swinging her legs like she's on a park bench and not the marble countertop of an exclusive restaurant. Exquisitely dressed in head to toe red as always, she smiles at me as I approach.

"Lilith?" I say, hesitantly. No way is her presence a mere coincidence.

She keeps swinging her legs as she studies me with her head cocked to the side. A smile plays over her lips as if she finds this amusing.

"Are you here for dinner?" I probe.

"I'm here to see you. Don't tell Luke if he doesn't already know. I need you to remember what I said," she whispers conspiratorially, as if he can hear her the whole way in here.

"What you said when?" I wrack my brain, trying to process her cryptic statement.

"I am not your enemy," she clarifies with a roll of her eyes, as if what she is saying should somehow be obvious to me.

"Of course not, Lilith. We're friends," I reply.

She is always interesting, but this is downright bizarre. She jumps down, landing perfectly on her five-inch stilettos, and comes to stand not just in front of me, but well inside of my body buffer zone.

"*I've* never lied to you," she states emphatically.

"I know you haven't. I trust you." I hold her eyes and nod at her. I'm not sure where this is going, but it seems important to reassure her.

Her eyes well up and her lip quivers just the tiniest bit before she grabs me into a tight hug and whispers fiercely in my ear, "You are the only one who has ever defended me. *You* are everything that is good in this world, and the next. Remember this, bestie."

She pulls back and grabs my hand, tracing a shape into my palm as she says, "Remember to trust me when the time is right."

She meets my eyes, closes my fingers over my palm, nods once, hard, then spins on her stilettos and rushes out.

I look down at my palm, but seeing nothing there, I wash my hands, attempt to wipe the bewilderment off my face, and head back out to Luke.

I hope he doesn't ask me about Lilith. I don't want to lie to him if he does, but there's also no reason to tell him. I hope she's not in any trouble. Although if anyone can handle themselves, it would be her.

I slide back into my seat and flash Luke a smile just as the next course is set before us. He narrows his eyes at me slightly and asks if everything is okay.

"Of course, must be the bubbles."

His eyes shoot to my champagne glass, which is half full, and then back to me.

Chapter 41

How very interesting. She didn't lie, but she also didn't tell me the entire truth. I search the surrounding area with my mind, but all I can sense are my people that I have used to set up a perimeter and Lilith. Everything seems as it should be. Now we just have to wait for the last move, and it will be checkmate.

Lieshe studies my face, gauging my reaction. Today has been perfect. Every step was orchestrated to shape her feelings for me. I've been devoted and charming. And, I'll even admit, I had fun. Seeing my favorite city through her eyes breathed new life into even the boring old museum.

People say it would take years to see everything in the Louvre. I've seen it all countless times as I wandered the long corridors, marveling at the great beauty humans are capable of producing. And the deadly destruction. So many examples of both.

Perhaps if I study the beauty long enough, it will drown out the utter depravity and wickedness I've endured since time immemorial. Evil does not stem from me. I don't make humans do anything. I merely exist in the shades of red that were created, just like all the brushstrokes in the Louvre.

I am chaos, the force that spins the system ever outward, in a constant battle against the inward momentum. Without opposing forces, the system would collapse. Rather than appreciate that their very existence hinges on this delicate and fragile balancing act, humans take and take and take.

A wicked smile curls my lips. I give and give and give. Thankless. Loveless. Sentenced for all time. I've seen oceans of sin, yet it's me, *me*, who is punished. My eyes begin bleeding black, my anger pushing up against my skin, my normal temperature skyrocketing.

I pick up my champagne to take a sip to calm myself, noting the way the tiny bubbles begin to roil and enlarge as the liquid moves toward its boiling point. I set the flute down without taking a sip before the glass cracks from my heat.

Someone is calling my name, but the sound barely registers. I clench my hands, forcing down my power and rage. Folding in on myself, pushing my true nature down deep when it claws at my surface to be released, is a slow and painful battle. The restraint I have built up over the years is a hard lesson learned. Existing in this plane calls for extreme control.

Never being vulnerable, never once having anyone to share my pain, to love me, has left me empty—forged in fire, hammered into shape, and hardened 'til my exterior is steel. The process repeated, until just like steel that has been annealed too many times, I'm brittle. I've been fractured inside my seemingly impenetrable armor.

A sound breaks through the pulsing in my head, the thrumming in my veins. My head snaps up as something touches my hand. I look at it. Small, pale, cold against my heated skin. It's so fragile, I could disintegrate the bones and sinews and turn the blood to dust with barely a thought.

I'm tempted, *so tempted*, to wreak destruction on this touch like a moth's wing. But the sound comes again, and my eyes flick up to its origin. And there is her face, her eyes, the yellow green of my own reflected back at me, pulsing in the low light of the fancy fucking restaurant surrounding me with bullshit.

Seeing those eyes and hearing her use the safe word I had given her quiets it all, giving me peace. Instant peace, like I haven't experienced since the beginning, fills me. All it took was her touch and the only human voice to ever say my true name.

"Luke, are you okay?" Her words float to me, full of concern, caring.

I give a small laugh and parrot her words back to her, "Must be the bubbles."

She gives me a tight smile back, both of us relieved when the final course is delivered. Lieshe cuts into a piece of the exquisitely prepared rare steak. I stare in fascination as she takes a bite, wraps her lips around the fork, and hums in appreciation at the flavor.

A drop of the decadent finishing sauce clings to her lip and drips off, landing on her knife. She looks down, and without thinking, picks it up to swipe the drop off with her tongue.

I hyper-focus on the small pink tip darting out and skillfully cleaning the handle. All I can picture is her licking a black pearl of my cum off my cock in the same way. The vision triggers a tsunami, wrecking my tightly held control.

I'm done with restraint and the trappings of this damn world. I need her in *my* world where we can live by *my* rules, free from the constraints imposed on us here. I'm ready to be done with tonight's events. Though the guest of honor has yet to arrive, I know just how to pass the time.

I hold up my hand, and a member of the waitstaff immediately responds. I flick a black card into my hand and without tearing my eyes away from her lips and that damned tongue, I say, "Clear the restaurant."

The waiter is stunned, sputtering over my request. "Sir?"

My voice drops an octave; I hate repeating myself. I am

dangerously out of patience. Switching to French and over enunciating each syllable, I say, "*Évacuez le restaurant.*"

His mouth opens and closes like a fish until he stammers out, "Sir, we cannot simply clear the restaurant."

I tear my eyes away from Lieshe's wide-eyed stare to look at the man who dares to tell me no.

"You can and you will. Call Frédéric and tell him Luke Devlin is here, and then clear this fucking restaurant," I instruct him with cold, clear confidence.

He snatches the card from my hand, backs away, and scurries to the kitchen. I count in my head. One. Two. Three.

Raised voices reach my ears from the kitchen, followed swiftly by the manager coming to the center of the restaurant. A satisfied smirk settles on my face as he announces, "Ladies and gentlemen. Please remain calm. My sincerest apologies, but we must immediately evacuate the restaurant."

He repeats himself in French, holding up his hands at the protest of the patrons. An alarm begins to sound for good measure and that gets the people up and moving. Lieshe and I remain seated, letting the world swirl around us. The chaos brushes over my skin in a comforting caress.

The older couple from our earlier elevator ride passes our table, and the gentleman shakes his head at me with a small grin, winking as he walks on by.

I sit motionless, watching the questions play across her beautiful face. It's a damn good thing she has no idea how she has affected me tonight, how close I came to breaking, or how easily she soothed my beast.

She can never know. I must win, and that leaves no room for emotion or vulnerability. She is so close to falling for me, and now I will push her over the edge. But I will not, cannot, love her back.

After the last soul leaves the restaurant, I stand up and smooth down my jacket. I face the table, look at her with my feline smile, and pick up her knife with one hand as the other reaches out and clears the table in one swipe.

She screams and jumps up out of the path of the flying debris. "Luke! What the hell are you doing?"

I let a dark evil laugh out. "Oh, *mon petit chou*. What have I told you? I do whatever the fuck I want. Get on the table."

"Get on the table?" she squeaks.

"Get. On. The. Table." I step menacingly toward her with each word.

Her heart rate spikes, and I can smell her arousal thicken the air between us. I knew she'd like a little fear to go with her pleasure and pain.

Backing away from me, she stumbles back onto the table. I walk into her space, forcing her to sit up on it in retreat. Her eyes flick down to the knife and back up to my face. She swallows hard.

"Wh-what are you doing?" The slight quaver to her voice shoots straight to my cock. I could eat this up with a fucking spoon.

I push her shoulder, and she falls back on the table, legs hanging off. I move to stand between her knees, nudging them apart to accommodate me. Leaning over her, I drag the dull edge of the knife down her lips and chin.

Her pupils blow wide, and her chest heaves. Without taking my eyes from hers, I flip the knife in the air and catch it, this time angling the sharp edge against her skin. Her breathing turns shallow as she tries to remain motionless.

I trail the knife over her throat, softly enough to leave her skin intact yet hard enough that she is worried I am not. Despite her best efforts to control her movements, her breathing hitches, catching the point. A loud moan escapes me as a pinprick of crimson appears over her heart.

"So fragile. Delicate," I murmur as the knife glides further down between the swell of her breasts and reaches the top of her dress.

I stop for a second, loving the tension and wonder in her eyes—the fear and the trust. Chaos and order are perfectly balanced, for now. The anticipation on which way this could tip pushes me to continue, wondering which will be sweeter —the journey or the reward.

The knife bites into the thick satin of her gown, loud in the stillness of the now empty restaurant. Her eyes flick down to follow the trail.

"Lieshe," I rasp out. "Eyes—"

"Always on you," she answers, meeting my molten gaze once more.

I don't want her to follow the path of the knife, rather I want the anticipation, the fear, the wonder to bleed over into her pleasure, coalescing into pure, raw need. Lust—another of my favorite sins. I lick my lips and taste her feelings in the air itself. Its fucking delicious.

I continue to draw the knife down, the satin giving way to reveal creamy skin and stunning curves. Her hands are clutching the sides of the table, knuckles white. As the tip slides past her belly button and over the sweet soft swell of her belly, she tenses, catching the tip of the knife again.

"Careful darling, I'm barely restraining myself as it is," I grit out.

I'm enthralled by the contrast of her red blood. I dip my head down, licking the drop with the tip of my tongue. Staring into her eyes, I make a show of drawing it into my mouth. I swallow loudly and let out a deep hum of appreciation.

"I am going to fucking devour you."

I rest the knife on her belly, so I have use of both hands. She lets out a breathy moan as I grab the two sides of the shredded dress and rip down the rest of the material, the rending pulling a gasp from her lips. The dress falls away, as if presenting her on a bed of white satin. She's my blasphemous bride, but my queen needs red.

Picking the heavy handled steak knife back up, I flip it up into the air again and this time catch it by the blade. I use the handle to tease her nipples, drawing circles around the tightening peaks. I trail it pack up to her mouth and tap her lips.

When she opens her mouth and extends her tongue, I know she is open to my plans for this knife. I place the handle in her mouth and watch her suck it, cheeks hollowing, tongue swirling. My cock grows even thicker, wanting to find its way home inside of her heat.

I pull the knife from her mouth with a pop and drag it slowly down her body. Down her throat, between her breasts, circling her navel, and then down the slope of her belly to her mons. I tear my eyes away from the path of the knife to meet hers.

Her pupils are blown wide, surrounded by golden rings. Her breaths are short, sharp. As I stop my descent, she impatiently shifts her hips. I smile and say, "Are you my eager little slut? Does your cunt want to be filled? No matter what it is?"

She bites her lip, scared to answer. Scared to give permission to the dark side she so clearly craves, has always craved. Oh, what a creature she would have been if her spirit hadn't been suppressed from such an early age.

"Words, *ma Reine Rouge*. I want your words as much as I want to devour your soul."

"Yes," she chokes out, flushing crimson.

"Yes, what? Yes, my filthy whore wants to be filled with anything?"

"Yes, my Lord. Please!" Her cries fill me with anticipation. Moving to my world is going to be incredible.

I slide the handle down over her mound and circle her clit, causing her to cry out. I rub the thick knife handle up and down through her folds until she is thrusting her hips upward, desperate. When she is wanton, breathing hard and tossing her head, I ease it inside of her opening.

"Spread your legs. This is a damn vision, watching your pussy eat up this knife. *Bon appetit, jolie chatte.*"

She draws her legs up, balancing her heels on the edge of the table, giving me a beautiful view of her pussy gobbling up the large handle. I pull it out as she whimpers in frustration, bringing the knife up to the light. I hold her eyes as I lick the cream off the handle.

"Your fear is fucking delicious," I murmur.

Bringing the knife back down, I begin working it inside of her further and further. Watching it disappear in her sweet entrance surpasses every damn painting and sculpture at the Louvre. I have never seen a more beautiful sight than her cunt gobbling up this knife handle, pulling it in for more.

"Not fear," she pants out. "Trust. I trust you."

Knowing what is about to happen, her saying she trusts me tugs at where I suppose my heart should be. I have no conscience, no soul. I am incapable of love, but hearing that she trusts me is like plunging this knife into my gut instead of her sweet pussy.

Shaking my head hard, I push the thought away. There is too much at stake tonight. Winning is the only thing that matters right now.

I tighten my grip on the blade as she clamps down. With

my free hand, I grab her ankle and shove her leg sharply back, giving me even more access and a far better view. I'd rather think about this.

"Fuck, look at your greedy cunt eating this knife. I can't wait to sink my cock into you," I rasp.

A loud moan spills from her lips as she arches her back off the table.

"Oh, my sweet whore loves my filthy words. Be a good girl for me and cream all over this knife, and then I'll shove my dick in you. Is that what you want? To be filled up by my thick cock? Have me paint your insides with my cum?"

My words push her over the edge. Her pussy clamps down on the knife so tight I can hardly continue to thrust it in and out. I tighten my grip on the blade, determined to have her finish. My blood drips down my arm and off my elbow, but there is no stopping now.

Awareness of the chaos about to ensue on the ground snags my attention. Ah, the white knight has arrived. Perfect timing for my finale. I keep the blade well covered by my palm and fingers, but slide my thumb up to strum over her clit, pushing her orgasm higher.

Her mouth falls open in a silent scream as her whole body seizes up. She is lust incarnate, and a more beautiful sight I've never seen. She is meant to be my queen, and I, her king.

I withdraw the knife and throw it into the pile of debris I swiped off the table. Frédéric is going to be furious. I cleared his restaurant and then made this lovely mess, and the carnage has just begun. Good thing he owes me.

Not allowing her a chance to recover, I collar her throat with my hand and haul her off the table. I force her back against the large windows that overlook the city. A human looking up from the ground would not be able to distinguish what is happening. But he's not human, not anymore. And this view is just for him.

Releasing her, I admire the contrast of my crimson bloody handprint over her slender pale throat as she stands there gloriously naked.

I don't bother undoing my French cuffs or even my shirt buttons. I shuck my jacket, savagely rip off my tie, and tear my shirt off, buttons and cufflinks flying.

I need to bury myself in her. Now. I spin her around to the window, both so she can see the night skyline of Paris and to give those below a better view.

I lean into her ear and demand, "Let go of all your fears. You are mine now. Nothing can touch you, not even death. Put your hands up on the glass."

Dropping my pants, I push her front against the windows. She gasps at the temperature contrast of the cold glass and my molten body plastered to her back. I can't help but thrust with my dick buried in the seam of her ass.

I take a step back and pull her hips with me. This angle highlights her curves, back arched. I kick her feet wider apart and line my cock up at her entrance. I can feel his eyes boring into us from the ground below. With a wicked grin back at him, I impale her in one hard thrust.

She clenches down at the sudden intrusion, tugging on my magic cross piercing delightfully. I slowly pull out, making sure she feels every barbell along the bottom of my cock, and then slam home again. The pace is brutal, punishing. The primal scream from the ground below that reaches only my ears has my dick throbbing harder.

His pure rage fuels my desire, my revenge, my need to win. I wind her hair around my fist and pull her head back, arching her back further. She struggles to find her balance, sweaty palms slipping on the glass. The struggle makes me burn hotter.

With my bloody hand, I retrace the raven I had drawn on her back so long ago, infusing it with fresh power. Below, I write the safe word I had given her, my true name. I need to get her safely home, and then this can be our every waking moment. Ruling the world, both above and below, as we indulge in every dark fantasy.

I hope the sacrifice that is coming will ensure her safe passage. The thought of losing her tightens my chest in the oddest way.

My attention is piqued when two unexpected visitors blip onto my radar, causing my hips to stutter. Realizing who they are has me laughing darkly. Oh, this is going to be fucking epic. As the humans would say, let's get this party started.

I reach around to grasp her swinging tits, marking them with my blood, pulling cruelly at her nipples until she is mewling like an alley cat.

I could have let the gash on my palm heal in an instant, but I want to paint my queen red. My own masterpiece, worthy of the Louvre. I leave a bloody trail down her belly and find her clit, rubbing circles while I continue to pound into her from behind. I'm rewarded with a flood of arousal.

I change my angle so my piercing rubs directly over her g-spot. "This pussy was made for me. I am going to claim her for all eternity. Come for me. *Viens pour moi, mon amour.*"

Spasms start deep within her, racing to the surface like the shifting of tectonic plates to destroy me in her earthquake. Incoherent words spill from her lips.

In response, I flood her like a tsunami, unleashing wave after wave inside of her. I pull her hips sharply into mine, bottoming out inside her tight channel, to release the last pulses of my orgasm at the entrance to her womb.

All of her—I am claiming all of her.

"You are so damn beautiful," I pant out.

"Luke," she moans, as her pussy ripples around me. "I'm so full. It's so hot."

"Yes," I hiss. "Touch yourself. Come for me again, *mon amour.*"

I grind deeper into her, keeping myself hard for her to chase her pleasure. I can only imagine the sight she must make from the ground. She has one hand against the glass and one hand on her pussy, her face contorted in ecstasy— painted in my blood. To me, a vision. To him, a nightmare of his own making, the end of not just his world, but *the* world.

I can taste victory as surely as I can taste the lingering sweet copper tang of her drop of blood clinging to my tongue. I let myself drift into her mind, feel the emotions swirling. The lust overrides her fear of heights, her craving for my darkness to take her deeper and push her higher.

I let myself experience her orgasm as it courses through her, a bright spark starting low in her belly and rushing out through her limbs like a wildfire out of control. The sudden rush of oxytocin, accompanied by her questioning her feelings for me, wondering if this could be love.

I pull back from her mind with a self-satisfied smile as she writhes on my cock. Checkmate is in my grasp.

Chapter 42

Luke Devlin has wrecked me physically and mentally. I'm wondering now if he has also emotionally. There are times when I think I could fall for him. Sometimes I think I would be crazy not to.

So, why does something just seem off? Sometimes when I peer into the windows of his soul, I sense there is something sinister hiding from me, peering back from its hiding place in the shadows. Something not Luke, but ancient and dark, using him as a soulless vessel. But how could that be?

The devastation McVladam left in his wake may just be too much to open my heart up again so soon. Or maybe I am guilty of self-sabotage. Not allowing myself to take a chance on what could be the most incredible romance of my life.

Or maybe, a small voice says inside, maybe there is something off about Luke, and that deep down in my gut, an instinct or sixth sense is trying to warn me away. But Luke is so dazzling, so all-consuming, that I can't even analyze myself. I'm left not knowing which thoughts are my own; what is real, what is imagined. Maybe this is all just one big waking dream.

He has shown me so many facets of himself that I still don't even know who he is. Is he a performer or a business owner? A player or a one-woman man? That small voice pipes up again and asks, is he even a man? I can't help but smile as I answer, he fucks like a god.

Far below on the ground, something catches my attention. "Luke, what's going on down there?"

He pulls me back against the heat of his chest and looks down over my shoulder. He drops a kiss on it and then fetches his jacket and pulls out his phone. Speaking in rapid, clipped sentences, he barks an order and then hangs up.

"It seems you have a rather persistent admirer. He's giving my men quite a run for their money."

"What? McVladam is here? In Paris?"

Luke snorts. "McVladam? He's been trying to get to you for days, but my security has intervened. I won't tolerate a man who won't take no for an answer. Your safety will not be compromised by whatever this asshole's name is."

He taps out something on his phone, gives it to me, and places his hands on my shoulders.

"Lieshe," he says with a small shake. "Listen to me and do exactly as I say. Now is not the time to be foolish, stubborn, or brave. For once in your life, let someone take care of you. Let *me* take care of you. You are going to walk out the exit behind me and take the elevator to the third level. I just put the entrance ticket on this phone. You must appear calm. When you get off the elevator, there is Gustave Eiffel's apartment. Everyone will be looking through the viewing window. Walk right past them."

"Wh-," he cuts me off with a finger over my lips.

"Trail your hand along the wall just where the bottom of that window is. Round the corner and you will feel the metal will change. Be sure no one sees you and then push on that panel, right over the rivets. A door will open just wide enough for you to slip in. Wait for me there."

"Wait, what? How do you know this? What if you don't come?" I cry out.

Luke crushes me to him and whispers fiercely in my ear,

"I will be there. I will always be with you, *ma Reine Rouge*. For what is a king without his queen?"

He pulls me by the hand and snatches up my dress, throwing it to me. I try to put it back on while he yanks on his pants, but it has no way to stay up; the white satin is ripped to shreds.

"Luke, I can't look calm walking around naked," I say.

He flashes me his signature feline smile and holds up a finger to signal me to wait. He ducks out of the restaurant and is back in no time.

As I'm still trying to pull my decimated dress around me, he grabs a knife from a nearby table and cuts off a strip of the tablecloth. He uses the remnants of the dress and the makeshift belt to make a messy skirt that at least has my bottom half covered.

Next, he pulls a T-shirt from the gift shop bag. He drags it over my head, and I thrust my arms through the holes and pull it down. He drapes his jacket over my shoulders.

I peer down at the shirt that says *I heart Paris* and nervous laughter erupts. I'm hysterical, emotion overflowing into uncontrolled sobbing giggles.

He stands there for a moment, amused. Reaching out to cup my face with his hand, he says, "Lieshe, love. I need you to pull it together."

His soft touch and quiet words calm the chaos. I lean into the touch that has centered me more than angry shouting ever could. It's like Luke can read exactly what I need and know precisely what will make things worse. I've been yelled at, demeaned, and scolded enough in my life. Soft words and a sweet touch make all the difference to me.

I still and take a deep breath. "Ok. I trust you. Third floor, window height, funny panel, wait for you."

"Good fucking girl," he growls and pulls me in for a

fleeting yet panty scorching kiss. All cinnamon heat and fire. I can't help but whimper when he pulls away. He drags me by the hand to the coatroom, where he grabs his hat and cane.

"Really dude? You need your hat and cane right now?" I hiss at him.

He just chuckles and then guides me out the back exit. "I might need to pull a rabbit out of a hat. Bring up your elevator ticket so you can move through the line quickly. I'll see you soon."

I glance down at my strange outfit once again. "But Luke, people are going to know something is up."

"This is Paris. No one cares about your eccentric outfit. Now go!" he urges with a small push.

I attempt to act normal as I join the queue. I nervously keep messing with the phone, worried that I will somehow lock the screen and lose access to the ticket. I keep my ears trained behind me, listening for any clue as to what's going on, but I'm too high up.

Too high up, I repeat to myself in a panic. And I'm going up higher! I've got nothing to ground myself with in this moment. I can't envision my feet sturdy on the ground when I'm in the air. My already frantic heart gallops and my breaths become shorter. I don't know how I am going to be able to get on to a crowded elevator to go up even more.

The next group boards, and I realize my palms are sweating and my hands are shaking. I remember I'm supposed to be blending in. I wrap my arms around myself under the jacket, hiding my trembling hands. The action wafts Luke's cinnamon scents up to my face. The dark and spicy fragrance hits my amygdala and hippocampus, where scent and memory swirl together.

Flashes of Luke flit through my mind's eye. That damn

feline smile, his absolute worship, the craving for darkness he stirs in me. The pure sin of him. I bring the collar of the jacket up to my nose and inhale deeply. I catch sight of the panty "pocket square" and laugh out loud, the final release I needed to break my rising panic.

The next group of waiting passengers steps forward; I scan my ticket and shuffle to the back corner. A commotion starts up, and the ticket attendants start yelling to the crowd. The other people in the elevator turn back around to see what is going on.

Taking a page from Luke, I say, "Oh no, looks like we need to get off!"

As the others shuffle off, at the last second I hit the door close button and shoot up to the next floor on my own. I steel my nerves, knowing now I need to get to the safety of the meeting spot.

I think, what would Lilith do? She would walk off this elevator like a boss. I give myself a firm nod as the ding announces I'm at my final destination. I calmly walk out, head held high and shoulders back, and blend in with the crowd.

Too bad I can't swing by the champagne bar and grab a glass of the bubbly to calm my nerves. I step past the groups gathered at the windows peering into the famous apartment and start running my hand along the edge of the wall, just as Luke instructed.

A commotion starts behind me, and I hurry my steps without running. I'm almost to the corner when the workers start shouting. I keep my gaze fastened to the outside wall of the apartment, knowing if I look out over the city below, I won't be able to rein my panic in at this dizzying height.

I just have to make a few more steps to round the corner. To distract myself, I count them: three, two, one. I make the corner, but before I can breathe a sigh of relief, I am stopped short by the sight of the back of a security guard.

Fuck! I continue to slide my hand along the wall, careful to keep it level. The guard tilts his head to listen to the radio's incoming announcement. I tiptoe forward until I am almost on top of him. I have maybe two more steps before we collide when there is a subtle change under my fingertips. I pull my hand back to find a stylized raven on the rivet.

What the hell? I push the strange marking and sure enough, the panel swings silently inward. Running on blind trust, I slip into the apartment and close it again behind me.

Sliding down the wall, I let my shaky legs splay out in front of me and indulge in a full-blown panic attack. I can't hold it off any longer and all of this adrenaline has to go somewhere.

I hyperventilate until my hands cramp up and the room spins. I allow myself to envision every crazy doomsday scenario my mind can conjure, from the Eiffel Tower falling over to McVladam bombing the whole thing.

My brain takes every fear and negative thought it can think of and swirls them together into a miasma of chaotic killer nonsense. Time passes; I have no clue if it's thirty seconds or thirty minutes. All I know is that I am sitting alone with panic sweat evaporating off my body, slightly nauseous after the massive adrenaline dump.

But the purge was cathartic and as my heart returns to normal, my brain reboots and I start thinking logically again. I inspect my surroundings, taking in dark wood paneling and chintz furniture. Being in this space that has been frozen in time is like tumbling down a rabbit hole.

There aren't any obvious cameras, but I can't help but wonder if a security guard is going to come bursting through to arrest me. Common sense would have me stay in this one spot, unmoving, but just like Alice, curiosity gets the best of me, and I can't help but explore the apartment that most only get to see from the observation windows.

The windows! I need to be careful that I'm not seen by the other tourists even if there are no cameras. Dropping to my knees, I crawl along the wall toward them, trying to catch a glimpse of any onlookers. I sneak my head around a corner and see the windows, but no faces peer back at me.

Emboldened, I continue crawling closer until I'm right underneath. I strain my ears for any sign of the people who had been on this level, but I hear nothing. I rise to my knees and peer through the glass at an awkward angle, trying to remain hidden.

I see nothing and no one. I lean forward to find a completely abandoned third floor. My knees are starting to protest, so I stand up and walk to the other windows. I am not sure whether I should be worried or relieved that there seems to have been an evacuation.

Just how dangerous can McVladam be? What if Wren was right about everything? Maybe he really is a serial killer who followed me here from Baltimore. Oh shit, what if he killed her, and I didn't warn her because I was jealous and heartbroken?

Silent tears stream down my face as I worry about her safety. We have been friends for years. How could I not have said anything to her?

I have been so distracted by Luke. What a selfish and hateful thing to do. If she is hurt, I'll never forgive myself. She was never anything but kind and funny and loving.

Is, Lieshe, is! I correct myself from slipping into the past tense thinking about her, refusing to even consider that there is a possibility she could be gone. And it would be all my fault. I grab the phone Luke handed me out of the jacket pocket and desperately try to recall her phone number.

It's no use, though. I cannot recall the long string of international numbers that have been programmed into my phone for so long. I pace the small apartment, my appreciation for being in a time capsule gone, replaced by desperation to know what the hell is happening.

Luke has created an all but impenetrable field around her. The only way I've been able to get close to her in a public space is to be in particle form. His home has been surrounded by his bodyguards at all times. So, the sudden shift in security detail that allowed me within sight of her clues me in—he wanted me to see the two of them in that window.

Which is how I know tonight is a trap.

It's one that I have no choice but to willingly walk into. This is my swan song. If I lose tonight, nothing else matters. Bargaining her soul has been the lowest moment and the biggest mistake of my wretched existence. I am all in on a chance for one lifetime together. Just one.

If she doesn't say she loves me first, she will belong to him while I walk this earth alone forever.

This night will test me like never before. As I walked up to the Eiffel Tower and saw her pressed against the window with that monster behind her, I fell to my knees as he sneered down at me. Why he chooses to punish me, both in the beginning and now, I cannot fathom.

Surely no sin can weigh as much as the punishment that has been heaped upon me, over, and over, and over again. In my long tenure on this damned planet, I have made a few dear friends, but the pain of losing everyone became too much.

I remember back many years to the great Hesiod, one of

the few humans to have ever not only heard my story but believed it. The Archaic period was one of the golden times I was privileged to witness.

The legend of Prometheus's punishment was inspired by mine. Whereas, he had his liver eaten every day, my heart is destroyed repeatedly. Both of us are doomed to a never-ending life sentence.

And then Lilith came along, inspiring the story of Pandora and capturing poor Hesiod's heart. He didn't stand a chance. If only she was as good as Pandora. But unlike the story she inspired, she left nothing for him, not even hope. I shake off the memories of the great Greeks and focus on the present day.

Despite the centuries that have passed, my odyssey remains the same. I must win the fair maiden's hand and defeat evil. I walk to the elevator to the restaurant where I saw her last. I am thankful he had somehow had the historic landmark evacuated. This battle will be bloody enough without spilling an innocent's.

I board and am engulfed by her rose scent. Mentally, I push out the decaying cinnamon and sex that pollutes it. I flash pictures of her smiling at me through the centuries from some of the good times we have had together. Despite every lifetime ending in anguish, I do have some glimpses of happiness together. Those fleeting moments make the loss all the more bitter.

I dig deep and muster the last of my strength, the last shreds of my soul. Everything that I am will be put on the line for her tonight—for us.

The doors open to the second floor. Not a soul stirs, further confirming my suspicions that this is a trap. He wanted to break me with his lewd display earlier. It is not the worst thing he has put me through, and I doubt it will be the last.

I walk through the restaurant and take in the one table that has been destroyed, shaking my head at his inability to even have a meal without causing chaos and devastation. As I reach the back exit, I find his men waiting for me.

I crack my neck and smile. Ten humans to me seem like fair odds and will help me burn off some of this rage. Spreading my arms, I stand tall, showcasing my large frame. To their credit, Luke's men are highly trained, probably the best mercenaries money can buy, and don't so much as flinch.

Good thing I don't plan on fighting fairly. Just to be an asshole, I smile at the biggest one and beckon him forward. He drops into a fighting stance and performs a series of martial arts kicks and punches meant to intimidate me. I remain motionless, watching his approach with an amused smile.

Right before he makes his final impact, I vaporize into particle form, causing him to go sprawling. One man gasps in surprise, but the rest are too highly trained and have probably witnessed a fair amount of strange sights under Luke's employ.

I re-materialize behind the man who gasped and twist his head with my hands, his neck breaking with a satisfying crunch. Before his lifeless body drops to the ground, I am already onto the next man. I blink in and out of solid form with my hand wrapped around his heart, pulling it out of his chest, still beating.

It has the desired effect, making even these hardened killers glance around in concern. Their fear only fuels me. Every man I kill, I envision having Luke's damn face.

I let myself drift into berserker mode, reliving my time

spent with Norse warriors. I channel the trance-like fury they taught me and focus in on one second at a time—kill, spin, shift, rip. I am so consumed I barely notice the additional men flooding in around me.

With an inhuman howl, I shift into my beast form and switch to tearing their throats out. Quick. Efficient. Deadly. A I may also enjoy the fear reflected in their eyes right before they die. At last, my final partner in the macabre dance of death falls. Exhausted, I shift back to my human form and look around to see I am entangled in a mass of bodies.

I extricate myself and try to walk toward the elevator, but the ground is slippery, covered in blood. I make my way to the car and take it up. As I walk out onto the third floor, I am surrounded by silence. I set my senses to high alert for the danger I know must be surrounding me.

I spin in a slow circle but see nothing. My head snaps around at the sound of the elevator doors opening again. The single occupant turns, and for the first time tonight, I am truly afraid. Missing pieces click into place as I realize I have been betrayed.

Chapter 44

LIESHE

I couldn't figure out how to reopen the panel. The main door is locked. Just as I am about to throw a chair through a window and find out what the hell is going on, Luke slips in the secret entrance, elegantly tipping his hat and cane at me.

"Luke! What is happening? Everyone is gone, and I was so worried," I say as I run and wrap him in my arms, nuzzling my face into his hard chest.

"Things are even worse that I thought. He is completely unhinged and violent. He killed my men."

The color drains from my face. "He what? I mean, yeah, he's a bit of a stalker, but a killer? Really?"

"I'm sorry. I imagine this is such a shock. You are so incredibly lucky he didn't kill you. He's been leaving a trail of bodies behind him, even in your hometown." Luke holds my face in his hands, concern filling his eyes.

"Wren tried to warn me about a killer at home. I should have listened. This is just so bizarre. How did this happen to me?" I wail.

"A star that burns this bright will always capture attention. This is who you are, who you have always been. Gathering the lost, spreading love. Of course, he was drawn to you. I'm only thankful I got to you in time, Lieshe."

"I should have warned Wren," I say as a single tear rolls down my cheek.

"Why should you have warned Wren?"

"That's why I came looking for you in London. She had sent me a picture of them together after I left him in Scotland. I thought he was just a con man. I didn't think her life could be in danger. I would have told her."

Luke's face falls, and the color drains from his skin.

"Luke, you're scaring me. What's going on?"

"Wren texted this morning while you were sleeping, and I told her that you had met someone and moved on to Paris. She must have said something. It's all my fault that he followed you here. I've put both of you in harm's way."

"We have to find her. We have to save her," I gasp.

"Stay here. I know you're scared and tired. I promise as soon as this is over, I will take you away from all of this. But right now, I need you to be my brave queen. If you see him coming, I want you to go to the bathroom and push against the back wall. It will open to a ladder that leads to the top observation deck. Repeat it back to me."

"Luke, no. I can't do this again. I can't hide and wait to see what happens to everyone I lo-, everyone I care about."

Despite the urgency of the situation—the danger—his face lights up. He picked up on where I stopped myself from saying love. He sweeps me into his arms and claims my mouth, tongues clashing, breathing each other in.

He breaks the kiss but keeps holding me tight as he says, "I can't save her and worry about your safety at the same time. We can't go back and change the decisions either of us made. All we can do is try to save her now."

"Yes, of course you're right."

Guilt punches me in the gut. I'm worrying about myself when I should also be worrying about Wren. I trust Luke to get to her if she is here, but fervently hope she is not. That instead, McVladam has left her safely behind somewhere.

He steps back and gives my shoulders a small shake,

saying, "Do not come out if you see her. He may try to use her as bait."

His words twist in my gut. He presses a quick kiss to my forehead and then spins, knocking the secret door open with his cane before slipping back outside. I race to the windows and press my face against them, peering out into the night.

A lone figure exits the elevator. As they step out into the light, my fear is confirmed. A shadow emerges from the darkness and steps behind her, grabbing her by the shoulder and spinning her around.

"Wren," I scream and pound on the glass with my fists. "Wren!"

She stumbles back, and her pursuer steps toward her, emerging into the light. It's McVladam, blood running down his body in rivulets like a warrior of old. His eyes burn amber. He is yelling at Wren, but he doesn't look angry. He looks bewildered.

I am desperate to know what they are saying. I look around for something to break the glass, needing to know what the hell is happening.

Chapter 45

VLAD

"Miss Field?" I am shocked by her presence here, still not quite believing she could have betrayed me.

"Wren. All these years and you could never even call me by name or think of me as anything other than your servant," she spits at me.

"Wren? I don't understand," I utter in disbelief. Her family has served me for centuries, a vow made generations ago.

"Can't you see? Can't you see that *I* love you? I've always loved you. *She* has never been worthy of you. You don't even know her. You love the idea of her, of who she once was. She is nothing but a whore."

I recoil at the venom in her speech, shaking my head in confusion as she continues. I protest, "What? No."

"Yet you run after her like a fucking dog in heat. I am the one who has been *faithful*. I am the one who has worshiped you. I am the one that can make you happy." She is seething, screaming as spittle flies from her mouth.

She paces and reins her voice in. Spinning back to face me again, she speaks slowly, as if to a child, "The first girl. The only girl in generations. And they never let me forget it. Oh, no, I was reminded daily of what a failure I would be and what a disappointment I was. Questioned how I could serve a master as great as you when I was nothing but a female."

Her voice is rising again as she paces back and forth, arms gesticulating wildly. "My spirit was beat out of me. I trained until my hands and feet bled. I studied *you* until you were all I knew. I lived and breathed *you*. And when my grandfather died, I thought I would be free. Surely my blood, sweat, and tears had proven my worth to my father. He would recognize my absolute devotion to you and that fucking vow."

She gives a bitter laugh. "But oh, he was worse. So much worse. When he told me he was going to use the only valuable thing I possessed to create another heir, a pure male heir, to serve you, I knew what I had to do. And I had no tears left to mourn that sick fuck's passing."

I reach toward her, devastated. "Wren, please forgive me. I had no idea. I would have protected you."

"Would you have? But then, who would have been your spy? Who would have watched *her* for you until it was time for you to go to her? You wouldn't have saved me. You would sacrifice everything for her. Everything! Me. You. You'd sacrifice the whole damn world. I found my own path forward. I am finally going to have the love I deserve, my own happy ending." Her tirade is unhinged, her eyes wild and darting.

I see Luke come up behind her, stalking her like a jungle cat. He stealthily pulls the top of his cane up, revealing a hidden dagger.

"Wren."

Her name falls from my lips as a broken whisper. I see what is coming in slow motion, lunging forward to try to save her from his clutches, knowing I'm too late. This plan has been put into motion well before this moment.

He knew exactly how tonight would play out. He took

advantage of a sick and love-starved, lonely girl, but I am not innocent in this. I was too wrapped up in my story, my own unending pain, to appreciate the value and suffering of someone else. This may be the most painful lesson yet in my wretched existence.

In startling slow-motion clarity, Luke fully unsheathes the hidden knife, the runes etched into the blade glinting in the moonlight, and places it at her throat.

He whispers into her ear, the dark words drifting to me on her exhale, "I told you the price would be steep."

As the blade slices the long column of her neck, understanding dawns in her eyes too late, at just how grave her mistake in trusting him was. Just how steep the price is of their bargain.

I catch her as she falls and lower her to the ground. Helpless, I try to keep her life force in even as the pulsations slow. Her heart frantically beating as I attempt to stem the torrent of blood that spills forth.

Wren's lips are moving, whispering. I place my ear next to them to witness her dying words.

"Tell me you love me. I need to know someone loved me," she chokes out.

I do the only thing left to do and respond to the dying wish of a tragic life. I put my forehead against hers and whisper with all sincerity, "I love you, Wren. I love you."

I open my eyes to meet hers, to witness her life fading away. She deserves more, but this is all I can give her. A futile attempt to show her she is not alone. Not unloved. I drop my head onto her chest and listen to her broken heart stutter and stall, then stop forever.

The useless black organ I thought was long since dead inside my chest shatters with a loud crash. At first, I think the scream that pierces my ears must be coming from me, but as I spin around, with Wren still clutched in my arms to find where it is coming from, I see Lieshe in the distance, looking at me with abject horror through the shattered observation window.

Too late, I realize what has happened. All Lieshe can see is me, clutching a very bloody and very dead Wren. I know exactly what this looks like. Luke Devlin is nothing if not a performer who knows how to stage a show.

Behind me, I feel myself being surrounded by more of Luke's men. And I realize I played into his trap. The first wave of men was meant as a distraction leading up to this main event. Wren and I unwitting players in the center ring of the circus he has made of our lives. What he is willing to sacrifice has no bounds, no humanity.

My desperate plans, my love, my devotion—nothing was enough. I was never going to defeat him. All hope is lost.

I don't know if I can fight them. I have no heart, no soul, no reason to live. I welcome the pain promised in their eyes, the punishment to be delivered in the lines of their bodies. It is the least I deserve for the suffering I have caused and that abject failure that I am. Nothing can compare to this exquisite pain that fills me from the loss of my *Roză*.

One of the men pulls out a sword and steps toward me, lining up for a kill strike aimed at my neck. At least I will have died trying to save my love, as I think this time, I really might die. I've never been decapitated, and with Luke here, I think he may finally collect my soul. The blade sings as the mercenary pulls the sword back to deliver the fatal blow.

I bow my head and close my eyes, picturing kissing my sweet *Roză* in the garden the first time I had ever laid eyes on her. I can smell her rose scent, feel her soft lips on mine. I feel the warmth of the sun as it smiles down upon us.

I could not choose my life, and now, after seeking it all

these years, I am powerless to stop my death. But I can choose to die with the memory of her taste on my lips. My last heartbeat will echo the depth of my devotion to her. The light in her eyes will be my last conscious thought.

And in this final moment, as hundreds of her incarnations over thousands of years flash before my eyes, I know with a certainty carved from my flesh—I would choose it all again. Endure every torment, swallow all the pain, just to be with her one more time.

I whisper her names, a litany of love and loss. Each one seared into my memory just as it is inked into my flesh. They fall from my lips like the perfect rosary, wrapping me in the shadow of her embrace.

A sudden shout breaks the spell. My eyes snap open to see Lilith has caught the sword midswing with her bare hand. Pulling it from the man's grip by the blade, she says, "Oh, no. He's mine. I've been waiting for this shit for centuries."

She flips the sword in the air, catching it by the handle in her left hand. With a few fluid figure eights, she tests its weight and heft. Dropping into a fighting stance, she angles the blade at me. Everyone falls silent, watching the drama unfold.

"This is for calling me into this damned existence," she whispers as she stares into my soul, calling my sins into account.

Gabriel and Jophiel appear behind her. Their presence makes me realize I really am going to die. I whisper to the night, "Forgive me, my love, my life. Forgive me."

I bow my head to Lilith. My sins are stacked at my feet like cordwood, awaiting someone to set them ablaze. With a fierce battle cry, she lunges forward, aiming for the poor decimated organ in my chest.

I remain motionless, welcoming the final blow, surprised she didn't go for the more dramatic decapitation. I have no fear because the sword cannot destroy my heart.

It's already gone.

Chapter 46

LIESHE

The shattered window gapes like vicious jaws, a portal to an alternate reality that cannot be my life. My arms ache from the effort of smashing it with an end table, yet the sensation is nothing compared to the visceral pain consuming my chest.

My screams are stuck on repeat, a constant wail erupting from my throat like a siren. I just watched him kill Wren. I saw Luke and his men, even Lilith, try to stop him, but he just went after her. It even looked like he had been trying to drink her blood, bent over her as he was, covered in red.

Wren is dead. McFuckface killed her, and it's all my fault. I didn't warn her. I led him here. An innocent woman is dead because of me.

As I try and fail to make sense of what is happening, Gabe and Jo step out of the shadows into the death tableau before me. I blink, hard. But there is no mistaking them as they rush toward everyone.

How on earth is Jo here? She is supposed to be with Anna at Grimm. And how the hell does she know Gabe? What in the actual fuck is going on? Are they all in on this great charade? Co-conspirators in some strange game someone is playing with my life? Nothing makes sense.

Luke bursts through the secret door and pulls me away from the window. I can't tell if I'm still screaming or not as he drags me through the apartment. My gaze is riveted to the window as I stumble along. I vaguely feel my shin strike a piece of furniture as we bolt, but everything is so surreal it doesn't even phase me.

He pulls me into a tiny bathroom and then pushes the back wall open to reveal a secret passage. He puts me between him and a ladder. I stand there, unmoving, unsure where to look now that I can't see out the window. The only thing I can think of is, Wren is dead.

He spins me around and places his hands on either side of my face. His eyes search mine, bouncing back and forth between them.

"Lieshe. Look in my eyes. I need you to climb. Remember, I told you I would take you away when this was all over?"

I feel the stickiness of his hands on my face and know it's Wren's blood from his struggle to stop that monster. My friend's blood is coating my face. I can't understand what Luke is saying. All I know is Wren is gone.

She's dead. It's my fault.

The two thoughts chase each round my mind. A great sob works its way up my throat and out of my mouth.

Luke gently shakes my shoulders. "Lieshe. Lieshe! We need to leave. Now!"

I nod my head, my teeth clacking together like a nutcracker. "Yes, I'd like that. Let's leave now."

And I would. I'm ready to go with the one constant in my life. My only anchor in a sea of lies and conspiracy. Gabe, Jo, McFuckface. Was any of it real?

Luke spins me around and places my hands on the ladder rungs. I start to climb, focusing on one thought. *I'd like to leave now.* We climb and climb, his warmth surrounding me as I move up hand over hand, step over step on the industrial rungs, eventually exiting into the summit.

The night sky over Paris is so breathtaking that I forget to be afraid. I turn to Luke as the wind catches his jacket, lifting it off of my shoulders and sending it flying off into the night like a bird.

Luke pulls me into him and rips my T-shirt down the middle. He reaches out and traces something in Wren's blood over my heart while chanting. The words make the hair on the back of my neck stand up and the air shimmer around us. Darkness pulses at the edge of my vision.

"Luke, where are we going?" I whisper.

"What do you know about dark matter?" comes his cryptic reply.

"Dark Matter? Is it like the space between?" I reply, confused to say the least at this turn in conversation as I stand, traumatized at the top of the Eiffel Tower.

He grips my face urgently, pulling me into his intense stare and whispers across my lips, "Dark matter is all that is unseen. The gravitational pull that holds the very universe together. You are my dark matter, Lieshe."

I drown in the endless black of his eyes as if they are the gravitational pull he speaks of.

"Do you remember when I said that not even death can touch you now?" he asks.

"Yes," I reply, my voice a hoarse whisper.

"Come with me then. Let me take you away. Let me take care of you. Let me love you, Lieshe."

I stare into Luke's eyes, searching for an answer I'm not sure I want to know–who is Luke Devlin? But what I do know is yes, I want someone to take me away. Someone to take care of me. Someone to love me.

He holds his hand out, and as I place mine in his, I shiver at the heat of his touch. I break away from his intense stare to look out over the city of Paris one last time. Turning back to face him, I step into his warmth and wrap my arms around his neck. I feel no fear as I tip my lips up to his and lose myself in his cinnamon flavored darkness.

Luke scoops me up bridal style, and without breaking the kiss...

We jump.

Epilogue

VLAD

I wake with a primal scream, pulled from deep unconsciousness by her soul leaving this plane. I flail in panic and rage.

"Calm down," Lilith's calm, cold voice comes from the recesses of the room. "She's not dead."

"How do you know?" I wail, filled with anguish.

"Because I know where she is," she replies, sounding annoyed.

I stagger to my feet, ripping off the bandages around my chest. Despite my rapid ability to heal, a vivid puckered purple scar covers my heart. I run my fingers over it, then stalk through the shadows, picking Lilith up by her throat and slamming her against the wall.

"What have you done?" I growl.

She grabs my hand as I squeeze her throat. Her face turns purple, yet she smiles, throwing me an inexplicable wink.

I drop her to the floor with a scowl, where she collapses, laughing her childlike giggle in between coughing fits.

"Me? I saved the fucking day, you twat." She wipes her streaming eyes, hysterical.

"You tried to kill me!" I rage.

"Oh, relax. I saved your life. You were about to be decapitated, and I wasn't sure you would survive that. I took a calculated risk. I knew exactly what I was doing, and I risked my own fucking neck to do it."

"You should have let me die. I've failed again."

I fall to my knees as they go weak. One lifetime—I had asked for one lifetime, this one, with my love. I am a failure. I couldn't even complete my vow of taking him down with me. Why am I still here? Why couldn't Lilith have just let me die?

"I didn't do it for you. I did it for her. Or did you forget who I am?" she says.

"Never. I know exactly what and why you are. And I know you will never forgive me," I reply.

"You are such a typical man. This isn't about you. It's about her. She's the only friend I've ever had. She is the only one who deserves to be saved. You cursed her as much as you've cursed me. I saved *you* so we can save *her,* jackass. Now get the fuck up and act like the man she needs you to be."

As unorthodox as her pep talk is, it makes me stand up and take in my surroundings. As I see the thick stone walls and feel the power that surrounds me, I realize where Lilith has brought me.

Luke thinks he's won, but he hasn't. Not yet. I'm home now. We'll bring this fight to my territory, and I will win. I *will* have this lifetime. He thinks he can play me and deceive her, but he doesn't know the first thing about her.

She'll see through his lies. I have every confidence in my love.

"Wait for me, *Rozǎ*. I'm coming for you," I whisper into the night. The game isn't over yet. I turn to face Lilith and declare, "Check."

A Message From The Author

My Dark Darlings—

The second chapter of the longest love story ever told is only possible because of you. Thank you for all the love and support you've shown me and the *Immortal Redemption* series. I hope you love where this world has gone, and I can't wait to finish this journey with you. Although we'll bring Lieshe's story to a close in book three, a few characters from this series are demanding their stories be told, too. So, rest assured, this world will continue.

I never dreamed of becoming an author, but now I can't imagine anything else. When my mom became sick, I lost myself. Writing this story, with pieces of her woven into the world, helped me find my way back. And though writing and being an author takes time away from my family, I know I'm leaving an incredible legacy for my children. They see me chasing my dreams, and they even help with everything but the reading! So, if you receive a package from me, know that my children are learning to follow their dreams, too—because of you.

Special thanks to my husband, my children, the real-life Lieshe and Mindy, and my dad. Without this core group, book two wouldn't exist. And, as always, thank you to my mother. She would be thrilled to see all of this. One of her biggest fears was that ALS would consume my life. Though I advocate for ALS every day, I've chosen something else to be my life—my kids and my books. It's a damn fine choice.

Lauren—you've been my rock. Your support and encouragement are unparalleled, and I appreciate you more than you know. Thank you, my friend. I hope you love seeing your sweet kitty's name immortalized in print.

Follow me @CassandraElizzabeth and keep an eye on cassandraelizzabeth.com for updates and to subscribe to my newsletter. And finally, please help support indie authors by leaving a review.

My Eternal Love,
Cassandra

About The Author

Cassandra Elizzabeth is an exciting new indie voice, known for her immersive storytelling and vivid imagination. Her writing journey started when she could not find the books she wanted to read. Cassandra weaves themes of self-discovery, friendship, love, loss, and acceptance into a tapestry of macabre and spicy fiction, with a dash of murder, mayhem, and mystery. When not lost in the world of words, Cassandra can be found talking to the flowers or spending time with her family.